FORGED IN FIRE

Val Vayro

Copyright © 2018 Val Vayro

All rights reserved

For Neil Vayro.
1980 - 2014

Foreword

Weaving a tapestry of time, so different from our own in most respects, this book is the result of many years of research, into a family that happens to be mine. It began as the year 2000 Census was made public, and thankfully, could be done mostly by computer, although it did necessitate some visits to the three nearest Records Office. Looking at original material was fascinating. At one point, I had the actual probate document of a will in my hands from 1770. You're not always allowed to see the original as so much is now on microfilm, but I must have been lucky.

My parents accompanied me in the early days, which began with a rather large gravestone for a family of Hutchinson with the names I was looking for. I learned very quickly it was not my family, as this family could afford a gravestone and my family could not! It was an extremely hard life for most people, but being a Blacksmith guaranteed employment, a certain respect and income, if customers paid up!

The dialogue that I have used is a mash, of Yorkshire, some online dialect help and some reading I did about the Swaledale dialect, which is apparently quite different from 'normal Yorkshire'. They call it 'Swardle'. I have tried to give a flavour' of Swaledale with some words and speech patterns, but please don't be offended by my offerings, if you are a purist. Just have patience and enjoy the experience'. The vocabulary is usually decipherable.

I hope you enjoy reading it.

Part One

1781 - 1795

MALLERSTANG

Chapter 1

1781 Alice Fothergill

A snowdrop : A daycent lass 'as keeps hersen tidy an clean, an helps her mother of a neet, instead o' bein' gaddin' abaht wi' th' young chaps.

(Original Illuminated Clock Almanack)

Alice was an excited young woman. And she had every reason to be. She was more than excited, because there was a chance, just a chance, that she would be going to Saint Luke's Fair in Kirkby Stephen, very soon. Her life had been a quiet one so far. Too quiet. She was thinking this, and had been thinking this, for a good while now. She needed to know more about life. She'd been cooped up for too long!

She'd never been to the Fair, even at her age, but she'd heard exciting stories about it from her mother, who also had never been, in all her life. And, in turn her mother had heard it from her father, who had given her a watered-down, but exciting enough version, for 'daycent' mothers and daughters, who were mostly kept safely at home, and Alice was most certainly decent. She spent all her days on the farm and never went anywhere, except maybe to visit her sister now and again, and she was beginning to worry that she would die an 'old maid.'

It just wasn't fair that boys had all the excitement. The world was all wrong. And she'd noticed that as a girl she was very much ignored in company, whereas her brother wasn't. It was unusual for a boy to sit in the corner and take up quiet pastimes. They were all noise and swagger and just *couldn't* be ignored. When she was younger she'd tried acting like her brother but that just got her a telling off: a lecture on 'how young ladies should behave,' and another on how she'd never attract a husband behaving like that. So, she'd sunk back into the shadows.

All in all it wasn't a bad life: just a boring one. The longed-for outing all depended on her older married sister, Elizabeth, and whether she and her husband would take her, or not, as the case may be. Alice and Elizabeth had tragically lost both their parents, their brother and both sisters and for a short while since the last loss, Alice had been living at Southwaite Farm, her family home all her life, with outside help, and her mother's friend, old Peg as a chaperone. Her sister's husband Will had taken over the lease so she could remain there and had sent men to help on the farm. It was still too much work for her. So now she heard herself saying, what she thought she would never say. She needed a man.

A life as a lonely, unmarried aunt was too bitter to contemplate. She'd given it some thought and come up with the solution. Where better to find a man than at the Fair? There would be men enough there, she was sure. She could have a good look round and choose the one she liked the look of. That was the plan. That was how many young men found a wife, she knew that. Talking to her sister, she laid out what she wanted. She'd found that you had to be straight with Elizabeth, or she would sometimes twist what you said. Was it intentional? She didn't know. But she did know that it was annoying.

"Now why would ah have said that?" she wondered many a time. She knew fine well she hadn't. The last incident was when Elizabeth had promised, faithfully, to visit her and bring the babies (as she called them) so Alice could dote on them, as she loved to do. And what happened? There was no sign of Elizabeth on the appointed day, while Alice gazed longingly down the road for the sight of a pony cart.

Elizabeth did, however, turn up two days later. Alice hid her disappointment. She didn't want to stop them coming altogether, and hugging the youngest child to her, she took the other by the hand and led her into the scullery for a treat of homemade toffee.

As they sat together in company, Alice thought it was as good a chance as any to ask her sister for some advice. Speaking in her usual thick Swaledale accent, she asked, "Sister. How did thee knaw Will was the one f'thee?"

That was a question Elizabeth hadn't expected, but one that was easy to answer.

"Da said he were a gud man and so that were awl."

"Da found thy 'usband f'thee?" she asked, incredulously.

"Aye," Elizabeth replied, lowering her eyes, and with a smile said, "but ah was not disappointed."

Alice let those words filter through, before she continued. Now she'd begun she would press on, with no fear or embarrassment. At least, that was her intention. Firstly, she needed to ascertain if her sister was willing to collect her by ponycart.

"Ah need a man, an' mun find a gud'un at this Fair," then she quickly added, "if thee'll tak uz. If ah's goin". She went on, "Dost thee ken o'any gud men who's in need of a wife?"

"Well Alice, ma honey bairn, that do depend on what thee wants in your man.

"Honey bairn? Ah isn't ain o' thy bairns Elizabeth," she interrupted, smiling at the words her ma used to call her. Elizabeth carried on, ticking off on her fingers. "Aither, is it addlings, ye want, the brass he has and can mak? Or are ye luckin' for a man who be lovesome or do thee want a bonny like fellow and be man-keen. A bonnyish fellow ese ezey on t'een."

She paused for a moment, to let Alice think. "Awl three wud be gud, but actilly dear sister, ah wants what thee has." Elizabeth stood, gave her a long look before she smiled and quipped, "Thee can't. He's mine. Then turning away to collect the children, she left Alice looking at her sister, with a look that said, "You are not funny."

The visit had given Alice much to think about. She hadn't really thought yet about what she wanted in a man, so she did now. She started by discounting good looks. That was the least important thing. But she qualified this with, unless he was slovenly, too smelly, had a huge nose (she had a mistrust of people with noses that were too large for their face), or was in any other way disagreeable, or unappealing. That was a shock to her because she did care about looks after all. But not to the exclusion of everything else.

The next thing was his earnings. Brass was always good to have. Her father had kept them well provided for, but he worked long and hard on the farm for that. Her ma had complained many a time that a farmer's wife never saw her man. She saw many other men, labourers on the farm, that she cooked for, almost as much as she saw her man. Still 'gud addlings' would make life a little easier. No, the most important thing was that he should be 'lovesome.' He must love her, and in turn, she would love him. Now she had some sort of idea, she could have a good look around at the Fair.

It had been settled that Elizabeth and her husband Will would collect her the day before. But for now, she had life to deal with. Alice lived very comfortably. The land and farmhouse were leased, with Elizabeth's husband Will having taken over the lease for now. That was another reason why Elizabeth needed her sister to 'find a man', as he would then take over the lease, and release them from this added expense.

The living accommodation was generous, with two sitting rooms and a kitchen downstairs, as well as a scullery. Upstairs there were three bedrooms, with another room that had a staircase from the yard next to the hay loft. Any farmhands who worked continuously for them slept in that room, but not now. There was a stable, a calf house and byre, and a shed for the cart. The pig also had his own accommodation. And, in front of the farmhouse was the garden, full of potatoes and onions at this time of year, and the flowers and herbs she grew for ailments as well as for pleasure. She loved the uninterrupted view over the Mallerstang valley, and if she had a spare minute, she stood and gazed over it, at any time of the day. The cost of the lease for such a large residence was not small, but it would make a very suitable home for a growing family.

Alice had been pushed headlong into the practicalities of a farming way of life and had quickly begun to find out that there were jobs that must be done. The two hundred sheep were to take to the hills for the winter. The five cows were to milk each day. The stirks were to put to pasture or feed. The winter housing had to be cleaned and their hay meadows managed. Hens and geese were to manage daily, and their eggs collected. The pig also needed management.

Her brother-in-law had found a couple of lads to do the work, but they didn't have the knowledge or experience to fully take over a farm. So, with Will's agreement, Alice sold the wethers, (the castrated male sheep) and the bull. That made almost £60. Her sister, seeing she may not have a chance as good as this again, took this as payment for the rent that Alice wasn't paying.

Alice still had the stirks and the two calves for market eventually, a pig, the milk cows, as well as a horse and a Galloway. That was all she could manage. But she wouldn't starve.

When her father had died and his probate had been released, his estate was worth £148, which was an extremely healthy amount for a small farm.

'And,' thought Alice, 'I'm a good prospect for a wife. I have brass and I have stock."

It remained to be seen if that would be enough. She shivered as she pulled her thick shawl even tighter around her shoulders. She was standing in that small patch of ground she called her garden, looking over the Valley. A full round moon was suspended in the darkness, its face peering down at the Earth and providing an eerie glow. Before sunset she had admired the trees with their brightly coloured coats of red, yellow and gold, and the brightly hued carpet their shedding had caused. With one last look at the pinpricks of light in the sky, she turned and walked back inside her cottage.

She was not lonely. She never had time to be lonely. And she had plenty of kin to love. Her sister Elizabeth had children that she could lavish her affection on, and she did. Her father's family was large and so she had many cousins her age too, one being her favourite. This cousin, William, had recently found himself a wife, a flame-haired beauty from Thorns at the top of Swaledale, Jennet Hutchinson. He was considered a very lucky man as there was no shortage of suitors at her father's door. It seems she had everything required for a good wife. She was beautiful, kind-hearted, thoughtful and hardworking.

At this wedding, on a warm Tuesday in late spring Alice had met Jennet's one brother and one sister and had been in their company for the full day, but, as it is at weddings, she couldn't remember much about them. There were too many people milling around and Alice wasn't one for crowds. After the marriage they'd set up home at the farm at Hanging Lund, a hamlet about six miles south of Kirkby Stephen, in Westmorland. The farmhouse was in a very remote place, tucked under the slope of Mallerstang Edge that towered above it.

Thinking about it later, Alice was surprised to find herself very jealous of Jennet. Her looks, among other things, made her jealousy hard to ignore and she had to work hard at hiding this. In Alice's eyes she was genuinely concerned that a man would not look twice at her ordinary brown hair with a face dusted in freckles: that they may not even give her a second glance.

"Alice, thee's a reet bonny lass," her family used to say, when she wished out loud that she wasn't as tall, or as freckly, or had such boring hair. 'So, they *would* say,' she thought.

'Ah didn't think ah was a denty-be-pretty sort, but ah muz be,' she sighed, thinking about Jennet.

William and Jennet's firstborn was a girl, named Sarah, born just over a year after their marriage. Their second child was due in a few months now and Will was hoping for a boy. And here was the second reason for Alice's jealousy. A family. A family of her own: not as an aunt or a sister, but her own bairn, or even two to love and dote on, and to sew for too. Thinking about it now though, where did a mother get the time to do her mothering? *Her* own life was full of work, and she had no family to care for yet.

She milked, she churned, she washed and mended clothes, she made bread, chased the geese to find their eggs. She grew vegetables in their long garden. She set the fires, trimmed the tallow candles, swept out the old rushes and spread new sweet-smelling ones when needed. She plucked and gutted chickens, skinned and gutted rabbits, and could make a stew or pie tastier than any she had ever tried, her mother had often said.

She did all the things a good wife did, without being a wife.

She'd waited long enough. Too long. She was now twenty-seven summers. Why hadn't her da found *her* a husband like he had for Elizabeth? It seems he'd chosen a good one there. Well, he *had* chosen a good one there.

Elizabeth had told her so. And she was the one who would know

Chapter 2

Saint Luke's Fair

'Niver tell a Yorkshire lass that you're unworthy of her. Let her find out for hersel.'

(Yorkshire Father's advice to his son)

Alice was a fairly modest young woman, if you didn't count her stews and pies, which were, quite frankly the best you would taste. It was her personal appearance that she felt was not the best, compared to others she saw. She had never considered herself pretty, but in fact she was. She was quite tall – not too tall so that she was taller than most men she met, but not a petite waif of a thing either.

Her eyes were her most striking feature, as deep blue as the early evening sky, in a face that was almond shaped, with a smile that lit it up, like sunshine on water. She was twenty-eight now, so it showed some of the lines of her age, but not as many as most. Her lustrous, long brown hair spread like a mantle round her shoulders, shining with rich hints of colour, just like the sunlight glinting on the copper pans in the farm kitchen. It was her only vanity and she brushed it with care, every night, singing to herself as she did. This colour complemented her complexion well - lightly browned with working outside and dusted with a few freckles over the bridge of her nose. She hated having to tie her hair up under a bonnet, but that was the rule when she was out, because of her age. She loved it loosely tied, and the feel of it around her shoulders.

She wore clothes that were plain but clean and maintained by herself as well as she could – plain skirt and bodice, stockings well mended and a shawl that had seen many years wear. In contrast to many she knew, she liked to keep herself clean, using water from the rain butt, rubbing her hands, feet and face with a rag and a jug of clean fresh water. Sometimes she spoiled herself and warmed the water, scenting it with herbs from their garden, kept for plants that had medicinal uses.

....

Saint Luke's Fair was two whole days of bustling people, meeting with old friends and catching up with their news, making new friends, trading wares. With plenty of eating too. For the men, and some women, there was drinking at the ale booths. For those men that wanted it, there was wagering in many forms: cock fighting, wrestling matches and anything else the men could lose money on. Wives dreaded their husbands leaving home with a pocket of brass and coming home with nothing but a sore head.If they were interested, as many were, there was whoring too.

And for the young and the women too, a theatre group usually made an appearance, mummers or puppets, with traditional tales, perhaps of Saint George and the Dragon, even sometimes Mr. Punch.

Alice had been told of sword dances but had not seen one and wanted to see one so badly that she could hardly sleep for the excitement of it all. Thinking of it with her naïve look at the world she wondered if it was dangerous. Did they dance holding swords? She had prepared well for the day, making cheese at the cheese press, collecting fresh eggs, churning butter. She'd also tied the garden lavender and thyme into delicate sweet-smelling nosegays that she hoped the ladies at the Fair would appreciate.

Because it was so far, Elizabeth and her husband had come to collect Alice the day before. It felt like a holiday, like Christmas perhaps, a day she did not have to work. Carefully putting the freshly laid eggs, butter and cheese she was trading on the cart bottom, she sat up alongside her elder sister, who appeared today to be in an unpleasant and unfriendly mood.

As the little fell pony pulled the cart and its wares along the track, she felt the rhythm of the wheels on the stony ground and despite the bumps along the rough way, it almost lulled her to sleep.

That day in late summer the heather fells were a blaze of dark purple on either side as they travelled purposefully along the narrow bumpy track. Even if the wind blew a little fiercely over the fell, the sun shone, and the birds sang. The small trees, stunted by the savage wind in winter and moulded into strange shapes, were silhouettes on the horizon. Alice felt a lift in her chest, her heart fluttered and beat fast as she thought about the excitement of the days to come. She was happy. Soon she would go to the Fair, and she went happy but tired, to bed, thinking about the pleasures ahead.

The next morning, she found out exactly why her sister was in such an unpleasant mood. As it happened, he, along with many men in the district, wanted to try a wager or two at a cock fight, and take a brew or two of the local ale. It always made him a little maudlin' and melancholy, she said, and difficult to rouse the next day. She said that he would be either singing or sleepy after a few jugs and didn't know which was worse. And without going into detail, she said, it sometimes made him a little amorous!

"Ee'll stink o'sup 'n be singing' and flirtin wi' the young lasses." she grumbled, "and winnet want to get up t'next morn."

"He'll be wantin kisses an'moare when we get hoame," she finished. "An 'ave telt im ah want nee moare barns."

As an unmarried woman, Alice had no idea at all what her sister was talking about and looked at her in amazement. Elizabeth had never volunteered such information before, and Alice felt honoured, in a strange way, listening to her sister talk about a club she had yet to join. Now the time had come, and she was staying with her sister for the event, as excited as any young child.

"Dear sister, will uz see t'Mummers?"

Elizabeth, her elder married sister, and supposedly immune to the excitement of such an event, heard the same in her younger sister's voice.

"The Mummers is there Alice and we shall be there. Thee's all ov a fluster girl. Calm theesel," she replied patiently.

Then, from Alice, who had no money of her own, "Dust thee think ah could have a new dress? What about the sword dancers? Shall uz see em?"

"My dear Alice, thee's a grown woman. Thee can see whatever thee wants to see," replied her sister, now with impatience. "There will be japing, and thee shall see all the sights and sounds of the Fair."

Although it was true that Alice was a grown woman, she was far from being able to make her own decisions. Until her mother had died, all that had been decided for her.

"I can't wait Elizabeth. I won't sleep."

It was too much, she thought.

Chapter Three

John Hutchinson - Thorns

"But Iron — Cold Iron - is master of them all."
(Rudyard Kipling)

John Hutchinson was a young man with prospects. At just twenty-one years old he stood head and shoulders above many his age — just like his father. He was well known in Thorns, and especially known by all the young women, with his hair the colour of a ripe field of barley that lay around his neck in wavy curls, and eyes the colour of fresh grass. He was handsome, and then some, but he always seemed to have a rather sombre look about him.

However, those who knew him were well aware of his sense of fun.

He had a trade as a Blacksmith, like his father Miles, and his grandfather before that and had almost grown up in a forge: had seen the bellows make the charcoal burn hotter, the anvil and hammer beat the metal into shape, even before he knew what they were. He loved the heat and noise of the smithy. The atmosphere was sometimes unbreathable and the heat often unbearable, full of clouds of hissing steam in that dark and poorly lit space.

But it was his life.

As an apprentice-Blacksmith John had spent much of his time bringing coal and other fetching and carrying for the first few years. Once he reached ten years, he had been allowed to use tools and make nails and other small items.

His da Miles had told him that making nails used all the skills he would need, and that it was good practice.

Miles had been a journeyman for years, travelling and learning his craft from more experienced Blacksmiths and had spent some time in the Valley before moving the family to Thorns when John was young. Now Miles had his own forge there and a strong young man to help him. It was what he did, and he was proud of it.

He had a good business and was kept busy. A Blacksmith was always busy. The local lead miners were very needy of their services – picks, shovels, hammers and wedges, plugs and "feathers" used for splitting the rock. These were all made by the Blacksmith. Shovels cut the peat used to smelt iron ore and to keep them warm in winter. Farmers needed Blacksmiths too, and so did their horses. There were large jobs like mending carts and wagons, and small jobs like making the nails and the ironwork for coffins. They made wheel bonds for the cartwheels, provided horseshoes and fitted them if needed, mended tools as well as made them, and tools for the women too, like cooking pots and pans. The Blacksmith was at the heart of every village, and John knew that his father was respected because of what he could achieve with his hammer and anvil.

Thorns, where they lived, was a hamlet of grey stone at the top of Swaledale, without the shelter of the valley sides, and not far from the township of Kirkby Stephen, over the fells.

At the edge of the cottages stood the smithy, with living quarters alongside, built from rough unhewn grey stone and a roof covered with misshapen stone tiles. The walls sweated cold in the winter snow and rain and weren't much warmer in the summer. Of light there wasn't much, as the windows were small, so less glass which cost 'brass.' The cottage had a dirt-floor, spread with rushes that Elizabeth his mother swept out and replaced with fresh now and again. Peat and wood burned smokily in the stone fireplace as coal was kept for the forge fire, and there was a large iron cooking pot, added to daily, suspended above the fire on a heavy iron chain. Hanging in the chimney too was a large side of salt-cured, smoked beef, ready to last them through the long, gruelling winter days that were coming.

The kitchen was the main room but was so low that Miles and his son could not stand upright, except between the big oak beams that crossed the ceiling. His mother Elizabeth, being much shorter, didn't have that problem. There had been another member of the family - his elder sister Jennet, who had been married the year before to a Fothergill from the Mallerstang valley, and the families had enjoyed celebrating together. They now had a beautiful baby girl, the image of her mother, and another baby soon to come. The family visited regularly because Jennet was a dutiful daughter, but she also missed her mother.

Miles was a tall man, head and shoulders above his son in law William, with a rangy, lanky body, whose slight build belied his strength. The rest of the family were blond haired and fair skinned, but not so Miles. He wasn't quite a red head, but had hair that was a soft red, much like Jennet. His colouring meant that if spent a day in the sun, his skin glowed red, so it was just as well that his occupation kept him indoors for most of the time. Pale blue eyes looked out from this face, half covered with a bushy beard and a smile was never far from his lips. None of his three children took after him in looks, but it was said that he was the image of his own father. Two children had inherited the blond good looks of their mother, thick fair hair, green eyes and skin that seemed to soak up the sun, except Jennet who favoured her father more.

Miles and Elizabeth slept in a small room off the kitchen, with their younger daughter Elizabeth sleeping on a pallet in the corner. John slept up in the loft, which was often cold and draughty when the wind whistled and danced through the gaps in the stone roof.

The same stars that Alice looked at were visible to John through these gaps, but he fell asleep trying to avoid seeing them, covering his head to keep in the warmth. And some nights he just stretched out in front of the peat fire and stayed there the night, where it was warm even if not too comfortable. Away from the kitchen door, past the smelling heap of household rubbish, was the midden, not a very sanitary affair, but better than some. Here the night soil was put and was used by the family through the day. Periodically a layer of dirt was added to the hole but in very wet times the water skimmed down the slight incline behind and over the soil, bringing a smell and perhaps human waste with it. Sometimes the men just took a shovel and simply dug a hole somewhere behind the building, or among the small clump of trees beyond.

******

It was evening and Miles strode wearily into the kitchen, out of the endless rain that seemed to hammer into him on the short walk home. Being the apprentice, John had to stay behind to rake out the forge fire for the evening before he was allowed to leave making it ready to be lit the next morning. He entered the room, seeming to bring with him a whirlwind of pure energy that radiated his youth, just as his father radiated his exhaustion.

Dodging the low sturdy beams, Miles went straight to the rough wooden table, sat on a wooden form and leaned wearily on his grimy elbows, while John, when he entered, threw himself onto the old settle by the fire. Resting his feet on the raised hearth and facing the fire he took off his boots and rubbed his poor feet ferociously. A full day in heavy boots took its toll.

"'What's ter eat?" he grunted, in his thick Yorkshire dialect. "Ahs fair clemmed."

"Ah'm fettlin it now" sighed his mother wearily.

His father said nothing but waited silently until a wooden plate of hot greasy mutton stew was put in front of him, together with a chunk of roughhewn bread. He started guzzling it down before John had even got to the table.

"Tak thee mucky boots off," shouted Elizabeth, without looking at him, "and sit thee sen down."

He dragged himself up from the settle and came to sit opposite Miles, devouring the greasy mutton stew as if he'd not eaten all week, then carefully wiped his plate, like his father, with a hunk of bread, until there wasn't even a drop of gravy to be seen.

After a brief period of silence, punctuated with the sounds of good appetites and more than a little slurping, while Miles attacked a second plate of stew, came the following from an excited John.

"Saint Luke's Fair soon. Appen ah could gan this time?"

"Use your gumption. How can thee both go? Da must go. Mebbe next time," answered Elizabeth, regret in her voice. Shaking her head she said, "There's work thee mun do."

So, he grumbled but gave no argument.

While John ate his second helping, and even after, Miles talked about the Fair and what he would do, with John sulking in the corner.

That night Elizabeth did what mothers do, and persuaded her husband that it would be to his advantage to have John there. Not only that: he was persuaded that it was his idea to take him. John would be able to watch the horse and cart while Miles was enjoying a flagon of ale, having a wager, and many other things the men got up to at the Fair when their wives were not there.

As the sun came up, Miles got ready the low wooden cart with its iron spoked wheels, and their beautiful dales pony, old and docile, but strong and capable of pulling a fully loaded cart for many a mile. They may have had goods to sell but it was ale, gambling and women that drew men to these occasions mostly.

The visit to the Fair meant that Miles could 'kick over the traces' a little and enjoy the sights and opportunities, not forgetting Dirty Maggie's ale.

They travelled slowly, their large wooden wheels rumbling along the stony pathways behind their only livestock. She stood a full fourteen hands high, with a head that was straight and neat, and broad between the eyes. Her muzzle was fine and her ears incurving to the head. Although strong, her body was short, her muscles were apparent in her quarters and longish neck and as John looked at her strong withers and strong sloping shoulders, he knew she would never let them down.

John loved her, spending any time he could spare rubbing her down with straw, brushing her silky mane and tail, feeding her and making sure she had fresh water. She had a good appetite and hay had to be plentiful. He loved the feel of the warm breath that snorted from her nose as she nuzzled carefully from his hand. He had known her all his life and apart from his feelings, it was his job to make sure she was looked after. She was an important part of their business and would not easily be replaced if something should happen to her. That time would come eventually, but it would not be because John had been derelict in his duty.

John and his father were going to market with shovels, picks and cooking pots. His mother Elizabeth never left the village and never had, in all her years. That was the normal state of affairs for village wives and this visit was merely a diversion for Miles as he had all the work he needed.

Elizabeth had packed a basket of food to last them the journey and throughout the day, wrapped in pieces of rag: bread, smoked bacon and potatoes cooked in the oven. To wash it down was a stone jar of Elizabeth's own brewed ale.

Aware that the journey would take them almost half a day, they had set off before sunrise. As the first rays of September light were breaking the horizon, John, sitting up front next to his father, watched the morning sky gradually lighten. And then it began to rain. He lifted his face to the large drops of water and thought it wasn't surprising, but it meant they would be even colder when they arrived.

The road from Thorns to Kirby Stephen took them over hill tops and through inhospitable countryside until it levelled in the valley. There was no shelter for them from the strong gusting winds that could make cheeks and ears sting, but not so much today. As the sky lightened, he noticed a few bedraggled sheep grazing on the flank of the hillside, a rocky outcrop of limestone and the bracken that had changed to its autumn colours, with some heather still showing its purple. Through the marshy ground covered in reeds, they had to travel slowly, hoping the wheels would not stick. Gradually the narrow track became increasingly steeper and the reeds were no more: just short stubby grass. Although he had done this journey many times, he was always a little anxious as the steep track tucked into the side of the hill, following the contours of the land, and he knew just how steep the drop was on his left-hand side. This time, because of the heavy mist, he couldn't see it, even though he knew it was there. The cloud was so low that visibility was poor, and they both trusted the sure foot of their pony and his father's experience of the way.

As they travelled John let himself dream about the future and think that this Fair was maybe where he would meet a lass who was what he wanted, and not who his mother thought he should have. There was a significant difference!
His ma had brought lasses that were good cooks, pushing 'suitable' young women his way often, and that was fine, but there hadn't been one who he thought he wanted to spend his life with.
His da had told him there would be women a plenty, and all he had to do was choose. But how would he know if they would make him a good wife?

He would have to find one someday. And soon. And not just for him. It was important that a stock of children be reared, to help in the old age of the grandparents at least. As well as the parents.
He'd thought about this a lot. She would be bonny, but not too

bonny because he knew what problems that could cause. One of his friends, Danny, had a wife that was very pretty, and according to Danny it was a continual headache to him.

"Ah wish ah'd bin warned," he often sighed to John. At first Danny had been so proud that other men were looking at her, but when he saw her looking back he had revised his opinion. It had cost him a few bloody noses too because he didn't trust anyone who spoke to her in case they tried to lure her away from him. It was a terrible way to live together.

His advice to John had been, "Diven't choose a lass that's ower pretty. Thee'll rue the day."

John had decided that she would be quiet and respectful, not loud mouthed and coarse like many of the young women he had come across. Come to think of it, Danny's lass could be a bit like that, but Danny considered her to be sweetness itself.

She would look as if she could take care of a man. That sounded good, but he had no-idea what that meant, or what that would look like.

The next one was easy. She wouldn't be so young that she didn't know how to run a household like some of the silly young things his mother had tried to press on him.

He would need to look around with the right kind of lass in mind.

He mentally ticked them off.

Pretty, but not too pretty.

Quiet and respectful.

Capable, whatever that meant.

Not too young. Not too old either, he hastily added.

They would be there for two days and to John, that was time enough for everything. Miles' father had been born near Kirkby and his family lived nearby so they were going to be calling, and maybe sleeping on the cart overnight, if it didn't turn too cold.

They pulled up at the edge of town and made sure that the pony drank her fill from the river. After taking care that all was still securely on the cart, they led the tired pony to the edge of the market square, as near as they could, and hitched her up carefully, although they both knew from experience that she would not wander.

The whole square was alive already with so many sights, sounds and smells that it was impossible to isolate any one thing that caught your attention, John thought.

"Tak care ower John. Watch them what wants thy brass," warned Miles. "Niver tak thy een off it, or it'll gan."

John was more worried about his da's brass, but didn't dare say.

"Never worrit theesel. It's nee problem for me, da."

And they parted company.

As no buying or selling of goods could take place unless it was at a Fair or market, they were obviously busy places. This was a Trade Fair, and as usual there were many businessmen trading livestock, cheeses, hardware, and other products. The noise was something deafening and it usually took an hour or two to become acclimatized.

There were sheep bleating from the pens ranged along the roadside, geese cackling, hens squawking and roars of raucous laughter coming from the alehouses and beer tents as men took a break to eat, drink and exchange stories. This was where his father would be spending a few hours before placing a bet on a cock fight and losing his hard-earned shillings. There was music from street performers, a hurdy gurdy man, sellers shouting that their goods were the best, as well as children playing in the street, screaming and shouting above the din.

As he was inexperienced, John was always fascinated by and a bit in awe of the women who hung out of the windows at a certain renowned lodging house in Kirkby. They were to be avoided; his father had warned him. They promised the one thing that men wanted, and then robbed them of their goods and money, often without delivering on their promise.

Also to be avoided were the many guileful and well-trained pickpockets, who could relieve you of your brass and be gone without you being aware of their thieving actions.

There were many other things to see, but first and foremost John was interested in the food. He loved black pudding and beef sausage, and quickly saw someone selling parcels of the delicious food, fried, and producing such a smell that his stomach was clawing its way out of his mouth. It had been a long day since bread and dripping for breakfast and the small amount they had eaten on the way over. Roast pork was on offer too: delicious and succulent with crispy crackling skin. Before leaving he may have some of that, he decided.

But first he had to secure buyers for the goods on the cart that his father had left him in charge of. Farmers were always in need of what he had to sell, and it didn't take long. The cooking pots were of the best quality but less in demand, so they only realized a few shillings. Nevertheless, it had been worth making the journey.

Now he needed to make sure that this money didn't go on cock fighting or be lost at the bottom of a tankard. In other words, it was not to go in his father's pockets. His mother's instructions.

Miles had come with a few shillings to spend, and he was told not to spend any more. Any money made was meant to go towards the quarter's rent.

John, having finished his business, wandered about and through the crowds, listening to some and avoiding others, all the time making sure that he was not the subject of a pickpocket. Stopping in front of a musician playing the hurdy gurdy, he enjoyed the rhythmic sound for a while, feeling his feet want to move in time to the music. Further on he heard the shout ring out, "The best wool in England for the cheapest price." He saw little children playing, while trying not to drop their candy, for it would be a long time before they got more of the same.

Stopping next to a small knot of men, smoking pipes and talking to, or rather listening to, one of the many travelling men who came to the Fairs, passing on news from the rest of the country, John was particularly interested in one piece of information. A new bridge had been built it seemed, of cast iron, over a river.

Right over a river, and a wide one at that, they said. How was that even possible? *And it was* an arch bridge too. The first one to be made this way they said. He couldn't believe it would stay up.

The amount of iron needed to make such a bridge. Where would they get that? What a sight, but not near enough for him to visit.

"Nay, niver across a whole river," said one.

"Aye, and it needs mending already. The size of it's so great."

There was more talk about the war over the great sea, in America. It was a revolution, those that knew said. England was fighting to keep their lands there, or something like that.

He only knew his way from home to Kirkby and back again. If he'd been in the Militia, he might have had to fight in the army, and travelled. But he wasn't hankering after that. He loved to be just where he was now, but he could share in some of the excitement, just listening to the drovers and other travellers telling about it.

There were crowds around them, and they waved their arms and used their voices to give listeners a feel of the action. It was obvious they'd told these stories many times already, and they loved this feeling of importance.

Strolling around the fair, eating his delicious food, he chewed as slowly as he could to make it last longer, hot grease dripping down his chin and onto his shirt, and a mug of Dirty Maggie's ale in his other hand.

Should he buy a small trinket for his mother? He wished it were for his girl, and that set him thinking about his mission. Everyone knew that Fairs were a clever way of meeting others and beginning a courting that could end in a marriage – even a hasty one.

So, with that in mind, John cast his eyes carefully around the square, scanning each group of people with interest. He felt he would just know it when he saw the right girl for him. Not that young woman coming towards him. She looked at all who passed and knew she was turning heads. She was dressed in all finery and frippery, and looked like she would spend all his money before he had any. And she had a look of Danny's lass!

Nor that woman walking over the square. She was dressed like she belonged in a bawdy house, and she was coming straight towards him. Time to get away. He turned quickly to change direction, and as he did, caught sight of a young woman, selling her last few eggs to a grateful customer, turning towards him just as he turned towards her.

He liked the look of her. Where had he seen her before?

She was good to look at. Pleasing on the eye, his da would say.

She was dressed neatly too, and without airs. Her hair was hidden by a matronly bonnet, brightened with a ribbon of duck egg blue, but as she turned it fell and he could see her hair glowing as it was caught by a stray ray of sunshine. And then he remembered where it had been. Where'd he'd seen her? It was at his sister Jennet's wedding where he'd seen that wonderful hair before, framing the pretty face. He thought she was his brother-in-law William's cousin, a Fothergill, but he struggled to remember her name, if he ever knew it.

He decided quickly that she was the one he wanted to get to know and hoped he hadn't left it too late. That last time he hadn't been looking for a wife, but things had changed in the past two years, almost three. He was most definitely looking now!

In a perfect example of synchronicity, Alice had noticed the man across the square as he had noticed her. She'd glanced at him and then looked away, carrying on with the job in hand, but she'd made some observations already.

He didn't seem to be selling but was walking leisurely around, if a little unsteadily, so she knew by that and by his slightly flushed face that he had been tasting the brewed ale at Dirty Maggie's, the name given to the local inn, a good while ago, and staying now for ever probably. Elizabeth had warned about the effects of this brew on the local men, and to avoid any she thought may have sampled it. It would be very obvious, she said.

Maggie was the toothless old crone responsible for this brew. Even though the business of brewing and selling ale was a profitable one, she seemed to prefer dressing in rags, and dirty ones at that. She smoked a clay pipe, and in a phrase that Alice used of such folks, was a stranger to clean water and a wash rag, or to any water for that matter. As she walked past, the pungent aroma she left behind her almost made your eyes smart, even more so than the usual person. But you could forgive her all that because her ale was said to taste like no other, and no-one had been able to brew any half as good. Maggie herself said she would take the recipe to the grave. A few brave men had tried to court her for the sake of the recipe but had given up when the task proved just too impossible even from those like her, who also didn't like using a rag and clean water.

By now Alice was feeling quite hungry, so looked around for somewhere she could eat. Eventually finding a pocket of grass at the edge of the square to sit and eat the bit of food she'd brought; she took off her thick shawl and spread it on the ground. Elizabeth was nowhere to be seen, but she wasn't afraid of being alone here. Standing and talking seemed to be weary work today.

The bread from her kitchen was a little stale but the cheese and lump of bacon were good. That and a cold potato, baked in the fire oven, made a feast. A mug of Maggie's ale would have been good to keep out the chill but knew she couldn't. Someone would see her and tell. That was a fact.

As she sat and chewed thoughtfully, she felt a shadow at her side. How did she know who it was before she looked up? The man who had caught her interest before. She thought he had a familiar look about him but didn't know why.

He asked her pardon to sit down next to her, but at a respectable distance, and kept his face turned to the front, not looking straight at her.

From here she could see, as she snatched sidelong glances, that his face was weathered, even for such a young man. She thought him to be about twenty-five or so, just younger than her. A lock of corn coloured hair had escaped from his cap, falling in a curl down his forehead, and he constantly pushed it back from his face as he ate his lump of pork, covered with what looked like delicious crispy skin. Her mouth watered at the sight of it. Seeing her eyeing the pork, and noticing that she had only plain food, he leaned towards her and asked, "Good day to thee miss. Would thee like to try a piece."

Astounded at herself for even contemplating sharing food with an unknown man she nodded, and accepted the food he offered, unable to keep the sheer pleasure from her face as she tasted the delicious morsel.

"That be truly kind of thee. But I've nowt t' give thee," she said, more shyly than usual.

The words came to his lips before he even thought of them and he replied, "A smile would be enough for me."

She was blushing too hard to smile and kept her head down so he couldn't see.

He was a working man of course, as she could smell hot iron about him. 'A Blacksmith,' she thought. His clothes said the same. They were dirty and could have done with a good shake at least.

And then without a word, he gathered up his things, doffed his cap, and went, striding across towards the centre of town.

She watched his back as he went and was surprised but very pleased when he turned his face towards her and winked, showing eyes glittering like emeralds, a smile that changed his whole face, and changed he

Chapter 4

Courtship.

"I ne'er was struck before that hour

With love so sudden and so sweet.

Her face it bloomed like a sweet flower

And stole my heart away complete."

(John Clare)

It was now late afternoon and getting cool so Alice felt it was the right time to leave the Fair and make the walk to her sister's house. It was raining, but not too much. Even so it made the road 'a clarty mess', she told Elizabeth.
She was even more glad to get to her room at the very top of the house where it was cosy and comfortable. She took up her supper, cold chicken pie and a few pickles from the kitchen and lit the fire that was set ready for her. A luxury she thought, not having to set it herself.

Her sister had four children, from nine years with the youngest being only a year old and she loved spending time with them, but she was so, so tired tonight.

And she had other plans, wanting to spend the time on the new bonnet she was sewing her sister as a surprise for Christmas when it came. She lit the two candles she'd been given, when daylight could no longer reach the small window under the eaves, hoping to make them last.

Alice was a neat and very competent needlewoman but had to concentrate even more tonight as thoughts of the fair-haired young man she'd seen at the Fair were making her a little careless. Finally, she left her sewing when she was too tired to see her way to stitch, and brushing her hair for twice the usual time she wondered if she would see him the next day. It took her a good while to fall asleep, and this night, for the first time in an age, she dreamed of her ma and da.

It was a family occasion, but there was no sign of her brother and sister, gone for almost as long. As is usual with dreams, there was a strange turn to events, as she found her grandparents, who she could not even remember, were present too.

Nevertheless, she woke full of memories of the dream and feeling very hopeful that her day would bring her all that she now wanted.

Her sister had promised she would spend the day with her as there was indeed a theatre troupe visiting and jugglers too. A treat she thought. There will be singing too. She loved singing.

And of course, he might be there.

The next day although slightly better, the weather was still not good. In the early morning clouds darkened the sky then rain showers promised to make the ground even wetter and muddier.

As Alice had feared, despite her promise Elizabeth was not keen to go out walking in the town, especially with four children in tow, although the two oldest were really enjoying the Fair under their own steam. Alice, employing a tear or two she had found often worked in these situations with Elizabeth, gently reminded her of her promise. Once it was agreed she was almost dancing with excitement as they wrapped up warmly with thick shawls and bonnets to walk the short distance into town.

Now she needed to talk to her sister about the events of the day before. Best not to leave it a complete surprise.

"Sister. Ah spied a lad yesterday ah thowt ah knew."

"Let uz knaw if tha sees 'im today."

"And sister, ah woz leet-heeaded, he woz so bonny."

"An that's thy want. A bonny man?" Elizabeth walked faster, in front of her so Alice couldn't see the signs of amusement on her face.

She saw him as soon as they turned the corner, dressed in no different clothing, no better than yesterday but with a cleaner face, at least looking sharply around and scanning the crowds for something.

Nudging Elizabeth's elbow to let her know, they both watched as he found what he was looking for. His hand went up and he strode over the square – towards an older man. His da perhaps she thought, nothing alike in looks but there was something that spoke to that relationship as they went into the alehouse together.

Alice was bitterly disappointed that he hadn't been searching for her but if she could have heard the conversation inside the tavern she would have been better pleased and would have blushed with embarrassment.

Once inside John grabbed his father quickly by the arm, led him to the ale tap and blurted out, "Da. One of them lasses out there is reet bonny."

"Oh aye, an which one is that?" asked Miles, quizzically inclining his head with its weather reddened cheeks, and then tipping John a wink and a smile. He knew full well which girl John had his eye on. He'd seen the shy looks passing between them and fully approved his son's choice.

"Ye'd better speak to her then," as he handed him a flagon.

"An whit will ah say? Ah've nowt t'say. Whit can ah say t'a pretty lass like that?"

"It'll cum t'thee. Diven't worry. Or juz tell her she's bonny. They like that."

John had heard it said that his da liked the ladies and this seemed to be proof, from his own lips.

The day began too slowly. He'd seen her looking at him. How could he speak to her? He needed to at least begin to get to know the lass better and want her to be interested in him, although from the morning before he already felt that she was. The secretive looks she'd been giving him when she thought he wasn't looking were proof of that.

He walked slowly across the square once more. A misting drizzle had replaced the heavy showers, and everything was damp and cold but thankfully, not soaking wet.

Standing still for a while, he weighed up his next actions and then thought that it had better be done now and quickly.

Striding quickly over to the stall where Alice and an older woman were looking at cloth, he stood near waiting his chance.

"This'd be grand fur a bonnet sister but t'blue would mak sich a bonny gown."

"Oh Alice, William wuldn't like me te spend on such fancy clobber. Ah've nee need o' that."

Looking at the beautiful fabric, Alice burned for something new for herself beholden as she was to her brother-in-law for every penny. "Summat plainer fer uz?" she whispered, hopefully. "Wot think tha?"

Elizabeth took a long look at her sister's clothing as if she hadn't seen it before. And what she saw, *really* saw, made her realize how well she herself was dressed in comparison. Alice's dress had a plain skirt well mended, with a bodice that had been let out as Alice had grown in years and other places. Sighing, she realized that if she was to find a husband she needed to at least have one new dress. Remembering how generous their da had been when she herself was looking for a husband, she answered kindly with, "Ah can manage t'get thee a length o't'wool, but not t'muslin. An a lang o'cotton for t'bodice."

Feeling excited now Alice leaned forward and lightly picked up a corner of the fine wool cloth between her fingers. It felt so dainty in her hand and would be so easy to sew. She pictured the finished gown: a skirt from the fine wool in a shade of green and a new bodice in white, buttoned at the front with a drawstring neck. It would have an overskirt gathered up in a patterned cotton because she had some of that at home. She was not to have muslin but what she could have was more than she dared ask for. Her sister was being very generous.

Watching it carefully measured, cut and parcelled around with string was a treat in itself. Gratefully picking up her parcel she turned quickly to be on her way wanting to watch the theatre troupe, when suddenly she collided with a tall body standing so near to her that they were the same shadow.

She'd just enough time to scream in anguish at her beautiful dress being ruined before she had even begun sewing as her parcel fell to the ground.

Quick as lightning a hand reached down and grabbed it up so quickly that the wet stones didn't spoil it. Not too much anyway. Looking up to thank the person who was handing her precious parcel back to her she found herself looking into those same eyes, emerald green, but strangely tinged with flecks of gold that she hadn't been aware of the day before.

She found she was trembling while her heart began to pound in her chest. In fact, she felt quite light-headed and had to grab the nearest support to stop her from sprawling over the cobbles. She said later that she was glad that it had been Elizabeth's arm she'd used, and not the man's.

"Ah was all ov a'dother," she said to Elizabeth.

Taking charge of the situation, and pressing any advantage he had, John took Alice's arm to steady her, and felt her trembling. Was that good or bad? He had no clue.

"Whar's thee bound tee lasses?" he asked them. Then putting on his best voice he said as confidently as he dared, "If thee want t'see t'Mummers the speeches have started," continuing with, "and ah will see you and your friend are safe in the cludder an out o'yon clarts."

"Tha wud, wud tha?" spoke her sister raising her head from making payment and seeing who was standing next to Alice.
'Oh Alice. Thee has done well there,' thought her sister. 'A good catch.'
Speaking to this striking young man standing there looking very sheepish, she announced, "Ah can say now, that I know thee."
They had all met at John's sister Jennet's wedding almost three years ago and now Alice knew why he looked a little familiar. With relief she knew now that he was a respectable man.
Elizabeth took charge as she always did, making Alice feel very inferior. She wasn't happy about this side to her sister's character and found her very bossy and controlling, often telling her so but she realized that this wasn't an occasion to complain about it.
'Let her get on,' thought Alice. 'See what she can do.' She stood meekly beside her sister and waited.

"Come wi'uz Sir, an' we'll talk," her sister ordered.

"Go this road, oot o' t'blood o' t'cock fight. Thee wadn't want it t'sowk in thy good duds."

What he really meant was, "Let's go this way so you don't see me da lounging against the grey stones of the building, watching and cheering on the fight and hoping to win back some of the shillings he had already lost." His mother would be patiently waiting and hoping.

And Miles had possibly or even probably, spent it all.

Alice felt her face flush and redden and burn with a blistering heat of embarrassment but also touched with anger. Did she have no say herself? But, nevertheless she gracefully complied, and they walked briskly together over the muddy square through a light drizzle falling from a dirty sky.

Alice walked on one side of him and her sister on the other, carrying one child and leading another.

John was anxious and beginning to sweat in spite of the cold of the day. He couldn't believe what he'd done or that he was being allowed to spend time in this young woman's company.

Alice was able to look more closely at this very good-looking young man. But she felt a bit ashamed for him because of the clothing he was wearing, although he didn't seem to care. His knee length breeches were worn into holes as were his stockings and his linen shirt was more coloured grey than the white it had been when his mother had first stitched it.

Elizabeth was pleased that Alice seemed to have snared this, very suitable young man herself and knew that at her age there wouldn't be many more chances, if any at all.
How Alice hadn't remembered John, Elizabeth didn't for the life of her know. He was so handsome and worthy of remembering she thought. So he was a Blacksmith. It was good that he had a trade and Blacksmiths were always busy and well respected. He seemed to want to avoid the cock fighting that was on show, but she had her own thoughts on why that was. He thought highly of his mother and respected his father she found in conversation. What more was there to say? Alice seemed to be extremely interested so Elizabeth took on the role of matchmaker and chaperone.

They spent a pleasant afternoon at the Fair watching the Juggling and the Mummers Play. The smell of the beef sausage was so tantalizing that Elizabeth bought a piece for them to share, with John refusing to take any. He'd spent his money on a small silver spoon for his da to give to his ma.
And now taking control once more, Elizabeth said if he was interested in a courtship it would be a promising idea for him to

visit Southwaite the following week. She herself would be there. He was interested, of course he was, but he was also rather alarmed at how fast things were developing.

John was sure his own father Miles would approve and his mother too. He hadn't taken much notice at Jennet's wedding but he wondered why not. As for Alice herself, true she quite liked the look of him. He was rather dirty and unkempt but she knew she would change that. And if she had her own man she could sew and cook for him too.

The rest of being a wife, the more intimate details she would have to learn. And that was what was worrying her more than a little. Now she had no ma she'd have to ask Elizabeth!

As for John as he stood in the fading light of a late autumn afternoon he knew that she was the girl for him and that he wanted to set up home with her as soon as he could, if she was willing.

Chapter 5

Marriage and the early years 1782

"If equal affection cannot be
Let the more loving one be me,"

(WH Auden)

Very soon they were betrothed with the families' delighted consent. John's parents were pleased he had found a 'daycent lass' and so was his friend Danny, but he warned John again about marrying such a 'bonny lass'. He was having great problems with his lass, he said, and the men who followed her around. John was a little concerned to hear that, as Danny's Mary was nowhere *near* as pretty as John's Alice. If Danny was to be believed he would need to be careful.

It was agreed by both families that after marriage the sensible solution would be for the couple to live at Southwaite with John taking over the farm lease, despite having little experience of farming. Elizabeth was very pleased with this as it would release her husband from paying for the lease of Southwaite, but it would leave his father Miles rather shorthanded in the smithy. Not wanting to stand in the way of his son's happiness Miles said he would make do and probably start an apprentice.

Alice sat in church with her sister Elizabeth and family hearing the Banns being read in Saint Stephen's Church Kirkby Stephen on Sunday 3rd March 1782, and the next two Sundays, while John heard the Banns at St Mary's Muker.

They would both rather have been married by license as it was less public that way but they couldn't afford the cost and John's parents wanted it done 'properly'.

She heard herself described as a single woman of this parish and John a single man of the parish of Aysgarth and was grateful that their ages hadn't been revealed because she was aware now that she was older than him by six years. But what she felt now was that it was no-one else's business.

All would be well.

They would be married on Thursday 21st March (1782).

As a particularly good needlewoman Alice had sewn herself the dress she had imagined at the Fair that day at their first meeting and also the customary shirt for John, although because of the brief time she'd had some help with that from a neighbour.

Since that day they had spent some time together, sometimes but seldom, alone. It was often the case that a baby was on the way before the wedding day and this was considered useful as a proof of fertility but Alice was determined she wouldn't shame herself in that way. Before the sun began to rise on her wedding day Alice was up taking care of her usual chores, feeding the geese and collecting the eggs.

"Hold on my chicks. Givover peckin' at uz. What a cletch thee be," she spoke softly to the brood of young birds.

After that she looked in on the pig, they were rearing for slaughter the next year and gave him the slops and other such disgusting rubbishy treats that a pig likes. He wasn't noticeably big yet she considered and would need lots of fattening up over the spring and summer. Young Harry had already milked the cows and given them some fresh hay so that was one less job for her to do on this exciting day.

She'd spent the days before cooking and baking for the friends and family who would expect something to eat, and among many other things she'd made a large mutton pie which was usual at wedding feasts.

Thankfully, the day was breaking clear and dry, with just a powdering of fresh sparkling white frost on the high hillside. It had been a bad winter with snow so deep that some weeks it had been impossible to even go to Market. An unusual steady thaw from the beginning of March had meant that most of the snow had now gone but still lingered in huge amounts on the hilltops and would not truly go for a month at least.

Alice had been glad of the geese and the eggs and meat they provided that winter as well as the smoked and cured pork that everyone laid down for bad weather if they could afford to.

Quietly she busied herself in the kitchen singing softly to herself and laying out the food for later. This morning she had thought of her father and mother, and wondered what they would have made of this. They may perhaps have married her off sooner to a match of their choice, and shuddering at the thought she said to herself, "Well, it may have been a good marriage. Who would know now? At least I've had a say in it"

She thought of the years she'd spent without them both, but there was no point dwelling on that. She could only hope to have some influence over the future that would be changed for the better for them all.

Her brother-in-law had risen early to collect her for church in Kirkby Stephen. She was nervous and felt her poor stomach turn over as she thought about what lay ahead for her. Once she was wed she became her husband's property. The fact that she had no father or brothers made no difference because they would have had no say anyway. She would be at the mercy of the man she was spending the rest of her life with. She prayed to God that he was a good one. She thought she'd chosen well but you never can tell.

Dressing carefully she brushed her long brown hair once more and tied on her bonnet. As she left the farmhouse she visited their small flower garden and picked a posy of the only flowers she could find this early in the year. Walking head held high, she departed out of the garden towards the cart and her new life.

....

Much earlier that day, over in Thorns John's mother Elizabeth had made sure that she and Miles were as well turned out as possible. John had a new white shirt sewn by his bride-to-be, as was the custom. He would keep it all his life and would probably wear it every day. They had all washed with a jug of tepid water and a clean rag. The best 'going to church' clothes had been retrieved from under the bed and given a good shake to remove vermin. Mother Elizabeth had treated herself to a bright blue bonnet that was almost the colour of her husband's eyes. Struck with a romantic notion, she remembered her own wedding day. There had been some challenging times, and some babies that were not to be, but there had been many good times too. Miles was a man of few words but she knew he loved her. That was all that mattered.

As they had much further to travel and had to cross the high lands between Thorns and Kirkby, setting off before it was light was the only way they could make sure to be there on time. Thankfully, the moon was full and bright shining like a beacon on the hillside, illuminating and lighting the way. They had only travelled a mile or two when feeling every one of his fifty or so years, Miles leaned forward in his seat and kneaded his knuckles into the base of his spine trying to ease the aches. The day before had been harder than usual trying to catch up or even get ahead of his work so that he could be away for this important day. Managing without John was going to mean he had to work even harder. An apprentice would be willing, but young and inexperienced hands.
Steering their faithful pony over the way she knew so well, he guiltily longed for the journey, and even the day, to be over.
Sitting by his side, many thoughts were fleeting through John's head too. He'd been lucky enough to secure a position at the forge in Outhgill in the Mallerstang Valley near their home in Southwaite, with the Master Blacksmith, but he would also have farmwork too.

John was an uneducated man but had a natural curiosity about the workings of many things. He'd never seen the need to be able to write before now and certainly couldn't read, but he'd been practicing something for quite a while. He wanted to be able to write his name in the Church register instead of merely making a mark. Both he and Alice had asked their own parish clerk to provide a copy for them at the first reading of the banns, and they had dutifully practiced, on the ice, or the wet ground, with a sharp stick. It was a matter of pride for John, and Alice wanted to please her husband. Writing your name was a sign you were better than those that couldn't.

At 10 o' the clock in front of the high altar table, the young couple were married with their families around them, on that sunny wintry morning at St Stephens Church, Kirkby Stephen. The ceremony was witnessed by sister Elizabeth's husband Will Harker, and by the church clerk, Edward Cowperthwaite, who obligingly witnessed all the weddings as he had to be there anyway.

As they came out of the church, after a brief spell of weak winter sunshine, the sky darkened, and spreading clouds blotted out the daylight.

On the cold journey back to Southwaite, Alice rode with John and his father, mother and young sister. Pulling her warm shawl around her, she thought about the rest of the day, and the rest of her life. The journey gave her ample time to do just that.

It was tantalizing.

What kind if a husband would he be? She hoped she knew the answer to that one from what she already knew.

How many children?

Would they be happy?

Once back to their home the celebrations would begin.

It wasn't long before there was raucous singing and some dancing, plenty of food, and to Alice's embarrassment, much joking at the young couple's expense about what would be happening later that night.

It was like a dream Alice felt. She didn't seem to be able to spend much time with John but looked after their guests, providing plenty of food and ale. Her mutton pie was remarked on, and John was gratified and relieved that she was at least a good cook.

The scraping and squealing of the fiddle's lively tune were a constant noise and at one point Miles insisted that she and John lead a jig around the room. She obliged but felt that she didn't like all eyes on her and was glad when she was allowed to return to her other duties.

While his mother spent her time helping Alice John and his father seemed to be drinking more and more. In fact all the men were drinking jug after jug of ale and some of the women too. And then without warning a few would call on the fiddler, break out into very loud singing, and then swing their partners around knocking into others and spilling drink on the rush covered floor.

Her brother-in-law William, Elizabeth's husband, in company with many others, was finding it difficult to keep his feet. His words too weren't making much sense and slurring into each other. Elizabeth sent daggers to him through her eyes but he was oblivious.

In a corner, Jennet and her husband, solicitous of his very pregnant wife, were nursing their baby.
Throughout all of this noise and seeming happiness Alice thought about the choice she had made and hoped her choice had been a good one.

Family left for their long journeys and only neighbours were left. Finally at the end of a lively evening with much whistling, shouting and loud jeering, the two left to go upstairs to their bedroom. John had bid everyone a courteous good night and Alice more embarrassed than she could ever have imagined had kept her eyes lowered to the floor. She picked up her favourite woollen shawl, the one that had been her mother's, and leaning in towards her new husband, she felt his body warmth and his arm snake round her waist and she knew then that all would be well.
At the same time John was also thinking about the future. They had a new life together a hard one, like it was for everyone, but he had a skill that would always provide a living — more than farm

labouring at least. Blacksmiths always had work. He had a wife to provide for now but he knew that she was a hard worker too very pleased to have him as a husband and would do all she could to make his home life comfortable. It was a little disappointing that she was not yet having a bairn but that would soon be remedied. now they were wed.

Chapter 6

Early Married Life ~ Alice 1782

"There is nothing nobler or more admirable than when two people who see eye to eye keep house as man and wife, confounding their enemies and delighting their friends."

(Homer)

Alice found very quickly that married life was very similar to unmarried life. She had the same work to do with only one important change, and that was providing them with the child they were both wanting. Every week she carried out the tasks the same as before in the farmhouse in Southwaite where she had grown up. It was still a full two weeks before Christmas. After milking the few milkers they had and feeding all the beasts John made sure he had the time to do an extra but very important task. She'd never forgive him if he didn't. He knew that well enough. So off he went into the neighbouring woodland blanketed now in a deep cover of snow. Although it was well after dusk this fresh fine snow, like crystallised ice, sparkled and shone by the light of a very helpful full moon. He'd already scouted the area to which he was relatively new, and had spotted an old Oak, its trunk split and blasted by a storm some years ago it seemed. Now taking up his axe he split away one side of the trunk and hacked himself a decent sized log, leaving another for a neighbour if they should need one. This was dead wood and should burn well he knew. "Alice'll be well pleased with that," he said aloud, congratulating himself. They hadn't been wed long and all he wanted to do was to please her. Attaching ropes to the heavy log he used his horse to pull this very important festive log over the snow-covered ground towards their cottage. The cold was striking him through and he wasn't one for seeing the beauty of nature, or he would have remarked at least to himself at the effect of the snow twinkling like the stars above. Or the tall trees with their snow-covered branches showing shapes that looked like huge creatures outlined against the moon lit sky. But he did notice footprints that he recognized as a fox's and determined to make sure their geese were well defended. When he was not far from their door and could see the windows lit by candlelight Alice came out and joined him, her thickest winter shawl covering her head wrapped tight against the cold. Strong leather boots kept her feet dry but her petticoats were dragging through the snow and soaking up water like a wick. "Aye, tie on them ribbons lass," he ordered Alice and watched as she tied coloured ribbons all over the log. Then walked the few steps to the door. Everyone who helped with the Yule Log was supposed to have good luck in the coming year and who didn't want that? Dragging it in together they laid one end in the fireplace. A blessing was said and then wine was poured over it to make it feel welcome. After lighting it with a torch they stood back and watched the flames curl around the log as the fire took hold.

"Let us all have good fortune this year, lass."

"Aye, let's," she whispered to him. The good fortune they both wanted was a bairn.

He knew that Alice had been out herself collecting greenery to decorate their home on this their first ever Christmas together. That morning she had told him, "Now John. Don't thee be fetching holly for ah's getting' it meself, this very day." She went on, " An' I seed sum Ivy too."

"Will yee be making a Kissing Bough, my darlin' wife?"

"I will, if I can mak the time," she smiled at him. Of course she was. She already had the ribbons and candles and had earmarked the very greenery she needed to make these ornaments which would be hung one above the door and one in the kitchen.

"An then thee'll gi'uz the first kiss," he laughed.

"Ah'll gie yee as many as thee wants," she laughed back.

"Whit abaht the young lass helps in the dairy parlour? She's very comely," he said. And immediately he knew he'd gone too far with his teasing. A cloud came down over his young wife's face and she turned away from him. 'Why dis ah always dooa that?' he remonstrated with himself.

"Ah Alice lass. It were ainly a piece o'mischief." And then he saw her face. She was laughing at him.

"Ah nooah that John Hutchinson. Do you think ah would allow her near yee if ah thout thee couldn't be trusted?" She laughed out loud and walked away into the kitchen.

He knew she'd already begun the bough because he'd seen it tucked away in one of the outhouses. It was near to being finished and only needed ribbons and candles to be attached.

At last it was Christmas Eve. She had sent him out to collect the ivy and holly she'd seen and together they made sure that the mantel and the window frames were well covered.

"Well gooa and fetch them John. Thee nooas where they is, ah've nooa doubt," she smiled at him. He grinned back and hurriedly leaving the kitchen he returned in a scarce two minutes carrying the biggest and best kissing boughs he had seen and he told her so. His mothers were all that he had to compare with and hers were remarked on in all of Swaledale. Each of the two boughs was composed of five wooden hoops making the shape of a ball. This had been artistically and carefully covered with Holly, Ivy,

Rosemary, Bay and Fir. It wasn't the first time she'd made these as this had always been her responsibility even before she had married. But now she was making them for her husband, and that was special.

She was a wife now. Not only a daughter. Smiling with contentment she took red apples stored away from Autumn and hung them from red ribbons inside the hoops. To finish she put a candle inside the ball at the bottom.

"What about the Mistletoe?" John queried. She shyly produced a bunch, and he hung some from the bottom of each bough.

Again he said, "E'en better than ma's." And now, paying attention to the next job he took a Kissing Bough and hung it in the porchway before the front door. The evening was off to a particularly good start. The second bough was hung in the main room off the kitchen.

The next morning Christmas morning they looked out of their small, frost-covered bedroom window. There had been another good covering through the night and the valley was drowned in snow, but John still had to get up and see to the milkers. Ducks and geese had to be fed too.

They had a few neighbours who were mostly farmers and whom Alice had known all of her life, the nearest one being Peggy Carter, an old widow. She and Alice's mother were old acquaintances and had helped each other out in the past after both losing their husbands.

They went to Church together that day ,not far, just along the road, in Outhgill and took Awld Peg with them to this small church that had been renovated by 'The Lady Ann'. This particular morning it was full of farmers and their families, as well as farm labourers, those who were working in other professions, and those who were being kept by the Poor Law. The Church was, in fact, fuller than Alice had ever seen it. "Would thee look at that," her Peg spotted, "Ower there. Next t't'awld lass wi nee teeth." There were many who could have fitted that description, so she looked all around. "Ower there lass," she spoke in an exasperated voice. Alice looked again, more carefully, in the direction Peg was nodding, and she saw what she meant. A woman stood there, clothes in rags, face the colour of the dirty roadway, but round her head she wore a headband of many different coloured ribbons. "She's ain o' the Travellers Peg," Alice told her. "Aye she is," Peg replied. "But she's thy da's sister tooa." Alice looked open mouthed. This was something new.

"She left to join the Mummers afore she could be wed. Ah was niver sure if aah believed it or not. Thee da teld awl that she was meant t'wed an awld farmer of hereabouts, but she craved a different life. She ain't bin seen here for more'n twenty years now. An there she be"

"Ah want to ask her home wi'uz. Aye, ah dooah."

Alice approached the dirty old woman, politely introduced herself as the old woman's niece, and asked her to come home with them. That was the first time. Next, she begged, but the old crone was still adamant.

"Jus for the day? Thy brother would 'ave been so happy."

The woman stood before them in her rags, but proud and upright. Hearing the words, she realized her brother was dead. She hadn't known of this. But still she wouldn't come. She had made her life, she said, and she was happy. She was just visiting the old places today.

Feeling that she had let her da down, she left the Church and solemnly walked the way home. But as soon as they walked through the door and shed their wet outer garments, they began the serious business of the meal. John had killed the goose. Alice had plucked it and saved the feathers for a pillow and then stuffed it. And soon the smell of goose roasting on a slow spit on the fire wafted through the house. They had potatoes, carrots, and parsnip, roasted in the fat from the goose with batter pudding, and the gravy was made from the giblets. To follow of course there was plum pudding. Alice's ma had been old enough to remember a dish called, 'Plumb Porridge,' which was a sort of soup, made from a shin of beef, thickened with bread, dried fruit sugar and wine added, then seasoned with mace and nutmeg and she had talked about it every Christmas Alice remembered.

The Yule Log burned in the hearth. Visitors came that evening and were embraced under the Kissing Boughs.

"Dooah thy neighbour John Alderson play the fiddle?" John asked.

"Well that he dooah."

"An will he be callin toneet?"

"Ah believe he may."

And he did. He brought his fiddle and played for the whole evening. There were songs such as, *'I saw Three Ships'* and *'Fare thee Well'* which allowed for a great deal of dancing, and other tunes that were well known to many. As they had to rise early the next morning, being farmers, the visitors left at a reasonable hour, apart from Alice's cousin William, married to John's sister Jennet. They were staying the night with John and Alice, which was fortunate, considering the weather and the potential problems travelling to Hanging Lund, further up the Valley.

Once all others had left the four had a warming drink of mulled wine.

Alice and John rose early to carry out their chores, and then Alice cooked a hearty breakfast for her guests, as was expected, and for any farm hands who were helping out over Christmas.

Goose eggs had been collected and two each prepared, as well as slices of ham that had been smoking in the large chimney place. Hunks of fresh bread and home-made butter added to the meal, together with ale brewed by Alice herself.
"I can scarce walk dear sister," Jennet complained.
"Do not blame me dear one," Alice replied. "I did not force the food down thy throat, she laughed. "Thee needs to say, NAY."
"She cannae say Nay,' her husband laughed.
Crossing the room towards her, Alice put her arms around her, and patted the bump that Jennet was so clearly showing. "Keep that dear bairn warm," she said, smiling.

Although some would have no work over the Christmas holiday, which did not end till 12th Night, the 6th January, if you were a farmer, with beast to look after, you always had work to do.
Over these twelve days they enjoyed as much as they could. There were evenings when the fiddler played, and evenings when they sang all the songs they could remember. In tune or not, it didn't seem to matter. They enjoyed it all the same.

One night they played *Snap Apple,* where john fastened an apple to the end of a stick and a lighted candle to the other end, suspended from the ceiling by a string. Players had to attempt to take a bite from the apple.

Alice had tried. Others had tried. But the only one who could accomplish this was John.

"Ah, dear wife. Thee must bow to the greater mastery of thy husband's greater teeth."

On 12th Night all greenery had to be taken outside and burned or risk a year's bad luck. And who would want to risk that?

Alice and John now occupied the cottage alone.

At the back of the home was the heap of household rubbish, to be seen outside everyone's home. It may have been a little further to walk to dispose of anything, but at least it was not in plain view, and the pig got most of it. The midden hut was further away. But often it was just a walk into the open air, with a spade if needed.

Inside the farmhouse it was fairly comfortable, with a table and chairs and a wooden settle beside the fire.

The peat fire smouldered and sent smoke into the room when the wind blew a gale outside, or even when it didn't, and it whistled down the chimney, with a ghostly moaning sound.

Alice spent a lot of time outside in the small vegetable garden so necessary for their survival, next to the narrow beck of spring water that provided this necessity for them and their neighbours. Planting would have to start soon and later she would attempt a herb garden, she thought, with plants she knew had healing properties. Cooking as usual was on the fire, with the large cooking pot she was used to, dangling over the heat. In the evenings when they were sitting on the old wooden settle that had belonged to her father's family, in front of the fire, sometimes eating there, she felt most content. The fire gave out pinpoint light and they only had tallow and reed candles, but she felt warm, cosy and content with him beside her.

He was her rock, so strong and always dependable. Yes, she had to persuade him to wash more often than he wanted when he came home. A bucket of water from the water butt was the place for that and was always ready at the back of the house. He was as black as the night sometimes when he came home, and a little dirt went a long way.

"John Hutchinson. Don't thee be cumin in here with thy dirty boots, and dirty duds, and dirty hands," she shouted at him, as he walked towards their door.

He smiled at her and made a show of running to the door where she stood, barring him, hands on hips and smiling, despite her words.

Many an evening this was their way, and it often ended with him picking her up, and twirling her round, with his dirty hands and dirty clothes. And she loved it.

Sometimes he would walk past, and doff his cap to her, saying, "Hello good lady. Is thy husband home?"

And then, undressing down to his shirt he would plunge his head into a tub of water and rub the dirt away from his face and hair with his hands, shaking his head like a shaggy dog, with water droplets landing on anyone who was near enough. The whole business usually took less than five minutes, which was just as well in the winter when he had to break the ice on the top of the barrel. On days that were too cold he washed indoors with a dish of water and a rag, and those nights went to bed much dirtier than she would wish.

There was sometimes a little soap. Stockings were washed and breeches changed as he undressed to his undershirt. He couldn't understand her needing to wash so much. In that she was rather unusual, she knew.

Days passed, weeks passed, months passed. He looked forward to coming home to her, and the good meals she could prepare with very little money. He was proud of the fact that she had a plentiful vegetable garden, and that they also had a herb garden.

Neighbours called to see if she had anything for this ailment, or that ailment, and sometimes went home with a little something to add to the cooking pot.

In fact, it was almost time for St Luke's Fair when she felt a strange stirring in her belly. A fluttering as if there was a butterfly caught there. She had wondered for the past two months about the changes in her, as her mother had never spoken of such things. So, having no experience of this, she couldn't be sure. Best to say nothing, she thought, until it was more noticeable. But, wanting advice, she consulted Old Peggy, who, having digested all available information, looked at Alice, smiled and agreed.

"Aye. There's a bairn. By Eastertide 'appen," a year after they had been wed.

The next month was one of the longest of her life, and in the end, she just had to tell him. The air was buzzing with her suppressed excitement. How he hadn't picked up on her mood she didn't know.

In the end, "There's a bairn comin," was all she said.

He wasn't stunned into silence. He didn't shout with excitement, or lift her up, or show that he was in any way pleased, for the whole of five seconds. But then she saw the smile that lit up his face, the one she'd seen the day they'd met at the Fair.

"Well Alice, lass. About time" he whispered into her neck and kissed her forehead and throat.

How proud he was, as well as rather relieved, that there were going to be children. A married man had to produce children to prove he was a man. And a wife had to have children. It was her duty. But he was just so happy for them both.

And now it was all she could think of. Every morning she looked down and marvelled at how big her belly could grow. As time went on her ankles swelled. Sleep was becoming more difficult. She was so tired.

What would it feel like?

What would happen?

How would she know?

There were so many questions. And she knew nothing. She'd asked Jennet of course, but got no information there, or from her sister Elizabeth. Telling her she would just know, was no help at all. What would she know? They'd both survived the experience, a number of times, and didn't seem daunted about going through it again. But they were either unwilling or unable to describe it.

And she had no mother to ask either. She remembered her sister Jane being born, in this very house, in the very bed she shared with John. But she'd been sent out walking, with her brother John. And when they had returned, much later, their mother was sitting up in bed, smiling, with a baby in her arms. That was the only experience she had. Her mother had looked tired, but happy, as Alice met her new sister for the first time.

She spent her evenings now mending the holes in John's pockets and had sewn a full set of clothes for her baby, as well as for the crib. She couldn't wait until she had a daughter she could teach to sew.

Holding her belly with both hands, 'Oh it's so heavy' Alice complained as she walked around her small garden that morning looking over the valley. It must be near her time she thought.

It couldn't be too bad surely.

There were many children born in the valley in her time and before and if it was so bad an experience she figured there wouldn't be so many children.

She carried on in her sublime ignorance waiting for her time to become a mother until she was as knowledgeable as any mother. Now she knew all about this big secret.

And how wrong she'd been she thought afterwards. How could a woman go through that time after time – like pulling a loaf of bread through your nose, was the only analogy she could think of. Why didn't men have this torture? The bible said it was woman's lot because of original sin and Eve eating the apple. Well, Adam had done it too.

Their first born was a boy, on a spring day in April 1783. The birth had been painfully unremarkable and Old Peggy had helped to deliver the squalling baby into the world. Alice looked down at him feeling that she could spend hours and hours gazing at this little person so perfect and so beautiful. Even if his face was a little scrunched and wrinkled to her he was perfect. She ran her hand over his downy little head breathing in the smell of him and stroked his dark hair wisping round his forehead smiling into his innocent blue eyes that could hardly remain open. This tiny being now depended on her for nourishment and love. He was so helpless, wrapped tight in his swaddling clothes. She would love him all her life and all of his.

The birth had all happened while John was working and home he came to the cries of a baby in the house.

"A bairn. Cud thee not wait for me," he laughed, picking up the baby from its mother's arms and walking over to the window.

"Well now, I did try, "she replied, pretending to be affronted at the suggestion. "He was in too much of a hurry to meet his da."

John, hearing the word "he" realized he hadn't even wondered if he had a son or a daughter so excited was he at the idea of either.

"A lad. A boy. My boy," was all he could say over and over. His first born was a boy and that was wonderful.

Three days later on the Sunday following his birth as was the custom, they all rode in the cart pulled by their faithful Galloway, along to St Stephen's church in Kirkby Stephen. The weather was kind. The trees were beginning to cover their bare branches with leaf buds and tiny baby leaves of a beautiful green.

There was a feeling of contentment as they travelled along the road together, John driving the pony and Alice holding her baby very closely still mesmerized by the innocent blue eyes that looked up at her. He'd done nothing except feed and sleep so far, with most of the sleeping through the daylight hours as young babies do. Alice was so weary but strangely excited at the same time and even anxious. Her anxiety came from the realization that she would be responsible for this human being for a good many years to come – keeping him safe, fed, clothed, and happy.

They sat themselves down at the back of the church, front pews being reserved for those who paid and looked around for family members. Her sister Elizabeth and family were there, as well as John's sister Jennet and her family, and grandparents too.

There had been no discussing names. He was named after his paternal grandfather as custom dictated, the proud grandfather sitting in the church with them. And he became Miles Hutchinson, in St Stephen's church where they had been married.

Life continued much as before for John but for Alice another layer had been added to her life. She helped with the small livestock, cooked, baked, washed clothes, and she now sewed, much more than before. John divided his time between the forge and the farm and they were both busy. Fortunately, baby Miles was so content that she could spend some time too on her vegetable plot that had produced fresh food for them the past year.

As she stood outside listening to the sounds of the country in the ice scoured gorge, on a spring day as bright and clear as she had ever seen, she heard him gurgling contentedly to himself lying in the wooden box John had made for him.

The sun's rays beamed on the hillside and as the afternoon drew to a close she looked up and watched the clouds run across the south facing slope, sky like over excited lambs.

And she knew then too that there was another child coming. She was a little concerned, worried even, that a baby would be a yearly occurrence and really hoped it wouldn't. She even laughed at herself imagining walking into town with at least twelve children in her wake. But she knew very well that it was every woman's duty to have children and that they would do their bit in turn as soon as they were able. How good it would be as well to have family to help you in your old age, she thought.

She half hoped this next one would be a girl eventually helping her around the home. But it didn't really matter which. She was looking forward to cradling the new bairn in her arms and crooning songs to them both.

Now that John had proved himself by producing a boy as his first born he seemed a little underwhelmed at the news a second time, but she knew that was just his way, and that he was just as proud. Their new babe was born in the October of 1784, just after St Luke's Fair and it was the girl that Alice had hoped for. The summer had been a warm one, unusual in the Valley, and Alice had suffered for it, dragging herself around the garden, unable to bend to dig up any potatoes, and trying in vain to sweep the floor of the farmhouse.

Feeling the now familiar pains she was relieved that the process had begun. Again thankfully it was an unremarkable birth with no complications, and the midwife pronounced both her and the baby to be in rude health. She was out of her childbed and on her feet again immediately.

She was needed.

This baby being a girl, had to have Alice's mother's name Mary, and

Alice knew her mother would have been so proud.

By now young Miles at just over a year old, was attempting to walk, hanging onto her petticoats as she tried to work, stumbling along beside or behind her with his tight little fists hanging on as firmly as he could. Sometimes he let go and stood wobbling and unstable, his arms out by his side to attempt to balance and looking down as if he couldn't believe his little legs were holding him. Then when he realized that she was gone falling to the ground and crawling after her.

He'd been much less content since new baby Mary had been born, not wanting to share his mother's time with a stranger, and his cries often woke her after Alice had spent time and effort getting her to sleep.

"Hush my babe," she whispered and sang softly to him a song she remembered from her young days , and one that always seemed to soothe him.

"The ewes and their lambs with the kids and their dams,
to see in the country how finely they play,
the bells they do ring and the birds they do sing
and the fields and the gardens are pleasant and gay."

Early Married Life ~ John

Being a Blacksmith was all that John had ever wanted to be, even though he had to spend a goodly piece of his time on the farm. He worked for a master Blacksmith at Outhgill but couldn't wait till he had his own forge like his father.

He also wanted to be a father. And once they were married he set about as often as he could trying to make this happen. His wife was willing if inexperienced but that was just as well he thought. He had begun to wonder if there was a difficulty. He spent long days in the smithy and weekends or more on the farm so was weary and worn when he came home. His new wife was always there with a meal as soon as he entered the home and he devoured it ravenously as if he had never eaten. He was very thankful that she was a good cook.

And then one night Alice gave him some news that was guaranteed to make his face light up: news he had begun to think he would never hear.

"A bairn? Aboot time," he whispered into her neck, kissing her forehead.

"Yes," she agreed. "It is."

The next few months were an agony of waiting for him and he saw how Alice was worrying over the birth. But it was not for a man to worry. Women had that all sorted.

Once the babe was born he felt Alice's contentment, watching her looking down at the boy as she nursed him, softly singing a song he had never heard her sing. The smile on her face as she looked up at him said it all. They were both happy and they were both content.

Summer came and went. Winter too with its blanket of white covering the hills and the valley. The next spring John became aware of something different about Alice. She didn't bustle about like she used to, darting here and there, like a fieldmouse he used to think. You thought she was in one place but she'd already moved to another. Now she seemed to be in one place all the time. she couldn't bend and dig without tremendous effort or walk into the village to market. If he had been more observant, he would have noticed perhaps how pale she was, and how she was growing thicker around the waist. But he didn't. His life was full of smithing, sleeping, loving and eating. He just thought that Miles was tiring her more than usual.

Of course another baby was due. The signs were all there to see. John was just as proud as last time but felt that it wouldn't be right to show his feelings as a man so kept them hidden, until the child was born that is.

After that he couldn't hide them.

This baby, a girl, was born at the time that his sister Jennet had her third child another Miles in the family. He always looked forward to their visits and he liked her husband James as a brother having no brothers of his own but with two Miles it was going to be confusing in the future.

Being the father of a daughter he found to be a totally unique experience. He'd held Miles many times and liked to take him outside talking to him under the stars, but he found himself drawn even more to this little scrap who scrunched up her face and eyes when she cried as if she were angry with the entire world, waving her little fists about when Alice loosed her from her swaddling. Her little round face peered at him with her eyes that seemed green like his and his mother's, even though Jennet said that a baby's eyes changed colour as they grew and "everyone knew they were always blue to begin with." These eyes which he swore were green, looked up at him and held his in a lock as he looked down at her not wanting their eyes to part. A feeling swelled in his heart causing a great warmness to spread throughout his chest. He felt a tug of love in his insides and a lifting of his spirit. Gently stroking her head, he kissed the tip of her nose, and whispered softly in her ear that he would protect her always. She had his heart and she always would.

*****

Later that year John rode the horse that had been Michael

Fothergill's along the road one night thinking that his work was worth more than he was paid. But it was so much of the same work. Day after day after day. The same thing. Over and over. He was tired of being the underdog and knew he was capable of more than was being asked of him. He wanted to prove himself. But a Blacksmith's work was made up of many repetitive works that were none the less important. He forged horseshoes, he mended pans, he ironed the clogs that everyone wore. He was good at ironing cartwheels. What he wanted was to be able to create his masterpiece. And so he plucked up the courage to ask the Master smith. The piece he wanted to make was a scrolled gate and that was particularly difficult.

"Master. Ah's toiled 'ere w'thee for a reet gud stint. Does uz graft please thee?"

Looking up from his examination of a horseshoe he'd just made he replied, "Aye John. Thee's a reet grand Smith."

"Ah want' t'fettle ma masterpiece."

"Tha'll hav't'finn thy own iron."

"That's not a bother for me."

Telling the Mastersmith what he was going to make, he realized the enormity of his task.

Oh well, he'd do what could do. Master Simon said he might have time to give him a bit of help: not strictly the done thing.

John foraged for iron to use and gradually he put by a little, gathering a store so that he could use it to make his piece. It would take some time.

Maybe he would wait. Waiting was so easy. All he had to do really was breathe and each day would pass followed by the next and the next and the next. But while he waited he grew more content with this new life. Alice made a comfortable home for them all and as a husband he had no complaints. He felt she was as fond of him as he was of her. After all, he'd chosen her at the Fair that day. She just happened to be there. That was what he thought anyway. But she had always felt that she had chosen him. He was the 'lovesome lad' she had wished for, and had made appear, wasn't he?

Love manifests in many ways.

Chapter Seven

Onwards together

"Grow old along with me.
The best is yet to be."

(Robert Browning)

Standing in the kitchen one day over a tub of hot water and John's linen shirt, (he only had two, and was wearing the other), Alice felt the now familiar butterflies in her stomach. She'd been moderately pleased that there'd been longer between bairns this time. Breastfeeding had been extended, on advice from old Peggy, and that had helped for a few months. She had a boy and a girl now, but just knew there would be many more additions to the family before she was done.
"Ah. We go again,' she thought.

It was once more at the time of St Luke's Fair in October that she had realized there would be a Spring baby.

Their second boy, Michael, was named after Alice's long dead dear father. and he was born in April 1787.

Now there were five of them in this lovely new family, which included a baby and two children aged four and three, who were very lively and very hungry. The little vegetable plot was even more important, and the cow still gave them milk. The calf was growing and would be slaughtered the next autumn to provide meat for the winter, salt cured, smoked in their chimney, and hung at the fireside. With John's wage they passed life reasonably.

The two older children played outside most of that summer, in the dirt of the vegetable garden. They dug patiently with their bare hands and loved it even more when a shower made the ground soft enough to dig and make shapes.

When he had time John had made a little toy for the children, a hoop and rod for Miles, and hoops on sticks for Mary.

As well as this Mary played contentedly and imaginatively with a stick tied round with rags that she called her 'babbie', while Miles played boisterously with his iron hoop and stick, rolling it backwards and forwards along the garden, racing after it in a vain attempt to outrun it until it hit a bump and fell over in the dust.

Like all children they loved being outside, whether it was wet or dry. On fine days Alice took the children and walked along the lane to meet John as he came home from the forge, with Miles running ahead to be the first to greet his father. She loved the smell of the outdoors. The meadowsweet in summer. Wild daffodils in spring.

The smell of leaves when the trees were wet after a shower of rain. Familiar smells were comforting. She even loved the smell in the air after the animals winter housing was cleared out.

'Good, fresh horse shit', they called it.

At night, the two children slept together soundly on a straw mattress, while baby Michael slept in the pine cradle box made by his father that had been vacated by his older siblings. He was a happy baby too, looking much like his brother Miles, and didn't need much attention.

'Thankfully so,' thought Alice.

He smiled at anyone who looked at him, kicking his legs and waving his fists in enjoyment. Mary had watched her mother looking after baby Michael and tried to do the same. She was a little mother to him, one day trying to carry him out of his bed, into the garden. Happily, Alice realized what was happening and prevented any calamity by catching him as he slipped from her arms. Mary cried, and Alice felt like crying, but Mary didn't do that again.

In the country days were marked by the sometimes-cheerful sound of morning and evening church bells. Alice did wonder who rang the bells, thinking you would need to be very strong to do that. They must be very big and heavy to lift. How on earth could anyone ring them at all?

The weeks were marked by attendance at Church when possible, and the visits of and to family.

Longer periods of time were marked by the seasons, the birth of children and special occasions, such as Annual Fairs. There were also other markings of time for families in the form of baptisms, weddings and burials.

And so time passed.

The summer of 1788 was a very dry one, a drought even, in the Mallerstang Valley where there was usually so much rain. The lack of rain became a worry, and everyone did their bit, praying for a downpour.

Streams dried up. Sheep and cattle were dying because of the unknown lack of water. This lack of water meant that the hay harvest had been poor. There just wasn't enough to feed the horses. Because of this the valley, which had once been an important thoroughfare, became a black spot for horses and carts. Fewer and fewer came up the valley that summer because of this terrible drought. And so, with less horses needing shoeing every two weeks there was less work for a Blacksmith to do. John and his master felt the effects.

But John's family kept on growing.

"There's summat I need to tell thee," said Alice one evening, as they sat together companionably on the settle.

"Soon we'll have another mouth to feed."

She'd waited to tell him, and had been loath to pass on the news, not knowing what his reaction would be, but it was hardly her fault, was it, she thought? It definitely took two, and some night she felt she could be discounted completely, as she was so tired and almost slept through it.

Happily, he was happy.

John was always happy with his family. It was what he'd wanted, and he hoped there'd be many more. His own family had been quite small, and he'd missed having brothers.

They had their second daughter, again in March of that year, a girl with hair as dark as anyone had ever seen, and eyes to match. They named her Elizabeth, after John's mother.

Now the Hutchinsons had four healthy children. Not every family could boast four live children in four births.

Baby Elizabeth slept in the wooden cradle that had seen much use, and Michael transferred to the bed with his parents. Miles and Mary continued to share the straw mattress and seemed comfortable enough.

No-one could prevent the bugs though as straw was a home for many, but that was just the way things were. And bites were a normal feature of everyday life.

Although many exciting and important events were being played out on the world's stage, the inhabitants of the Mallerstang parish only heard of any news if the vicar imparted it after evening service. And he only heard of it from the drovers who passed through the valley. And they only heard it from other traders at larger Fairs who had heard it from others nearer the capital. It was passed down through many hands before it reached Mallerstang, or anywhere in the north of England. This particular year the vicar told them that there were troubles in France, (wherever that was), a prison, with a strange name, had been overtaken by the common people, and they carried the heads of two important men on pikes. Confusing, but it was of no relevance to John and Alice. They hardly knew where the next village was. One night Alice asked, John, "What dust thee ken aboot the gannins on in that country the Reverend axes uz t'pray for

"Well, awld lass," he began as he usually did, "ah's glad they's ower the sea. That's all ah can say."

And she had to agree with him.

Chapter 8

A Forge of his Own

"I see the smithy with its fires aglow,
I hear the bellows blow,
And the shrill hammer on the anvil beat
The iron white with heat."

(Longfellow)

At six years Miles was a sturdy, strong boy, old enough to earn a few pennies himself. A local farmer was pleased to have him fetch and carry around the farmyard and do some bird scaring. John wanted him to learn his craft as a Blacksmith too and was waiting for the time he could begin an apprenticeship, which would be soon he hoped.

Miles was a little worried that he would not be able to scare any birds, and that they might like him too much.

"How duz ah fright the birds da?" he questioned.

"Dee whi thee allus diz. Run and shout aaargh," laughed John.

Summer this year was peaceful and warm, engendering a feeling of peace and calm, while eventually autumn with its usual burst of colours and its misty, sometimes frosty mornings, gave way to a very severe winter. For a period in December no coaches came up the valley at all. So now there was another reason why there was little work.

Finding it more and more difficult to provide for his growing family, the master Blacksmith gave up his smithy, and the journeyman, James Farraday, made the difficult decision to move them all to London.

It was a journey of hundreds of miles and impossible for him to afford himself. The reason for London was because of the help of his Church, the protestant sect that had split from the Church of Scotland, and they would find employment for him. Paying for their transportation, and their settling in once they arrived in London, made the move possible.

Faraday had left because he couldn't earn enough to keep his family, but John still thought that he would be able to turn things around and make a living. He didn't want to believe there was no money to be made there when he had the luck of having a smithy almost handed to him. He'd always had dreams of running his own forge, and here it was for the taking. Never mind the reasons why he shouldn't take it. He was blind to those.

So one late spring evening, as Alice stood outside, washing the youngest children down with rainwater after an exceptionally muddy playtime John came hurrying along the lane, his handsome face was normally creased with worry, but this time it was glowing with hope.

"Alice. Me bonny lass. Ah has some news for thee. The journeyman is gannin to London and the Master Smith is leavin.' He says the forge is mine if ah can pay the rent!"

She wiped her wet hands on her overpetticoat, just in time, before he picked her up, swirled her round and covered her in kisses.

"John Hutchinson, whatever be thee sayin,'" she laughed, but a note of worry had crept into her voice.

"Just what I do be sayin.' Blacksmith in ma own forge, if uz can pay the rent."

"And can we?" she asked, ever the voice of reason.

John turned away from her so she wouldn't see the worried look on his face.

"If ah dinnot tak it, then mebbe no wan will. Then ah'll hav nee job."

"There's allus plenty t'dee here John Hutchinson. The hay isn't bein cut. What'll us feed the beast in the winter?"

"That lad Harry'll hav te work harder," but he knew she was worried because that was when she gave him his full name.

That night John talked and while she mended Alice listened.

He didn't know why the Faradays were leaving, he said.

Maybe they had family in London, he said.

The dream of having his own forge wiped out anything else from his mind. It was a chance for him to make something of himself, and he wanted to take it. He was willing to gamble on himself and downplayed the risks. He just ignored them.

They would rent somewhere to live too and move the family from Southwaite. John's father and mother, Miles, and Elizabeth, had decided to move from Thorns and join them. His father Miles was suffering from the bone ague and had given up his work. They had some brass put by and would manage.

"Why did ye not tak thee da's forge," Alice asked.

"Ah was ower late," was the answer.

"But John. Duz tha think uz mun leave. Caan't uz stop?"

"Alice, owld lass. Ah muz be reet near t'smithy f'graft."

It seemed they must go then. What her husband said, she must do.

There was a lot to think about.

Alice's sister Elizabeth was not happy about John giving up the lease to the farm, but it was his farm now, so she had no say in the matter. That was the law.

"It be a bad thing he be doin' Will," she moaned and complained to her husband. She had no control over this decision and was finding it hard to accept. She was a woman who liked to have control herself.

But he was a man and could do what he wanted.

John ploughed ahead, selling most of the milk cows, keeping only two. The remaining sheep had to go too and were left with a neighbouring farmer who would sell them at the next sheep sale. They had fifteen pounds cash in hand, a fortune, as well as the sheep money, whenever that came. And for that they would have to trust their neighbour.

John and father Miles made the journey together to Kirkby Stephen applying to the Manor Court to lease buildings in Outhgill for both families. The information was duly recorded in the Manor Court Book and the tenants were given a copy of the lease to the land in return for the promise of a payment of rent.

Miles and Elizabeth had larger accommodation, with a dwelling house, stable, field and outbuildings. John's was more modest, smaller than Southwaite, but with enough room for all. And what was best thing for John was that the smithy was right next door. He would have no more long early morning walks to work or no taking their horse when he had other work to do. John was delighted. It was just what he wanted. A new start. He would show everyone what a craftsman he was.

But for his poor wife, this move meant her leaving the home where she and all her family had been born. She'd lived there for twenty-eight years and had seen her parents and her siblings die there.
'Ah well,' she thought. 'It's an unlucky place to live, to be sure,' trying to make light of the situation.
She was uneasy certainly, but he was her husband and he wanted to go. She may not want to go. She may feel this to the core of her being. But she had no choice.
It sometimes felt, when he talked about it that he *had* to go. She could see a fire burn within him when he talked of his plans. His cheeks burned, and his eyes looked at her but through her, with a feverish look. In his mind, he was somewhere else but here.

They made their plans to leave.

For John it was exciting.
He was so obviously keen to go : on edge and tense, agitated even. He hurried Alice along, not letting her spend any time going over her memories. This was someone else's dwelling, and he wanted to live somewhere that was his.

For Alice the whole business was heartbreaking. She made a huge effort and attempted not to cry, but it was made worse when her husband was so delighted to be leaving. Going through from room to room she remembered important events that had happened over her life, both happy and sad. But she had to go. She had no choice. She'd made her choice on the day she married him and now no choice would ever be her own gain.

They put all they could on the back of their cart that warm summer morning. Neighbours helped and Alice said her goodbyes. Leading the cows along behind to the village of Outhgill, they passed the stark ruined castle of *Pendragon* Castle, built on a mound, overlooked by Wild Boar Fell to the southwest and Mallerstang Edge to the east. Its crumbling turrets and ramparts lay in the shadow of these steep hills, on the banks of the slow-moving River Eden.

As children Alice and her brother John, and friends too, had played among these ruins, running in and out of the grey stone walls, playing hide and seek, taking great care not to fall from the turrets and ruined walls. It was well over a hundred years since the Lady Ann had restored and inhabited this castle, and its ruinous state was partly because of its age and partly because of locals plundering the ruins for the useful grey stone to build their own houses and cottages. Once she was gone it had quickly fallen into disrepair, a bleak reminder on the skyline of its previous majesty.

Alice remembered the old tales she'd heard many times from her father as a young girl. The legend was that the castle had been built by Uther Pendragon or "Terrible Chief Warrior," the younger son of King Constantine and supposed father of King Arthur.

It told that Uther Pendragon needed the river Eden to change course and fill the ditch around the castle to make a moat. He was unsuccessful. He did divert it, but it did what rivers do and reverted to its original route.
A well-known rhyme that all children knew from a very early age told the story.

"Let Uther Pendragon do what he can.
Eden will run where Eden ran."

On this warm day, the short journey was rather pleasant. How particularly beautiful was the valley in summertime, she thought. She'd always enjoyed long walks there before she was wed, along the riverbank where sheep grazed to "Lady Anne's Highway," the road that Lady Ann Clifford had travelled between her five castles.

Walking along beside the cart with young Michael walking beside her for part of the way, Alice bent to pick sweet-smelling wildflowers, especially those that were useful for herbal remedies. She was learning more about these from Old Peggy and knew which could ease fever, and which could ease lung disease. She knew which could ease the ague, and which were useful for many other ailments. Meadowsweet was particularly useful for many things.

Alice was grateful that she'd been able to take some items of furniture with her that had belonged to her parents – the two clothes presses, a wooden settle, a table and chairs, as well as two beds. There was also quite a lot of bed linen, eating bowls and the like, and other utensils. All of this would have been her brother John's if he'd lived. Mary and baby Elizabeth were riding the cart atop the blankets, while Miles, even at his young age, took charge of the cart and John rode their horse alongside.

The weather was still good when they arrived and unloaded the cart. Father Miles had done the journey the day before so he could give them help today. As the sun began to set that evening, they were settled in their new home, with John grateful to be living so close to his parents again. Alice could envy him that, as she'd been an orphan for a number of years now.

It was a smaller cottage, with nowhere near as much room as they had at Southwaite, but with all her family things Alice would make it a home.

The next morning, surveying the plot they had, she was pleased to see that she had plenty of space to grow her vegetables, such as she could, like potatoes, onions, turnips and maybe even some carrots. There was space enough for a few herbs too.
Once the family was settled, with a house, stable and garden right next to the smithy, there was no more travelling to work each day. Miles and Elizabeth had the same, as well as two fields. They had a couple of ponies to feed and house.

Now John had his own smithy, he really felt he needed another pair of hands to do more than a seven-year-old boy, his son Miles, could do. He didn't have the wealth to pay a journeyman, all he could afford was an apprentice. Board and lodging was an apprentice's pay, and as it happened there was no shortage of strong young men in his family keen to learn a trade.
Alice ever the voice of reason, wanted him to wait and see how much work was coming his way, but John was insistent. He hadn't told her why Faraday had left, and just hoped that when word got around about his skill, business would increase. With this in mind he took on his wife's nephew Edmund Harker to live with them, son

of her sister Elizabeth.

This capable young man had spent many days with John already, and had watched how he worked, already wanting to learn the trade and was waiting for his opportunity. He had no wish to follow in his father's trade as a farmer, and as a strong young man of ten years, he was keen and eager and learning fast. An apprenticeship was for seven years so he had plenty of time.

His mother and father were not best pleased as they'd expected him to follow his father farming, but they gave in, as Edward, his brother, at fourteen years, was keener than he was to work the farm.

There was enough work for now. The new Blacksmith was well received, partly because of his father's reputation but also because John's work and his worth were known and recognized by everyone. At present, his son Miles was mostly occupied with filling and carrying coal and water, but when working for his father he wasn't earning anything to help the household. He was sent out that next summer, when he could be spared, to drive horses for the local farmer and help with crops or hay or chop wood and earn a few precious pennies that were important. It was a lesson John taught his boys that they should always work. They weren't poor but neither were they well off. Yes, John had work, but jobs had to be completed for a Blacksmith to be paid, and that took time. And people were not always in a hurry to pay.

Bills were presented, usually verbally, and accounts settled on market days. Sometimes agreed payment was in kind, such as a new shirt for John, a new set of clothes for one of the children, a clutch of eggs, a rabbit for the pot. Everything had value and everything was usually valued. Everything that is, until someone tried to settle their bill with a bird cage containing three big black crows. It wasn't even a metal cage, but a wicker one, so no good at all. And what was he to do with three wild, rather feral crows? The noise from them was rather frightening, Alice said, and made the young ones cry even more.

Needless to say, that customer was told that any more work would need to be paid for 'up front.'

Life carried on much as before, until something happened that was out of the ordinary, and gave the village something to talk about, as well as lifting their spirits.

It was one summer's evening, while pummelling washing in the tub, she heard, or thought she heard, music: the sound of a fiddle being played. The sound was coming nearer, very fast and very lively. It wasn't unheard of before this for there to be music in the valley. Fiddler Coaty used to play for families and had been in great demand before he'd left the valley for Swaledale. Now it seemed there was music once again. She stood and watched with her hands still in the water, waiting until she saw a man coming towards her. The fiddle bow was sawing the air, but slowly and gently now, and she thought she recognized the tune as "Greensleeves," a favourite of many.

A man dressed like a tinker with a huge bushy beard, came strolling into the village and stood in a clearing, his playing livelier now, tunes that Alice hadn't heard before. Hearing the music, neighbours came out to see what was happening, and it wasn't long before everyone was walking his way – adults of all ages, and children too. The music was an invisible magic mist, swirling round them, ensnaring them, refusing to let them go. They were its captives but willing too. It was hypnotic. Alice felt her feet tapping despite her not telling them to. She wanted to dance and looking round the assembled crowd, she could see that she wasn't the only one. She caught sight of John leaving the smithy unusually early tonight as he made use of all the daylight he could. She and waved him over, as grimy as he was with the day's toil, sweat marking thin tracks from his brow and down his face, looking exhausted.

Miles, Mary and Michael stood beside Alice, and were entranced. Elizabeth lay on the ground, crying again. Old Peggy was hitching her feet, in time to the tune, caught up in the spell, her face a mirror of everyone's there. Except, not everyone had most of their teeth missing, save for one front peg.

It worked its magic on John who strode over to his wife, tiredness forgotten, and circled her tiny waist with his arm, his shirt sleeve pushed up showing his strong forearms, black, like his face. But she couldn't care. She wanted to dance. Taking hold of his hand she circled round him smiling up into his green eyes. He wasn't a dancer, had never been a dancer but was mesmerized by the music, and the atmosphere, and the whole feeling that this was something to be enjoyed, that things like this did not happen much and that he ought to make the most of this happy moment.

The feeling spread like a fever. Couples danced, some children danced, and others ran among and around the dancers. Some tunes were fast and some slow but all were enjoyed, and the fiddler seemed to never tire. The song they seemed to love the most was *"The Twa Sisters."* He sang it as he played.

It told a story that they tried to sing too. After hearing it they joined in with him as well as they were able, but they just preferred to listen to the fiddler playing and telling the story.

"There was twa sisters in a bowr,
Edinburgh, Edinburgh
There was twa sisters in a bowr,
Stirling for ay

There was twa sisters in a bowr,
There came a knight to be their wooer.
He courted the eldest wi glove an ring,
But he lovd the youngest above a' thing.
He courted the eldest wi brotch an knife,
But lovd the youngest as his life."

There were many more verses but none could remember them all. Villagers disappeared indoors and came back out with mugs of ale. This seemed to charge the atmosphere even more, with smiles and laughs and shouts and whoops and whirling partners around. Men and some women too, smoked a clay pipe as they listened and watched. Old Peggy had found herself a dancing partner, a widower she'd known for many a year, and with knowing looks and winks, John and Alice smiled at her, letting her know that they approved of her partner.

They had nothing, but their enjoyment of this simple entertainment was all they needed to make everyone happy with what they had. The fiddler played on, his bow scraping and squealing well into the evening till the birds had gone to roost, the sky previously red with the setting sun, was turning dark blue and stars were beginning to twinkle. Tired children were sent to bed although unwilling to go, while the grownups of all ages stayed on, to dance, clap and sing to the rhythmic music he played, tune after tune of gaiety and merriment. They danced and sang while he played the fiddle and ensured the music carried on into the night. Husband danced with wife and couples swung each other to the time of the music.

Then breathless, they stood bent at the waist holding their sides, dragging in great lungfulls of air, and waiting for the music to begin again. Cares were forgotten or diminished and all that mattered was the music which they hoped would never stop.

But it did stop. Saying he could play no more and laughing when he was begged by all there he put down his bow.

Over a drink of ale and food he told his story.

He was from north of the border, a Scot, and once he spoke, they could hear the difference in his tone.

"Ahm in danger ay prison at haem fur nae respectin' th' sabbath."

His name was Jack Tam and he had been travelling for the past year, enjoying the itinerant life.

"Aw ah need is a little scran an bevvy, an a scratcher fur th'nicht, anI'll be oan mah way."

There was no shortage of food offered to him, in payment for such an evening. A neighbour gladly let him sleep in the sweet-smelling hay of his hay loft and Old Peggy made sure he had plenty to eat and drink before he left. They all begged him to stay for another day or even two but he was not to be persuaded.

It's nae fur me. Ah needs tae be oan mah way. Travellin' is mah life noo."

The next morning he was up early to get a good start and many waved him off. He was heading for York and left with a baked potato, a heel of bread, a good chunk of cheese and one piece of bacon, tied in a cloth. Peggy made sure he had a good draught of her ale before he left the village. The fact that he was going seemed to have put a blight on the feeling of the night before. They begged and made him promise that he would come their way again. He did promise but who knew what would happen?

Tasks that had been abandoned the evening before were taken up again. Alice finished her washing.

"Come on awld lass. Let's 'ave a dance," said John when he arrived home the next evening. He took hold of her and whirled her round, while she smiled and laughed up at him.

"Aye. What a night that was."

"Aye lass, it was," he replied, winking at her but thinking more of the end of the evening, once they were all in bed, and he had her in his arms and all to himself.

That day, and for many more afterwards, Alice, along with other villagers, found herself humming the vibrant tunes, and tapping the floor with her feet as she worked. It was like they had all been infected by a fever and they were unable or unwilling to shake off its effects. The older children were to be heard singing the songs. The visit of this man had done so much for the morale and happiness of everyone, and it was talked about for days, weeks and months to come.

Summer ended, winter blasted through, the yule log was burned at Christmas, although a visit to church was impossible. And Alice realized she was expecting their fifth child, in the tenth year of their marriage.

Chapter 9

Family Life

"It's a good hoss that never stumbles.
And a good wife that never grumbles."

(Old Yorkshire Saying)

After the usual bad winter, a late Spring wind roared in over the hillsides, blasted its cold way along the dykes and whistled through the cracks in Alice and John's cottage. Winter had not been the worst, but neither was spring the best. Looking up into an ash-coloured sky, John pulled on his leather boots, dragged his heavy greatcoat tightly around him over his breeches and waistcoat and left the relative shelter of the house, taking his son Miles along with him, together with his apprentice, making sure they were warmly dressed.

He wondered when he left the cottage if he would have another son or a daughter when he came home, that evening, because she'd said it was about her time, and he could see that it was. A person couldn't get much rounder, he thought with a little chuckle that would have made Alice very angry indeed.

They walked together to the next-door smithy; the air now thick with falling snow that he hoped was going to be short-lived.

Walking towards where he spent most of his days he no longer noticed the clutter and jumble outside the doors of the smithy: old iron, cartwheels, tools, wood: things that were going to be useful to him at some time in the future. Opening just one of the wide doors and stepping in, John toed impatiently around a pile of horseshoes, untidily spread in his way.

The order came. "Mek way Miles, an' tidy these lumps o'iron ower lad." He barked this harshly at Miles, who'd been given this same order many times. Now John was determined. "Stack 'em in yon corner. Now."

The old iron would be reused when necessary. Nothing was wasted. Probably not for his masterpiece now. He'd lost the will for that. As he walked further into the smithy across the cobbled floor, John's eyes became more accustomed to the darkness inside. A horse collar hung from a hook on the wall next to some scythes and hayrakes that were for sale.

He walked further into the gloom to where his anvil stood, on top of a massive section of old oak. And there was the fire pit, with the bellows behind. A large water trough to quench the heat and cool any tongs that were too hot to handle was near, as well as a plentiful supply of coal for the fire.

He had taken to quenching the fire each evening to save coal, but it only took minutes to have a hot fire going. Here was everything he needed.

Taking off his great coat, he hung it on a metal hook on the wall and tied on the long leather apron that covered his chest and reached his knees. Once lit a blast from the bellows, worked by Edmund his apprentice, roared into the fire until it became white hot, and he made a start on the day's work.

His first task was a sad one. Ironmongery was needed for the coffin of a local lass who had died in her child bed. Her parents had brass but it made John think. That brass hadn't saved their daughter. He'd rather have his family than all the brass they had. Next a brace of hinges and locks were needed for the chapel door. Nails were needed so he let Edmund practice his craft, with much hammering and shaping. The skills needed for making nails were the staples of a Blacksmith.

They worked without talking until the church bells chimed the hour for the end of the morning. Talking was of no use. Who would hear it here?

A break for smoked pork and a piece of mutton pie with a hearty drink from the clean water butt was followed by the main event of the day – the ironing of a set of cartwheels for his brother-in-law,

Elizabeth's husband. They would be paid part in coin and part in kind, with a new undershirt for John and a new shift for Alice, sewn by Elizabeth's eldest daughter, who was at eighteen years old, an accomplished seamstress.

The first task for this was to measure the wheel to make sure he had a proper fit: a little smaller than the wooden wheel.
Meanwhile Edmund had the fire going and was pumping the hot: the forging heat, to make the metal bend. Then, laying the strip of metal over the edge of the anvil he hammered it to make a curve: hammering and curving until he had a wheel of iron.
While he was finishing this Edmund had begun the next task, outlined to him the night before. It had just needed a nod of John's head towards the doors to send him outside, to clear some ground of snow and light a fire. Miles was left inside stoking the fire while John and Edmund carried the heavy iron tyre outside and placed it into the ready lit fire. John knew, as all Blacksmiths knew, that the iron would expand in the red-hot heat, so when he judged it was ready he quickly placed it on the wooden wheel and used the snow to quench the fire, shrinking the iron and attaching it to the wooden wheels with nails.
It was the work of a master to make sure the wheelwright's work was not spoiled. But John was a master. He knew his trade. He

would do the second iron tyre the next day as the evening was almost upon them and they were losing light.

When he and Miles, together with Edmund, burst into the cottage that evening, hurrying out of the bitter cold and the squalling snow, there was still no new baby. But there was a plate of mutton pie with potatoes and a warm welcome from Alice, Mary and Michael, but crying still from Elizabeth. Dashing the snow from their cold frames, they all three sat at the long table, just vacated by the children.

As usual, the young Elizabeth was complaining, thumb in mouth and hanging onto her mother's skirts, even though she was nearly three years old. She was a child who was hard to please, very often crying, or miserable, and didn't play with the other children. Alice had stopped trying to make her smile. She would do so in her own good time, she thought.

The next week, although cold, was dry, with a sky bright and clear, making trees blaze with diamonds of melting ice. Throughout the day the spring sun glinting off the snow was blinding, but the beginning of the working day was still in darkness.

Once dawn had broken, the second iron tyre had been made, and William had borrowed a neighbour's cart to collect the pair. He was well pleased, as he always was, with John's work and was greatly confident that John would make a blacksmith of Edmund. The first year of his apprenticeship had gone well. As well as that Miles was nine years now and already showing his talents.

A further two weeks saw the weather improve beyond all measure. And this time the baby made his way into the world in the early hours of a dark morning, giving John an experience he had not yet had.

Alice had been uncomfortable all day and knew now what to expect. This was her fifth child after all. She went to bed that evening, lying on the straw bed, with the children on a bed in the corner and Elizabeth lying beside her. She still hadn't managed to make her sleep elsewhere and she was too big now for the cradle. John was so tired that he was fast asleep in a truly brief time, but Alice lay on, trying not to make too much noise and wake anyone. Lying until she could lie no longer,

"It's time," she groaned to Mary. "Go get Peggy."

Unable to prevent it, Alice let out a long deep moan, followed by a groan and clutched at her stomach that was now doing its best to expel this poor child from the comfort of the womb.

Rubbing his eyes wearily John woke and took in the sight and the terrible sounds before him.

"Nip on sleep by t'fire. Their dooant want ta see dis," said Peggy taking in the scene with her experienced eyes as she came hitching into the room.

Seeing Alice writhing in pain was enough for him. He did as he was told, carrying the children out of the bedroom and next to him by the fire, and she heard him talking to the children, telling them all was well, and to go to sleep.

After a long night of pain and thoughts that she wasn't going to survive this time, it took a further five hours before this baby made its appearance: another boy.

Desperately trying to stay awake John found it impossible, and was woken by a baby's shrill, keening cry. Peggy had sent for the midwife just to ensure all was well, and it was.

Entering the bedroom, he saw her weak smile. But now he noticed too her face bleached as white as the clean shift she was wearing, A stray lock of hair was straggling across her eyes, and she raised a weary hand to push it behind her ear.

"A boy," she whispered. "He should be John."

According to tradition, he *should* have been John, after the baby's father, but this time they surprisingly departed from tradition, and called him William.

There was a small church at Outhgill, also restored by Lady Ann at least a hundred years before, and this was where the christening was to be held, at Sunday service. As the family walked together,

Miles at ten years, a young man already earning money to help keep the family, strode out in front while Mary at eight years, walked Michael five and Elizabeth three, down the lane in the spring sunshine. Baby William, wrapped in a warm shawl, was carried by his father, as Alice was still too weak to trust herself not to drop him.

Meeting family at the little church was a happy occasion and was to be a double celebration. Two Williams were being christened, a Hutchinson and a Fothergill. Born cousins, to hopefully become friends.

For spring, it was unseasonably mild, and as they stood outside the small church waiting for everyone, they enjoyed the feel of the sun on their skin after another harsh winter. The weather had changed remarkably quickly, and this last month the cold icy blasts had given way to warmer, milder breezes, bathing them with a feeling that was most welcome but very unusual. Buttercups, cowslips and other early spring flowers were beginning to cover the grass with a hint of the colour to come.

Winter's snow had melted so fast that streams and the river had been turned into torrents of fast-moving, icy water, tumbling frantically over stones, swirling and eddying with the current and carrying with them anything that got in their path.

Adults had been swept to their deaths in times past and you had to be so careful even in the summer.

"Gan canny near the beck," John shouted to his little family as they walked along.

It seemed that all four families had taken advantage of this unexpected, mild weather and packed a basket with food.

The four families with their children almost filled the small place of worship as there were now nineteen children, including the two babies, the eldest now twenty herself but working as a kitchenmaid so now unable to come.

After the service the women laid their shawls on the ground, the children played, and Alice remembered the first meal she'd shared with John, all those years ago, almost ten in fact.

There was racing, chasing, laughing and some small amount of fighting: really just an argument or two over who had won the race, as children do.

Their parents talked and ate, watching their children and enjoying these few hours of freedom from work and worry. And Alice silently gave thanks that none of her bairns had been taken into the arms of Jesus. She knew that they were fortunate and silently remembered her brother John, and sister Jane, and their suffering before their passing.

Back home, and the children asleep, after a day when everyone was happy and carefree, even for a short while, Alice slept in the arms of her loving husband, and wondered when he would want to resume his efforts to increase his family. She knew that if she hadn't been in her childbed just this week, he would have expected that pleasure from her tonight. A week or maybe two, she thought to herself, with a wry smile.

....

Life was the same, but it was also quite different. Now she had five children. Keeping them all clean and clothed was a constant battle. Mary was only eight, but already she could thread a needle and darn socks for her da.

She would not wash clothes without soap. It was a useless venture. Her weekly tasks were as follows,

Scrub white clothing inside then outside, and rinse with cold water. This was done for the females in the house.

The next week she did the same for the men in the house.

The third week she swept the dirt floor, cleaned the fireplace, and then the cooking pot until she got some sort of a shine on it.

The fourth week and fifth were the days for washing any bed linen and shaking and the straw mattresses to release any vermin.

By the time she got to the sixth week she was washing and mending for the boys, and the next week for the girls.

She tried so hard to keep up this rota. She felt it helped, as it emphasized she did not have to do it all: at once.

She also had meals to make, tableware to clean, mending and sewing, tending the small vegetable plot, looking after William and Elizabeth, making sure those who were leaving for work had some snap to take.
But all this work took its toll on Alice.
Where she had once taken immense pride in her cleanliness and her hair, now she hadn't the same time or energy. Her once beautiful hair was laced through with coarser grey, and she didn't see the need to brush it so often. She didn't have many clothes, and still wore the clothes she'd worn for the last ten years, well mended. She had three shifts, two petticoats, two bodices and an overdress. More than enough for her, she thought. Around her shoulders she wore a kerchief when she went out, to protect her neck from the sun, and to keep her warm in winter. John still wore the shirt she had sewn for him for their wedding day, even though he did have another. His breeches were mended and so was his jacket but he took little care about his appearance. Like many he had few clothes and wore them continuously.
Keeping the children clothed too was a struggle as they grew. Mary was learning to sew and did the mending already. Alice just

couldn't envision a day when she would be able to ask Elizabeth to do the same thing. Both boys' and girls' shifts were passed down, not bright white, but grey. Even the oldest wore clothes passed on from older cousins. If they bathed, then they usually did so wearing their clothes, so all were washed together, either in the beck or in a barrel with soap, together with cold water from the water butt. Son Miles was the proud owner of a new shirt Alice had made for him that had taken her all winter to sew. Having new clothes was an unusual event indeed. Maybe Michael would be next.

What was just accepted was the lice that covered everything. They were everywhere and just a part of life. Another thing was the ever presence of rats. Alice couldn't remember being so plagued when she lived at Southwaite, but here they raced around the rubbish heap, around the floor of the cottage when everyone was in their beds and even sat on your feet when you visited the midden. Baby William had been bitten in his bed one night but seemed to have taken no harm from it. The older children didn't even mention when it happened to them. They chased them for sport around the pig pen, where they knew there was a nest under the shed, and tried to whack them with branches, but weren't fast enough. They always got away.

Underlying all of this Alice knew that things were vastly different. The money was gone, spent. The animals were gone: either sold or slaughtered. All they had left now was one milk cow, a horse and pony, and the sheep they'd left behind to be sold.

Chapter 10

The Leaving

"I hear there are people who enjoy moving. Sounds like a disease to me."

(Jan Neruda Prague Tales)

That wonderful, warm spring and long summer was followed by an equally wonderful mild autumn and winter, with John seeming to have work enough to keep him and his apprentice busy.

Despite promising Michael a shirt (in her mind only) this winter Alice was working on a dress for Mary, sewn from fine russet woollen cloth woven by the weaver in Kirkby and bought with her egg money from the last year.

She hoped that she would be able to do the same for herself. To have a new dress would be a wonderful thing.

They were all glad it had been a milder winter as the stone cottage walls did little to keep out the cold, and Alice felt it more these days. Going outside to the midden on a wintry morning was an ordeal that must be endured, but a bucket inside was better in the really freezing weather.

Once again married life produced another of its gifts and it didn't take as long this time before she knew. The first signs of spring brought with it the feeling that was now all too familiar, having experienced it five times before. A year since the warm spring day of William's christening she was carrying another child.

But this time, it was different. She felt different. She was always tired at the end of the day, but now she felt exhausted. For a good while, she had felt that there was no strength in her limbs, and she found the normal business of the day increasingly difficult.

Despite her burgeoning waistline her dress was becoming slacker. She wasn't eating much. She just had had no appetite, even though her days were as busy as they always had been.

After a seeming flurry of work through the last winter, John had been taking stock of his situation. Work was slow. Even the usual regular jobs were thin on the ground. Counting up from his tally written with chalk on the door to his workshop, he'd been shocked to see how little work there had been for him. In the last month, he had shoed one horse, mended one pan and provided ironmongery for one coffin. And as far as he could think it had been the same the month before.

He had finally come to a realization: the same realization that his previous master and the Journeyman James Faraday had come to. He knew he'd been a fool.

There was no longer enough work here in this quiet valley for a Blacksmith. Could he finally admit, even to himself, that there hadn't been enough work when he'd taken over the lease? Probably not.

His decision meant more far-reaching changes for his family.

But he was the one who made the decisions, and they had to follow. That's just how it was, he thought.

He determined that he needed to go where his skills would be in greater demand. And that would mean a shake-up for all of them. His father, who had previously lived in Swaledale, still had contacts in the area and had heard there was work for a Blacksmith in the village of Thwaite.

Less than two years since they'd uprooted from Southwaite now they had to uproot themselves again. But this time they had a longer journey to take.

John stood outside the smithy he had taken over and thought about the gamble he'd taken with Alice's inheritance, and how he'd lost. Now he had to leave the quiet Mallerstang Valley and travel to an area where there was more industry – lead miners and farmers, who needed the services of a Blacksmith. He could no longer rely on travelling coaches with horses to shoe, and the odd mending job.

Deciding there was nothing for it but to speak up, he waited until after supper one evening. Sitting next to Alice at the table as she sewed in the light of a rush candle he began, in a serious tone, "Alice, awld lass."

She knew by his tone that that there were important things to come and had an idea what. She wasn't blind or daft.

"Yes, awld lad." She replied, smiling at her own choice of words.

"Their norrz ah'ed gran'reason to tek this smithy."

"Aye John." She replied, looking down at her sewing, not wanting to look him in the eye. "As thee said."

"Bur naw ther's neya mooar fettle."

"Why's that husband?"

"The coaches. They've stopped coming."

"So, what will uz do?"

Now he could not look at her. He, with his arrogance and ambition. had brought this on them.

But then he argued with himself, saying that a man ought to have ambition.

"Ah need fettle, an' the smithy is dead."

"It's a great pity that we left the farm," she added, and then bent to snap off the end of her thread with her teeth.

She had tried not to sound judgmental. She had to go where he went. Her star was always tied to his because he was her husband

and because she loved him.

But they would have been able to feed their children if they had stayed.

She had wondered why they ever had to leave Southwaite. Things could have continued as they were. But John's ambition and grand plans had meant his believing that there would be no time left for him for the farm. He would be so busy being a Blacksmith, which was all he wanted.

"So, what now?" she asked him.

Sighing a long sigh as he put his head in his hands and shook his head slightly, he replied so quietly, almost whispering, that she could scarcely hear him.

"Wi've to leve."

"Where to? Where to?" she asked, a note of hope creeping into her voice. Could they please be returning to Southwaite and leasing a small farm? That would be her dream.

"Back t'Swaledale. Thee seh ther's fettle enuff fer Blacksmiths wi' t' lead mines theear. We'll be orl roeight theear."

Putting down her sewing, she finally looked up at him. He was worried, she could tell. He was shamed that he was having to have this conversation with her, but she couldn't let him feel so.

"Well, who could have known it wouldn't work out for thee? Thee's worked reet hard. None could'ave done better."

With relief in his eyes, he reached over to her.

"Naw uz pretty miss, it's tahhm for a kiss." he said, smiling that smile that still melted her heart.

"Aye," she answered, thankful that the problem had been dealt with. "It's kiss time.

Swaledale was where John's father Miles had been a Blacksmith, and where John was born, in the hamlet of Thorns at the head of the dale. Miles knew there was plenty of work now the lead mines were doing so well. After enquiring about a position word had come back through Miles that a Blacksmith was needed in the village of Thwaite.

But this meant of course that John could not have an apprentice, so Edmund, Alice's nephew, would have to return home, his plans of being a Blacksmith now thwarted.

It was less than two years since John's ambition had uprooted them from Southwaite, full of hope, and even excitement. But now he was uprooting them again. The feelings about this move could not have been more different.

He waited until the beginning of summer so travelling would be easier. With rent all paid up and sad goodbyes said, old Peggy who had come with them from Southwaite, was so unhappy to see them go that she almost decided to go with them, but realized she was too old to make the change again. And, to tell the truth, she said, she and her 'dancing partner' had become close and were company for each other.

Standing outside the smithy he had worked at, John's mind went over the gamble he'd taken.
The gamble he'd lost.
He'd staked all they had and the stakes had been high. Most of Alice's inheritance was now gone. Now he was leaving the Mallerstang Valley completely to travel to an area where there was work.
But his poor wife was leaving all she knew.

With all his worries he hadn't noticed that Alice was not as busy about the place as she usually was. She was listless, had no energy and had to push herself to complete even the smallest task. If he had noticed, he would have put it down to "havin anuther bairn."
Yet again they had a new life ahead of them. Alice looked at the wooden presses that she remembered her mother using, and the wooden settle that she had sat on for many years with her father and others of her family who were all now gone.
Once more the family packed up all their belongings onto the cart,

to be pulled by their fell pony that the children had named Sorrel. Once more pewter, brass, earthenware, bedding, mattresses and the old family bible, as well as her father's old pine settle, were loaded onto the cart. This time Alice walked through the days before in a daze. She hadn't lived here long, but it was the valley she was going to miss. John did his best to be cheerful, but his demeanour just emanated the bitterness he felt. Why couldn't he have his dream? He *had* worked hard. It wasn't all his fault. Once again he gave no more thought to Alice.

Everything they had moved from Southwaite came with them as they left for Thwaite.

Birds sang as they left, but it was a sad day as they left Outhgill behind. Alice was leaving all her family in the Churchyard at Kirkby Stephen, and her sister, who was married to a Mallerstang man.

But it was no time to be maudlin. They had a new life ahead of them, yet again.

John hitched up the pony to the small wooden cart and leading it out to the roadway off they started, back towards Southwaite. Walking alongside Miles and Michael patted the pony's strong shoulders and talked to her as they travelled. As he rode the horse that had belonged to Michael Fothergill, out of the Mallerstang valley, past the spring blossoming wildflowers and trees beginning to bud their leaves, John remembered how it had been with his father's pony, and how well he'd looked after her.

Although it was early summer, as they began the ascent to cross into the next valley, the mist and low clouds were soon apparent. Keeping close to the hillside, following the narrow track as he had done many times before, they made good time on the journey. It didn't rain but the air was damp and so were their clothes, letting the colder temperature on the hillside leach into their bones. Birds, startled by their movement, flew up in front of them, their wings beating a tattoo in the still air.

Crossing over the hill, they rode along past the hamlet of Keld and down through Thorns, where John and his parents had once lived, then travelled past the hamlet of Angram, and along Angram side. By early evening they were entering the small village of Thwaite. Their future home was a few hundred yards outside the village, at the hamlet of Scarr Cottages, on the road to Muker.

There were only a few dwellings at Scarr Cottages, one of which was a small farm, joined in a terrace. They didn't look as old as those in the Mallerstang valley, and Alice dared to hope their dwelling was better appointed than the last one they'd lived in. She was down from the cart first, John helping her down. Walking through the door she could see firstly a large room downstairs with a kitchen and pantry too. She couldn't haul herself up the steep stairs but reasoned there would be just as much room there. The windows were still small, and there were some holes where draughts would bother them in the winter, but Alice thought it would be easy to sort that. It was habitable at least. She should be grateful for that.

Everything that had once belonged to her mother and father was brought in off the cart. The straw mattresses were carried upstairs by John and Miles, together with the two wooden presses containing anything they weren't wearing, which wasn't much, and some bedding, wrapped around their earthenware. They had their table and the old wooden settle which were carried in and put in position, together with the eating implements, pewter and brassware they had brought with them. Alice thought it was beginning to look like a home. Still in place, hanging in the dirty fireplace, was the cooking pot, soot-blackened, dirty and rusted inside.

Picking up the old besom that stood forlornly in a corner of the room, Alice managed to sweep the stone, flagged floor.

"And look Mary,' she shouted to the one who would be the most invested, 'Look. This will be much better'n a dirt floor, covered in rushes."

And then she began to cry. The enormity of her situation was gradually sinking into her bones. Dashing away the tears and turning aside so no-one could see, she moved slowly to put some food on the table: food they'd brought with them. It seemed like an age ago that she had been standing in another kitchen, but it had only been hours.

Unaware of this undercurrent of emotions, John managed to light a fire. Thankfully, a small amount of coal and wood had been left. The room felt damp inside and needed heat to air it out.

Water was in plentiful supply, as across the lane, right in front of the cottage, was a beck and a waterfall. As she looked over the way and saw Mary with the old, sooty rusted pot, trying to clean it in the running water, the tears came again. They fell, and she didn't know why. Alice could see that Mary had made some improvement to the pot, but not a lot.

That prompted John to say, "Ahl see what's liggin around t'smithy. There's boun to be a pan browt f't'mendin then forgot."

Wiping her eyes on her petticoat before turning round, she warned, "Best look out for the bairns, with that water so close."

"Aye lass, we will that."

Looking at her pale, lined face and weary eyes, he still thought she was the prettiest lass he knew. He also knew that he didn't tell her enough and vowed to put that right.

Tired out with travelling, Alice gathered the children, took some covers and went upstairs to sleep. John fell asleep in front of the small fire he had managed to light, but it had very soon burned out as he slept.

Work for John was to be at the smithy in Thwaite and he would walk the short distance there each day. He felt guilty for the poor lad Edmund, taken on as an apprentice, who'd gone back to the family farm, but his parents at least were pleased. Miles would come along with him and help where he could, still yearning to be a Blacksmith like his father and grandfather.

The following day, being a Sunday, gave them time to organize themselves as best they could. Kind neighbours called, bringing a little something to eat, even though they didn't have much themselves. There was bread, some dumplings, baked potatoes and a little news too, making Alice feel that she would be more at home here than she had previously thought.

She tried her best with Mary's help to organize the house, kitchen and pantry, while John sorted the sleeping. The boys and Elizabeth slept on tired out still from the day before. They had enough room to stable Sorrel their pony, as well as their horse Dandy, and could take them to the common ground through the day. That became a responsibility for Miles too as well as helping his father at the smithy.

John's next all-important job was to see what work there was for him. He walked along to the smithy where he found, after talking to the Blacksmith, that he was wanting someone who could take over most of his work. He would pay him a wage to begin with, he said, and see how he got on. The Blacksmith was a good age, had only girls in the family, and his apprentice cum journeyman had just left for the industrialized world of Lancashire.

Full summer was welcomed. Meadowsweet blossomed, wildflowers bloomed, heather was a purple mist on the hillside among the yellow gorse. Miles worked at the forge and as well as his duties with Sorrel and Dandy managed to find a little time to help a local farmer. He needed to earn brass too at his age. Mary helped at home and seeing how tired her mother was, did much more than was asked of her. Michael, at six years old, managed to earn a penny by bird scaring in the fields. Elizabeth, four, played seemingly happily in the dirt. How that girl had changed! And William, at just over a year old, was toddling around, hanging onto his mother's skirts, just as the others had, as she tried to make meals.

John missed his parents so, quite soon after their move, they visited them in Outhgill. It was still summer, and the air was beginning to warm. As they left home early that Sunday morning, they were all in particularly good spirits, even Elizabeth, who still cried a little. Singing birds and a colourful butterfly or two in the hedgerows made Alice glad to be going back to the countryside she knew, even if just for a visit. She'd told no-one but she'd been so homesick, even though she had no-one to visit.

It was the valley she missed.

The journey once more was slow and leisurely and for part of the way the children jumped down and ran alongside, until they were tired. Then John lifted them up in his strong arms and swung them behind him onto the bed of the cart. Mary skipped along, now and again stopping to pick wildflowers: putting some in her hair and picking a bunch to give to her grandmother. Michael, true to form, was either walking along in a daydream or chasing butterflies and bees, managing to get himself stung in the process. William and Elizabeth rode in the back of the cart with Alice, all three of them sleeping for a good part of the way.

Alice was glad she'd managed to have a short sleep as it wasn't a comfortable ride for her. Her dress was now very tight and there was little time before the child would be born. If it was a boy, she wanted to call it John, and it would be Alice for a girl. But there was no way they could know that now. The well-worn baby clothes that had seen all her children and her sister's children arrive, were ready for the new arrival, as well as one piece of new clothing she had sewed, whatever it be.

John rode along, thinking of the words his father had spoken to him, before they left Outhgill. A boy, no matter what age, needs to feel that he has the approval of his father, and if there's praise, so much the better. When they last spoke, before leaving, Miles had told him how proud he was of his accomplishments, and of his family. Only a few words, but those words were enough. A warm feeling spread across his chest, like sunlight, and sustained him all throughout the journey that day.

What pleased Grandfather Miles too was that both older boys, Miles and Michael took after him, with sandy hair, even though John could not have had any influence over that.

They spent a few hours together because that's all the time they had, and when they left they took away with them one of his mother's rabbit pies to eat along the way, as well as home brewed ale to wash it down, both adults and children. It was a long way to go for such a short visit, but it had been a necessary one for John and Alice.

By the time they reached Thwaite the moon was lighting their way and the stars shone in the clear, dark blue sky. As they pulled up outside their home Alice thought about the many times she'd stood outside on a night like this at Southwaite, looking upwards at the lights in the sky, to where she'd been told was Heaven. Tonight she wondered about it again, while John unhitched Sorell and gave her hay and water and a rub down.

Tumbling tiredly into bed as soon as they could was the next thing. The wooden crib was still occupied by William, but he would soon have to vacate this. John very carefully carried the four youngest children into their beds, two straw mattresses, and Miles joined them.

The next day was a beautiful warm day in midsummer and work as usual. Alice walked along the lane to the ditch side and picked an armful of Meadowsweet, breathing in their strong fragrance as she walked back home. Having brushed the floor again, she strewed fresh reeds and the fragrant herb all over the floor, to make the stuffy room as much like summer as possible.

While visiting Miles and Elizabeth the day before she'd been aware for the first time in a long while how they were all not as clean as they should be.

Her petticoat was in a sorry state, and she was determined that once this baby came, she would sew herself another. And it would be beautiful. But in reality she knew that it would be drab and serviceable. What was the point of a gown that's only purpose was to look pretty. It had to be warm and hardwearing. The pretty green woollen gown she'd been wed in was worn into holes these last ten years, being worn every Sunday, but she would remake it for Mary, she thought.

As she stood outside the doorway, looking into the lane, and arching her back, she felt the discomfort of the precious burden she was carrying, wishing she could just set it down for the shortest time, and pick it up again.

She stood kneading her knuckles into her lower spine, but as they probed the ache they gave no relief. She cradled her bulging stomach with one hand and used the other to shade her eyes from the low morning sunshine. John had left early and she hadn't heard him go. Looking down the lane she thought she saw him but wasn't sure. Dropping her hand she disappeared inside, ready to give the children their breakfast of barley rye bread and oatmeal porridge, but busy Mary had beaten her to it. She'd pulled up the settle to the table and everyone was eating contentedly, their bellies still half full of rabbit pie from the evening before.

At the Smithy John had a big job to do, but one he'd done many times before. He must get on with ironing wheels for Dick Trot, a nearby farmer. Miles worked the bellows into the fire to increase the heat to heat the metal so it could be worked into a wheel rim. They carried on in companionable employment, with only the ring of hammer on iron punctuating the silence. It was a waste of time trying to converse as the hammering made it impossible to hear, and what would the two talk about in any case? All Miles wanted to know was if he was doing the job properly and John would tell him if he wasn't. And standing watching John was the best way to learn how to do things well.

Once the wheels were ironed Miles was sent away to drive horses for Farmer Dick and then home to collect Michael. The two boys were going bird scaring, hoping to earn a duck egg for tea.
John stopped for a short while at midday, and ate his meal, sitting outside on an upturned barrel, in the warm summer sun. No sound could be heard except the birds in the hedgerow behind and a cow calling to her calf over the way.
In the azure blue sky wispy clouds floated slowly above them in the slight breeze. It was a day as perfect as any could be. A man should be proud that he had three healthy, sturdy sons, as well as two beautiful daughters, a caring, good wife, and a way of earning a living for all of them.
And he was. Life was good.

Chapter 11

An Era Ends

"Grow old along with me.
The best is yet to be."

(Robert Browning)

The weather didn't hold fair for much longer. Across the sky, storm clouds spread, a dark grey blanket that covered the earth as its shadow blotted out the light. Fat raindrops dropped onto the dry ground, collecting into rivulets that filled the ditches. Gardens were watered and rain butts filled.

For John work made him happy. For Alice it was daily torture. She knew she was near her time. She was tired. She was more than tired. She was exhausted. She was worried. She hadn't felt like this with the others.

After visiting Miles and Elizabeth she had vowed to herself that they would be cleaner: that they would have new clothes. She had sent Mary to see a dressmaker in Muker and asked her to visit. The outcome of that was Mary and she were to have a new dress each. John had said it was possible, so she didn't worry about the cost.

Next it would be Michael, and then maybe John would have his turn.

But for now she had her laundry to do to, so, putting water from the rainbutt on the fire to heat, she filled the tub with a little more water from the stream, got on her knees and began to rub shifts and shirts in the warm water. Soap was an important ingredient, and she wouldn't wash clothes without it. It was a waste of time. Grated into the water, it miraculously changed the colour of her skin. After scrubbing the shifts, both outside and in, she plunged them to rinse in icy water: heavy work for anyone but for Alice it was impossible. Bending over the tub she felt the first signs that this child wanted to be born. And then she fell forward, unconscious.

The next thing she knew was that she was laid flat on the ground outside, by the stream, with their old neighbour Jenny urging her to push for her life. Elizabeth was standing, watching the process, and crying for her ma, holding Mary's hand, as she'd carried William across to find her ma.

It was too long. It was too hard.

"Come on lass. Get this bairn out," soothed the old woman, stroking her head.

Out in the open air!

Finding the strength from somewhere deep within she finally managed to do just that.

"It's a boy," Jenny shouted, as she held the baby aloft for his mother to see, but Alice's eyes were closed, and she heard nothing. After that she slept for three days.

It was June, and Meadowsweet was still blooming along the ditches. Jenny made soothing warm drinks of this concoction for Alice, and tried to get her to nurse the baby, but she could not. John's sister Elizabeth was able to wet nurse the child so he wouldn't starve until Alice was able to sit up and try herself, but the babe had to stay in Kirkby Stephen

Mary did the best she could. The washing had been finished, the children and John fed and Mary had made a tasty vegetable broth most days, with potatoes and bread.

And Mary's dress had been made. It was beautiful, and she so deserved it.

It was two weeks before Alice dragged herself up and out of bed for most of the day.

July was a wet month, and so the summer reverted back to a damp one in Swaledale. The baptism had been a hurried affair, and nothing like the last wonderful family day, with Alice not even present. John was the name chosen, even before he was born, in line with tradition.

By the time the seasons changed the family were on an even keel once more. Mary was minding toddler William and helping her ma. At ten, Miles was working all day at whatever he could find. He was never one to be downhearted and managed to find some work most weeks with farmers and his father. And now Michael was six he wanted to help out too.

But Michael was a dreamer, and dreamers find it hard to concentrate on the job in hand. When left to a bit of bird scaring, he thought of what he could be doing at Farmer Dick's. And when he was at the farm his mind was in the clouds with the birds. His da said that he ought to think more.

"But da ah'm allus thinkin," was his answer to that one.

He *was* always thinking. But not about the right thing.

He thought about running through the long grass before the hay had been cut. He thought about chasing the farm dogs, but he'd stopped after they started to chase him. He thought about riding horses, but wasn't big enough for that yet, and he could hardly wait. He thought about just spending time thinking.

He wasn't as keen as his brother had been to be a man and earn his own brass. He could wait.

He helped his mother dig up the potatoes from the garden, but this was really just picking up one or two at a time and carrying them inside to Mary who prepared them for the pot.

Being a farmer and working outside was all he wanted to do, not spend time somewhere dark and noisy like the lead mines.

He pushed his hair away from his pleasant face and looked up at the sky, feeling the damp mist on his face and loving the feeling of freedom in the open air. He couldn't explain how he felt and why he felt that way. He just did.

When he took in the latest potatoes baby John was crying. Old Jenny was bouncing him on her knee, but it wasn't making him quiet. He wondered why she did that. It would make him bad tempered too, he thought, if he was being jiggled about like that, and baby John seemed to agree with him. Jenny carried John outside and his wailing brought Alice over to him.

Michael knew that didn't work for him either, but babies must be different, he thought.

Alice took hold of the baby and went inside to feed him and comfort him. At only a few months old baby John was thriving and was already eating a little gruel, but his mainstay was the milk that Alice gave him. William was still little more than a baby and hadn't been walking for long. He wasn't a happy baby and spent a lot of time grizzling and whining. Sometimes she had them both at the breast together.

As soon as Alice turned her back on him, he let out a piercing scream and wail until she was within his eyesight again. There were times when she walked out of the door, and kept on walking, knowing the children were safe, because she couldn't bear the sound.

It was not usual for a man to worry about his wife's abilities as a mother, so John was in ignorance of the problems that were making Alice weary and worn. He failed to notice that she wasn't eating, that she was paler than normal, that she was thinner than she had ever been, despite just having had her baby. Men didn't notice such things.

He'd just taken a beehive as part payment for a piece of work and was talking enthusiastically about it to Alice. She nodded and smiled and said nothing. Mary was to take charge of it, he said, next spring. Honey could be taken to market, he said, and she agreed. Honey could be used in puddings, he said, and she agreed. And honey was really good to eat he said, and she agreed.
He was pleased with this latest piece of trade and oblivious to the undercurrents that were tugging at his family life.

Winter came early. Snow came down in small icy flakes from an ash-coloured sky and settled on the hillsides in a growing blanket of white. John left the cottage early each morning, rubbing his cold fingers to keep them warm. He needed to make sure that Sorrel, their pony, as well as the horse Dandy, were warm enough and had enough hay in the stable. He wondered if they would have to let the horse go.

This particular morning when he put on his great coat and boots and left it was still dark, but the moon and the stars lit his way. As he walked on, he hoped that Alice would be in a better mood when he returned later that day. She was so different to the woman he'd married, and he wished she wasn't. She had no time for him, and he wouldn't force himself on her, not like some men would. He knew she was worried about another bairn, but a big family was all the better, wasn't it? There would be family to look after them when they got older.

He loved all his family. The boys were all different. Miles was a Blacksmith. Michael was a dreamer but wanted to be a farmer. William was just finding his feet, and John, well, he was just a baby. As for the girls, Mary was a mother hen, looking after her chicks, but Elizabeth was a different matter. She was still rather testy, often bad tempered and didn't want to help anyone. For a while she had been better tempered but not anymore. She was self-centered and would do nothing to help anyone, and at four years old she was the most demanding of the children. None of them had been as temperamental as she. She had a temper and she showed it. If she didn't get what she wanted immediately she let everyone know that she was not pleased and she was so vocal that sometimes even Alice was afraid of her daughter's outbursts.

Yes, they were all different.

That summer of 1795 came and went, and Thwaite enjoyed a fleeting period of drier warmer weather. Autumn brought the usual harvest and the slaughtering of the livestock. If desperation set in, they had the vegetable garden, but work was more profitable here. At least John had been right about that.

And Alice's new dress was almost ready.

Life was better than it had been, since the move to Swaledale, but maybe it was time to see if their neighbour in Outhgill had sold the sheep that had been entrusted to him.

A journey back to Outhgill was made, with John astride Dandy, thinking he may as well make use of him as they wouldn't have him much longer. It didn't take long to discover that yes, the ewes had been sold, but that had fetched far less than was expected. They were worth at least £20, John knew, but he was handed only £10.

"It were a bad year," was all that he was told.

They'd been duped, and by someone who was supposed to be a friend. Once more, money was at the root of it. Not being in a position to dispute the figure, or the reason, he had to regretfully accept the money, and curse both himself and the farmer, who had been a friend and colleague of Alice's parents for years.

So that's the price of trust, he said to himself on the journey back. But at least they had some, if only half, and it was better in his pocket now.

Alice wasn't well. She hadn't recovered properly from the last birth, couldn't even look after her children and it was left to Mary to do that. She couldn't prepare meals. She wasn't capable of doing any household work. She was a shadow of her former self. Although she tried to do the tasks she had always done she found it impossible. Mary, at ten years old, did the best she could. The next year was difficult for them all.

She'd tried, she'd really tried, but it was all too much for her. She was tired and had the cough she'd heard coming from her father, a sign of the malignant disease that had taken him. Her chest hurt when she breathed, and she had night sweats and chills. Some nights her sweats were so great that she got up from bed and dried herself at the fire. It was when she began to cough up blood that she knew that things were bad.

"John, thee muss let uz tell the bairns," she begged.

"Tell them what, awld lass?" he asked, pretending not to know what she meant.

"Aw John. Thee knaws. Ah's sick, an' getting' sicker. Ah muss talk to 'em."

He heard the pleading in her voice and agreed.

"Divent frighten them lass. Thee's got a ways t' gan yet."

She didn't argue. There was no point.

Calling her children to her, "Mah honey bairns," she began. Then she held them each tightly, kissing their foreheads. "Each o'yee has to mak theur own way in life," she continued.

Now each child was looking at her intently.

"Look out for each other," she went on. "Thee all knaws what's right and what's not. Dee what's right. The way we've raised ye. 'onest is allus best.'"

When it came to it, she couldnt tell them she was leaving them. It was too painful. She would just pray for a miracle.

She worried about them having no mother – especially the little ones. And baby John was less than a year old. She hoped she would last a little while, just to be with him a little longer.

Not knowing how long she had, she tried to carry on as normally as possible for as long as she could. It actually took a further two months before she had to take to her bed.

John and she slept on their mattress now, in front of the constant fire, sleeping in his arms through each long night, making him leave her each morning, promising she would still be there when he came home.

She kept her promise. John rushed home once the daylight had gone and he could no longer work, but he knew that someone would fetch him if she took a turn for the worse while he wasn't there.

Later he described it as sleepwalking his way through the whole thing. He knew she was dying, but how could he know that, or even believe that? Just the look of her thin strained face, as white as if she'd been covered in flour, and the wrists that were so thin he felt they would snap like a stick, was proof of that. She ate nothing, except a spoonful of gruel each morning, and never left her bed, except to use the chamber pot. She was aware enough to know that Mary emptied this every morning for her, but Mary would have done anything for her mother.

Yes, he knew she was dying, but he didn't want to know. He knew he would be saying goodbye, yet he couldn't believe she was going to leave him. She and he had been together for only twelve years, yet he couldn't remember what life had been like before he met her. She had lost her mother, father, brother and sister, and now she was going to leave too.

He'd never been one for Church, but this made him feel even more that a God could not let one person feel so much pain and suffering. In all of this, at least he had all his children, and he would keep them close.

Summer was over when Alice left them.

As she lay next to him that night he could feel her bones through her shift, angular and sharp. When he woke early that morning, she was still warm, but no longer breathing. He kissed her forehead, got up, walked to the door and looked outside, across the beck to Thwaite Edge. The air was completely still. It was breaking dawn. And she was gone.

He let the children lie.

There was time enough for tears.

Later that morning the local good woman was fetched and John sent the children outside. She had things to do, she said. What she was really doing was the laying out of their mother. Washing her, cleaning her, changing her clothing. Alice would have been proud of how clean she was. John was adamant that she would be buried wearing her new, dark green, fine woollen dress.

Mary took William, John and Elizabeth for a walk along the lane, and told them they were to think that she was their mother now. She would look after them.

Then they had sat with Alice all through the morning, Mary holding her hand, now cold, while John went to the carpenter for a plain wooden box. All the way there, as he drove Sorrell along, pulling the cart, he was in a fugue state. He didn't want to believe it, yet he must. There were things he had to do. His family must be told. Her sister must be told. The church must be told. It was Monday. And she should be in the ground by Friday.

On the way for the coffin he made a major decision. Alice knew no-one here and had only moved to be with him. Her family were resting in Kirkby Stephen Churchyard, and so he decided that she would lie there too.

Through Elizabeth, the vicar was contacted and permission given.

On a warm summer's morning, the family made the journey back there, just two years since they had left, but now they were carrying Alice in her plain pine coffin.

They had a burial service, although Alice would probably be cross at him for wasting the money. He wished he had the brass for a headstone but he could save for that.

A hole had been dug and she was placed in it, with family standing round, and her sister Elizabeth saying a prayer after the Reverend. John couldn't bring himself to say anything.

Alice was laid to rest in St Stephen's churchyard, Kirkby Stephen, with a small posy of flowers, like the ones she had picked herself for her wedding day. Staying there until the late afternoon sunlight cut through the low clouds and cast long shadows on the grass, the family eventually began their journey to the home of Miles and Elizabeth. For the younger children it had been a day out in the open air. Elizabeth (or Betty as she was now known), William and John didn't realize the implications of this day. Mary, Miles and Michael were more subdued. Leaning on his father, John barely managed to walk.

Grandparents Hutchinson spent the evening trying to persuade John that he should bring his family to them. But John's emotions were too frozen to let him make any decisions. They talked well into the night, and only the children slept. Thinking how lucky he was to have both parents still, by the time the sky was beginning to brighten he had come to a decision of sorts.

Miles and Michael were working most days. That left Elizabeth, William and John for Mary to look after. Elizabeth was enough work for one body. She was a child who screamed and stamped if she didn't get her own way, and only Alice had been able to deal with her. So, he made the decision to ask his parents to take William and

John and look after them, until he could do it himself.

A year-old baby would be a handful for his mother, at her age of fifty-six, but he knew she could manage. He just knew she would. Mary would deal with Elizabeth for now. At least that would mean John could still earn his money for a while longer, and none of them would starve. For if they were not careful, hunger would creep up on them, a slavering dog, sitting at their table.

He had to work.

Book Two

1796 - 1837

SWALEDALE

Chapter 1

New Beginnings

"The chief beauty about time is that you cannot waste it in advance."

(Arnold Bennett)

The family settled once more, but without Alice.

Mary looked after them as best she could. Baby John and William were settled with his ma and da, who he didn't thank enough, or tell them he loved them enough. He resolved to put that right. That left five in Thwaite, including John.

That winter had been very severe from November 1795, right through until March. Listening to folk he heard it said, if you could believe it, that in January it had been colder than anyone could remember. How pleased he was that he'd already made the move to Thwaite as there would have been even less work in Outhgill for him now.

As the snow melted on the hills in a warmer February there was flooding, until the snow came again, right through March. It was deathly cold, making it a struggle to keep warm. On the coldest nights they had slept on the one mattress for warmth, in front of the fire, prompting Betty to say, "Juth like ma."

The autumn before had been exceptionally wet, even for rainy Swaledale, so now the ground was saturated and frozen.

It was a long, cold, miserable, hungry winter.

Working as long a day as he could, by the light of the forge fire or tallow candles in the late afternoon, John believed that all he did was work, but then he remembered to be grateful that he had any work at all. Mary fed them with soup, potatoes and bread, and the smoked beef they had put by. Sometimes old Jenny brought them an onion pie.

They went mostly unwashed, these very chilly days, but Mary was determined they would be clean come Spring.

She'd asked her da if there was any money to make a new shirt for Michael. Not yet, he'd said, secretly thinking that any new shirt Michael had would very quickly not look anything like a new shirt. He would rather this new piece of clothing went to Mary. Girls cared much more about their appearance. He was resolved. He would give the money to Mary, but only if she promised not to let Michael be the one to waste it. There was plenty of time for that.

Keen to settle his family after the sorrows of the past months, he was aware of the heavy weight in his chest that seemed to grow even heavier with every passing day, and he dragged it with him wherever he went. He hadn't married for love, but he'd very quickly grown to love her. And now there was supposed to be a life to live without her. Whatever happened in his life now, that would not change.

The days gradually lengthened, and spring began its journey across the land. Grass sprouted and animals were once more sent out to feed. Sorrel and Dandy had spent their winter in the outbuildings, with daytime journeys when necessary and possible. Work was plentiful. Rent was paid. New clothes paid for, and John was sporting a brand-new shirt and waistcoat, courtesy of Mary!

Today was a special day. They were going to visit Outhgill. Mary persuaded her da to wash properly and she supervised the washing of Betty. The boys had to assure her they would take a cloth and at least get their faces wet.

After an incredibly early start they arrived.

His mother presented them with a meal of cold mutton pie and potatoes, and ale of course.

"Ma, this is a pint of ale like nun uther," and he raised it to his lips, while taking a sideways glance at Mary. He didn't want her to feel she wasn't feeding them. She was only eleven summers, and was doing the work of a grown woman, every day. Nevertheless, the substantial meal prepared by his mother was very welcome.

Alice was the main topic of conversation. It was what John needed, as he didn't talk about her at home. Mary and Miles listened to the talk about their mother, about events before they were born. How they wished their da would talk to them like that.

Talking over and bellies full, with a further supper, they settled down to sleep somewhere, anywhere. Mary was delighted to see her two youngest brothers, so she bedded down near them. Being so young when he left, baby John knew none of them and Mary found that hard to understand. Now he was almost two years.

The next morning, they visited the churchyard and left a posy of flowers for Alice, before setting off for home.

"Why dooant thee stop 'ere longer, begged his mother. "We've room a plenty, and food too."

"I must work ma, or we'll be hungry afore the winter."

"Thy sista Jennet will be wantin ta sithee."

"She'll be welcome ta cum n'visit."

It was heartbreaking for his parents to see how alone he was, how much he missed Alice, and they couldn't be happy knowing that he was not.

'You can only be as happy as your saddest child,' was a saying. And how true it was, they thought. But there was nothing they could do, except support him by looking after William and little John, with Jennet's help.

Chapter 2

Children

"Come away, O human child!
To the waters and the wild
With a faery, hand in hand,
For the world's more full of weeping
Than you can understand."

(The Collected Poems of W.B. Yeats)

Mary set about cleaning when they got home. She needed to keep busy. There'd been enough for her to do without thinking of cleaning. But now she took up the old besom and swept the stone flagged floor, while John lit the fire. Michael was told to make sure that Elizabeth didn't wander into the beck but of course it was he who wandered about, looking up at the hillside and the sheep and the animals he might find there. Miles helped with the fetching and carrying.

The next morning, early, John walked into Thwaite, and began his day's work.

At the moment he was managing, with Mary. After all she was eleven summers old and believed quite capable. But still, he hoped he hadn't overestimated her abilities.

It was late spring now and the weather in Swaledale was comparable to the weather in Westmorland. The snow had all gone, apart from a little in the hedge backs, and according to folk lore that meant there was more to come. The beck was cold and clear and was where any washing took place. It was also used downstream as the privy by the males in the family. No-one liked the privy, because of the rats, but Mary and Elizabeth were not going to use the beck, under any circumstances. They would rather use a chamber pot.

True to folklore, the snow did return, and there was more. In the month Of May, when Summer should have been thinking about making an appearance, about half a foot of snow fell in Thwaite, making a hard life even harder. And once the snow had gone the rain returned, leaving a covering of ice that made it hard for even a horse to travel.

One morning, trudging on the way to work, lifting his face to the huge wet drops and feeling them trickle down over the bridge of his nose and off his chin, he heaved a deep sigh. Then carried on walking the short distance to the Blacksmith's.

There was no work for Miles there at the moment, so he'd looked elsewhere. Both he and Michael were old enough to bring in something, even if it was only a few pennies. They couldn't play all day.

Here the local farmers had all the help they needed from their own families. But there was an opportunity in a quite different occupation in this part of the country. The dale was teeming with lead mines. At twelve years of age, it was about time Miles had a full-time occupation, and so he was lucky enough to be set on as an ore dresser. Walking up to the mine with the other local boys, and some girls, every morning, he spent his day at the surface, dressing the ore, separating lead ore from the dirt and rock. He arrived home, tired and dirty, but well pleased with himself, telling Michael all about his day's work, "with the men." He made about three pennies a day, but the work made him feel like a man.

Walking over the moor to the mine early that first morning he'd been eager to begin, and walking back, with his hands sore and his back stiff with the bending, he felt good that he was making money for the family but he had truly little choice in the matter. Each day was harder and harder, but he couldn't give in.

He was a man now and a man had to work.

Michael was just seven and had managed to get a penny or two bird scaring and chopping wood. But he'd spent more time trying to catch the birds than actually scaring them off, creeping up on them, as carefully and quietly as a cat. They flew away eventually, but not before they'd done the damage he was being paid to stop them doing. So that job didn't last long.

He wasn't really big enough to drive horses, so he couldn't wait till he was old enough to go to "proper work." But for now, his father had put him to work digging over the little plot of grass he'd leased over the track next to the beck, and they would try and plant some potatoes.

Elizabeth, now called Betty by the family, was still what was called a 'twisty' child and spent much of her time grizzling and crying, looking for someone to give her comfort: never content, never laughed, seldom smiled and she had always been so. She perpetually dragged around the stick doll made for her by Alice, that she had called *Babbie*, raggy and dirty now, but she never let it out of her sight. She slept with it, ate with it and spent all day long with it. She'd been just five years old when her mother had died, but she didn't talk about her at all.

It was Miles who talked about her the most. Miles had known her the longest, twelve years, and had been the first born. He'd been special, and he missed her.

But Mary felt she was almost invisible because she was just there. She made meals, looked after Betty and Michael, did some washing. She walked to the village for a penny loaf every day and some milk. She worked so hard and did so much that people almost forgot she was there, taking her for granted and expecting her to be always at hand.

As for John, he had little time to think about anything except making sure he did enough work for money for the rent of his cottage and pastureland, and enough money to feed them all for a few weeks at a time.

Chapter 3

Peggy Pedley

"A woman as flirts for fun lessens th'market price ov her virtue."

(Clock)

The Hutchinsons were one of only a few families living at Scarr Houses. In one of these cottages lived a young woman, Peggy Pedley, still with her mother and father and with her own daughter Ruth.

She'd been baptized Margaret, but no one had ever called her that for as long as she could remember. Peggy was the name she always went by.

John had been on his own now without a wife, for almost one year. The time had passed, and he didn't know he had endured it, but he had. Mary looked after them all as best she could and tried so hard with her sister to temper her bad moods and make her pleasant. It was an extremely hard job, but John thought she was making some headway there.

He slept with Miles and Michael, huddled close for warmth and hadn't thought of replacing Alice, but he had thought about having a woman close again. It would not be for love but would be for comfort. And he needed some comfort.

He'd noticed Peggy walking to Thwaite, sometimes with Mary, with her little girl beside her. He'd even begun to compare her with Alice in the looks department but said to himself that he would choose Alice every time.

Peggy was shorter than Alice, and as she walked, her basket on her arm or swinging by her side, she exuded a confident, swaggering air that made all the men look at her. Her hair was very deep brown and lacked shine. A brush would probably have remedied that. It was long, as was always the case, and the odd times he had seen her with her hair down he thought how much more appealing this made her face. But it was usually pushed up under a blue bonnet, tied under her chin.

He could see she had more covering on her bones than Alice, making him wonder what that would feel like. Her shape showed that she had more of the womanly attributes, and he wondered too, what *that* would feel like.

Waking from his daydream he was shocked that he could think of another lass in that way. He hadn't seen it coming, and he didn't seek her out, but she wouldn't leave his mind no matter how he tried.

Peggy was very aware that the young men, and those not so young, watched her as she walked into the village, determinedly swaying her hips, basket on her arm. She knew, too, that the women whispered about her as she walked by.

She could just imagine the talk.

"Thee knaws aboot that un?"

"Aye. Aye ah dee. Dis thee knaw she's gor a byebegit and nor t'mense t'keep herself out o' t'way o' menseful folks."

"Leuk," whispered one of the company, as she knocked her companion's elbow with hers. "Thy Jack's een 're poppin."

And so it went on.

She wasn't a 'bad girl.' She'd just made the same mistake as some others before her: the same one her own mother had made. Peggy's baby had been born before she could make sure of the marriage. It was because she'd never looked or acted shamed or sorry that she was treated as if she wasn't decent and could never be respectable.

She was eight years younger than John, but he felt like an old man anyway, at the age of thirty-six years. Even though he didn't really want her, as he convinced himself, he believed she would never look at him. She would want a younger man, with no children to tie her down.

But she might want some company.

And that was as far as his thinking went, and with that he was as guilty as anyone about considering that she shouldn't be in decent company.

Peggy's mother had other ideas. Her daughter now was twenty-eight summers with no husband, and no prospect of one. Many wouldn't have her because of her "situation": little Ruth was three years old and a lovely child but often shunned too.

She could see that John seemed a respectable man, trying to look after his family. And his children were manageable and growing up. She didn't know about the two youngest staying at Outhgill, but that probably wouldn't have made any difference. She had a plan, and she would see it through.

She would arrange that they would get to know each other and then watch how it went.

Her plan was for Peggy to offer to help in the house and with the children while her mother looked after little Ruth. And for that, John would make her mother a new cooking pot.

It seemed a reasonable arrangement.

And Peggy was to take over the cooking and all of Mary's tasks.

Running along the lane when she heard this, Mary was happier than she had been in an age.

"Ah can leave now da," Mary uttered breathlessly as she burst into the cottage like a whirlwind.

"Where's tee ganna gan? Diven't be daft."

"Daft? Thee disn't need us. Ah's free o'this."

"But Mary. Ah can't let thee gan."

She was adamant. Leaving the lane where she had been talking to her father, she walked up to the only large house in Thwaite, Kearton House, and asked if they needed help. She was determined to make something for the family.

"Duz thee need eny help lady? Uz can fettle 'ard' n ah kna a' to keep our house."

"And what age ist thee girl?"

"Thirteen summers," she answered, adding one on for good measure.

"Thee's a canny un. Ah knaws thee and thy family. Thirteen thee says," looking her in the eye. "What does age matter if thee can dee t'job?"

Stepping aside she invited Mary inside for a trial, and she began that very day.

"Thee can start by cleanin' t'brasses ant'hearth. Then us'll see."

She was taken for a trial period for four shillings each month, and she had her meals with the rest of the staff. It was a fortune to Mary: a good deal of money for a girl of her age to earn. She was determined to make a success of it.

Peggy Pedley went to Number 3 Scarr Houses every morning and dressed Betty who had settled down considerably, made everyone oatmeal for breakfast, put up something for Miles and John to eat at midday, and did any other thing that was asked of her. She ate at home with her little girl and mother, and then went back later to put together something for everyone to eat at supper time.

All was going well, but after two months John had a dilemma. At their last visit to Outhgill, he could see that the two young boys were getting the better of his parents. His mother was old, and she was tired. Granted, she hadn't had a large family of her own to wear her out, but she was too old to be rearing a family now. He could send Mary there to look after them: not a clever idea, and he thought better of it. But because things were working so well with Peggy John decided that William and little John could come home. He didn't know what a huge surprise, and not a welcome one, that would be for Peggy.

But changes would be needed. To look after the young ones, Peggy would need to live-in with them. And as further payment for this, a deal was done for now that John was to make a griddle for her mother's fire.

Peggy loved her work. In fact she didn't consider it work. She daydreamed that the handsome man because he was still that, was her husband. She put together a supper each evening, usually a cold meal, made the young children go to bed, and sat with the others downstairs, on the settle, in front of the fire.

Peggy was now part of the family. She'd made sure that she was and had made herself indispensable.

As part of the package her little Ruth had moved in too as Peggy spent all her time there now. Mary, Betty, Ruth and Peggy slept upstairs, and so did Mies, Michael, William and John at the moment. Two were just babies still, at three and four years old but a curtain was hung up in the sleeping room upstairs, dividing it into two. On one side were the girls, and on the other the boys.

John was to sleep downstairs, on his own mattress, which would be dragged into the corner during the daytime.

There was room for them all upstairs, eight in total, sleeping on three straw mattresses. And that left enough room downstairs for a little comfort in the evening for everyone, in front of the fire.

The evenings were drawing in, and the late summer sun, even though bright, hung low in the sky. The fire smouldered but still gave out sufficient heat at present, but it wouldn't be long before the wind would whistle around the building and find anyway in it could through the many holes and cracks. This dwelling was more substantial than the last, but still left a lot to be desired in the way of keeping warm.

When temperatures really began to drop, they wore all the clothes they had, but sometimes even that wasn't enough, and this winter wasn't the worst – was even mild compared to earlier times. It was just a matter of keeping moving through the day and huddling close through the night.

While John had an advantage, as the smithy was warm, Miles was outside in all weather, dressing lead ore. Mary, too, was fortunate that hers was indoor work, but her hands suffered sores and chilblains from being constantly wet.

She'd been working for half a year for her original employer and received her half-yearly payment of twenty-four shillings. The feeling she had when she handed it over to her da was one she had not had before and could not even describe. He was adamant she keep some, so she did, but used it to buy some new tableware.

Now there was something else being offered to her. There was the possibility of a live-in position in Grinton in a much larger establishment. Her employer, Mrs Carter, had a sister who was the housekeeper there, and she was looking for a reliable kitchen maid. She and her father considered it carefully, and now that Peggy was "helping" so much, they felt that it was possible. After being given such a good character by her present employer, the position was hers, and Mary was so proud. She was still just given four shillings each month, with her necessary clothing and her keep, as she was so young, and "in training" but with experience she would be paid more. And she was close enough to visit home when she was allowed any time of her own - Sunday afternoons. She was working, she was not to feed, she was not to clothe. And Peggy, in effect, had taken her place.

Days followed a regular, steady rhythm. Peggy made breakfast and some snap for John and Miles. Michael was sent out to find work at the farm. Children were sent out to play.

Peggy walked to the village for a penny loaf and some milk, then spent the day with her mother. Evening time Peggy put some sort of meal together. Then the younger children were put to bed. Miles was asleep even before that after his day at the mine.

That just left Michael. He was nine summers old and should have been working more regularly. A local farmer had been persuaded to take him on as a farm hand, against his better judgement, as he'd seen Michael in the village, chasing the geese.

He wasn't lazy. He wasn't work shy. He was just a dreamer.

Time spent under a daylight sky, summer or winter, in any weather, or evenings spent under a canopy of stars, were what he dreamed of.

Being hemmed in, being confined by walls, he couldn't easily tolerate.

He loved the horses. They were two fell ponies, strong shouldered and faithful, and capable of pulling any plough.

He loved the cows, docile and friendly, with their long tongues and eyelashes, and learned how to milk them.

He loved the geese, but they didn't love him, chasing and pecking after him.

But he hated the pigs. They were fattened up for slaughter only and would eat absolutely anything. They were rough and loud and he found nothing of interest in them.

But he still felt that maybe he could be a farmer. Maybe he could work with animals. Maybe he could work outside, instead of in a smithy, or in a lead mine. There wasn't really much else to choose from.

He began his new job and slept at the farm in the stable with the ponies, looking after them very well.

Meanwhile, Miles had been doing well at ore dressing. He was almost fourteen years old, and an opportunity came about for him to work at the smelting mill. John was against it, but Peggy said it would be good for him.

"It'll mek a man o' im, John. That's wha' thee want, in'it?" she whispered one night.

"Ah doun't knoah" John replied after considering for so long Peggy thought he'd gone to sleep. "E'se's ower yung t'be deein' such graft."

"Why doan't thee let 'im 'ave a nip on ta see a'e'does?"

She was wheedling and coaxing now: so much so that John didn't know if it was what he wanted at all but was persuaded to let Miles go. He would sleep in a hut near the workings with the rest of them and come home for weekends. Miles was so pleased that he could be making more money, or so he thought, that he never even thought about the time he would be sleeping in a hut, on the hillside.

And Peggy had her way. Evenings were spent, just her and John, in front of the fire, on the old wooden settle, while the younger children were upstairs, in bed.

They talked little. John wasn't a great talker. Peggy sewed and mended, but not a lot. Some nights he had to send her to bed so he could sleep after a hard day's work.

But he became increasingly comfortable in her company and liked the feel of a warm body beside him. He even began to think that she was a homely, good sort, and that he could do much worse.

"A bite ter eat, John?" she would ask.

"Aye. Ahs fair clemmed," he would answer.

One evening, after this exchange, she leaned in close and whispered to him, "Owt else tack thee fancy John?"

Not sure of the lie of the land, and if she really was offering more than food, he turned and looked at her. The look on her face was the key to the situation. She couldn't have made it any plainer. John was a man unused to such wiles and answered with a grunt, that sounded like the affirmative.

Thinking that she may not have a better chance, she took his hand and placed his arm around her waist.

"What about that then?" she whispered, her mouth close to his ear so he could feel her warm breath.

Immediately, he snatched it back, as if it had landed on hot coals, but for that fleeting few seconds, he had appreciated the feel of a woman's body, soft and warm and pliant.

Her bonnet was tied but hung down her back, leaving her long hair loose. She had taken more care since living here and had brushed her hair until it shone.

Continuing her gaze, she looked straight into his eyes, and he was unable to help himself, feeling as if he was somehow bewitched.

He lifted an arm that now no longer seemed to belong to him. It moved, slowly, of its own accord, and took hold of her ample breast, his hand circling the warm flesh he could feel under her bodice.

"What abaht this?" he countered, whispering into her ear.

He could feel her soft, warm body beneath her clothes: her heart beating faster, and her breathing become shallower as he worked his hand around her breast, kneading, squeezing. He looked again at her face, and her eyes were now closed. He lifted his other arm and began to work her right breast under his strong fingers. Squeezing and rolling her nipple between his fingers, he felt her body stiffen under his touch. Lifting it from her bodice, he touched it with his lips and then very gently licked and sucked at the mahogany brown nipple that became more prominent as he did so. Feeling her body arch slightly, he knew she wanted him to go further.

This wasn't love. This was need. He was taking what he'd been missing for a year: the comfort and love he'd had nearly every night with Alice, and Peggy was very willing to let him.

He knew what she was offering.

He gently took hold of her, lifted her off the settle, pushing it aside, and laid her down in front of the fire. Parting her legs with his knee and lifting her petticoat and shift, he was met with no resistance. She was breathing faster now and seemed to mould her body to his. As he lay on top of her and entered her, she gave a soft moan, holding him close to her, wrapping her arms around his body and arching her pelvis to meet him. He dealt her swift strokes, thrusting deeper and deeper. With a grunt, he let go and rolled off, leaving her uncovered, dishevelled, and frustrated. For Peggy, it was over too soon.

'Maybe next time,' she thought. She knew there were going to be many more next time; now she had him on the line. She climbed the stairs to bed that night, happy, having achieved what she'd been working towards. She'd played the long game. Now it was just a matter of time. She'd fallen with Ruth after just once, so she knew it wouldn't be long.
Unsurprisingly, after about three months of these nocturnal activities, she had some news for him.

"There's a bairn comin," she told him one evening, when they were alone. The same words Alice had used when they were expecting their first. His face took on the look of a startled, hunted hare.
"Well, what did thee expect? Thee's been takin they pleasures for mony a neet now."
"Aye," he replied. "So uz 'ave. So what's t'dooa naw?"
"John Hutchinson. Thee knaws what's t'dooa naw," she spoke angrily. "Thee wudn't leev uz wi'a bairn an' orl t'shame t'boot."

So that was it. He knew he'd been played and caught: a fish on her line. He would have to marry her now. It was just over a year since Alice had died. Alice, who he hardly thought of now. And that thought made him feel more guilty. But he soon thought through the situation, as he lay on his mattress after sending her upstairs.

The brain is particularly good at rationalizing events and looking for answers to problems before being asked.

It was simple. He needed someone to look after his family. A man can't do that, and work were his thoughts. He needed someone to warm his bed, too, and provide what had been missing.

And he had found 'someone.'

So now he had Peggy, whether he wanted her or not. She could do all of those things, but she was nothing like Alice.

She was shorter in stature with more flesh on her bones, and an ample bosom. The Swaledale winds had weathered her round, agreeable, rosy face with its dark eyes, leaving it a light shade of brown, in summer and winter. Her face was dominated by a nose that was a little too large, and eyes that were a little too far apart, but her dark, dark eyes looked earnestly out of a face that despite her features, came together in a more pleasing fashion than you would think.

But, where Alice had been gentle and kind to everyone, Peggy was more intolerant, and apt to raise her voice for no apparent reason. She had a loud raucous laugh that his mother later said, set her teeth on edge, and made baby John cry. He startled like a baby rabbit whenever he heard it. His eyes would pop, and his face would curl up to cry.

If fate hadn't put them together, John may never have looked at her; who could say what may have happened? Actually, it was her mother, not fate. And Peggy herself, of course.

The news of the forthcoming marriage was a surprise to his parents, coming so soon after the loss, but having seen the lay of the land they'd tried to warn him. He didn't want to hear.

It was no surprise to Peggy's mother. Ruth had made a great friend in Betty and wanted to live there 'forever'. John and William were content as long as they were fed. They couldn't remember a mother's love, and although John's mother had tried her best, she was too old to cope properly with two young boys, so she had left them for their own company.

Everyone accepted the new life: some with pleasure, some with misgivings and some with actual indifference.

Chapter 4

Another Marriage 1796

"Did yo ivver see a step muther as liked t'huzband's bairns better ner her awn?"

(Toddles)

Despite her deficiencies in other areas, Peggy was from a religious family and had a strong religious belief.

It was true that Ruth's father had got away unscathed, and there were various rumblings in the village over who he may have been, but Peggy's uncles were 'God fearing Methodists' and pressed John for a marriage in Low Row Methodist Chapel. He held his ground and wasn't to be persuaded. His parents wouldn't come if it was to be held there. So, it was not held there. Simple as that.

On the morning of 10th September 1796, which was a Thursday, Peggy, her daughter Ruth and Peggy's mother, walked together along the road to Muker and St Mary's Church. Peggy carried a bunch of late wild-flowers and her best "go to church" dress and blue bonnet, having treated herself to a new white ribbon for the occasion. Best it was white that day, as it would never be white again. Betty and Ruth held a few flowers in an attempt to be flower girls. It was really a pitiful affair. But nothing could knock the smile, or rather grin, from Peggy Pedley's face.

It was a fine start to the day for the time of year, with a cloudless sky of azure blue, promising a pleasant walk there and back. That was to change later in the day. You could never trust the weather, his mother always said. Why should you? It was always changing its mind!

There were no friends, and no big celebration this time, just close family only. Jennet could not come, and Alice's sister Elizabeth refused to come. It wasn't a popular match, but it was a necessary one. Everyone knew why, though no-one spoke of it.

John could have refused but he was not that sort of man. He said that to himself, over and over. He was not that sort of man.

Throughout the whole event Peggy was like the cat that got the cream, and privately congratulated herself.

"A've dun it. E's mine naw," she said to herself as she walked back from church, holding onto his arm. Her mother was delighted that her wayward daughter had finally caught a man who would marry her. Many would not have. It rained so hard on the way back from the church that the family looked as bedraggled a bunch of people as ever was. But not even that could dampen Peggy's spirits. She had her man, and she would make of him what she wanted.

That Christmas was one of the coldest in living memory. Villagers talked about it at length, wondering when the cold spell would break while old folks compared memories. The beck in front of the cottage was frozen and they had to break the ice for water. At least Miles didn't have to walk to work in this weather, John thought, and he hoped that Michael was warm enough. But he had the young ones to worry about now. He had worked for his father when he was still quite young, so didn't think it wrong to expect his children to do the same.

What he'd forgotten or was purposely not thinking of, was that he'd had a mother to nurture him still then. They did not.

As well as being remarkably cold the winter was a very stormy one. The walls of their modest home took a battering from high winds but not much harm was done. The wind howled and moaned whistling around the walls and down the chimney, while stepping outside you were likely to have your feet blown from under you.

Eventually snow bleached across the hillsides, driven by those remarkably high winds, and landed in drifts outside their door, making any form of travelling take at least four times longer. Even the horses found it too difficult.

Sorrel, the fell pony, was happy in her stable, with John taking care of her now that Miles was working at the mill. But Dandy the horse, inherited from Michael Fothergill, had gone to her new owner two months before, when John had realized he was going to need money for this new wife and family.

Feeling sorry for his two older boys who were in less comfortable straits in such a bad winter, John talked about having them home.

"Wood thee gi'uz extreur fettle ta doa, when ah'm 'avin thy babby? Nay John. Ah can't be deein it."

He was easily persuaded.

Not that she did much 'fettle' now anyway.

He knew that Peggy consistently showed a hard side, even with her own child. Sometimes especially with her own child.

But then there was a soft side too. He loved to see her with the girls on her knee, singing softly and caressing their hair.

If only she would brush it though, he thought, remembering how Alice had taken such care with her hair, and with Mary's, in the early days. He was being selective with his memories, as always, when he thought of Alice.

Peggy's time had come and gone. She lay in bed, nursing her baby son, looking down into his sweet angelic face. Stroking his face and bending over to kiss the downy hair on his fair head, she thought how she could see his father in this face, and a touch of her father

William too, long gone. She lay wondering whether this life she had chosen would bring her what she wanted. It ought to be better than the life she'd had. Now she was finding that perhaps it wasn't.

She'd heard some talking.

There was a young girl, Peggy Nilson, now living in Thwaite, who'd got herself into trouble, but was managing very well she'd heard. It seemed she had everyone looking after her needs. The parish were paying for her laying in and a doctor for the birth.

A doctor! Who needs a doctor for a birth?

Butter, and a loin of muton were given to her at Christmas.

Even her John, her own man, had asked the parish for four shillings and sixpence for bread for her. Why was it any of his business, she'd like to know. What was it to do with him?

She didn't know, or at least she hoped she didn't know.

The baby of Peggy Nilson's, called John, had been born a few months after their first born, which meant of course that she'd fallen for a bairn just before Peggy had told John of theirs.

She wouldn't ask him because she didn't want to know.

If it *was* him then the girl wasn't making him pay, but was letting him get away with it, which was even worse.

Maybe he was just being a good neighbour. That's what she hoped.

The christening of the new baby had been held as usual, at the first Sunday service after he was born. Peggy wanted to call him John, after his father, but there was a difficulty as there was already a son called John.

"We'll call him Jemmy then," she countered, "after thy grandfather James."

"Jemmy?"

"Aye, Jemmy. It'll dooa," sighed Peggy. She couldn't even give her son the name she wanted, so how she resented the boy who already carried this name.

Marriage wasn't bringing her the life she'd expected, that was for sure. She even felt it unfair that she was expected to do so much work, looking after another woman's children. But she got on and did what she could each morning, which wasn't really much. The floor hadn't been swept for months. There had been no washing done. The children were filthy, and so was she.

Then once she was able to, she picked up baby Jemmy, called for Ruth, Betty, Will and John, and walked along Scarr Houses, to her mother's.

Ruth and Betty skipped along the lane together, scampering all over the place, like two young pups. Will and John began pebble throwing at each other but were sharply brought to heel by a shout from Peggy. They knew even now not to anger her.

Ruth ran in and was at home straight away, diving on her grandmother, who enveloped her in a tight hug, but Betty was shy, and unused now to such shows of affection, hiding herself under Peggy's petticoat. The boys were as they usually were, ignoring everyone and rolling on the floor, fighting, shouting and landing a kick on the shins now and again.

And this became the daily routine.

Breakfast when she could be bothered, then along the lane to her mother's, taking the children home just before John arrived home. Her mother, who hadn't much herself, would sometimes give her an onion pie which Peggy passed off as her own, despite there being nothing in their home to produce such a meal.

But as far as John was concerned he didn't care who'd made it. He didn't care about much, except maybe his children of course.

And even then, some days were so hard to endure that he wanted to forget about everything.

Thinking back to his life in Southwaite, and the man who had lived there for twelve years, he didn't know where that man had gone, but he'd gone, and there was nothing left. Life with Peggy was a compromise.

He needed her and she needed hm. But there was no love. At least not from him.

Then he reminded himself that he hadn't married Alice for love. However, somewhere along the road, love had appeared. So maybe things would get better. Or maybe they wouldn't.

He found that he really didn't care.

One thing Peggy did do was to make sure the children went to church, and then to Sunday School, when the weather allowed. The parson's wife ran a class every Sunday, and in it she tutored the children about religion, and a little bit of reading and writing, based on Bible stories.

Because it was church Peggy made the children have a quick wash and put on their least ragged clothing.

Betty and Ruth loved the stories, and the reading and writing, but the two boys were less keen. They had to sit still, which was a tricky thing for them, never having done much of that,

They were expected to answer questions too. They squirmed and fidgeted, until Peggy gave them the eye. Then they sat still for a little while.

Miles and Michael, when they were home, were expected to attend too. They would rather not, but John insisted, remembering how long it had taken him to learn to write his name for the Church marriage service, and wanting his children to have at least "a bit o' larnin'."

"It won't do thee nee harm," he insisted. "If tha's a bit o'larnin, then thee's a reet grand lad." And when they complained, as a reward he gave them a mug of weak ale each before they left to go back to their respective employment.

As for Jemmy, the two girls made a great fuss of this baby, and treated him almost as a plaything, carrying him around carefully, laying him down to sleep, and picking him up and shuggling him when he cried.

He seemed to cry more and more as the weeks went on, but that could have been because of the sores on his bottom from wet clothing. It was a frequent problem with babies, Peggy said, but John didn't think it had happened with the others when Alice was in charge. In fact he was sure it hadn't.

Jemmy had started to eat a little gruel and Betty was the one to spoon it into him, while Ruth watched.

The more time she spent with the quiet, amenable Ruth, Betty lost her bad temper.

Jemmy's mother had very little to do with him, except feed him and sometimes change his dirty clothes, covered in urine and worse. At the end of every day they were all soaked but were put to dry by the fire for the next morning, or rinsed out in the beck if they were dirty. That was the custom. It was believed that urine was somehow able to treat sores, a sort of antiseptic, despite causing them in the first place. Old wives believed that the urine had some sort of antiseptic properties and helped to keep away illness.

Sitting nursing him was one of the pleasures of being a mother her mother had told her, having left out any mention of the initial soreness that made it far from pleasurable. But knowing you were responsible for keeping this tiny defenseless creature alive was the pleasure and the pride.

That very wet summer came and went. Daily trips to the village for bread, milk and sometimes butter, kept Betty and Ruth occupied, and now William, who was four summers, walked along with them. They were lucky if they had shoes but were more likely to be wearing clogs, as did most people, ironed at the smithy. They loved the walk together along the lane and across the bridge into Thwaite, speaking to neighbours as they walked. Everyone knew them and everyone spoke.

Sundays meant church if possible, in Muker, and on Mondays sometimes the market. The girls thought it was a treat to go there. Bedtime was whenever Peggy was tired of them.

Baby Jemmy slept in the wooden cradle John had made for his first born , Miles. Spending his time between working at the smithy and cultivating a small vegetable plot at the edge of their pasture strip, where they were growing grass for hay, kept John more than busy.

The cold, wet weather had an unexpected consequence for one of the family. Michael was usually warm and snug in the stable, with a bed of rushes and heather. The farmer's wife had gifted him some extra clothing, now too small for her sons, and a couple of blankets. But this particular night he was woken by a cold so bad he couldn't get his breath. He had never, ever felt so cold. Looking up, he saw the stars through a sizeable hole in the stable roof, and his bed and everywhere around him was soaking wet. The ponies had taken no hurt as they were bred just for this type of weather, standing together and keeping each other warm.

Almost paralyzed with the ferocious cold and wet through, he made his legs take him out of the stable and stumbled into the open under the dark night sky. The last few nights there had been poor shelter, and he'd been lying on a bed of wet heather, with no cover, allowing the insidious damp to leach into his poor young bones. The ponies were better looked after than him because he was the one to do it. When he visited the farmhouse for his meals, he had said the roof was leaking, but no-one had expected it to fall altogether.

He shivered and shook so badly that he couldn't control his limbs, so he sat down on the ground outside the stable, in the dark, looking for someone to help, but seeing no-one. Dawn broke. The winter rain continued to fall heavily, forming rivulets along the edge of the field where he sat. A strong wind gusted, blowing through the bare branches of the treetops and around where he sat, bringing rain drops that hit his skin like needles, and burned where they touched.

He was there for some time, hearing the cock crow and the doves wake, unable to stand or walk. When finally the wind dropped and the rain abated he was able to pull himself to his feet and stumble along the muddy path. It took him most of that day, stumbling and sometimes crawling, to make his way to the edge of the farmland and the roadway. The Farmer had cursed Michael when his ponies were not brought to him but felt very guilty when he saw how the young lad had been sleeping.

As for Michael, if he'd been in his right mind, he would have turned the opposite way, to the farm, and would have been welcomed into the warmth with a good, cooked breakfast, as usual.

But all that was in his mind was to get home.

Jim Calvert was the one to find him, and, making him lean on his arm, managed to take him all the way to the rutted track. There they were able to find someone who could take the young boy home.

"Eee. Thou'll no' make auld bones," cried Jim trying to lift him onto the cart. "Wher'll we tak thee young lad?

"Scarr," croaked Michael. "Hutchinson", was all he could say.

"Ahh. Thee's a Hutchinson? Ain o' John's lads. Ah'll see thee home."

And he took Michael right to the door.

Chapter 5

Good and Bad

"No two losses are the same."

(Author)

Young Michael was home, and his father was so pleased to have him there. He was only ten years old after all, and the whole situation made John feel very guilty. It was his fault that Michael had been sleeping and living in such wet and freezing conditions for the past year. What would Alice have thought? He knew that she would never have allowed this to happen. She would have made sure that he was warm and dry and would have visited often. And farmer Dick Trot felt equally guilty. He knew he should have listened to the lad.

John had been only once, right at the beginning. And now young Michael was paying the price. He only hoped that the boy survived. Looking after disabled people was not something that Peg was good at, but her mother was. Now she took her rightful place as a grandmother, and it was she who nursed young Michael back to full health. He lay on a straw mattress next to the fire for two weeks to get some warmth back into his bones. Once he was fit John wouldn't allow his stepmother Peggy to send him back to the cold damp barn and insisted that he stay with them, sleeping upstairs once more with the rest of the family. And Michael was glad to be back home with his family.

Dick Trot did his bit and delivered fresh milk every day and eggs too when he had some spare. He told John that Michael had a job with him for as long as he wanted.

Peg already knew there was a second baby on the way when Michael was brought home but she kept it to herself, not telling John till Michaelmas.

Jemmy was only eight months old by then, and the new baby was due before Easter her mother thought, before Jemmy was even one year old. She also thought that it was far too soon to have another child, but it was too late for that. She would need to speak to her daughter after this baby, and make sure that she kept it at the breast as long as she possibly could. Old wives knew that kept the babies away a little longer.

Peggy wanted a girl, and she got a girl: a tiny spelk of a thing with a scribble of dark hair. She was born on a damp, miserable morning in early February, and as tradition dictated, she was called Jane, after Peggy's mother.

She bothered no-one and lay quietly and content in her crib, looking around her, with eyes that were alert and all seeing, or so it seemed. Now Peggy decided that it was even more difficult to manage without her mother. So once again, she didn't. She and the children spent most of the day with grandma, and then returned to their own home just before John came home. Her poor old mother was tired of being a servant to her own daughter, and for little or no thanks, so she decided to show her that life was going to change. The next day when Peg turned up at her door, with the five children and a baby, her mother was in bed, complaining of having been unwell through the night.

"Thee'll needs must make thy ahn meals Peg. Ahm so ill ah can hardlys move."

"Oh ma. How can ah dee that wi'six bairns."

"Dee what we all dee. Thee'll cope."

"But ah'm so jiggered ma."

"Dooant be sa soft. Thee's young wi plenty o' oop. Ah's awld and uz owld bones ache."

Peggy stood there with Ruth, Betty, William, John, Jemmy barely walking, and baby Jane, knowing she wasn't going to win this one. She turned towards home. Thinking better of it she turned back and went inside. Putting down baby Jane on the cold flagstone floor, she sent the other children outside to play in the lane. She lit the fire and made her mother a warm drink. Then she broke a piece of bread from the loaf she'd just bought, put it with a lump of hard cheese, and gave this meal to her mother, who thought, "Well at least that's a start."

After that Peggy took the children back home and gave the same very modest meal to them before sitting down to nurse baby Jane. The next day she visited and her mother was still saying she was unwell. It was a realization to Peggy that other people needed care too and that perhaps she would have to think of others. Maybe her mother was tired of looking after them all now. A husband and six children were a lot to look after. It was a hard lesson to learn.

After a decent interval of time, almost a week, her mother walked slowly and cautiously along the lane to her daughter's home, and was welcomed, if rather grudgingly. And her mother, seeing a slight change in her daughter, showed her how to make an onion pie, and a vegetable broth, agreeing to help her look after the children, from time to time.

The newest addition to the family, Jane, a pale, thin baby, was not the least bit healthy looking. She had a pinched, almost old look to her face. Her arms were twigs on an unhealthy branch, ready to snap if you weren't careful. There was a transparency to her skin and her complexion was even fairer when set against the darkness of her hair which sprouted unevenly on the pale skin of her head. Thankfully, she was a placid baby, and didn't cry or grizzle much, but she wouldn't have received much attention if she had. Jemmy toddled all around the cottage, in his dirty shift, arms outstretched for balance, as toddlers do, falling over a much as he was standing. For a child so young he seemed to have rather large feet and that ought to have steadied him a little but it didn't. He was at that age where everything had to be chewed, and so put in his mouth. The flagstone floor provided many things for him to experience as it was rarely cleaned. He'd almost choked on the end of a reed one morning having fallen with it in his mouth. Lying there he was making guttural sounds and whistling noises were coming from his throat when Peggy just happened to walk into the room. She picked him up, hung him upside down and slapped his back. Once he was breathing properly she simply put him back to the floor, to wander, crawl and perhaps make the same mistake again.

The four older children by now were fending for themselves, eating when they were hungry while Peggy made a show of having some sort of meal for John in the evening. She could make an onion pie now, and a warming broth. But she was happy, more than happy, to carry out her wifely duties at bedtime, with an abstinence of a week after childbirth. It was what bound her to the man, and he to her.

The circle of life went round as it should and Father Miles, still living in Outhgill, passed away in March at the age of sixty-one.

He'd lived a hardworking life and was still doing some smithing when he died. For all that, it was a respectable age but the son was heartbroken to lose the father who'd been his partner in many things. The burial was at Kirkby Stephen and his mother paid for a service. She was a strong woman but was grateful that she had a son to support her through the service and at the graveside, as well as a daughter who made sure she was looked after. Throwing earth in over the coffin, John suppressed a tear. Men did not show that kind of emotion.

His mother tried too, but with less success. Jennet was pleased that she'd been able to persuade her mother, with the help of her brother, to go and live with them at Hanging Lund, not far from Outhgill: a solution that suited everyone.

John sadly went to the Manor Court and ended the lease his father had taken out back in a more prosperous time. The parents' home was emptied, and all contents shared with Jennet having those items her mother wanted to keep.

Taking charge of his father's tools made John think of all the times they had worked together: the times they'd shared. The small pony cart which was given to him had memories that hurt. The pewter, brass and bedding mostly went to the girls, but John asked for some bedding. Theirs was full of holes by now.

His sister Jennet knew she would have given Alice a memento, but she was determined that strumpet Peggy was getting nothing.

Now John needn't worry about his mother and Jennet would have some help. She had six children still at home and the family farm where she lived with her husband, Alice's cousin, needed more help than ever before.

When he was home from the forge John had to spend some time on the piece of land they'd rented from Christopher Metcalfe. It was just over the lane in front of the beck, right in front of the cottage. Here he tethered Sorrel and successfully grew his crop of hay and even a few vegetables. Things were sprouting well this early summer in the warm weather.

Michael was home for good. Or at least for a good while anyway. He had no inclination to go back to the farm, even though he loved animals. That was a fact. Always had. So, John set him to looking after their fell pony, Sorrel. He'd tied her onto a long hemp rope, so she could eat her fill, while on the days that she was needed he hitched her to the cart, talking to her while stroking along her nose and letting her snort her warm breath into his hand. But he was eleven years of age now and needed more than ever to be earning money for the family. He was downhearted that his love of animals wasn't going to do that anymore. Because he hadn't gone back to the ponies, Dick had reneged on his promise to John and had employed someone else.

Now there was only the mine, but it was a long way to walk each day. Miles was fifteen years now and was doing the work of a man. Instead of making the journey each day, he lived in the miners' hut and brought his money home at weekends. His workmates gambled among themselves, and money changed hands regularly but so far, he'd managed to stay out of it, and keep his.

Children came to this family very easily. They'd been wed for only two and a half years when their third child was born.

Eleven months after Jane came a boy: small, sickly and weak. He arrived in a snowstorm with old Jenny, their near neighbour, in attendance. The vicar came to their cottage and the poor bairn was baptized Edmund, living for only thirteen days.

Losing a child was something that John knew nothing about but neither did Peggy. He wondered how he was supposed to feel when they buried this little scrap in his tiny box. But in truth he felt nothing, although he couldn't say if it was with grief.

He just felt nothing. Ever.

Carrying the little plain wooden box to the churchyard, he placed it in a recently dug grave, along with another villager. Only he and Peggy were there. Standing for a short while beside the grave felt like the right thing to do, but no one said any words: then they left.

His mother had warned him, all those years ago, before Miles was born. He remembered her very words and thought them rather harsh at the time.

"Don't get too fond o' them afore you're certain they'll be stayin'," she'd told him.

So many babies died in their first few months. It was just a fact of life. He was here, and then he was gone.

Peggy had gone on with her everyday activities. She'd hardly had time to recognize Edmund's face, and certainly couldn't remember it. He wouldn't nurse because he was so weak. He just slept or whimpered rather in his little wooden box that was like a little coffin. And then one morning, after he had been on this earth for only thirteen days she knew she knew he'd gone.

She hadn't looked at him all through the night. The end result would have been the same, she told herself. And she was right. But she'd left him till the morning, gave the poor little soul no comfort, no mother's warm loving embrace to ease him. Not knowing if he was in pain, or how much he suffered. She wasn't condemned for this. Babies died all the time. There were always plenty more to take their place.

Miles was now sixteen. He was a lead miner, his da having decided not to send him to the Smelt Mill and worked as hard as any of them at the Scattersgate mine. Working underground for the past two years he was now an experienced miner, spending his days boring his way through solid rock, following the vein or ore, breaking it out hundreds of feet below the ground, hammering at the rock with pick and wedge. The tunnels and passages were very narrow with just enough room for him. The work was arduous and unrelenting. And he was constantly saturated. Water dripped everywhere. Most of his working hours were spent in wet, soaked clothing, stiff with dust and clay while even the walk to his working place underground was through ankle deep running water. A shilling a day would never be enough to support a family, but good enough for Miles to take home to John and Peg. He walked home over the moor each weekend and wished he was going somewhere else. He wouldn't miss home because there was nothing to miss. He still missed his mother and tried hard to keep a picture of her in his mind, but it was getting increasingly difficult to do. Their days at Southwaite were often in his mind, and he wanted nothing to do with Peggy. Apart from that Miles was reasonably content with his life. Weekends were spent in the local Inn with his miner friends, where he spent both time and money. John, remembering his times at Kirkby Fair with his father, didn't begrudge the boy, but thought that maybe he didn't need to be there so often. When the little money that Peggy gave him ran out, he came home, but there was really nothing to come home for at night. He slept upstairs with the young children and could hear Peggy and his father downstairs, doing what he tried not to think until they both fell asleep. And wished that he could not. How had his father forgotten his mother so soon? Why had he taken up with Peggy? His mother had been gentle and kind, and everything that Peggy was not. And now he could see that she was getting fatter so that meant that another baby was coming. This little cottage was hardly big enough for them now. When would the babies stop?

Baby number four for John and Peggy came the following year, in the early autumn of 1800. The few trees were turned russet and yellow, while early morning was marked with low clouds and heavy mist. Peggy was well used to the signs now and when to call on her mother to help with the birthing. Miles had been right.

Michael watched all of this, but without thinking of the consequences. He was only thirteen years old. He'd needed to earn a few pennies at least, so there was nothing for it but to go back to the farm. The walk each day had him across the fell and he sat for some time most days in the heather, watching the birds come and go. He learned their calls and their song, and he practiced them on his walk, knowing every species of bird on the fell. He found nests among the heather but left the eggs be. Never would he take any of these eggs and never told anyone where they were either. His life was quite simple. He worked at the farm, and he loved animals. In his naivety he didn't think about where babies came from or why they came. He saw these things happen, but they were on the periphery of his vision. They didn't matter. It made him happy too working at the farm because he was able to eat with the farm hands. Wonderful meals they were. If he could rise in the morning and join them he had a proper breakfast, like the cold meat he had yesterday. Some days it was cheesecake or fruit pie. He'd never had fruit pie till then. The next meal, dinner, was a plate as full as you wanted, of hot meat pie and vegetables. That was yesterday. and today they'd said it was going to be boiled beef and dumplings. He loved being a farm hand!

His sister Elizabeth, or Betty as she preferred now to be called, was eleven years old. If she hadn't been so useful to Peg, she would have been sent out to work. And Peg's daughter Ruth was the same age. Together they washed clothing and made a decent job of it, cooked plain meals, or more often assembled items to eat. Grandma Pedley had taught the girls how to make dumplings and other simple dishes.

They helped Peg look after the boys, who were now eight and six, and helped care for Jemmy three, and Jane two. John and Will were earning a penny or two, bird scaring now, and Will was old enough and strong enough to drive the horses. This had been what he'd been waiting for. There were more stomachs to feed, but at least some of them were earning money.

Peggy sent Ruth for her mother when she felt the pains begin, and the bairn was born just a few hours later. John had taken heed of his mother's warning and wouldn't go too near this bairn until he was sure she was staying. She was baptized Peggy, and this time he'd managed to persuade his sister to bring his mother from Outhgill. It wasn't too far. He was pleased they'd made the effort, and it made him feel that at least they were trying to accept Peggy. The family once more made the usual walk along the road by the river from Thwaite to Muker, and up the hill to the church. It was mid-September, and the sun was low in the sky. If people were thinking about the time they walked along here with Edmund in his tiny box, they didn't speak of it. Life was cheap, and there were plenty more children to take the place of those who couldn't stay.

Chapter 6

Family

"What fascinates me are the turning points where history could have been different."
(Hilary Mantel)

Later that year they had better news.
Mary moved back to Kirkby Stephen and visited her family at Scarr Houses along the way, bringing money for John from her wages. She was John's first-born daughter, and he missed her so much. On her visit, he'd loved listening to her telling them all about her years as a kitchen maid and about the big house she'd lived in for the past few years. But there was always more to tell.
She didn't tell them that her real reason for leaving had been the unwelcome advances of the master of the house.

She was a strikingly pretty, shy young girl, with blond hair and green eyes, like her father, a radiant smile, and a dimple in each cheek that made anyone give her a second glance. It had become increasingly difficult she'd found, to ward off the man's advances, and threatened with dismissal she'd decided to leave but not before she'd managed to obtain a written character from the mistress. She heard from the other girls that she hadn't been the first who had needed to leave. They reached a compromise.

She was seventeen now and was looking for paid employment as a kitchen maid. She wouldn't earn much but would get board and lodgings and a few shillings each week that she would bring home when she could.

She had the name of a good family in Kirkby Stephen, to whom her mistress had written, and she was all set to begin work there the following week. This would pay her £1 each month, and she would send most of that to her father, she said. Working there she would be able to see her mother's cousin Will now and again and be able to reminisce about her mother; maybe finding out more about John and Jane, her uncle and aunt and Alice's brother and sister, who had died so young.

John and Peggy had been married for five years now, bringing up three children as baby Edmund had died. Bringing Alice's face to mind was something that was increasingly difficult for him to do but seeing Mary had helped him to remember.

They had only been married for twelve years a lifetime ago now. And now he had another lifetime to live, with Peggy.

That summer was the usual wet one, and John struggled to bring in a crop of hay for Sorrel. Betty had planted potatoes and onions as her mother used to, so she could make tasty, filling broth. And they were rearing a piglet, in partnership with two other families in Scarr Houses. It lived mostly on potato and onion peelings, with the household rubbish from the other families. Young John and William walked the lanes looking for anything the pig would eat. Large wild plants, dead mice, or even live ones, wild apples and as much grass as they could pick and carry. Potatoes and even turnips snagged from a neighbour went over the fence into the pen. The trouble was that as she grew bigger, she ate more. John set traps for the rats, and she ate her share of those too.

"Good job, pigs eat awt," said Peggy, throwing the rubbish over the fence John had put up.

Looking over the fence, John laughed. "If we cud an all, life wud be allus easy, but a plate o'grass and dead ratten wadn't feed us."

"What abaht snaggers and mice," she countered.

"Get the pan on," he laughed. "Me mouth's watterin."

"Thee's a barmpot," she laughed back.

They kept the pig around the back of the houses so they could keep a better eye on it, and it wasn't long before the children were beginning to consider it some sort of a pet. A name had to be given, and they called her Bella. This year had been a dry summer and farmers has done well. On his little piece of land, John grew grass for hay, and this small patch of land gave up enough vegetables for them all. They had potatoes and onions, and there was a patch Jemmyevenings and back again as she was grazing her patch bare. He was working back at the farm and was lately helping with the hay harvest, which was heavy work for such a young boy, but he was sturdy enough and did what he could. Scything had begun early that morning, while the dew was still on the grass.

Because it had been a dry summer the farmer had gambled on it continuing to remain dry and had decided to windrow the cut grass instead of cocking. Not being strong enough to wield a scythe Michael was put to work that afternoon with a hay rake, turning the cut grass into rows along the strip of land. This week his father was earning more as a mower than a smith, helping Dick Trot with the hay, so was working alongside Michael. The boy made every effort to impress and was proud that his father could see how hard he worked, wielding the rake as expertly as any grown man. Seeing his father glance over more than a few times, then give a wink and the smile that utterly changed his face, made Michael glow with pride. Even if it was for only a few pence a day, at least he was working outside, and his father had seen him.

After that pleasant autumn, winter came and went. An unremarkable one with the usual amounts of snowfall in Swaledale, giving just enough for the children to enjoy. Sorrel stayed in the old building next to them, and Michael made sure that she had heather to lay on, saved from the summer months. The small amount of hay they were able to harvest that autumn was all she had to eat, and John wondered how much longer they could keep her. Farmers brought their sheep down from the hills and lambs were appearing that late March.

Jemmy was three now, and more or less outside in the lane all day, 'free range.' He just always seemed to find something to do: mischief, usually with the face of an angel. Jane toddled around, always with a runny nose and cough. They both had suffered a bout of the runs, down their legs, around their feet. It seemed that many in Scarr Houses were suffering, and it was particularly troublesome for the very old and very young, who could die from it, and often did. As Jemmy and Jane were recovering, it passed to baby Peggy, who was just over six months old. She could sit on her own, and that was how she was left, sitting on the floor of the cottage, while effluent ran from her.

"Howay Peg. Look t'this bairn man," John spoke in a commanding voice to his wife, who seemed to be totally ignoring this child's distress.

"Aye John, but she's just gorra bit o' t'skitters, jus' like t'others."

Peg picked her up to try and do something about the situation, but all she could do was take off the clothes she wore, and wrap her in a shawl, until her clothes were dry once more. She sat there wailing, and waving her arms to anyone who might pick her up and give her some comfort.

Jane, at two years old, didn't know what was happening, but sat with her and showed her the stick doll Peg had made for her. Baby Peggy took it and put it straight in her mouth, gnawing on the wood, to ease her swollen, painful gums.

No-one was worried. She would be well, just like the others. They were so certain. Unfortunately, she began to deteriorate.

Soon she was no longer strong enough to sit up unaided and had to be laid in her crib, too weak to nurse and either wouldn't, or couldn't, eat or drink.

Dehydration sets in very quickly with the young, and so it was with baby Peggy. Peggy tried to make her take a spoonful of something, but she was too weak. When she began to sleep most of the day John had wanted to get the medical man, but Peggy was against it. How he wished now that he had. Her breathing became so shallow that it was hardly possible to see if she was breathing or not. Until finally, she was not.

John had held this precious little bundle close and had made her smile, and even laugh as she'd looked up into his face. He'd listened to her gurgling, soothing herself to sleep, in her little bed, the one that he'd made all those years ago for Miles. He'd watched her, with love, as her mother Peggy sang to her and stroked her cheek, and with Betty, who loved her and played with her, showing her the stick doll called Babbie and feeding her gruel from her finger. He'd watched Michael, so nurturing, taking her outside on crisp, cold snowy evenings, tightly wrapped in Peggy's shawl, holding her up to see the stars. Watched her look at the snow as it fluttered to the ground and as it melted on her dark eyelashes and warm downy cheek.

They'd loved her for over six months.

She was theirs for those six whole months.

It seemed a long time.

It seemed like she was staying.

She *was* staying, they all thought.

She should have been staying.

She was already part of their lives.

She was their sister and would always be with them.

And they were all wrong. And, oh, how she was missed.

Peggy was meanwhile doing her usual regular job of producing babies and it seemed no time at all before another baby arrived. The birth was in October (1801), just a few months after baby Peggy had died.

Peggy wanted to call her Peggy again, after losing baby Peggy so young, but John was against the idea.

"At cannit abide it Peg," he growled. "Ower Peggy is gon. Divent call this ain the same. "

"It means we'll allus mind her. We'll 'ave 'er still."

"Peggy, ther's umpteen mooar names theur could choose. Why dis 'un? Why jont dis 'un when ah dooant?

"Awh John. She's named for me, and there mighn't be anither lass," she reasoned.

She got her wish, and the new baby was the second of her name, but *nothing* like the first.

This Peggy was quiet, with wispy, sparce hair, looking at a distance as if she had no hair at all. She seldom cried and was able right from the start, to soothe herself to sleep. Her features were quite irregular, which did not augur well for her to be a pretty child – crumpled nose, wrinkled cheeks, thin lips, and a strangely pointed chin, for a baby. She did have the look of little Jane about her.

Peggy used to look at her and wonder where her look had come from, how she would turn out. John just looked at her and saw his beautiful daughter.

Now there were again eight children living in this small house, including Peggy's first daughter Ruth, with Miles home at the weekend. Including parents made that eleven. They were squeezed in, three to a bed upstairs, with John and Peggy downstairs.

Ruth had been working hard, helping Betty with the younger children, and now she resented it.

"Don't wanna live 'ere no more," she complained to her mother. "Gonna see if Gran'll have uz back."

Gran was delighted to have her granddaughter back, but it didn't make much difference at Hutchinson's, apart from giving more work to Betty, who would have loved to go with her.

At twelve years old Betty was working at home, cooking, cleaning if she could, and looking after the younger ones. They could not have managed without her. She was doing all the jobs Mary used to do, and Peggy was brought in for. If they could have done without her, she would have been sent away to work in someone else's house for money. Alice would never have recognized the present character of her second born daughter. She was a million miles away from the bad tempered, twisty child she had been and had turned into a helpful, caring young woman.

Jemmy was a typical four-year-old, looking healthy and sturdy, with an angelic face belying all the trouble he could cause and all the mischief he could find.

The things he loved to do were simply disgusting, such as hiding in Bella's pen and frightening anyone who came close enough to hear or creeping through the long grass and jumping out on unsuspecting passersby. Another trick of his was climbing onto the privy roof and piddling on anyone below. At first, they thought it felt like rain, until they looked up at the sky, full face, and realized it wasn't. He would also jump off the privy roof and into the path of anyone using it giving them a fright.

Pelting neighbours with fresh pig dung as they walked along the lane was one of his favourite pastimes of the moment. And that meant he had been chased by many an irate neighbour brandishing a besom or worse, shouting out what they would do if he caught him.

All Jemmy did was turn to them as he ran, laughing aloud, fleeing away from a certain beating if he was caught.

It was as if he had no control over his laughter. He just couldn't help it. It seemed to well up in him and explode in a huge grin and a loud giggle that made people even angrier with him.

They all knew who he was. He didn't even try to hide but they would've recognized the laugh anyway.

He was just a boy, and a young one at that, but if he'd been caught, he'd have been soundly whipped by anyone who caught him.

On the very few occasions anyone managed a landing blow, Jemmy only laughed in their faces and ran on.

The whole of Scarr Houses was outraged about this terror in their neighbourhood and John was constantly stopped by neighbours who'd had enough.

"Use t'belt on him."

"Gi' 'im eur thrashin'."

John had never used a belt on his boys and wouldn't now. He knew it was wrong but couldn't help but secretly think that his boy was showing a bit of spirit.

"It's not the way," he said to Peggy. "Da niver did to me, and nor will us dee t'Jemmy."

"Ee's ower waywad. Ee'll cum t'nee gud, and whit will thee say?" moaned Peggy.

"Ee's anly a lad, an' lads get into bother."

"Mark my words, John Hutchinson."

"Ee's still under my een, and allus will be."

"An is that gannin tee keep 'im out o'bother? That lad's got a look in 'im een that spells trubble t'thee an me. Mark whit ah's sayin' t'thee, John Hutchinson."

John ignored the warning; one of many given and many heard about a multitude of events and went in search of Jemmy once more, finding him sitting on the front step of their old, blind neighbour Jacko.

Looking up, with a face that "wadn't melt butter", as the saying went, he found himself being taken by the scruff of the neck and dragged home.

Jemmy knew better than to resist his da and he resigned himself to his fate. He knew already that his da wouldn't beat him. He never had despite what he'd done.

"Ere lad. Get that bucket an'shovel. Thee has a job t'dee. Howk all that from Bella's pen and throw it onto uz land. It'll dee the veg gud."

Christmas Day that year was on a Friday. It came and went, with a trip to Muker church, after a breakfast of bread and oatmeal gruel. The girls had a new stick doll and John had made the older boys some jacks, and a hoop and stick for Jemmy. The one he had made for Miles all those years go was lost or left behind at Southwaite. Peggy and Betty made a meal of boiled beef and mutton from the weekly market in Muker. Peggy had managed to walk the mile there on Wednesday. With the potatoes and vegetables, it made a tasty dinner. Potatoes were crisped in the hot fat and batter pudding made it a full plate.

The last few harvests had been poor, so prices had gone up and people had suffered. To provide more food John had an idea that he put to Peggy after they'd eaten.

"Wit abaht havin' sum geese Peggy? Uz'd 'ave eggs, a'mean now an'then. Bella's not fatting up much, and she gans next spring. We can put 'em int' pigpen," was John's suggestion.

She seemed quite keen, as there was little work attached for her.

"Geese is easy t'feed. They scratch abaht and eat little wild thins, an grass."

"Ah'll see abaht it then," he agreed. It was decided.

It had already been decided. He'd already seen about it, and the deal had been done, but Peggy needn't know that.

Jemmy, Jane, William and John spent the rest of the day outside, pelting each other with snowballs this time, and making a snow house. Enjoying all the things children do in a few feet of snow. Miles, Michael and Betty watched, itching to join them, and finally couldn't resist it. Ruth came along too, and all the children living in the lane joined them, the Harper children, and the Milner's, screaming, shouting, laughing and rolling in the soft powdery crystals that glistened like jewels when the sun peeped out. Occasionally there were some tears, when a snowball that was made with ice inside reached its target. But the older ones looked after the younger ones, while the parents stayed inside, in front of the peat fire, and drank a mug of ale. Some days are more memorable than others.

Chapter 7
A New Skill

"And in the act of making things, just by living their daily lives, they also make history."

(Anne Bartlett Knitting)

"I wanna larn to knit," shouted Betty, running in from the lane. She'd just been to see Ruth and was impressed to see her sitting on the settle next to her grandmother, a stocking already begun, and seeming to be doing very well.

It was a way that many took to earn a little more money, both here in Swaledale and in the Eden Valley where Betty had been born. In fact the main square in Kirkby Stephen was called "Knitting Square" because of it. Even the men knitted and helped to instruct their daughters and sons. Some could be seen walking over the moors to the lead mine, knitting the stockings that were sold at the local fairs. It was an occupation for all.

The wool was obtained at the local Fair or Market and then the stockings were sold back to the same person. It didn't make more than a pittance, but a little could mean a lot to a family that was sore in need of food.

Peggy had learned a long time ago, but hadn't done any for years now, and John had never learned.

"What abaht Miles and Michael, and the two younger ones. They cud an all," said Peggy. "But ahh aven't t'time t'teach ee."

"Granny Pedley will," shouted Betty, and turned and skipped back along the lane, to let Ruth know the good news.

They had enough for a small beginning, and it could not be wasted. Betty learned first, and then she tried to teach Miles that weekend. He'd seen many men coming to the mine with their knitting sticks going in their hands and was willing to try. Grandma Pedley took the blue worsted wool every time from a trader who collected the finished stockings on his next visit. She made a small amount of money this way and it helped. It therefore took a lot of persuading and wheedling by Ruth and Betty for her to part with some wool. They promised absolutely that they would produce the stockings when the trader came back. For this Grandma Pedley was going to pay them one farthing for two pairs of stockings. Grandma would make a tiny bit more.

Betty and Ruth were good knitters and had produced two farthings, one half'penny, and to them it was a fortune.

They wanted to get an old broiler chicken for family dinner, but "uz needs moar brass f'that," complained the girls.

Granma Pedley was one whole farthing richer by letting the girls into her knitting circle, for no extra work, so she said she would give them another month. This time Miles was included and after tuition and practice he walked over the fells each Monday with his knitting stick, coming back the following Friday with his finished pair of stockings. There were other men there knitting too. The hardest thing was trying to keep the wool clean but Betty saw to that when he came home.

With Ruth managing four pairs (she had help from Grandma although she did not tell), and Betty her three pairs, together with those produced by Miles, two over the month, this time they had earned a further one penny and a farthing. After a further month, the girls came home with the broiler chicken, some flour and a small pat of butter with the remaining earnings. It was enough to feed them all, and Peggy made a pie too.

It had been so successful that they had to continue. Michael was the next knitter that Betty set her sights on, but after many hours of tuition, she was left with a ravel of wool and no stitches to speak of. Michael was more concerned about the sheep that had produced the wool. There would be no extra income from that quarter. Betty knitted until the light had gone, then went to bed and knitted in the dark. Over the winter months she was very industrious, sitting together with Ruth and Gran, singing as they knitted. The extra money made everyone feel extremely useful. Miles was not a prolific knitter, but still managed to produce two pairs each month.

As for the rest, the two boys Will and John, were just not capable of sitting still to do any such thing. It was Peggy who taught them to knit a few stitches while rocking on their seat and stamping their feet. They loved the singing, which was more like a shout when they got involved, but it passed the time. And they produced a recognizable pair of stockings each, after a good while that is.

Betty had progressed from obtaining her wool from Granma Pedley, to getting her own from a trader. But she was disappointed that the money she earned seemed to be getting less in proportion to the number of pairs knitted. Asking around it seemed that this was the norm. Traders didn't like to pay out too much in one week. Still, brass was brass, even if it was spent when she got home. But they would eat better, with a few treats, that week at least.

Once spring came Betty was more inclined to spend the time outdoors, on their small vegetable patch, or taking Jane and Little

Peg to see the cows along the lane. Giving the two boys a small spade each, made by their father when Miles and Michael had been young, she put them to work, digging over the soil. Even Jemmy was made to be useful. She was the only one who could persuade him that what she wanted him to do was actually what he wanted to do. And so, he cheerfully fetched and carried, the boys dug and planted and Betty was happy. She had transformed from a miserable child with a noticeable temper who cried at the slightest thing, to one who was helpful, kind and generous. The change was remarkable. And no-one knew how.

Peggy and John were fairly happy too with each other. Their children were growing into useful young people, and they had long since stopped worrying about whether they were staying or not. That worry was about babies. Not grown children. The summer was reasonably dry, but the dales were never really dry. Wind roared down from the hills, sweeping the rain with it. And when it rained, it didn't half rain. It could rain for more than ten days at a time. Thankfully, this year was better. The lane was blossoming with spring wildflowers, until Jemmy picked them for Bella pig's breakfast. Their farming land across the lane was growing a good crop of grass, and Bella had her share of that too.

Jane followed Jemmy wherever he went, gabbling at him, words no one understood, as they walked. She idolized him and went wherever he went unless he could give her the slip. At five years old he was even more of a terror than he had been at four. Going out into the lane at the beginning of the day he wasn't seen, apart from coming home for a bite to eat, until darkness. Jane was left behind. He didn't want her getting in the way of his mischief. If his parents had known what he was up to he would probably have been whipped this time. Even he, at his early age, wondered why they didn't come for him and drag him home. But they had a lot of bairns. They mustn't miss one, he thought.

Market day was an important day for everyone. Peggy walked along the lane from Scar Houses to Muker, with Jane and little Peg hanging onto her skirts, to see what was there, and to hear the news that the traders brought. Bella had been butchered and their share of the meat was hanging in the chimney, smoking, to be eaten next winter. Pelting people with pig dung was one activity at least no longer available for Jemmy. Passers-by were safe from the horrors of pig dung whistling past their ears, splattering their backs, or worse.

A part of the pig had been exchanged for four geese and a gander, and they were now living in Bella's accommodation. The geese were no trouble, scratching about in the dirt for what they could find, and the family all brought flower heads and grass for them to eat. A good lot of worms and bugs meant a good egg. Peggy had let the first few eggs hatch and now they had a few goslings but then they had to isolate the gander, so he wouldn't harm them.

Little Peg was only just walking, and falling over in the ruts, but Peggy couldn't carry her with a basket of eggs on her arm. Betty was at Ruth's, in a rare moment of free time, but was collected on the way past the door, and pressed into taking care of her little sister. It was late summer; the days were long, and the weather pleasant. As they all walked along the dusty lane together Jane continuously darted along in front of her, and then back again, to show her mother what treasure she had collected. A flower, a pretty stone. She even found a farthing this day and her mother eagerly pocketed it, telling her to keep her head down, and find another.

Lost in her own thoughts, Peggy was already aware that there would be a new baby in late winter, making this her sixth child and married less than seven years; her seventh, including Ruth.

John was a hardworking man who needed to take his pleasures. And he frequently did. Peggy wasn't always willing, but she was never unwilling. No wife could be. It was her role to provide the children, so they kept telling the wives at church. But the vicar didn't care about the toll it took on a woman's body as the babies kept on coming. He was quite old now, and his wife had only produced three children in total.

"Wonder how she's managed that? Peggy wondered.

But for Peggy the babies just kept coming. There wasn't any way to stop them, once they'd started, until the woman's body gave up and said, 'no more'. That was a good few years ahead for Peg. At least another ten, she groaned, with a possible eight more children. It would kill her.

The eggs were sold very soon. Butter, flour and bread were bought, as well as a peck of oatmeal for porridge and a few vegetables they didn't grow, for broth. Bones were obtained from the butcher to boil with their vegetables and, with their own potatoes and onions, and a pie or two, that would last them the week, all eight of them.

That night she talked to John about Sorrel.

They simply couldn't afford to keep her, she said.

The small amount of hay they grew could be sold, instead of keeping the pony fed in winter, she said.

The family needed the food more, she said.

Or, instead of the pony, they could have a cow, so milk and butter wouldn't need to be bought, she said. And cheese even.

It all made a good deal of sense. He knew that already. Their milk cows had been sacrificed since the move when food was needed. And when she told him her news too, he realized that another mouth would be to feed, eventually.

Some of the children were working and bringing in a small amount, but they were lucky, with John's occupation, as families nearbye were only a week or two away from starvation. These families lived from day to day, hand to mouth, hoping that they would have enough for the next meal, or asking the Poor Law Guardians to help.

John was proud that, even with all the children he had, he'd never had to go and ask for Poor Relief.

1803.

This new babe was born on a snow-covered morning, in early February 1803. Having used all the family names, they resorted to uncles, and so Christopher was chosen.

Little Peg was coming up to two years old now, had vacated the wooden box, used as a baby bed, and was sleeping on a straw mattress next to John and Peggy, with Jane, who was five. The birth was uncomplicated, and quick. Very quick. The fact that this was her seventh child probably had a lot to do with it. She'd just time to send Betty for her mother when she felt the urgency, but the baby was almost there by the time her mother had hurried along the lane and bustled inside.

"S'truth child. We need more warning or thee'll be birthin in the lane," laughed her mother, pleased that all had gone so easily.

"Better be quick as not," Peggy retorted.

Taking off her shawl, her mother shook the snow off it and took her grandson in her arms.

"Hast thee a name for t'little man," she asked. Peggy and John had talked about this, and she was pleased to give her mother the news.

"Aye, and a girl was to be Christian," she added.

"That's a pretty name for the next time, after thy aunt."

"Aw ma. Next time? How many more times?"

"Ainly the good Lord knaws that dowter, and he winnet be tellin," her mother consoled, knowing that her daughter was averse to the work these children brought.

She also knew that the family was not yet a large one, compared to many another in the Swaledale village.

Grandma made the food that night. Smoked and salted pork was added to a pan of boiled potatoes, with a little bread. John was greeted at the door with his mother-in-law smiling, holding the new baby in her arms. He had the same fair to ginger hair sported by his late Grandfather Miles, and his brother Miles, with the same piercing blue eyes. He was long, but dainty, with delicate fingers, and his head constantly turned, this way and that, looking for nourishment.

"This yan's a hungry yan," laughed Grandma. "Thee'd better get on."

Peggy took hold of him and put him to the breast, where he guzzled like a baby does. She looked down at him and stroked his head, which she liked to do, while humming contentedly to herself.

John was as proud of this son as he had been all those years ago, twenty in fact, when his first had been born. He looked at him and wondered what life would have in store for him. There wasn't much choice, he thought. Either the mines or the land.

Miles had grown into a strong young man with a life ahead of some sort. Maybe he would stay around here, or maybe he wouldn't. He was already showing some interest in a young girl in the village. Mally was pretty and had many admirers but she seemed to prefer Miles. However there was plenty of time, and plenty of girls. He considered himself too young to be wed. Better to spend time looking and enjoying the company of the girls who seemed to enjoy his. There was time enough to make any commitment. And he didn't want to do that. Like most young men of the day, he took his pleasures, and if she 'fell for a bairn' then he would wed her. But for now, he was fairly content with his life.

*****

This life was unrelenting. There was work and not much else. You worked if you wanted to eat. You ate if you wanted to live. That was why times like the picnic all those years ago, at Mallerstang, and that day last December, when the children were all playing in the snowy lane, were so precious and important.

John knew that children were important for the family, but he was different to most men his age. He knew that children were important, as a family. Yes, they helped in your old age, if you or they lived that long, but they also gave you pleasure and pride as they came along, and as they grew. He heard some talk as if life was cheap, but to him it wasn't. It was the dearest thing there was. Alice, Edmund and baby Peggy had been taken from him. He wasn't a praying man, but he prayed today that no more would.

The whole family went together to Sunday school now. This Sunday had been the baptism of Christopher, and after that they had stayed in the little chapel at Muker, and taken part in the lessons, all still learning to print their names, apart from John who was proud to say he could do that already. The oldest, Miles, Betty, John and William, had almost mastered that, if they had something to copy, and were attempting to read simple sentences about the Bible story of the week, with Peggy and John looking after the young ones.

This week it had been about a story Jesus told about a man in the bible, who helped another when no-one else would. John couldn't remember his name, but it was about a good man, he remembered. Now he was learning to read, and write, *"This is a good man."* What a thing to say about someone, he thought. What a wonderful thing to have said about you when you've gone. I hope someone can say that about me.

The children loved the pictures they were shown that went with the story. They were so colourful and like nothing they had seen before, of places they had never seen nor ever would. Some were printed and some were drawn and coloured by the vicar's daughter, who was waiting to take up a place as a governess. She would be so missed, thought John. The children loved her, and the grown-ups admired her. The older boys all blushed like beetroot when they saw her, and she pretended not to notice, considering their feelings.

So, Sundays were now looked forward to, and not dreaded. The walk along the lane to the chapel was an easy one, in any weather, and every weather held its pleasures. Spring and summer were good for picking wildflowers, either to give the teacher when they arrived, or for home, if picked on the way back. In autumn the young ones walked along, kicking the leaves along in front of them, from the few trees that were left. But winter was the best, like today. Snowballs, sliding, jumping in the deep snow, getting so wet that sitting for over an hour in church, and yet another hour at Sunday School, was uncomfortable to say the least. But the fun had been worth it, and the time sat, dripping wet and cold, went over so quickly, with Miss Ann in front of them, reading in her soft voice, and guiding their hand with hers, to make the marks on paper that she said had a meaning.

They dried out somewhat while sitting around the roaring metal stove fire, the only form of heating, but were just as wet when they arrived home, and all huddled, steaming, around the smoky peat fire until all were dry.

Chapter 8

Village Matters

"Envy is the ulcer of the soul."

(Socrates)

Peggy was a busy body who liked to keep an ear out to what was happening in the village. Every week she came in with something that made her increasingly unhappy with her lot. The latest news was of one of the Milner families. The children had sadly lost both parents to the Red Rash the year before, and since then they had been living with their Grandma, quite old and struggling to provide them with food and clothing.

Peggy couldn't see how that was different to the plight of many others who were also struggling. Old Hannah had asked the Parish for help, and, so the tale went, she was given enough money to provide all of them with a new set of clothes each. As soon as he walked into their cottage Peggy was there with her moaning.

"Aw John. It's not reet."

"What's up ma pet," he replied in a droll way.

"Thee knaws the Milner children?"

"Them that lost their ma and da t'year gone by?"

"Aye John. Tha knows whoa ah'm on abaht. Ah knaw thee dis."

He was beaten.

"What's t'bother awld lass?"

"Brass John. From t'Guardians, f'cleeas fert lot ov'em."

Peggy always made out they were poorer than they really were. She loved the sympathy from those who commented on her large family, but it wasn't really sympathy. They were well aware that she was married to the man who was guaranteed employment. She had a large family, but half of them were now working. Surely, they discussed, her children should be dressed better than they were. They looked almost like paupers, in rags and tatters. John just hadn't been asked by Peggy for money to provide better clothing. It didn't occur to him that they needed it.

"John, lad. We need brass f'cleeas fert'lads tooa."

Ah'll gi'it yer ower Peg."

And that's all it took.

But the probable fact is that had the Milner's not been given new clothing, then Peggy would not have thought about wanting any for her family.

John would never approach the Poor Law Guardians. He was too proud for that, and he knew they would give him nothing anyway. She still hadn't finished her moaning, even after the promise of brass from John. She's gone next door to share her thoughts with their neighbour who had the measure of Peggy anyway. He could hear her loud, coarse voice passing her thoughts to Jenny next door.

"It's not reet. Us gort nowt neither."

She watched with greedy eyes what the Overseers of the poor gave to families of the village, and begrudged any allocation of shift, dress, or any other item of apparel. Just last week it was Butcher Kitt who had his year's rent paid. Before that it had been Coty's boy who had been provided with clothing. She was never satisfied, even when John gave her the few shillings needed for a new dress. The cloth was bought at the market, and a dressmaker paid to make it. He thought about Alice, sitting in the evenings, sewing and mending for them all. Peggy didn't sew. She couldn't sew. It was Betty who did the mending and some little sewing for the young ones.

Betty also took the opportunity of washing their clothes while they were in her hands for mending ~ something that Peggy very, very seldom did. Betty could remember Jemmy and Jane being sewn into their shirt and shift for the first few winters, and their clothes were only washed when they had a dunking in the water barrel, fully clothed.

The dress was made but, ironically, she couldn't wear it yet. She would need to wait till this baby had made an appearance, or it wouldn't fit. Until then she had to make do with Betty letting out her old petticoat and bodice.

Her easiest accomplishments seemed to him to be producing bairns. It seemed to take truly little for there to be another one on the way. She was never unwilling to "be a wife."

Come Friday evenings, when Miles was home from the mine the little cottage was literally full to the rafters. Nine children, ranging from a few months to twenty years, plus their parents, were squeezed into the small space. Beds were pulled out at night and rolled up for the morning. Food was plain, but never scarce. Washing was not often done, and clothing was in tatters, but Peggy had seen the seamstress to provide new. They had a roof, they had a fire, and they had food in their bellies. Evening times Miles made the young ones laugh with his imitation of a cow, and Michael went through all the bird sounds he knew.

They were now young men. Saturday and Sunday were spent helping John farm his land or helping at the smithy. When there, Miles' mind wandered back to the time in Outhgill when he helped his da. He'd wanted to be a Blacksmith. What had happened there? He'd always enjoyed the hammering and shaping, and was learning a little still, but he knew he would never have been any good. His da was a Master craftsman, and he would never have been a Master. He knew that now.

Michael too was a young man, now sixteen years. He still worked for farmer Dick Trot and was the fittest and healthiest of all the family. The money wasn't as good but there were compensations. He worked in the open air and the meals farmhands were given were certainly worth it. There would be a time when he may have to take a place in the lead mine but not yet.

Mary too was growing up, away from them all, like many young women. She was seventeen now. How they all missed her and Betty thought often of the problem she'd told them about.

Betty was working at home, and at the age of fourteen years was taking on most of the cooking herself. Granma Pedley had taught her how to bake pie, and how to bake cakes on the backstone of the fire. She looked after the geese and collected the eggs. The young boys did what they could. Their major occupation, however, at ten and eleven, was pretending to be soldiers in the Militia, fighting each other, rolling around the floor to see who could land the best blow, or kicking each other under the table at mealtimes. John watched them in amusement. They both worked for farthings for Dick Trot and went scavenging in the fields looking for anything that was edible. Bird scaring, horse driving, were both things they could do.

The other boys had grown up much faster than these two, he mused. At eleven Miles had been working as an ore dresser. Peggy wanted them ore dressing at the mine for more money. Well probably it was time, he thought.

"Soon," said John.

But Jemmy was still the one to watch. The thing he enjoyed doing the most was terrifying old Ma Harker who lived along the lane. She was a good old age and partially blind, so couldn't see what tricks were being played on her. Creeping up behind her as she dozed on the settle, he would whisper in her ear, making her think that the spirits were talking to her. Or he would whistle in her ear, making her jump, so startled that her heart nearly stopped. In time she realized who was playing these tricks, and turned to chase him from the room, but he was too fast for her.

He continually wandered the lanes, looking for mischief. The farmer's drinking can was emptied, and its contents replaced with the contents of his bladder. Watching Dick Trot splutter and choke made his sides split with laughter.

Stones were thrown at the old brown cow on the neighbouring allotment, just missing, and not hurting the animal, but frightening her just the same.

He would have loved to start a fire with the sticks he collected, but didn't know how, so pretended he had a place to live among the gorse bushes on the hillside, sneaking a little food out and devouring it, peering out of his secret hide at the world around. He was above the smog of the village, away from coal fires and smelt ovens, and the air was cleaner. Up here he was solitary and happy in his own company never letting anyone know where or how he spent the day, except sometimes Betty. As long as he was home to sleep that's all that seemed to matter to his parents.

Betty thought that baby Christopher was delicious. He gurgled and smiled at her as she took off the wet cloth wrapped around him. By June he was four months old, and she would lay him on the grass and watch him kick his long thin legs with pleasure. She fed him with a mix of watery gruel mixed with cows' milk. Peggy no longer wanted to nurse him, but Betty looked into Christopher's eyes and watched him smile as he looked up into her face.
Peggy said her milk had dried up. Betty knew it hadn't. You could see.
Meanwhile John was as content as it was possible for him to be and so proud of his boys. Working in a lead mine was hard, dangerous work, and Miles was doing just that. Michael was working in the open air, on the land, as he'd always wanted to do.

Letting his mind wander to the forge in Outhgill in the Valley, he thought about how much he loved smithing. It was in his blood, but working for someone else was not the same. He'd been his own master once, and that was what he would love to be again.

That autumn moved on relentlessly. Rain was a frequent feature, and water was never in short supply.

One evening, as John walked back from the forge, his guilty thoughts went to Jemmy. He hardly ever saw the lad and wondered what he got up to. He was headstrong and that got him into trouble, but you couldn't help but love him. He'd promised many times that he would take the boy in hand, saying, "Ah'll mak a gid lad from thee."

But so far he hadn't. He hadn't even tried. Guilt was tempered with exhaustion. He was just too tired.

On this evening, moving along rhythmically with his strong stride, he looked up at the sky, suddenly dark and swollen with rain, and spattering his face with large fat drops that fell down his cheeks like a river. It was a cleansing, calming feeling, refreshing and cool. The rivulets made grimy streaks down his face, as they fell and gathered momentum over his nose, dripping and coursing, until his hair was drenched, and so were his clothes. He rubbed the rainwater over his cheeks, his eyes, his nose, his neck, then shook his head, like a huge, wet dog.

Standing perfectly still and raising his face to the torrent, he stretched out his arms to each side, as if in prayer, communing with the natural elements, enjoying the feeling of absolute surrender.

When he eventually reached home the rain was coming down absolutely vertically, bouncing off the ground like pebbles, making him so wet that he had to strip off his clothes to his undershirt. These were left on the stone floor for Peggy to hang on a bush to dry once the rain stopped.

He went upstairs and pulled off his shirt, changing it for the only other one he had, the one that Alice had sewn for his wedding gift, over twenty years or more ago he thought, without reckoning carefully as the task was too difficult. Then he pulled on a pair of breeches and went back down the stairs to be greeted by Peggy with a quizzical look about her.

"More work for uz," she whined.

"Jus dry 'em awd lass," he uttered wearily. "And mend the holes where the daylight comes in."

"Ower Betty will. Ah 'ave ower much t'dee."

John gave a short laugh and then looked away. He didn't want to anger her. Not tonight.

You didn't poke a wild beast for fun.

She put the breeches next to the fire that was burning all year round. Peat in summer. Coal in winter. And they soon began to steam with the heat of the fire, filling the room with a damp cloud. Grateful for the warmth, he sat on the settle that was pulled up next to the table in front of the fire and waited for his tea. Peggy had put it together, so it was basic rations of bread, cheese and what was left of the smoked ham, from Bella. He much preferred it when Betty was the cook. At least then he was usually offered something hot. He fell upon the plate and devoured it quickly, looking around to see if there was a possibility of more but all there was had been plated for Jane, Peggy, John, Will and Jemmy, when he appeared.

I must find out what's happening with that lad, he thought. He barely saw him. In fact he was hardly at home. He should be with the family and earning a little money if he could. That's what he would do tonight. He would go out looking for him and ……

Looking outside he saw the chilly rain still pounding the ground and changed his mind. The lad would come home when he was cold and hungry and then he would have his say.

Will and John came running in through the door, shaking the rain from their heads and clothes. Sitting alongside their father they began to eat the cold meal in front of them pulling faces at each other, trying to pull each other's hair and aiming fierce kicks under the table. They had always been close since those first few years living with their Grandparents in Outhgill and were never far from each other now. Jane and little Peg watched them in silence as they all ate, big eyes going from one to the other of the boys while Betty spooned oat mash into Christopher and tickled his chin making him giggle. The rain was easing now so John rose wearily and stood at the door. Their field of grass was battered and would need some dry days for it to recover enough to cut. Sorrel stood at the end of her rope, water dripping from her mane, but she was a fell pony and bred for such weather. Despite Peggy's entreaties, John had resisted selling the pony, or exchanging her for a cow. He knew it was a sound idea, but it had not been his, and so it was not taken up – yet. The time would come, he knew, when he would have no choice, and that time was coming soon. A cow would give them milk, butter and cheese but would also need overwintering. At least she would pay her way though. And the hay and oats that Sorrel then didn't eat could be given to the cow.

It had ceased raining, so he pulled on his jacket and set off down the lane, towards Dick Trot's farm. Better to put it off no longer. But, instead of an exchange, the cow was purchased with a barter: John promising to iron a set of tyres for Dick. And they kept Sorrel. Come springtime the Hutchinsons were the owners of a brown and white cow the children had called Meadow, tethered on the land where Sorrel still stood.

Betty meanwhile was learning the new skill of milking, while keeping her eye on Christopher, who spent his time rolling around on the ground nearby, in and out of cow pats.

One day when he was covered in cow dung she took him over to the beck, and doused him in the cold flowing water, while he complained very loudly. She came back to an empty bucket. Meadow had kicked over the bucket of milk, and so that effort, and that precious food, were wasted. Not wanting to admit to this one, she tried milking again, and managed to get Meadow to let down a little more milk, saying when she took it home that it was all she had managed to get.

The milk was always warm and creamy, and the children loved it, straight from the cow.

Betty's next job was to learn how to make butter. Grandma Pedley had some knowledge of this and gave some ideas to Betty.

So, Betty put milk in a tall jar. She found a long stick and cleaned it. Then she put the stick into the jar and stirred it round, and round, and round, and round. She sang the song she had been told would give her the rhythm and help pass the time.

"*Come butter come.*

Come butter come.

Peter stands at the gate

Waiting for a buttered cake"

After a good long while, and with an aching arm, she could feel the mixture thickening, until finally, after many hours, it was the consistency of butter.
"Butter. Butter," she shouted. And there it was.
Once a week this was now her job, and she was good at it. They now had milk, butter and eggs.

"Ah love Butta ma, bur us arms r'jiggered," she complained to Peggy. "Can thee tak a turn?"
"Wood their gi'uz extreur fettle when ahm avin a bairn? was the usual response.
Peggy was tired. She was thirty-six summers, she thought, or thereabouts, and felt like an old woman. The next baby was on the way. This would be her eighth, but she knew there were plenty with families bigger than this. Ruth, her first, with an unnamed father, lived with her mother along the lane, in Scarr Houses. With the growing brood she had, it was probably a blessing that her mother took care of Ruth for her. On weekends Miles came down from the mine, and he took food back with him to eat through the week. Baby Christopher and little Peg, just under two years old, didn't take much feeding. But the two older boys had voracious appetites, and the in between boys weren't far behind. Betty had a good

appetite too.

Jemmy raided the pantry whenever he came home from his forays, but Jane ate little. She was a stick thin, puny looking child – six years more like a child of four. She had a constant run from her nose, which she wiped all up her arm and across her cheeks. Whenever Jemmy appeared she trotted after him, as she had always done, wailing when he left her behind.

No-one made her eat. If she didn't eat then there was more for the others, was the feeling of some. Betty gave her attention when she could, but Peggy was her mother, and ought to be taking more care.

The hay and oats had been harvested. Meadow the cow was happy in her new environment and continued to give them plenty of milk. The eggs produced by their geese were often used at market to barter for other essentials, such as flour. Betty continued to knit a little and managed to produce the stockings required by the traders, but she was locked into a cycle, handing over stockings and collecting wool once a month. John and Peggy were unaware that she was putting away some of her earnings every month, and now had five shillings saved up. She couldn't spend it, or they would know she had it, so it was rather a shame when she saw some fine woollen cloth at the market that would make her a frock.

Peggy's new frock had been made months ago and was only worn on Sundays to go along the road to Church in Muker. How Betty would love a new frock herself. All her clothes had been hand-me downs from her cousins in Mallerstang, the latest being from Jennet's daughter, five years her elder, who had it from her own sister, so that by the time it got to Betty it had been well worn for ten years, and often remodelled. Betty was good with a needle, so she unpicked it, turned it inside out and remade it – again. She was fifteen now and had never had anything new. And that was nothing new either. *Most* girls had never had anything new.

But Betty had some money now. She alternated between feeling guilty that she wanted to spend it on herself, and guilty that she hadn't already spent it on the family. The thing to do was to speak to her father. Peggy wouldn't understand.

So, with John's blessing as he realized what a hard worker his daughter was, Betty had a new dress for Easter.

It was now March 1804. Peggy was near her time. Her back ached. Her legs were swollen and ached so much that she could hardly stand. Her belly was swollen, and everything ached. Even her heart seemed to ache with the pain of carrying this bairn. Grandma Pedley was called for late one night, and the next morning John had another son.

It was Peggy who gave him the name Edward, after an uncle on her mother's side. He had the colouring of his father, blond hair, and plenty of it and was alert right from the first minute.

"This one'll be lively," said Grandma Pedley. "He'll not sleep much." She was right in that respect. Where Christopher had been placid from the start, and now at just over a year old, still slept every morning and every afternoon, Edward slept little, and was awake every hour to nurse through the night. Both lots of wet and dirty cloths from the boys were rinsed in the beck if they were lucky, or often just dried in front of the fire. That was the usual thing to do.

John had made a second wooden box for Edward to sleep in, as Christopher still occupied the original. The new box had rockers on to try and pacify Edward and rock him to sleep.
It was Jane who spent her time doing this. Stick thin and puny with a face as if she had fallen into a bag of flour and a constant run from her nose, she sat on the floor, rocking, rocking, rocking her baby brother

And then one day there was great excitement! Well Michael at least was excited. The Constable had been to the house and left a paper for his da to complete. That would be difficult as no one could write, except John, and that was only his own name. It was for the list of those who were volunteering to defend the shores if Bonaparte did his worst. But you had to be seventeen. Not long, thought Michael, who was sixteen now, and looking forward to the chance to be involved. They needed men who could help others out of harm's way, move cattle and crops, gather up any arms and equipment and generally transport and feed the troops. It all sounded so exciting.

"Jus pit thee names on 'ere," the Constable had said. Michael thought he was almost seventeen. Would anyone know if he lied about his age? Probably not. So he, his da and Miles were the three names on the list. All that time at Sunday School learning how to write it had paid off. He would wait and see. There was a second list, compiled by the Constable. This was for any men who weren't in the militia or the Armed Forces but could be called upon to fight. Michael would have loved either, Miles was not so keen, and John couldn't leave the family. Joining the Local Volunteers for a while was all the excitement Michael came by, doing a bit of training. When you didn't have a job, it was paid employment, but it was boring, not really fighting, so he didn't stay.

Baby Edward had been born on Friday and on Sunday 25th March he was baptized. Standing outside, waiting for everyone, John could hear the water rocketing over the rocks at the small waterfall on Cliff Beck. They walked together across the fields, Peggy carrying baby Edward, Betty carrying Christopher, and John striding along with little Peg aloft on his shoulders, giggling and trying to put her hands over John's eyes, before coming to Straw Beck, and walking alongside it to Muker. It was breezy and the wind buffeted them, while there was still snow on the ground in places, but not much. Betty wore her new woollen dress, in a deep, rich red, and a thick shawl, while Peggy had squeezed into hers. Brisk walking kept them warm in colder temperatures. John and the boys were in the best clothes they had: with new shirts. Even Jemmy was with them today. He knew he couldn't miss a family event like this, much as he would prefer to be roaming the hills. There were another two children baptized that morning, and John knew the families well.

Waiting patiently until it was time they all drew around the font. Despite being a baby who grizzled for no reason, Edward seemed to know that the best was expected of him, and he slept throughout the whole affair, making Peggy even more dissatisfied with him. Christopher, who was as placid a child as you could want, cried the whole time, and little Peg pulled onto Peggy's petticoat, wanting attention, which she did get in some part from her father. Jane sat and couldn't take her eyes off the vicar, who had that mesmerizing effect on many, while Jemmy was thoroughly bored. The others were old enough to pretend, even if they weren't interested. The Vicar was Reverend Richardson, and he had baptized all the Hutchinson children after Jemmy, as the previous vicar, Lister Metcalfe, had died in 1797. Up till now Rev Metcalfe had lost three of his own children, from eighteen to thirty-one years in age. It was a village tragedy. His daughter Agnes still took a class on Sundays, to help the poor to read and write.

They stayed for Sunday School, with some like Betty now able to read a short simple Bible story. This week's had been about the tax collector, Zachaeus. The story of him climbing the tree to see Jesus had resonated with Jemmy, who climbed as many trees as he could. The younger ones were also quite taken by the fact that an adult climbed a tree for a serious reason. The pictures they drew were quite detailed because it was something within their knowledge. But all Jemmy could think of was that he wanted to be climbing trees himself.

They walked back alongside straw Beck and then over the fields to Scarr Houses. The wind had dropped but it was still quite cool. When they returned home John stood on the bank of Cliff Beck and listened to the waterfall again. Looking up at the hillside he saw sheep grazing, clouds racing across the skies like lambs chasing their dams, and he felt that he was a player in a much more serious game. It was the first time he'd felt anything like spiritual and felt that it was also a turning point in his life but didn't know why.

Life followed its usual rhythms, with everyone knowing their place. It seemed that sad events followed happier ones for John, and so it did again. This time it was the death of his mother. She had lasted seven years after his father, but at sixty-five, still living with Jennet she'd finally gone.

She was buried in May, at Kirkby Stephen, near her husband and parents, and now John felt that part of his life was over. He had no ties there. They'd been good, supportive parents, and he missed them both, but it was the circle of life. They'd both lived good lives, and must be in God's hands, he knew. This was how it was supposed to be.

Chapter 9

Illness on a grand scale

"Before you tell a grieving parent to be thankful for the children they have, think which of yours you could live without."

(Unknown)

Jane was the first to fall ill. She was so frail that any disease was able to gain a foothold with her very easily and without much effort. She never looked well anyway and had little energy to play with the other younger children so it was not noticed immediately. It began with her complaining of a very sore throat. Again this was nothing new, but when this turned into a fever then Peggy began to take notice. The rash, a sandpaper rash, was the tell-tale sign on her neck and face to begin with. The poor girl was so distressed. She ate nothing now and if she tried she vomited it back. She lay wrapped in a shawl, her whole body shaking with the fever.

As if that wasn't bad enough little Peg took ill too. This caused Peggy to run along the lane to get her mother and together they looked after the two little girls with cold compresses, trying to bring down the fever. There were other children in the village suffering too and some had already died. Little James Clarkson, only a few months old hadn't been strong enough to fight it. Then there was little Robert Harker the same. Agnes Mecalfe, the daughter of the Reverend Lister Metcalfe was also taken, and she was two and twenty years old. And there were others, from a few months to over twenty years.

Grandma Pedley looked inside Jane's mouth, and there was the other sign. Her tongue was red and bumpy, and so was little Peg's. They were sure now. It was the Scarlet Rash.

"Aw ma. Whit will uz dee? The power bairns."

"Pray Peggy, send up thy prayers, and look after the bairns."

Jemmy had been out for a number of nights. Due to the family being concerned about the two little girls, unfortunately, and sadly, he had not been missed. If he had been, perhaps they would have tried to find him. In fact, he was holed up, on Thwaite side, in his makeshift camp, looking out over the village.

It was August and fairly warm through the day but cooling down considerably at night.

He sat in his hideaway where normally he felt content but this particular evening he knew that everything wasn't right. He didn't feel right. Through the warm day he shivered, but at night he burned with fever. Perhaps he ought to go home. He wanted people around him, and he *never* wanted that. He wanted to go home to let someone look after him, but he physically couldn't.

He was seven years old, and he wanted his ma.

Lying back he looked at the pinpoint stars as they swam and moved around the sky, silvery fish in a dark pond. A voice came from the gorse bush next to him, speaking to him, with comforting words. Words he wanted to hear.

"Help is coming," it said. "Da's on his way. Thee'll be good."

He waited, and waited for his da, awake and then not awake. He called for his ma now and then, with a throat so sore he could hardly croak. He didn't even try to move. He was waiting for his da to come, his da who didn't even know where he was. The night saw him slipping in and out of consciousness.

Time passed more slowly than he could ever have imagined. By morning he was so thirsty that he sucked the morning dew from the grass around him.

Alternating between sleeping and waking he hardly knew how long he'd been feeling unwell. The days and nights were fluid, and after a while he barely opened his eyes.

Sleep was comforting, and how he ached to be comforted. He was a boy who shirked human contact, and yet he ached to be in loving arms, or in his bed at home.

And he cried, gently at first. They were silent tears, running from the corners of his eyes and down the sides of his face, as he lay on his back, out in the open air now. And then he was sobbing so loudly, and so deeply that his whole body was wracked with it. And when that subsided, he had no energy to even wipe away the tears. And he waited for comfort.

He was seven years old.

At home, his older brother Will was suffering the same fate, though he was fortunate and had the care and comfort that Jemmy craved. He was nursed, his temperature was brought down, and he was on the way to a recovery. Thankfully, the two young girls were mending and seemed to be over the worst of it. They were recovering, and so would Will, who was much stronger and sturdier. It was only then that they thought about Jemmy.

"In God's name. Three nights since that young uns been hame," said Peggy, angrily. " That lad'll be the deth o'uz."

"Wait till ah gets a haad o'him."

"He'll be hidin on the hillside," confided Betty. "That's where he be when thee looks for him. And he doesn't want to be found."

"Uz needs him 'ere, where 'e can help look after the young uns," Peggy replied, scathingly.

"Will's badly, so he needs to do Will's fettle."

John was angry, but also beginning to be a little concerned. This was the longest that Jemmy had been away from home, and he berated himself that he hadn't had the 'talk' with the boy before now.

"Tell uz where Betty an ah'll find him."

John stomped out of the room and followed Betty's directions. He was angry with her too that she hadn't told before now, but he couldn't stay angry with Betty for long.

Walking quickly along the lane and running now across the fields, he advanced to the bridge across Cliff Beck, over a small gorge, carved by the Beck out of limestone. It was a simple drystone arch resting on the limestone rocks either side and he had to be incredibly careful because it was barely the width of the length of his forearm. From there he climbed the hills up to Thwaite side, turning and looking back over the valley towards Kisdon. He could see at once why his young son loved to be up here, as free as a bird. He swept his eyes from one side to the other, noticing the village and Scarr Houses, and the lane between. Remembering his time at Thorns, when he was a young lad, how he loved to explore and find places where no-one knew he was hiding, keeping to himself, thinking he had the greatest secret, but he'd never stayed out all night. He hadn't dared to. The boy was much more of a daredevil than he'd been.

As he walked, he thought too about how he was going to spend more time with the lad. He was their firstborn, and seemed to have been forgotten so easily, with all the children who came after him. It was because he was so resilient, and independent, thought John. He didn't seem to need anyone.

Looking down into the valley he could see smoke from the village houses hanging over rooftops, but up here there was none. Unusually, there wasn't a breath of breeze.

Just ahead was the farm where Michael worked, Appletree Thwaite, on Muker Side. He looked up and saw a falcon, hovering, ready to swoop down onto some unsuspecting field mouse. A Swaledale ewe was standing in amongst the flowering purple heather and he could smell the faint honey smell and hear the hum of the bees collecting pollen and nectar. For a second it took his mind off his real purpose for being here. But only for a second. He carried on, striding through the heather, up and on to where Betty had directed him.

It was a warm day, and he wiped the sweat away from his face with his forearm. He was thirsty, and realized too that he hadn't eaten that day. As he walked, his mind alternated between worry for Jemmy and anger that he had them in this position. He should be at home, looking after Will and the girls. Who knew who would take ill next? It wasn't fair. And in the next breath he thought how free he felt, up here on the fell, away from work, and the worry of daily life.

It couldn't be much further. Up ahead he could see a copse, with something like a fire circle in front. He didn't know why, but he felt his heart leap into his mouth, and begin to race, thumping in his chest, faster and stronger than it should. Jemmy was only seven years old. His father should know where he was. What was he doing up here? As he moved closer to the copse he could see a figure lying across the opening. A hide carefully constructed so that no-one would know a person was there. And John knew who the person was.

He ran to the figure lying prostrate and still in the opening, picking him up. Jemmy was still conscious, and able to speak, but very weak. Sweeping him up in his strong arms, John ran with him down the hillside, to Thwaite, and to the cottage at Scarr Houses. But he knew himself that Jemmy had stopped breathing long before he reached home. He felt life leach from the boy but heard him whisper," Knew thee'd come. "

Peggy screamed and cried and screamed some more. Her son was dead. Why was he dead? How was he dead? He'd been fit and well, and sturdy. He'd been full of life. She wouldn't let anyone else touch him. How many mothers would there be who laid out their own son, she sobbed, at seven years. Guilt and shame made her blame anyone and everyone in the family.

John, for not being a better father.

Betty for not telling them where he was.

Will for not being a better brother. And so on. She was deflecting the blame from herself because she felt the guilt weighing on her so heavily. She was his mother, and she'd somehow let this happen. She cried, she wailed, she sobbed. She wanted the world to know how she felt.

John couldn't tell anyone how he felt. He was numb. He was broken. It was his fault. It was his penance for not looking after his family. He would never forgive himself. And he felt that God would never forgive him. Neither would Jemmy.

And, may heaven help them, they were still nursing Jane and Little Peggy, the first to take ill and the weakest to begin with, and Will. Peggy was no good. She sat beside the coffin, head down, tears rolling. Her mother and Betty continued to nurse the girls, keeping them supplied with cold water and placing a cold compress on their foreheads. Jane said it felt good and gave Betty a watery smile.

They did the same for William, but his terrible sore throat and rash were so bad that they were really worried.

"Whit abaht the medical man awld lass," John asked Peggy.

Her answer was the usual.

"Nee medical man iver saved anyone from t'Red Rash. They either gets better, or they dinet," replied Granma Pedley, in answer to John's question that Peggy was incapable of answering.

And that was that.

Will seemed to be making some sort of a recovery, and was half sitting up, taking drinks of water to soothe his throat. But while John was away searching for Jemmy he spiked a high fever. Laying in bed at home he seemed to lose the will to live. Betty nursed him, laying cold cloths across his brow, and singing to him sweet and slow, songs she remembered from her young days. They took heart from the fact that Jane and little Peg were now so much better. And Will was stronger than them after all. He had to be all right.

But he lost the battle, and that was that. The Red Rash took where it wanted. No-one was safe and everyone was afraid of it. No-one knew whose child would be next when it was around. Child or adult, of any age. It was all the same with this disease.

Peggy and John now had two of their boys, sharing the same coffin. Will was going to meet his ma, Alice. John tried to take some comfort from this, but it was hard because he didn't really believe it. Life would be easier if he did, he thought.

"Jemmy, Jemmy," was all that Peggy could say, over and over, between sobs.

Thinking back to what his ma had told him, about babies, not getting too close till you knew they were staying, John now had two boys, who couldn't stay. There was no bargain he could make with God to keep his two boys. They were long past babies, but they were still children.

The funeral was a burial without service, on Saturday 18th August 1804. Both Jemmy and William were laid to rest in Muker Kirk Yard. Peggy had wanted to call him John when he was baptized. She got her wish this time and he was buried as John.

The two boys were together in a plain pine box and carried to their final resting place by Sorrel. They were carefully lifted onto the flat bed of the cart, and John led the pony by its halter, as Will had done many times before.

He'd lost a wife and two bairns but these two boys who had outlived the dangers of childbirth and infantile diseases were now, at seven and twelve years old, gone. One Alice's and one Peggy's. His guilt over Jemmy was weighing him down, and he wanted to talk to him tell him he was sorry, that he hadn't deserted him. But in his heart, he knew he had. What father let his seven-year-old boy sleep out overnight, and not be mindful of where he was? Would it have made any difference, he constantly asked himself. The answer was probably no because Will hadn't survived. The difference was that Will was nursed, and loved, and cared for, and had still died, but died in the bosom of his family.

Jemmy had died alone, afraid, aware of the fact that he was extremely ill, aware of the fact that no-one had come looking for him. John felt that he deserved to die himself and wished that he could if it would bring back his boys. But nothing could do that.

This day was to be lived through somehow, as well as all the days after. He had to accept the fact that they were gone.

He vowed to be a better father, and a better husband, and to keep them all safe, forever. A man can vow that, can promise with all his being, but it doesn't mean he can keep that promise.

Standing at the graveside tears escaped his eyes and silently ran down his face.

Looking around he saw the same in Betty, while Peggy screamed for her boy.

Jane, at six years old, had been allowed to come, but the younger bairns had been kept at home. Granny Pedley had her hands full there, with Little Peg, Christopher and Edward, was his passing thought.

The journey home had been again in total silence. There was nothing they could say. Life went on.

The hay and oats were harvested. Meadow the cow was happy in her new home and continued to give them plenty of milk.

The eggs produced by the geese were a tasty treat and often used at market, to barter for other essentials, or a treat or two.

1805

Spring came in and brought with it the usual signs. The family continued to attend Church and Sunday School each week, with Peggy lagging behind to ask the reverend questions about the afterlife which of course he couldn't answer. At Sunday School Jane and Little Peg drew pictures of Jemmy and Will being carried up to heaven by angels.

John was a broken man, and Peggy was just as broken. She'd never been one to show her feelings, and had felt it was a weakness, but now she couldn't help it. Her feelings were quite plainly written on her face. She was unable to hide them and didn't even try. It was common knowledge that she was a hard woman, and that she didn't show her children any affection. But it was something she'd never had herself. Now she realized that these two boys had gone to their maker, without much of a kind word from her, she felt that she would ever be guilty of that.

She saw that her mother treated her grandchildren much better than she'd treated her children, and that was the crux of the matter. She hadn't been shown affection, so she didn't know how to show it in return.

Peggy and John went about the daily business of living, but they hardly spoke to each other for that week, or the next, or even the next. The hurt and pain were so raw that neither knew how to deal with it. Jemmy and Will were missed so much that their names couldn't even be spoken. John continued to blame himself and to think that if he had been a better father then Jemmy would still be alive. Peggy thought that she must have done something wrong, and that if she had called the medical man then Will at least may have been saved. The family knew that neither of these things would or could have changed anything but they couldn't persuade Peggy or John. For Betty it was more than difficult, as she was trying to be a parent to the younger children and also parent to her own parents. Miles and Michael were away through the week and weren't really able to put into words how that felt, never mind comforting anyone else.

At fifteen, Betty was left holding the family together, and it was too much. She couldn't take it anymore, and so she contacted her sister

Mary, who had been for the burial. After a short visit Betty decided that it was time to leave. She packed her bag and left with Mary, to go back to Kirkby Stephen and a place in the house where Mary worked, leaving Peggy with the responsibility she should have had all along. There she stayed for the next two years. Her responsibility was to herself alone.

Peggy was still nursing Edward, at only five months old, while Christopher was a year and a half. She only had Jane to help her now, and Jane sat very patiently with Christopher, spooning the oat porridge into him, while Peggy fed baby Edward. Young John was very subdued without his brothers, and for a good while had nothing to say.

At twelve years old he became an ore dresser at the mine where Miles worked. They walked over the hillside together Monday mornings, and back together Friday afternoons. But neither spoke about this nor wanted to speak about this. So it was never spoken of.

Chapter 10

The Healing Begins

"No-one ever told me that grief felt so much like fear."

(C.S. Lewis)

It was Thwaite Fair. Back end of the year and a busy time for all. No time for fun. There were eggs to sell, and Peg had tried her hand at making the butter, with more success than she'd expected.
The morning of the Fair was the usual great Hare Hunt. A pack of hounds were kept at Low Row to take part in endeavours such as these. Men dressed in their hunting pink, seated on their impressive horses, gathered in front of the local Inn who provided everyone with a drink before the bugle went, and off they set off.

Despite himself, John found himself watching, and feeling the tangible excitement in the air. Then he couldn't stop the guilt for allowing himself any enjoyment. It was a boulder crushing his chest. Peg was with him, in the village, carrying baby Edward. Christopher was carried aloft on John's shoulders, while Jane and little Peg walked behind, hand in hand. Young John was somewhere nearby, with some of the village lads. They were a smaller family now, but a closer family. The young children were too small to understand, but Miles, Michael and John missed their little brothers. They had stood and wiped away the tears at the graveside, and they had seen their father do the same.

It was a Saturday, so Miles wasn't at the mine. He'd watched the hunt set off and drunk a whole flagon of ale before walking back to the green. Pens full of noisy sheep were along the roadside, brought down from the hills to be sold.

There were the usual wool dealers who travelled the dales, giving out wool from house to house for those who wanted to make a truly little money knitting.

Lately, since the burial, Miles had seen a softening in Peg towards her children: *her* children, not Alice's. But he'd never been fond of Peg either, so, he couldn't complain. He worked so hard for this family, underground, dirty and wet, and now Michael had joined him. His farming life had ended after he made the simple mistake of leaving a gate open, but the consequences had been dire.

A field full of sheep had migrated to the roadway and down to the river. Some had fallen into the river that was swollen with the recent rains and had drowned before Dick Trot was aware they'd gone. Michael was frantically trying to put them back where they belonged, but it was more than one person's job. It was one man and his sheep dog who sorted it. Dick had lost five sheep, and that represented a decent amount of money lost too, he said.

Michael promised faithfully he would pay, but he had no money, so taking the job in the mine meant he could begin to repay the money weekly.

Miles worried for Michael because he wasn't as strong as him. He saw the lines etched on his face already, at seventeen years, and knew that Michael preferred farming, loved animals and hated mining. After his suffering with the croup when he was younger, his chest was weak, and he coughed up dirty phlegm. Miners' lung, it could be. He needed to talk to his da about getting him out of the mine before it finished him and wondered if the farm at Appletree Thwaite on Muker side, would take him on as a labourer again. At least then Michael wouldn't be breathing in the dust. The smog from the smelt mill was on the other side of the dale, even if it did lay low in the valley sometimes. Maybe in the spring, after the winter weather.

Peg was standing looking across the green, holding on tight to Edward with one hand and Jane with the other, while Little Peg stood just in front. She looked around to see where Christopher was, not wanting to let any of them out of her sight. She was a changed woman, a changed mother. Grief had softened her. She had lost four children now - three of her own. She didn't want to lose any more.

John thought often about Alice, and how she could never have let anything like this happen. Her whole life was her children. She would have been pleased that the girls were making their own way in life and that Miles and Michael were too. How she would have borne the loss of Will, he could not, and never would, even imagine.

Thwaite Fair was well underway. Peg had been going to sell eggs and butter from her basket but didn't want to let go of the children, so, for once they walked, all together, through the crowd, looking at the trade stalls, listening to the sheep sellers calling out for a buyer, watching a troupe of tumblers on the green, and being very wary of pick pockets. John had some small amount of money put by, so he threw caution to the winds, and treated the younger children to some sweet meats and candies.

There was a butcher's stall, full of beef, mutton, pork and veal, as well as live piglets in canvas covered pens and live chickens and hens. There were clothiers' goods, book, clog and patten stalls. There were haberdashers, with ribbons, laces, gloves and shawls. There were hardware men with scissors, pans, backstins, gullies, baskets, brushes and besoms. There was even a medical man selling remedies for all that ailed a person and seemed to be able to cure anything.

Drunken men came reeling and shouting out of the inns followed by much fighting.

Women screamed loudly at them, "Fetch the constable," and that seemed to stop the fighting.

Michael and Miles were treated to a mug of ale with John in the Black Bull, and they raised their glasses to their brothers Will and Jemmy. Only Peg seemed to get nothing.

Miles had seen her gazing longingly at some fine coloured, woollen cloth, held out by a trader to all the women who passed, and he wanted suddenly to do something for this woman.

He missed his own mother so much, and had never felt any warmth from Peg, but maybe that could change. With her protests in his ears, he took her arm, and led her gently back to the stall.

"Tell 'em what you want," he said gruffly. She looked up at him, looked back to the stall, and picked up the edge of a beautiful fine material, totally impractical. The fashions were changing, and the trader told her how beautiful this would look, high waisted and gathering beautifully. She could picture it perfectly. She wanted it so much.

But she quickly pushed it away, and picked up a thicker, fustian fabric, and asked for enough to make a man a pair of breeches and a coat.

It was for her John, who asked for nothing, and gave so much – to his children and to her. She had eventually realized that she had grown to love this gruff, beautiful man. And Miles was going to help her show it.

"For my John," she spoke, smiling up at Miles, with a radiant yet shy smile that showed a different face to the one he was used to seeing. Miles was more than astounded. He paid, and then together they took the material to a house where a woman lived who could sew such things. His own measurements would be perfect, he knew that. And he felt closer to Peg than he had ever, ever been.

Warning the children not to tell, they went back to the Fair, to find John and Christopher.

"Thy turn now awld lass," John smiled as he looked at her, and took her to the ribbon seller, who was shouting, "Ribbons for varra near nowt."

"For thy bonnet," he told her. She considered carefully and then chose a duck egg blue once more.

"Thy een be the same colour," he said, and looked into them, as if he hadn't seen them before.

She blushed and turned away, unused to this sort of attention.

"Get away, ye barmpot. What are ye blethering on aboot."

And this was the turning point. After eight years and seven children together, they were perhaps fond of each other, perhaps in love with each other, perhaps just used to each other and happy to be together. What had brought them together had also torn them individually apart. But they would use each other to heal.

John's new breeches and coat were proudly worn on their next visit to church. In the meantime, Peg had spent some time with her mother, begging her to help her learn to sew, so she could at least mend, or turn an old dress for Jane. She'd noticed how her first child Ruth, was better dressed because Grandma made sure of it.
'Not when I were a bairn though, 'thought Peg.
There had been enough fustian left over to make a pair of breeches for young John who was now eleven years, and she'd proudly shown everyone her handiwork. John had been closer than anyone to Will. Closer in years, and closer in life too.

And it was nine months after this Thwaite Fair, after the healing that had begun there, where John and Peg had found a new respect for each other, that their eighth child was born, in June 1805.
She was a golden-haired girl, with the palest of blue eyes and the sweetest of faces. With hair the colour of summer corn and blue eyes so pale that they were almost colourless, she was unlike anyone else in the family. Peg was given the responsibility of

naming her, and as John had used up all his stock of family names, looking back over her family, Peg chose the prettiest name she could, to go with "the bonniest lass", she said. It was Christian, after her aunt from Bowes. The family thought the name fitted her perfectly.

Christian was a perfect baby, placid and content.
She lay sleepily in her crib, and when she woke, she lay gazing, with her new eyes that were not yet focusing properly, turning her head towards any sound. The boys doted on her, just like Michael had done with their first Peggy. Young John couldn't stop himself from picking her up, even before she cried, dancing around the room with her, and taking her outside to see their cow, Meadow, in the field over the way, even though she was too little to know what she was seeing or where she was. Her little eyes were so pale that she narrowed them against the least amount of sunlight. Young John noticed that first and got his grandmother to make her a little bonnet to keep the sun away, so he could walk up and down the lane with her. It made father John proud to see how well his little daughter was looked after by her big brothers. Once more they had all become too fond of her too soon, as his mother would say. There was no doubting it. She was a beauty.

At first her blond hair was wispy, all around her head, but as it grew it curled into short ringlets that framed her face. She had almond shaped eyes, pink cheeks and a rosebud mouth. Kicking her dimpled legs, she waved her dimpled arms as she lay in her cradle, and when she smiled, she showed two dimples in her pink, round cheeks. She was the very model of what a healthy baby should be. By eight weeks she was sleeping through the night and if she did wake, she lay gurgling until she soothed herself back to sleep.

She was so special that Peg didn't want to dress her in the old clothes all the others had worn, so her mother made two new shifts for her, in off white linen, and cut some clouts that tied at the waist. They would be dealt with in the usual way, but not washed. At night she was firmly wrapped in the usual swaddling clout to help her feel safe and secure, in the old wooden cradle. Grandma was also knitting her a woollen dress for the winter, which was just around the corner.

The family had been knitting stockings all year for the Fair in Thwaite, due very soon. They could be sure of making a few shillings and even Michael had managed a pair this time.

At three months old, Christian was carried by her mother, to the Fair where everything had changed for her, and nothing had changed.

She was still a mother. She was still a wife, but there had been a shift in their relationship that had given her a certain lightness in her heart. She'd never felt it before, but she assumed it was affection and maybe even love, for the man who was the figurehead of all their lives. Life had changed.

Misery, unhappiness, discontent, they were in her past. She could not change that. Nor could she change her destiny. She just hoped that her future life would be kinder to her. She ached and cried still for the three boys and one girl she'd lost already, lying awake at night, guilt a huge rock in her heart.

As for John, he felt it as much as she. All those children had been his own. John wasn't a religious man, but he hoped that Alice was looking down on them all, from a safe place, somewhere close. And sometime, he would see her again. Till then, there was still a life to live.

He'd been lucky enough to find another wife, who seemed to have mellowed, and softened, and was even affectionate at times. She was still loud, and apt to screech out, but you can't have everything, he thought.

He could put up with that.

Chapter 11
Jane Has Questions

"The one who knows all the answers has not been asked all the questions."
Confucious

It was Sunday and all the family were at Sunday School, except for John. He regarded it as his time to relax and that he had done his duty getting them there. They all went, even the big lads. It was the only schooling they got, or ever would get, so they went. Simple as that.
But he couldn't have known the events that were unfolding this particular day.

Jane had been pondering on something for quite a while now and she needed an answer. Months ago, at Easter, they had been told that Jesus had come back from the dead to see his friends. He talked to them and walked among them and was as alive as anyone, the Sunday School teacher had told them. She was new and very young. At least once a month she had the same question from Jane.
"Miss, When c'n Jemmy and Will cum t' visit uz?"

And the answer every time, "It's not possible Jane. They have been buried and are now in the arms of Jesus."

But now Jane was determined.

"But Miss. Jesus cum back t'see his friends."

"Yes, Jane. He did. But ainly Jesus c'n dee that."

"An he said he w's cumin again," she continued.

"Yes Jane. He did."

"But Miss. If he can, why can't Jemmy and Will?"

Over and over again, until the poor young teacher dreaded Sunday coming round.

"Reverend. Ah cannit carry on with that lass askin' questions ah cannit answer."

"Whit question Agnes?" So she told him.

Jane was watching this exchange with interest. She waited until Miss Agnes had moved away and then approached her again.

"Ah canit answer thy question any btter than ah already hav'e. Thee'll have t'gan t'the Reverend."

'Next taim,' she thought. "A'll axe him the next taim."

A month passed, and Jane kept silent. Then she decided to have another try.

Walking up to Miss Agnes, she was quite surprised to see the older girl turn and walk in the opposite direction. So, what to do now? The Reverend was standing next to the window, watching this with interest, and hoping that she would not come to ask him the 'question'.

But she did.

"Reverend. Thee knaws mah two brothers died o' the Red Rash."

He nodded.

"Ah miss them so much. An ma still cries f'them."

He nodded.

"So ah want to knaw when they'll be cumin back t'see us."

"They won't be comin back for a long, long time. An before that thee'll have grown old and gone to join them. They's in Heaven, Jane, and Heaven is so perfect that they don't want to leave, just yet."

This was a new way to look at it. They just don't want to leave yet? She lifted her head to ask another question, but the reverend had already walked away.

"Cancel the lesson on Lazarus for now Agnes," he whispered to his daughter.

Walking home Jane pondered this whole affair. It seemed easy to her, but no-one knew the answer, except to say they didn't want to come back!

She'd have to try a different tack.

That evening, she sat beside her da on the old settle, and snuggled in, pushing Peggy out of the way in the process. She was only seven and still loved a cuddle from her da.

"Hey. Whit's thee deein bairn?"

"Ma. Ah needs t'talk to da."

With a loud hrrrmp, Peggy pulled herself up. She needed to visit the privvy anyway.

Jane squeezed her da's arm and proclaimed, "Da. I want t'visit Heaven."

John had just taken a mouthful of cold tea, and spluttered his drink over his shirt.

"Heaven Jane?"

"Aye, da. Ah needs t'see Jemmy an' Will."

Oh how he wished he'd had time to think of his answer, but he did the best he could.

"Lass, Where dis thee think Heaven is? It's a special place. Thee can't walk there. Thee can't ride there. Even if thee walked awl day every day, thee'd niver reach there."

She looked expectantly at him and wouldn't interrupt.

"And once thee gets t'Heaven, thee disn't ever cum back home."

"But da, Miss Agnes says ……."

At that he cut her short.

"Miss Agnes is ainly a bairn herself. She don't knaw."

But da. The Reverend says…………"

"Reverend?v Has thee bin botherin' the Reverend?"

"Aye da."

"An did he have an answer."

She nodded, took a deep breath and rattled off her answer without taking another breath. "He said that Heaven is see lovely they just dinet want t'cum back yet and that they'll cum back wi'Jesus but it'll be a long long time and ah'll probably be owld and deed mesel by then so ah'll be with them when they dee cum back."

Sitting there, red faced and panting, she waited for his response.

"Well lass. There you go." And with that, he shut his eyes, signalling their talk was over.

"Aye da. Ah just wanted t'knaw if ah could gan to Heaven."

He sat with his eyes closed for a good long while, then chancing a look, he opened one eye. She was asleep. And soon, so was he.

There was no more talk of Heaven from Jane for quite a while until one day Jane asked, "Ma, da, dis thee think there's toys in

Heaven?"

"Why's that little lass?" John asked.

"Peggy 'nd Edmund will want summat t'play with."

Peggy took this one.

"Ah expect the angels will've made a 'babbie' f'Peggy," (referring to the stick dolls the girls all had) an a hoop n'stick f'Edmund."

"But he's si little ma."

"The angels'll help him. Dinna fret."

"Thanks ma. Ah was just worried they would be lonely without uz."

Chapter 12
Miles

"It's all right if all you did today was breathe."
(Unknown)

Miles was now working at the smelting mill. And he was not well. His head was sore, his muscles were sore, his belly was sore, and it had been five long days since he'd been able to use the privy.

Michael too was complaining of the same, although not as much. He had joined his brother in the lead smelting mill and was suffering from the heat and glare of the furnaces, where the air was foul and full of smoke and they were breathing it in, constantly.

After doing the best he could finally, Miles had to accept that he was ill.

"Da, can uz cum and bide wi' yee a while. Ah's ill. Ah cannae eat so ah'll cost thee nowt."

John was willing, but it was Peg who was against it. More work, she felt.

But home he came. Pale and weak, he sat on the settle in front of the smoking, peat fire, holding Christian, content and happy on his knee, making her smile and even laugh as he bounced her around.

And then he thought of his ma. She was an angel then, and an angel now. She had Will now too. He was almost jealous that he would have to wait to see her. After three days of this self-pity and misery, he walked to the door of the cottage, and looked around. It was late summer and today, for a change, the sky was a bright blue, but with dark clouds on the horizon that threatened rain.

John was busy scything through the grass on their little patch of ground. Their cow, Meadow, was lying down, chewing lazily, her jaws working seemingly without effort. Christopher was sat at the edge of the narrow roadway, chewing on a stick he'd found. At his age, over two years, but not yet three, he wasn't sure what was food, and what wasn't. Jane was washing their plates in the stream while little Peggy splashed about at the edge.

'It's dangerous to be so close to water,' Miles thought, and began to walk over towards them, shouting at them to take care.

Edward, toddling around the lane, held out his arms to balance, as babies do when they first learn to walk. Looking down at his feet, as if he couldn't believe what they were doing, he fell onto rough stone and grazed his knees. Yes, it would have hurt a little, thought Miles, but he didn't need to scream out in pain like he did. At this, Meadow lazily turned her head towards the sound, while a flock of crows in the nearby tree, waiting to pick over the midden, flew into the air, startled by the high shriek. Peggy came running out, with Christian still at her breast.

"Can thee do nuthin, Miles. Thee be suppost t'be lookin arfer the young uns."

She was impatient, and worried, and this was evident in her voice as she shouted these words, pointing to Edward who was laid on his back, kicking his short legs in temper, like a sheep that couldn't right itself.

Jane jumped up and looked round, while at that very same time, Little Peg, who was playing at the side of the beck, rolled down the beck-side, right into the water.

John, working in the field, heard the shouting, lifted his head, and then ran over the field to see what was happening just as Little Peg disappeared into the fairly fast-flowing, but shallow water.

On his feet, Miles was there before him, running further downstream where he caught little Peg just as she was about to turn the corner and be taken even further down the beck. She spluttered and coughed as he pulled her out and held her upside down to let the water run from her lungs before holding her in a tight embrace, and whispering in her ear to let her know she was safe.

That didn't prevent her from complaining, and now she wailed,

"Ma. Ma,"

Peg had been rooted to the spot, and now came to life. She ran over and grabbed her daughter, hitching her onto her left hip, while Christian, who began to uncharacteristically cry after being deprived of her meal, was held on her right. Peggy gave Miles the look that was reserved for things she disliked the most.

"Miles. Thee be useless," she sighed.

It was he who had rescued Little Peg from the fast-flowing water, and he didn't know what else he could have done. After this, he felt that his family did not need him, and did not want him. Despite how ill he still felt, he went back to the Mill the next day.

Chapter 13
A Christmas Tradition

"I have a son who is my heart.
Daring and loving and strong and kind."

(Maya Engelou)

Autumn came and went. Miles was still feeling unwell but didn't feel he could complain to anyone. He suffered stomach cramps and muscle pains without complaint and told no-one.

Work at the smelt mill was hard and one of the most hated jobs was to clean out the long, horizontal flue that drew the poisonous fumes away from the mill and its workers, directing them to a chimney high on the hillside. The vapour condensed on the inside walls of the flue into lead and silver and had to be scraped off. This job was one of the worst jobs a lead smelter had to do, so it was taken in turn.

Now it was Miles' turn.

This day he'd been working at the second hearth for almost ten hours, waiting, once the fire had been damped, for the first flue to cool – a full day's job so that was for the morrow. He'd done this enough times before to know what a thoroughly unpleasant job it was, scraping off the lead, in the dark, cramped, very dusty and still hot, tunnel.

That morning he woke up in the mine shop where he slept every weeknight. Or rather he opened his eyes. He hadn't been sleeping. He felt feverish, and his throat was so, so sore. Nevertheless, he rose, shakily, and walked outside. A mug of ale had been left for him, and a heel of bread. He left them both and walked to their water supply, drinking greedily, then poured the remains over his head, rubbing his eyes and the back of his neck with the icy water, trying to motivate himself to begin the walk to the mill.

"Cum on Miles Lad. Thee's dun this afore," he chided himself.
"It's ainly a day's work f'thee."
The flue he was cleaning was an arched tunnel partly dug into the hillside and partly built above ground, covered with soil and turf. After quite a long walk he arrived at the flue, lowered himself into it, to begin the work he was paid to do: scraping away at the sides of the flue, taking off the flume that would then be re-smelted, he knew. And for a good profit, he was told.
He was so hot inside here, and it was hard to see. Scraping away at the sides, with the hot dust falling in his face and his eyes, making

them sting, made him think of Hell.

Maybe this is what it's like, he wondered. Hell could hardly be any worse.

He coughed as the thick dust fell into his mouth down to his lungs. Brushing it away with one free hand, he scraped at the flue side with the other.

Seeing as he was in Hell, he decided that it would be better to concentrate on something pleasant while he worked, so he forced himself to try.

"Ah. Dinah Alderson. Ah mun ha' a kiss from that pretty lass. Or mebbe even mooare."

Thinking that as he scraped and scraped made the time pass a little faster.

She lived along Scarr Houses, near his dad and Peggy. She was near his age, a little younger, and was a reet bonny lass, he thought.

"Ah's ganna get my kiss off her at the Sheep Fair, if'n she's willin'."

It was the usual thing for young people to use Fairs to begin their courtship, and that was how his ma and da had met. He knew that. Dinah had met his look and seemed as if she might be as keen as he, so what was to lose?

He worked then almost in a daydream, thinking about her light-coloured hair and blue eyes, and how her hips swayed as she walked along the lane. She had no brothers either, so he need have no fear that they would chase him. He was twenty-two summers old and earned a wage. Her father could do worse, he thought. The thought of her sustained him till the end of the day.

The job was finished, and he was home for the weekend, having left at Friday midday. He managed a few hours with Dinah at the Fair, but she'd more than one young man interested in her it seemed, and she liked the attention. He'd stolen kisses, and more. Dinah, it seemed, was very willing.
But it seemed she was going to make sure she had all the fun she could before she tied herself down to just one man.

He was still determined, and his next chance would be at T'Awd Roy, a social event that happened on the Wednesday next before Old Christmas Day, which was the 6th ^{of} January. It would soon be here, and then everyone would be celebrating, and he would have his chance once more.
But for now, he had the weekend to pass as he wished. He spent some time in the Inn at Thwaite, and some time at the forge with his da. They'd talked about going to Kirkby Fair next time. Spending

time with his da was something he hoped to do more of, now he was a man.

Over the following weeks he gradually began to feel more like himself and hoped he'd shaken off the terrible tiredness and belly aches for good.

And now it was winter. All was quiet and peaceful. Deep, sparkling snow blanketed the village, with a sky full of the promise of much more. Soon it would be the Christmas festivities that everyone waited all year long for.

Muker T'Awd Roy.

"Tis T'Awd Roy. Whit ave we t'give," asked John.

"We mun find summat," said Peggy, "but we've not much. Uz can de wi'out yon cheesecake, nee bother, but that's awl."

"Get it out, an see if tho can mak' an onion pie," John suggested, "and mebbe gi ' a piece o' smoked bacon."

"Not t'smoked bacon," argued Peggy. "Whit will uz eat this winter?

"Not t'smoked bacon," she said firmly.

She knew that if she put her food down John would agree.

"Well, mebbe not, but there mun be an onion pie," he traded. And then, to seal the deal, he coaxed her along with, "Thy onion pies be the best ah iver et."

He knew she loved flattery. Most women do.

On the night before the festival Miles and Michael went with Sam Harker, Jo Pedley, Peter Milner and four other lads, around the cottages of Muker, Thwaite and Scar Cottages, asking for donations of food.

"Din't forget thy aprons," shouted John. "Howld them out bi the corners so thee don't drop eny."

"An mak sure t'get plenty," he shouted, at their swiftly disappearing backs, as off they went, to collect food and drink for the festivities.

Later that night John, Peg and all the children travelled the mile along to Muker by the light of the full moon and the stars, through a covering of fresh, powdery snow. The night air was clear but very cold. There were tables in the four Inns groaning with all kinds of food and all were welcome to eat and drink as they wished. There was always more than was needed.

The next day too the marketplace of Muker was filled with tables full of these good things, free for everyone, like sweetmeats and fruit. There were outdoor sports too. Hurdle jumping, pole vaulting, hipsygypsy, and trotting matches. There was drapery and haberdashery for sale if you wanted new clothing for Spring.

But all dependent on the weather.

John was always pleased to see the fiddlers and wandering musicians because it reminded him of that day in Southwaite, years ago, so long ago, it seemed.

That night in the Muker Inn, all sat next to the fireplace, singing old ballads, while in the big room upstairs something else was going to be happening. It was dancing.

"But ower John, thee knaws ah cannee dance, and neither can thee," Peggy giggled, "but ah've got me byoots on, so thee standin on mah foot winnet hurt uz this tahm."
"Owld lass. Mind what thee sez. Uz dancing be the talk o't'village."
"That's reet," she laughed. "Nee body cud b'lieve it t'last tahm."
"Has thee not seen uz practicing?"
"Practicing?" She looked at him and wondered. She had seen him jigging about the smithy, and on his way to the privvy, but she thought it was either because he was cold, or 'bustin'.
The fact that he had perhaps been practicing was such an incongruous idea that she couldn't stop herself from sniggering a little. When he just looked at her and raised one eyebrow, the snigger turned to a cackle, and finally, when he did a short jig on the spot, she hooted with laughter.
All those around her were gazing in surprise, wondering what had caused cold hearted Peggy Pedley, (because the old folks still called her that) to be bent double, snorting with laughter.

It was 6 o'clock, so they went up the stairs, him leading her by the hand, then whirling her around, while others clapped their hands and stamped their feet in time to the fiddlers' tunes.

They managed a reel and a jig, and even *The Grand Old Duke of York,* before panting and out of breath, decided they'd had enough. The children watched them, half asleep, but wanting to stay awake for this exciting evening. Grandma held baby Christian who was fast asleep, and Christopher who wasn't but should have been.

Miles too had a particularly good night. He had planned to steal a kiss from Dinah, and this he had managed to do. Catching her round the back of the Inn, he put his arms around her waist and pulled her to him. Feeling no resistance, in fact entirely the opposite, he kissed her, long and sweet. Her body was warm and soft, as she moulded herself to him and he felt a heat rising through his body.

It was she who pulled away. Pushing him slightly, she stood breathless and disheveled, her hair falling around her face as she stood, eyes lowered, not meeting his eye. This was when Miles felt that she was the one for him.

It was a few days full of magic, like no other, and then on Sunday it was all over for another year.

Chapter 14

A story to tell: A lesson to learn.

"If you're going to tell a story, tell a tall story, or none at all."
(author)

It was a cold Saturday night. Everyone was home and huddled around the smoky fire, trying to keep warm. Blankets, covers and coats were made use of in an attempt to ward off the cold, and if you wandered too far away from the fire, you could see your breath. The younger children were trying to snuggle in but were beginning to whimper and cry. John could see the mood deteriorating so he went to the one person who could get, and keep, the attention of all present.

"Gi'uz a story, ower Mick."

"Ah Da," Michael groaned. But he'd been waiting for this request to come because telling stories was a thing he loved to do.,

Michael was a prolific storyteller, with a great imagination and he loved to tell tales of farms haunted by boggarts, and goblins. This particular night he excelled himself with a tale that made all of them shrink with pleasurable terror at the telling of it.

The story had all the usual elements, of things disappearing, milk souring, dogs going lame, and even the abduction of children. Peg and John weren't happy with the last but knew that it was just a story. Michael was good with words, and his description of a boggart was one that made their blood chill.

"The boggart was a squat hairy man, with long shaggy hair and eyes like saucers. The noise he made was like the baying of hounds." He grimaced as he gave the description, and that was almost enough for Jane, but she forced herself to continue to listen as Michael was sometimes very funny too.

Telling the thrilling, frightening tale, he looked around everyone in turn, holding their eyes with his, telling the story of the farmer and this terrible creature, the boggart.

Of course, the farmer was victorious. He always was in all tellings, but he had to employ a little subterfuge along the way.

"Oh, ower Mickey. Ah thowt the boggart had 'im this time," squeaked Peggy. The poor farmer must a bin owt on his wits."

"Tell it again. Again. Again." shrieked Jane and Edward, although Edward seemed a little unsure as he looked at Jane with wide eyes that seemed to say, "Are you sure?"

The stories were so good, and so well told by Michael, that listeners were led to believe, each time, that it was possible for the boggart to win. Being scared was good entertainment and terror was always the theme of a good night's storytelling. These simple dales people were often unsure in their own minds if these creatures were real or not. Many still believed in monsters and fairies and were easily persuaded.

Michael loved the atmosphere he created, and how everyone hung on to his every word. Being the centre of this attention was intoxicating, he felt. He knew he could tell a good story because he was always being begged to tell one, at home, at the inn and on the lonely evenings after shift at the mill.

"Mickey, gie us a story," they would shout. And he would gladly oblige, making the wicked boggart increasingly disgusting and frightening as the months went on, and his actions increasingly heinous.

Listeners covered their ears and sometimes their eyes and thrilled at the telling.

"Aaaaahhhhhhhh!!!! Nooooooooooooo!!!! was oft screamed out. "Watch out. Gan canny!" were words of warning for the farmer, from listeners, choked with fear, waiting to see what either he or the boggart was going to do next

Some weekends Michael never paid for one drink, so entertaining were his stories.

Another year passed. Thwaite Fair came. Thwaite Fair went. The years were marked by such occasions. Miles was feeling so, so tired now. He coughed so much that his chest ached. It was his turn again to clean out the flue.

"Let me gan," said Michael. "Let me tack thy place."

"Diven't dee that. Ah can't let thee."

But not listentening to his brother, Michael turned up at the flue the next morning, before Miles, and climbed inside. He was used to the job, but like everyone else, hated the work. It was a hot, dirty, dusty dark place. But at the end of the day, he felt good, and went looking for his brother.

Miles was laid on his bed, in the mine shop, eyes half closed, and clutching his stomach. It was a Friday, so Michael helped his brother home the long journey over the fell, with many stops on the way. By the time he reached Scarr Cottages Miles was exhausted, and so white that Peggy immediately dropped what she was doing and ran to help him inside.

"In the Good Lord's name, what has happened to thee? Thee's as white as a clout. Inside wi'yee, next t't'fire."

He was unable to bear his own weight now, and little Jane had to help them get him near the fire. After a violent bout of coughing too Jane noticed the red in his hand but said nothing. She didn't know what it meant. But Peggy did. Crossing herself, she knelt down beside him, and put her face next to his.

"Me bonny boy. What has thee been doin'," she said softly, not as a question, but as a note of comfort. Michael thought it was quite amazing to see Peggy, who was hard and unyielding normally, be as soft and caring as she was now with his brother.

"Gan and get thee da," she whispered to Michael, who was standing, statue still, looking at the tableau in front of him. He stood, rooted to the spot, and then something galvanised him into action. He turned on his heel and sprinted out of the cottage, along the lane to Thwaite, and got to the smithy just as his father was leaving.

"Da. Thee must get thi-ssen home. Our Miles is not his-sel. He's badly and as white as a clout and can hardly stand."

He didn't mention the cough, or the blood, but his manner made it clear to John that something was very, very wrong. It wasn't far back home, a matter of minutes before they reached the stone cottage. Christopher and Edward were playing in the lane with stones and twigs. Jane and little Peg were sat on the step, sent outside to play with their dolls, made of twigs and rags. Christian was inside, uncharacteristically crying at the top of her lungs. It was a cold day, but no-one seemed to feel it. Hurrying inside John saw a scene that would haunt him, and play out in his mind, for the rest of his life.

How had he not noticed how thin his son had become? How could he not have seen how ravaged his body was? In truth, it hadn't taken long for Miles to look so emaciated. The last week had been the undoing of him: unable to eat, or drink, and vomiting constantly. Now he'd rested a little, his face was no longer white. It had taken on a pallor of a lead hue. His head had been so sore all week and now he could hardly open his eyes. His body was clammy, his clothes soaked in sweat, and John could now see the tinge of blue in his gums. It was common knowledge that working with lead could make you sick, or worse, and the blue gum was proof. It usually didn't strike as fast as this, and Miles was young to be so badly affected.

The usual treatment was careful nursing, good food, and fresh air. But he was unlikely to get all, or any of these, here. And, it had never proved to be a successful remedy so far.

"Let uz be da. Let uz sleep," he begged.

"Have a sip. Eat summat. Thee mun get well," John whispered.

"Gan f'the medical man ower Michael. Tell'im he 'as t'cum," ordered John.

"Dr Rudd's a good man. He'll be 'ere, but let's try t'mak 'im more at ease," Peggy mouthed.

"Ave sum watter even if thee cannit eat."

"Ah cannit sup it ma."

"Aw Miles man. Thee mun 'ave summat."

Dr Rudd came, and after a short examination, told them just what they already knew.

"It's the lead lung Peggy. I think you already know that, John."

There was nothing more to tell. He'd seen so many men suffer the same way, but none as young as Miles. This was the tragedy.

They sat up all night with him. They whispered together about the signs they now realised had been there but had not noticed.

He'd mentioned to Michael that he'd walked into someone. He just hadn't seen them. He'd told him that he couldn't sleep, that he had seen his ma in the shadows and had talked to her. They knew about his aching belly, and other pains, and Peggy was now berating herself, loudly and often, until she was reminded to keep hush, as she remembered how she had treated him when he was at home sick the last year and had saved little Peg from drowning.

"It's not allus abaht thee Peggy," whispered John, impatiently. "It's abaht this bairn layin here."

Miles was still his bairn.

Miles lived another five days until early November 1806 at the age of twenty-three. He was John's fifth child to die. And his first born. The son he had longed for and been so proud to meet.

Once again, they'd all been dealt a cruel blow. He was grateful that Miles was free of suffering, how could he not be, regardless of how he himself felt. All pain would be gone, and he'd had plenty of that. He was with his ma now, who he'd missed ever since she'd gone, but that didn't make any difference to John. They had shared so much life together, and suffering too, and now he felt the guilt as his son, and another link with Alice was gone.

He didn't cry in public. It wasn't done but his eyes blurred when he thought about his brave boy. He looked up, trying to stop the tears falling. Will and Miles up there with their mother. He pressed his hand to his chest, to feel his heartbeat, and felt the cruelty once more, that it wasn't fair he was still here, and his sons were not.

Mourning this brother was a pain that Michael found hard to live through. They'd been close in age and for one summer they hadn't had to work on the farm or in the smithy. It was up till Miles was six years old. They had done many things together that summer as they were growing up in the Mallerstang Valley. Splashing about in the beck, trying to catch a fish for dinner, but never succeeding: throwing pebbles across the beck, to see who could get the farthest: chasing the sheep across the hillside, shouting at the tops of their voices, and getting the belt for it when they got home. They'd even managed to wander as far as the ruins one day, playing soldiers on the ramparts. And they never told.

It was their sister Betty that had put a stop to this. She was such a waily, needy baby that his ma needed help, Mary was only five years, but she was drafted in to help, and never got away. And Miles could earn some money now as he was five when she was born.

But Michael was only two years old when the freedom ended, so it was unlikely he had taken part in these escapades. It is more likely that he remembered the telling of them from Miles and Mary, and his memory placed him there too.

He missed Mary and promised himself that he would visit her as soon as he could. Shared memories were painful, sad but bittersweet. He would never, could never, forget his brother.

But he would have to try and find a way to live his life without him. Losing his ma had been his first loss. The first little Peggy had found her way into his heart too. Jemmy and Will – he'd cried when the Red Rash had taken them. But this was different. It always felt like Miles was a part of him. And Betty and Mary would be heartbroken, again.

His heart was breaking.

That cold, bleak day, Christian, Christopher and Edward stayed behind with Granma Pedley, but Jane insisted on going.

It was November and there was snow falling, soft and powdery, onto the frozen ground: Falling from a sky as dark and grey as the murky waters of the washtub. With a neighbour's horse pulling the coffin, it slid this way and that as they made the journey, to take Miles to be laid with the family in the chapel yard. They'd wrapped up as warm as they could as they walked alongside Miles on his last journey. As they walked Michael knew that Peggy was already well on the way to providing a replacement. The meaning of life seemed clear. Born, live, produce children, die.

In less than three months there would be a new little Hutchinson, boy or girl. Who could know? He could feel his heart pulsing in his throat and lifted his head to feel the crystalline snow drifting onto his cold face.

This time they could afford to pay for a service, and the vicar, Reverend Richardson, gave the address, mourning the loss of such a young life. Sadly, it wasn't an unusual occurrence, he said, and Michael knew that a friend of theirs, Thomas Pounder, another miner, had died the month before, at a similar age. Thomas' ma had sobbed and wailed in the churchyard when the body was laid to rest, but there was none of that for Miles. His ma wasn't there to sob for him. Peggy tried her best to 'behave', as John had called it, but she had known this lad for years, and he and she had come to some sort of a family relationship more recently, so she wept for the young lad who hadn't had the chance to become a man.

When T'Awd Roy came around they didn't join in this year. There was nothing to celebrate, and it felt that there never would be.

Chapter 15

1807 A Daughter Comes Home

"If you want to change the world, go home and love your family."

(Mother Theresa)

The snow fell and fell, lying over the hillside, a blanket of the purest white. The wind blew and whistled across the moor, through the village and into homes through cracks and crevices in badly built cottages. Some days, when out walking, it was almost impossible to stand upright. Clothing was permanently soaked through, and petticoats that were usually a few inches off the ground to prevent becoming wet, drew up the moisture from the bottom, like a wick. Being constantly in damp, or even wet clothing, was not good for anyone's health, and the winter saw off quite a few of the village's older inhabitants, as well as the very young.

The new Hutchinson baby was once more born on a very snowy, blustery day, but being a Saturday there were plenty of people around.

Grandma Pedley was doing her best, looking after the younger ones at her cottage, and a neighbour, the village good woman, was on hand for help.

But Peggy was experienced enough now herself to know she wouldn't need it. This was her tenth baby, after all: nine to John, and then her daughter Ruth. After an unexpectedly long labour, lasting all day, this baby came crying into this world at supper time, and it was a boy.

John spent the first hour just looking at him while the girls fussed over him. He didn't know if he was pleased or not.

What should they call him? Should they call him Miles? But he couldn't do it. It was barely three months since Miles had gone, but it was Peg who managed to persuade him.

"It were meant to be John," she whispered to him. "Your young lad's here again."

Born on the Saturday, he was taken to Muker church the next day to be christened, and Miles was the name that the vicar gave him. He looked nothing like his namesake. No gingerish hue about the hair, or pale blue eyes. He was dark, in hair, and eyes and even his skin had a dark tinge about it. He couldn't have been more different to his absent brother.

Peggy certainly had her hands full, with a baby, four children under six years old, and two older children, being boys, and no help at all with the children. Jane was only nine, almost ten, but she was doing much of the child rearing, while Peggy spent her time with the baby. Two months after Miles was born, an event gave them all some reason for cheer. Jane came running in from the lane, screaming that she'd seen Betty.

"Had away, thee's a barmpot," scoffed Peggy.
"Tis Betty. Tis Betty," she screamed, running into the house and jumping up and down with excitement.
Shuffling outside, Peggy peered down the lane, hand above her eyes in an attempt to see further. Little Peg looked up from playing in the wet dirt, and caught the excitement in the air, copying her sister, running around and screeching, although she hadn't a clue why.
And there she was.

Dropping her bag in the muddy lane, Betty propelled herself forward to Jane, running down the lane with her arms outstretched, to greet her.
"Betty. Betty. Betty. Betty," intoned Jane, like a mantra, as she ran forwards to greet her. They had almost both collided when Jane tripped over a large stone, took a tumble, and fell headlong on the rough ground, just in time for Betty to pick her up and comfort her. Remembering how thin Jane had always been, it was no surprise to Betty that she could feel the sharp angular bones of the child under

her shift. But she was still here, when it had seemed for a long while that she would not last the treacherous course of early childhood. Betty was eighteen years old now, and a young woman. Because of her employment, she was used to comforting children, and with her voice calm and soothing, Jane's tears had soon dried as pale stains on her thin dirty cheeks, a memory of the event.

Little Peg, having watched all with puzzlement, stood up and walked slowly down to meet them, unsure who this very kind person was. She held out her stick doll to Betty, who carefully took it, kissed it and gave the precious item back to its owner.

Little Peg was six now but didn't talk much. She had few words and because of that no-one talked to her. She had no need to talk. Jane got her everything she needed.

It was different with the boys. At four and five years, Christopher and Edward were much more vocal, and made sure every day that the whole street knew how they were faring.

They were boisterous little boys, who rough and tumbled, just like John and Will used to. But now, they had stopped, still, and were staring vacuously at Betty, who smiled back at them. It had not passed her attention that they were dressed in clothes that were more like rags, but then, in fairness, so were other village children playing in the lane.

Looking further on, she saw, standing in the doorway, a blonde haired beautiful little girl, thumb in mouth, holding onto her mother's petticoats, and hiding her head behind them when she saw Betty looking at her. Her face totally devoid of any expression. She was all but in rags too now, her lovely clothes grown out of. Peggy was nursing baby Miles as she stood there, breast exposed. Betty looked at all the children. Having spent the last two years working for a family in Kirkby Stephen and looking after their children, she knew now that both clothes and bodies should be washed regularly and that it would do them no harm.

She remembered how lazy Peggy had been and thought that was probably one reason the children were in such a sorry state. When she left her employment, they had given her some outgrown children's clothing for her brothers and sisters, and now she saw how greatly it was needed. But first, time to get to know them all again.

"Where's Michael and John?" she queried.

"Michael is at the mill, and John'll be choppin' sticks in the village," replied Peggy.

"I've some smoked pork and oatmeal cakes for us," Betty said, smiling.

All the children, apart from Jane, had good appetites. Food was always carefully shared. Fresh milk from their cow Meadow, and eggs from the geese, supplemented their diet. Vegetables, potatoes and onions, and sometimes carrots, were available from their small garden. They had eaten all their smoked pork so it, and the oat cakes were welcome.

When John came home that evening, he could not believe the tableau in front of him. The young ones were all sat on the settle, with Betty telling stories, Christian asleep on her knee, and Jane and Little Peg almost asleep, leaning either side of her.

The two boys were still wary but were gradually gaining ground and coming ever so slightly nearer with each few sentences. Michael would not see his sister until the weekend, but young John was so happy that he cried.

And old John, he couldn't believe his eyes.

"Betty. My Betty," was all he could say, and put his arms around her shoulders.

Betty had been a mainstay of the family when she left, and now she was back Peggy hoped and prayed that she would stay. That had been Betty's intention, and she saw now, how much she was needed.

She said she would stay but thought she would see how things were. She would not be as put upon as she had been in the past. Peggy would have to do her share.

That night she showed Peggy and John the clothes she'd brought. Some would fit. Some would be made over. But the children would have clothes for the summer that would be fit for the purpose of being clothes, and not rags. She even had a bodice and petticoat for Peggy, and a shirt for her da.

"Thee must be a good worker, Betty. Thee must be," John said, in a low voice, more to himself than anything.

"It were a house like no other," said Betty. "Ah wasn't a servant. Ah was more than that. And they were so good to me."

For a moment she remembered the wrench it had been to leave, and a tear began to form in her eye, but she dashed it away. This was the beginning of her new life. They had begged her to stay, but in her mind always was the picture of Jane, her hollow eyes in her thin, pinched face, following her as she left. Willing her, she was sure, to turn around and stay.

Now Betty was home she had already begun to make a difference. First, she'd gone to the inn in Thwaite and now had paid employment each weekend, cleaning and serving ale to customers. Because of where she'd lived and the life she'd had in the past three years Betty was appalled at the state of the cottage and the people living in it. There had been no mending done, no holes or tears stitched up, no letting out of clothes that were too small. Peggy hated mending, darning, or anything really. Her excuse was looking after the children. But what would it have cost her to spend a couple of hours each evening mending, as other mothers did, or not even every evening.

Betty worried about Michael. Of course, she worried about him, working at the smelt mill, hoping he didn't come to suffer from the lead disease like his brother Miles. And young John was only thirteen. He'd already worked some shifts at the mine. There wasn't much else to do. It seemed only a matter of time before he would be working there too.

That first Friday afternoon she walked over the fell with Jane, to meet Michael as he came home for the weekend. At the top of Thwaite Side, she paused for breath and looked back over the village, spotting Scarr Houses, and the inn, and other houses that she knew. Carrying on together they passed a mining hush, all stones and rubble. There were plenty of these scars on the landscape around here. They walked along together briskly as it wasn't the warmest of days for late April, and there was still a little snow on the hillside.

As Michael came striding down the hill he wasn't looking in their direction at first. Betty could see that he was lost in thought, and she knew what about. But as he got closer and saw who it was, he shouted out.

"Well. Betty? Betty? That caps owt. Our Betty. This be a good gay day. Eeh. Our Betty."

He continued gabbling.

"Eeh, ower Betty. Ah can't believe it. Where's thee cum from. Cum 'ere. Ah cannit ken what my een's seein'." Putting put his arms around her shoulders he hugged her tightly to him. This was just too good to believe.

They had walked home together, with Jane between them, talking all the way, about this and that, about day-to-day things, about how they felt. Betty let a few tears fall. Michael tried not to.

Betty had to go to work. She was good with people and could talk to anyone, never being phased by a man's words. Here they were mostly interested in their ale and not the barmaid. She recognised a few and chatted about their families, making sure they knew that she knew of their wives. It was the safest way.

It was late when she got back to Scarr Houses, walking along in the moonlight and remembering the times she'd walked this road before. She thought about Michael and how thin he was. Peggy was the same as always: coarse and vulgar, as well as lazy. But she made her da happier now. Life had a way of throwing things at you, in your face, and unexpected, but it seemed they had both come through.

Saturday meant they could all be together, at least for the day. John had no work to complete. Michael was home for the weekend, and the rest of the family were just pleased to see her.

She spent the morning with baby Miles before looking at the children's clothes and deciding what to do.

A pan of water was placed on the fire to heat and then added to cold water outside, deep enough and warm enough to be a bath: for the washing of bodies first.

Jane stood watching, scratching her head and other places, as they all did. Then she was lifted into the water. She squealed with pleasure when she felt the warm water around her: loving the feel of Betty cleaning away the dirt with a clean rag and soap. The washing of her hair, again with soap, was a different feeling because Betty used a small amount of something she called vinegar on her hair, and then washed it again with soap.

Her short hair was brushed. The clothes Betty had brought were taken out of her travelling bag, and Jane whooped with delight., before falling silent.

With a tremulous voice she asked, "When do they have to go back? How long can ah keep 'em?"

"For as long as they fit you dear Jane," was the answer, which caused Jane to dance around the cobbles, clutching the clothes tightly to her, in sheer and absolute pleasure.

Betty gave Christian the experience next, who was even more afraid of the event than Jane and had to be coaxed near the water. Betty lifted her up gently and held her as she was deposited into the fragrant liquid. Only when she heard the squeals of delight did she let go of her sister. She was going to cut the beautiful blonde bedraggled hair, so it was short like Jane's, but then said to herself, let's see how this goes. It was given a thorough wash and rinse, then brush, and as it dried Betty was glad she hadn't cut it: yet.

Little Peg was even more unsure about getting into the water. When Betty lifted her in, she screamed, this time with displeasure at the feeling of the water all over her skin, which was something she needed to get used to. But she still needed to be thoroughly washed. So, Betty soldiered on and completed the job.

Both Edward and Christopher were much dirtier. 'I didn't think it was possible', thought Betty, so she heated a fresh pan of water for them, making it into a game so they wouldn't rebel and jump out. She had brought plenty of soap, so she had thought, but it was proving to be inadequate for the task. It would be the first thing she would buy when she was paid.

Washing their bodies and seeing the lice crawling over them did upset her, but she knew that there had been a time when she'd been the just as dirty and just as 'lousy'.

Finally, she made sure there was enough water for young John and

Michael, leaving them to wash themselves. Her da and Peggy would have to wait. Their bodies were clean, and they had fresh, clean, lice free clothes, for now. To the boys it made no difference, nor strangely enough, to Christian, but Jane and little Peg were transformed, in appearance and demeanour. They twirled and danced around, looking at each other, smiling and laughing. And to Betty it felt good.

The next day was the turn of John and Peggy. She heated the water and left out the sliver of soap that was left. She was so so pleased when they took their turn. It would need to be a regular occurrence and maybe they would rid themselves of most of the lice. Every week was too much to hope for, but that was her eventual aim.

Next, she tackled brushing out the cottage and washing wherever she could. The flagstone floor was cleaned with water and the hard outdoor broom, and the whole place was instantly changed. It was still early in the year but there were some flowers to be had, so she picked what she could. But she remembered the old saying, "You can't make a pig stye into a palace": not overnight anyway.

Even the servants' rooms she'd slept in were much better than these. Early the next morning bedclothes were brought outside and given the shaking of their lives then hung on branches in the fresh air before being boiled, with shifts and shirts. Next the downstairs mattress was dragged out. Those upstairs would have to wait. It was broomed, brushed, shaken, but she knew she was fighting a losing battle. Bed bugs were the problem. Everyone had them. All the family here were bitten, but they didn't complain. It had always happened. No-one had the remedy.

And now the family had become a little more presentable.

The children were better dressed and the clothes they normally wore were made over where possible and made wearable by Betty's needlework skills. She spent time talking to Little Peg, encouraging her, making her talk, teaching her new words. She took the boys, with the three girls, for walks in the fields, showing them things about nature that she thought they may be interested in: birds and animals. Christian loved going with her and absorbed all the new information without seeming to need any reinforcement. The family was happy.

Chapter 16

1807 It's not Superstition. It's real!

"The reality is you will grieve forever".

(Elizabeth Kubler-Ross)

It had been a bad year for the dale. In Gunnerside there had been twenty-six deaths of children that year. The Red Rash had taken them all. And ten more in Muker and Thwaite: the most there had been for many a year. Deaths and burials were common, and parents grieved.

Baby Miles was six months old. It was August and there was a late hay harvest. Although it was very early in her time Peggy already knew that there was another bairn coming. She knew the changes. She just knew, after ten bairns. And this would be number eleven. She wouldn't tell John for another few months. There was no excitement now. No joy in the news. It was just news of another mouth to feed.

John still grieved for Miles but couldn't say how much. The young girl Miles had been seeing was now wed to another, and very happy, it seemed, with a bairn on the way. How could she move on so quickly, he'd asked himself. But he also knew that death was a fact of life, and that many young people were extinguished before they had the chance of living.

Thwaite and Muker Fair would be upon them soon. Something to occupy their hands, and maybe a little bit of their minds.

As the nights drew in and it became darker much earlier, it was usual for families to sit around the fire, knitting and telling ghost stories.

That Friday evening Peggy and Betty went along the row to a 'setting neet' with the other women, for scary tales, and knitting. Along at the Harker's house, where they were met, all were competing to see who could tell the most frightening tale. Many of them believed in fairies, witches and ghosts, so the stories told in the fire light shadows could be very frightening and made them huddle together for safety.

Once more the boggart provided the most frightening stories, but they loved being terrified as they knitted. They were there till midnight, and then Betty was declared the teller of the best and most frightening tale.

It was a short walk home, in the dark of a moonless night. After being terrified almost out of her skin, Peggy startled and looked over her shoulder more than once, jumping at the noise of the bats whirling around the roof tops or the owl in the tree. Grabbing hold of Betty's arm, she clung to her in the darkness, but Betty merely laughed at her.

"Give over. Thee's a barmpot," said Betty. "Thee don't believe them tales, do thee?"

"Ower Betty. Give ower. Thee knaws sum on't is true. Uz awl knaws tha."

Betty just laughed and thought how easy it was to frighten some people.

"Oh Peggy," she giggled, "careful o'that........"

She couldn't get the rest of her words out before Peggy left her side and ran as fast as she could towards their door. But even inside she didn't feel safe. It was known that witches and bogarts could come down the chimney. It would be a while before Peggy felt safe again. But she'd loved it, and so had Betty. It was good to feel something else for a change.

Peggy stood panting after her short run.

"Ah dee Betty. Ah dee believe in 'em. A'hve seen things as wud mak thee hair curl when ah was a young lass."

As it happens, the stories told in their cottage had been many times more frightening than those she'd just heard, Michael was a good storyteller, and so was young John. Thankfully, the very youngest,

Miles, Christian, Edward and Christopher, had slept through it, but little Peg and Jane looked at them with wide eyes and frightened faces as they opened the door, wondering if this was the boggart. "Mind it don't come down the chimney," Betty whispered mischievously to Peggy.

Truth to tell, they'd so enjoyed being scared to death, that they wanted Betty to tell them her tale. She let them beg for a while and then managed to get them both to bed, with promises of another night.

Once the youngest were asleep the grownups talked about the haunted house in Thwaite. Even John, who had more common sense than most, said that as he walked past it a shadow of fear came over him. One man was supposed to have had his hair turn white with shock when startled by something as he walked past this house.

Who knew?

To ward off evil spirits from the house when she'd come to live there Peggy had hung a stone with a hole through it, near the door. And she wasn't the only one. Most of the houses in Thwaite, Muker and Scarr Houses had either a stone such as this, or a horseshoe nailed by the door. She remembered being sent out as a child to find one that would do – one with a hole already in it. It had to be a found hole.

Peggy had both, the stone and the horseshoe, for good measure.

Church on Christmas Day was uplifting as they enjoyed singing the hymns and hearing the message of love and hope once more. T'Awd Roy came and went.

And the Hutchinson children, were delighted to receive a farthing each on Christmas morning. It was a wonderful gift, and they spent the day talking about what they would buy. Of course it all went on candy at the local shop. Jane and little Peg made theirs last for two weeks and only spent half of it. Jane took Miles' money and brought him back something suitable for babies. Betty, who'd provided the money, was delighted at the pleasure the children were getting from this gift. But Jane noticed that there hadn't been any for Betty.

"Share mine," she urged. "Why's thee got nowt?"

"Thine is thine," replied Betty. "I'm ower awld for candies," noticing with pride the generosity of her sister.

By now Peggy's belly was well and truly full.

"This bairn'll be a big'un," she whispered to John one night. "Mebbe it'll be the last. It mun be a boy. I feel it's a boy."

John said nothing. He knew that eventually their nightime activities would not produce a bairn, but for the moment he was just like other men, making sure that the purpose of marriage was adhered to, as it said in the marriage service. He was just doing his duty.

Peggy went into labour in the spring of 1808 and she was right. It was a large baby, who needed much encouragement to show their face. Her mother was with her all day and all the night. Her cries and groans were loud and pitiful, frightening the young ones, so Betty took them to a neighbour's and waited there for news. After waiting all day, she left them there and walked quickly along the row, in the dak of a cold evening, to discover what had happened.
 The baby was still refusing to greet the world.
"Betty. We mun have a medical man but Peggy says no," said Granma Pedley.
"What about the midwife," suggested Betty, and Peggy slowly nodded her head.
"She ain't gonna can push much more."
Taking a shilling from her own purse, from the money she had earned, Betty walked at a very brisk pace, into Thwaite, for the midwife. It took her a few hours and when she returned with Annie Guy, the local midwife, Peggy was done. Or so she said, that she couldn't push any more.
Thankfully, the midwife had many years of experience, and was able to see the problem and remedy it.

"That's your problem. He be arse first," she shouted. "Nee wonder he cannit be birthed, poor mite. Let's hope they're still wi'uz."

Using all the skills that she'd learned, she was able to turn the baby round, so that finally it could come into the world. It was not without its discomfort. In fact, it was downright painful. Both Peggy and midwife were worn out when, with a final push, a large baby boy made his appearance.

Peggy, although a strong woman, was almost unconscious, but she wasn't going to let anything happen to another child of hers. Not if she could help it. This was her job. Her role in life.

Both mother and baby were exhausted and there were days of rest ahead for both of them.

Peggy had been right. It was a boy. And he was named William, after his lost brother.

Chapter 17
Love and Hope

"The Course of true love never did run smooth."

(William Shakespeare)

It was uncanny. The new William was the picture of the old William: the same colour hair and eyes. But, where the first William had been an unhappy baby, always grizzling and crying, this one was a delight. He seemed to need no attention, which was just as well, as there was little to give.

John was still renting the same bit of pastureland from Antony Metcalfe for Meadow their cow, who had produced a calf the previous year, as planned, and the milk yield had increased. The calf was a bull calf, and would be slaughtered for food the next winter, helping to keep the family fed.

Peggy and John had tried to ensure the children hadn't got too fond of it, but of course they had. He had a name right from the start and was constantly petted and hand fed with the best grass. Christian had been allowed to name him, not realising he was, "a boy cow," as the others called him.

So, his name was Daisy.

They would have another few months with him, and then he would be led to the farm, where he would be butchered.

Meadow was milked outside every morning, with Peggy carrying the can over to the cottage, the usual way, on her back. She was still making butter, and John had made a paddle for her. She was wanting a proper churn, but John said they couldn't get one for nothing, and he couldn't make one. The butter was mostly for their own consumption now, and the children loved it spread thickly on bread. Goose eggs were another produce of theirs, and everyone loved having them cooked on a griddle with a little butter. They could also be exchanged for other forms of food at the local village merchant. Peggy had recently discovered chicory drink, and John was persuaded to let her have some.

The children seemed to be thriving. With Betty home Little Peggy was talking more and was able to recite a simple rhyme. With better food at home, Jane was now eating and so had put some flesh on her bones. Her face was no longer pinched and thin. This gave her a whole new look.

Christopher and Edward were two sturdy boys who loved to earn a penny bird scaring and made a better job of it than their older brother Michael had done at their age. The two babies, Miles and William, were only fourteen months between, and almost like twins. William slept and Miles was fussed over, and they had a cradle each.

Young John was fifteen now, and working at the mine, as there was no other work to be had. And Michael was still at the smelt mill. He hated it, but he had no choice.

That left Christian.

Betty spent as much time as she could with this little sister. She felt that there was something different about her but didn't know what. Her eyes were so pale, and her hair was almost white now. She'd never seen the like, and nor had anyone else in the family, but Peggy could hear mutterings from the old wives she passed on her way to the store.

"There's summat badly wi'that bairn."

"Aye, her's like not finished proper."

"Had away yee owld gossips," Peggy hurled at them, rushing past and dragging poor Christian behind her, stumbling and almost off her feet.

"Ma," she wailed. "Ma!" She wailed again. "Thee's yankin me arm. It's cumin off!"

Peggy finally stopped to see what was happening.

"Ye barmpot. Ah's not pullin' thy arm off!"

"But ma, ah din't say that. It's ma sleeve."

"Aye, all right, chicken." She knew better than to argue semantics with Christian, if she had known what semantics were.

It was Betty who realised that Christian couldn't see very well. If Christian was at the other end of the row, she didn't know who was waving at her, until they shouted her name.

Her pale, white skin burned in the merest sunlight, so she was either covered up, or inside on bright summer days. Apart from that, she was an intelligent girl, always asking questions about any plants she saw, holding them right up to her eyes so she could describe their leaves and flowers. At only three years old she knew the names of all the wildflowers that grew anywhere near their cottage and could draw a fairly decent copy of one in the dust, or with water and a wet twig, or with a chalk stone on the wall.

At Sunday School she was in her element. Once the teacher put a pencil in her hand, and guided her initially, she was soon able to hold it and write. Betty copied short bible stories in large print for her, and soon she was reading. Haltingly, but with increasing confidence she read to her older brothers and encouraged them at Sunday School with pictures from the story.

She was indeed the special child everyone thought she was when she was born.

She was too young to remember her brother Miles, and hadn't been born when the others passed, but she talked of them, often, as if she knew them.

One day Peggy heard her talking to someone in the lane, but when she went outside there was no-one there.

"Who're tha talkin' ta my chuck," she asked when she saw no-one.

"Just Gran," Christian replied.

Peggy knew that her mother was in Muker, so it couldn't be her.

"Din't thee be leearing to me bairn. Grandma's at Muker."

Christian came back with, "Nay. Not that Grandma. Tis Grandma Hutchinson."

Scoffing, and laughing right in her face, Peg cried, "It's not. It canna be. Thee cannit knaw Grandma Hutchinson."

"Why?" asked Christian.

"She's in the kirkyard at Kirkby, ower Christian. Dooan't be gormless!"

Christian took the reproach but didn't back down.

"But ma, she's tellin' uz she's lookin' afta t'lads, and baby Peggy actilly."

"Get away, ye brazzent bairn. Diven't yee be leearing abaht them bairns."

Peggy was having none of it. Her religious beliefs just wouldn't allow it.

"She says that heaven is pretty an breet: reet li t' Mallerstang valley on a lovely warm summer's day."

Peg's eyes were popping. What was this girl saying?

"Nee on'e iver talked t'thee abaht that place, ma honeybairn. An' thee's niver bin t'yon place."

"But Grandma says…." Peggy gently put her hand over Christian's mouth to stop her talking and guided her towards the cottage door. This was a puzzle, and Peggy was no good with puzzles.

"Christian, Dowter. Get thissen inside and give owr talkin like that. Thee'll be seeing boggles and barghaists next."

"What're they?", asked Christian.

Ignoring the question Peggy hurried her inside, worrying that if someone else had heard her daughter it would be so easy for her to be branded a witch, or even in league with Awd Scrat himself.

John came home that evening, totally unaware of what was in store for him. He was accosted in the doorway by Peg, who had found the day a great trial. Such a secret as this was extremely difficult to keep. Dragging him inside before he could disappear to the vegetable plot over the way, she could hardly frame the words she wanted to say. He could see and feel that she was overwrought, and that state of mind in Peg was not good. Standing still, beside her, he waited for the outburst, but it didn't come. Instead, Peg leaned in towards him, and very quietly and clearly whispered the words, "Owr dowter's addled in the heed."

"Ma, ah c'n hear yee."

Rocking back on his heels, John widened his eyes and looked puzzled.

"Addled?" he repeated. "Which dowter?" he asked, pragmatically.

"This yan," whispered Peg. She'd placed Christian in front of her, hands on her shoulders, pointing down with her eyes.

"Hush woman. What's the matter wi' thee?"

Peggy told him everything, while Christian looked at them both with her big, pale eyes.

"But ma, it *was* Grandma Hutchinson. Shi sez t'tell da she loves him. And that he was allus her bonny bairden, her bonny barne."

"Has she seen a fetch[1] d'yee ken?"

"Ah din't knaw *whit* she's seen."

"Neebody says 'bairden' hereabouts" he whispered.

"Da. Ah can hear thee," whispered Christian loudly back at them.

"She mun 'as heard it from thee ma. Ask her," John commanded.

"Aye, when ah seezs her," she replied and bundled Christian inside before anyone else heard them.

Peggy did not take kindly to orders!

John had not heard this word since from his ma's lips. She hadn't even used it to his children. It wasn't a word people used then or now.

"Fetch her back here Peg," he shouted.

There were too many in the cottage that might hear this. Christian was brought back and made to stand once more in front of Peg, whose hands rested on the girl's shoulders.

"Cun wi'me bairn, an we'll walk over t'tbeck,' he murmured," alang t't'falls."

She was delighted to have her da to herself: something she very rarely managed as there were so many of them.

"Aye da." She skipped happily along beside him, holding his hand, until they got to the point where the water rocketed over the stones, making a soft roar as it splashed along. Sitting on a rock he bade her sit beside him. She was content to just be there and sat beside him in silence, waiting for him to speak.

On the walk across John had been trying to understand what was impossible to understand, but now decided it just had to be accepted. He would never understand.

Holding her face in his work worn hands, he looked into her pale eyes.

"Thee has a gift dowter, but thee mun 't tell anyone else this."

"Why not da?"

How could he say that people might think she was a witch. His beautiful daughter.

"Thee mun't tell anyone."

"But da."

"And thee mun't speak o' it again."

"Ah had t'tell thee da. Grandma said ah had t'tell thee."

He remembered now, his ma's whispered conversations, seemingly to no-one, when he was a young boy, and his da's reaction when he asked him who his mother was talking to when he could see no-one. And now this that had been buried in his memory, made sense. Smiling down at her, because he didn't want her to think that she was in any way at fault, he laughed and told her about his ma, and what he remembered. It was important that she realised that they shared this story, because no-one else could be a part of it.

"Ah kna tha'il finn'it 'ard ta unerstan'. Thy ma and kin'll see summat fond in thy tellin', so, dinnit tell."

"Dinnit tell iver, da?"

"Thee n'uz can keep it t'thee n'uz," and he laughed.

She and her da had a secret to keep.

She could keep a secret, and she did. For many years.

******

There had now been two whole years without new babies. Two years for the family to take stock and get itself righted. Betty was now working at the village store. She'd had enough of being a barmaid and having the old men leer after her. Daytime work suited her better. Mary and Kit Clark owned the store, but were getting on in years, so they were very glad of the help, and Betty was such a good worker that eventually they couldn't do without her. She was able to take some of her weekly wages in food, and that helped the family finances more than money.

Peggy was teaching Jane and little Peg to knit. They sat together on the settle, knitting in time together, so that their arms lifted and fell together, and the rhythm helped them to keep going. Because of her poor eyesight Christian was not included in this, but she loved to hear the girls, as they sang while they knitted. Eventually she asked for a knitting stick, and taught herself, by listening to the others. Peggy wasn't hopeful of a result but was amazed at the work that Christian produced. It was neat, and there were no stitches dropped. The result was perfect. Adults didn't need to see what they were doing, but it was unusual for a child to produce work as good as this, especially at such a young age.

And now the time had come, and Daisy, the bull calf, so named by the children, was led away to be slaughtered.

"Where you takin our Daisy?" asked Edward, in a belligerent tone. He was the one who had spent the most time hand feeding the bullock with grass and talking to the animal. There was no way that John could tell him. No way at all. It would break Edward's heart. John said he was just taking him for a walk to the farm, to see if Daisy liked it there. Then he might stay there, he said.

Edward cried, and wanted to go too, but wasn't allowed.

John had been keeping a good eye on both his young boys after the terrible thing that happened to Jemmy and was very protective of them. He left it to Peggy to look after the girls.

The calf was duly butchered, and the meat cured then smoked for the winter. Although Edward and Christopher, or Kit, as he was now known, often asked after Daisy, they were told that he was now living on the farm and the farmer would not allow them to visit. He was much too busy!

"Back end" was followed by winter. It was wet and blustery, with gusts that nearly blew the tree down over the lane from their cottage. They spent a night in fear of that happening and were pleased to go outside the next morning to see that the winds had abated, and all seemed to be well. The roof was off the privy, but John could fix that. It was time for Meadow to be taken inside for her winter housing, and that meant that they would now be using up their store of hay.

And there was news of Mary.

She'd written to say she was visiting for Christmas. It was unusual for her to have any time away from work at this time of year, so they hoped that all was well. Betty knew what trouble she'd had at her last place of employment, so hoped that it wasn't more of the same.

It meant a lot to Betty to be able to see her older sister again, and she looked forward to the day, as did Michael for they would spend some of the time talking about Miles, and their memories. For John it meant seeing the daughter that he'd vowed to always protect, and now never saw. How could he look after her if he didn't see her? But she was twenty-five summers now, and a woman. Thank God, at least she seemed to be making her own way. His wish each evening as he lay before sleep was that she was happy. And thinking about things, it was well past when she should be looking for her own husband. Maybe that was why she was coming home? He still called it her home, even though she'd never lived there.

The children were washed and in clean clothes the day she was meant to be coming. The floor had been swept and the chamber pots emptied. Betty knew that Mary would be used to a cleaner environment, and one that did not smell of human bodies and excrement. The shock of that memory was still with her. Living as they did, just like their neighbours, they weren't aware of it themselves, but Mary and Betty had been used to having to keep themselves clean and help to keep a clean house for their employers. That was the difference now.

Christmas for everyone meant the yule candle and the yule log wrapped in hazel twigs as well as the traditional kissing bough. Peggy wanted a garland for the door seeing as Mary was coming, and the boys were dispatched to find holly, mistletoe and ivy, with a special warning not to eat the mistletoe berries as Peggy knew they were poisonous. The adults brought ivy and holly into the cottage, to dress it. And again, the children were treated to a small gift from Mary this time, a halfpenny each, enough to buy some candied sweets, and that was all they wanted.

Once the young ones were asleep, Mary, Michael and Betty reminisced about their time in the Valley. Their memories of their mother were shared too. John, too young to remember, listened with a wistful look, and asked more and more about her, what she looked like, what she wore, how she treated them. He only had Peggy to compare her to, and it seemed that she was a poor comparison, although no-one said as much. And Peggy realised that she couldn't compete with a dead woman, who could never now do any wrong.

It turned out that Mary was not there with any great news. She was just missing her family. That was what she told her father.

What she told Betty was entirely different. She was in love, as in all great love stories, with the son of the house. And of course, he loved her. They couldn't be together now because it would cause a scandal, but as soon as his father, who was now very ill and quite old, died, then he would marry her. Betty, a bit more worldly wise than her sister, despite being younger, knew that would not happen.

Mary told Betty all about him and gave her more information than she needed. Too much in fact! But Betty knew that the servant girl did not marry the gentleman. There was only one way this was going to end, and that wasn't well. She tried to persuade Mary, to make her see how she would never be happy and could end up being very unhappy: that her reputation would be ruined.

Mary retorted with, if that was the case, it was ruined anyway as she did not intend to make a secret of anything, and neither did he. She was adamant.

And so, on the day after Old Christmas Day, Mary began the long journey back to where she said her heart lay. The first part of the way she rode on the cart pulled by Sorrel and driven by her da. She was able to talk to him about the house she lived in. She would have loved to tell him more but had enough sense at least to keep it to herself. Then John made sure she was able to beg a ride with a carrier wagon. And it was three long years before they heard anything of her again.

Very soon after that Christmas, the Widow Alderson, passed on, at the good age of sixty-five. She'd been a help to Peggy and was very much missed. The children had usually visited her when they went along the row to their grandmother's, and she always kept a small amount of candied peel for them. They also had living in the row, William Harker, one of the Overseers for the poor for Muker and vestry clerk. It was one of his responsibilities, together with the Constable, to dispense relief. He didn't have much himself either but would not ask for relief. That was the irony.

Peggy had been forty when William was born, and John forty-eight. He didn't know where the years had gone. He'd been married to Peggy for twelve years, and to Alice for thirteen years before that. And as far as he could count he'd fathered eighteen children so far. And five of them were dead already. He knew that a Blacksmith's life was better than a miner's, who had a much shorter life, but there was very little more for them to do in the dales apart from farming. He worried for Michael and young John, one in the mine and one in the smelt mill. It's true that some people attained a great age, like Elizabeth Guy, who had lived till her ninety third year. And he wondered, and not for the first time, when his time would be.

Chapter 18

One for the Pot

"Each day hez its care"

(Yorkshire saying)

Because of the French Wars with Boneparte, the Militia, the local fighting force, had been reconvened, and many villages were having trouble filling their quota. All able-bodied men between the ages of eighteen and fifty were eligible for the ballot and if they wanted to duck this responsibility they had to find a substitute or pay a £10 fine, an amount well out of reason for the common man. John was exempt as he had children under fourteen years. Michael was still keen. It would be an adventure, he said, and he would be paid for his service. And what's more, the 'regimentals', the uniform they wore, would earn him the notice of many young lasses.

Muker Parish Overseers had been sent to Reeth and Marrick part of the Muker parish, to demand their quota, with differing success, and it was feared that substitutes may have to be hired. That would be great thought Michael, and he let it be known that he volunteered as a substitute if anyone needed him. He was twenty-one now and the right age he thought for some adventure. He waited and while he waited he once more joined the Loyal Dales Volunteers.

Invasion by France was a great threat to everyone and these men, as well as the Militia were the ones to stop it, or so they thought. But despite wanting to be involved, there was no opportunity for fighting for Michael.

He stood out in the field shouting, "Come on Boney. Do your worst!" And was lucky the Militia didn't take him away.

Young John had a new hobby, and that was poaching. There was always enough to eat but this brought them more meat. Poaching was actually a very dangerous occupation, and the penalties were severe, but John knew the gamekeepers, and they knew him.

One evening he'd bagged himself two rabbits and a grouse and was very pleased with himself only just managing to get home before the gamekeeper caught him. He'd sat for hours in the bracken on the fell, cold and hungry, waiting for that grouse. But it had been worth the wait.

The rabbits he'd snared and only got away with the crime because the gamekeeper knew fine well who he was and what he was doing. Because he was a local lad born in Thwaite, they cast a blind eye. If they didn't, he could be imprisoned for many years and maybe face the gallows. Some poachers were even deported to Australia. The rewards certainly weren't worth that. It wasn't as if they were starving. He just liked the excitement. He managed six rabbits that year but only one grouse. That was all he dared to do. Walking into the cottage in triumph the first night with a rabbit, he was king.

"Look ma. Look whit ah've got fo' t'pot," and he dropped it on the table as it was, tied by the legs but thankfully dead.

"Ower John lad. Thee cud a'been caught and 'prisoned," she whispered to him. "Did the Constable does not see thee walking along wi'this?"

"Dis thee think me a dunderknowl? Get it inta yon pot."

Peggy had seen her ma dealing with rabbit and knew what to do. Splitting the skin at the back of its neck she pulled the skin over and down, like taking off a piece of clothing exposing the dark, mottled meat. Slitting its belly, she dragged out the innards with her hands, chopped the carcass into small pieces with the gulley and dropped it bones and all, into the cooking pot hanging over the fire. Adding water, potatoes and onions, she stewed the meat while she made some dumplings. Her cooking had certainly improved, thought her husband.

At mealtime that night there were audible groans of pleasure and thanks to John for catching the animal and to Peggy for cooking it. "Thee gan canny, lad. Not all o'them gamekeepers is gannin t'let thee gan."

"Ah knaw da, but whee's ganna miss a rabbit or two? Eh?"

"It's nay the missin. It's the catchin – o thee. Not the rabbit."

On grouse night it was plucked, dealt with and enjoyed, without all the small bones that had made the rabbit a little pickier to eat. Betty took a rabbit to the store, and it was gladly exchanged for bread, sugar and a pound of soap for the family, and no questions asked.

That Christmas, at T'Awd Roy there was the usual market, and the usual sports, hurdle jumping and pole jumping, as well as trotting matches and shooting at a target in the lane. Bills were settled with the Doctor, Blacksmith, meal merchant, and anyone who had extended credit to the miners so far.

Fiddler Coaty gave of his best at the dancing, and Betty enjoyed a spin around the floor with a few interested young men. There was one who seemed more interested than the others, John Pounder from along the houses. But she was far from ready to settle for that yet.

A Mummers Play held everyone's attention through the daytime. It couldn't have been a better Christmas, and no-one could have eaten more than they did.

1810

Having had two years without producing a child, this year was to produce an addition to the family. Peggy knew by Christmas for certain, and even before. She was bitterly disappointed as she'd hoped there would be no more, but it was God's will, and she accepted that.

The year was passing. Spring had been wild and wet, but they'd passed a fairly comfortable winter, thanks to Meadow's calf, Daisy.

At Easter time there was always great excitement among the young. It was time to choose who would be playing the star parts in the Mummers Play.

Michael breezed in one evening, proclaiming very proudly, "It's the play da, and ah's t'be Lord Nelson this time, just like ower Miles was."

Young John was just as proud.

"An ah's t'be Saint George," he shouted, pretending to spar with a sword and an imaginary dragon.

Laughing at them both, Peggy pronounced, "Thee'll both be the best there be," and left them to it.

Costumes and masks were provided and worn, as they went singing and dancing their way through village kitchens.

Wearing the Admiral's tricorn hat, red sash and eye patch, Michael made an excellent Admiral.

Another, Mickey Jack, was Julius Caesar, in his toga: a bed sheet wrapped and tied, and a wreath of ivy around his head.

But young John was the proudest, wearing the costume of Saint George, waving his sword around and pretending to look for the dragon that he was set on killing.

Local children and their parents led him around the village, telling him where the dragon might be, and he played his part by pretending to be so disappointed not to find it. Finally, he disappeared into the smithy, and with shouting and roaring the dragon was dispatched. When he emerged, it was with the end of his sword burned by the dragon's flames, but really burned in the forge fire to add authenticity.

He was the hero.

After singing and drinking plenty of liquor they presented a sorry sight together with many more of the local young men. Getting home was going to be difficult.

"Ere, Mickey," shouted someone who seemed to have drunk less than the rest.

"Gie uz an arm." Taking hold of Young John with his other arm he led them along to Scarr Houses.

"Home now," he laughed. "'Ere's thy Betty. And a lovely lass she is too," he whispered to her taking his chance.

Michael heard and began to giggle. "Ower Betty has a follower," he snorted.

She kicked him and pushing him into the cottage she was going to slam the door when she changed her mind. Looking back, she gave John Pounder one of her sweetest smiles before gently closing the door on him.

*****

After the last two boys, the next baby born to John and Peggy was a girl born one warm afternoon at the end of May. When thinking of a name Peggy thought how much she loved the name Christian, so this girl was named Christiana. However, at the church she was christened Chrissey, and called that for the rest of her life. The baby crib had long since been vacated by William and now it belonged to their new daughter. Blond hair. Green eyes. Her father's daughter.

That evening, as they all sat around the table, eating a fine rabbit stew from one of young John's contribution, Betty sat with the newborn in her arms. Peggy watched her and recognised the yearning look on her face.

"Thee don't want a bairn yet. Wait till thee be sure of the man," whispered Peggy. "Diven't dee what ah did."

"Me, ma? Not me. Thee shouldst think on Mary, not on me," and as soon as the words left her mouth, she wished they hadn't.

At the sound of the name John lifted his head from his food and stared at Betty.

"Mary? What of Mary" he quizzed.

Betty looked from one to the other. Should she tell Mary's secret? It wasn't hers to tell, she knew that. But how could she keep this to herself?

So she told.

Everything.

And as she told, she saw the clouds come over her da's face, at that moment making him look like someone she didn't even know.

At first she wasn't sure how to phrase it, but then just blurted it all out, watching it fall like a stone, onto the table in front of her.

"Oh da. Ah cuddn't tell. She was so happy. "Ower Mary's in love with a gentleman, "she told them. "And she thinks he'll wed her."

"Wed? That'd be a miracle, and not gannin t'happen."

"How long has thee knawn this, ower Betty," Peggy asked through gritted teeth.

"Since the last time she were 'ere ma."

John looked down at his plate of food, slowly chewing, then slamming his fist on the table he almost screamed at her, "Afta all the truble secrets caused for ower Jemmy, and thee dis it agin. Ower Betty, we said nee more secrets. Thee shud niver 'ave agreed t'keep it fro'uz," mouthed John, his voice raw with emotion.

Betty was shocked. Her da had never lost his temper. At this present moment she was frightened of what he might do. Young John looked from one to the other of the two women at the table and then at his da.

Pushing the table aside he stood up, and said, "We'll be gannin now ma. Pack uz a bite ter eat."

John placed his large work-worn hand over his son's in a placatory gesture.

"Plenty of time," he said. "We wait till morning."

That night Peggy lay beside her husband and listened to him feign sleep. She knew he wasn't sleeping because she knew the sounds his body made, how he breathed when in the thrall of sleep: how he murmured and twitched when giving into the unconscious state. But this night even as he lay all night with his eyes closed she knew he wasn't sleeping. She listened for the change in his breathing that signalled him falling into a deep sleep, but it never came. He dozed for a short while but woke with a start, immediately wide awake again. It was a long night for them both.

And for Betty too it was a night when sleep was impossible. Had she done the right thing? She'd done the only right thing! But what would Mary think?

Young John alone managed to sleep most of the night. He was convinced they would be bringing Mary home, so was not worried about the outcome.

"Be reet," he said to himself as he settled down to sleep.

Both John and Peggy were awake when he decided it was time to push back the covers. Leaning forward for his boots and pulling on his breeches he turned to Peggy and said,

"She'll be coming back wi' uz," and Peggy did not doubt it.

Betty was up too and standing with young John at the cottage door. He'd harnessed their fell pony Sorrel to the cart and was ready to go. Setting off in the early morning light, they made a sombre procession, with Betty walking with them to the edge of the village. The guilt she felt for keeping this secret, and for telling it, gnawed at her insides. She knew that Mary would never forgive her, but what did that matter if she kept her safe. Mary was her older sister, and no-one but she was looking out for her.

The fell pony trudged over the hill, through the top of Swaledale, past Keld and down into the Eden Valley, to Kirkby Stephen. The journey would have been pleasant, had the reason been less serious. It was peaceful, they passed no-one, and bracken and heather lined their path. The odd Curlew or Merlin flew above them, and bedraggled sheep ran as they approached. Once they had safely negotiated the hillside through the early morning mist they stopped a while to eat the bread and smoked bacon provided by Betty. A fresh cooling draught from the fast-moving stream refreshed them and they set off again, along the drovers' road into the town.

Their journey had begun in the early light and now it was nearing midday. The town was alive with people walking or driving their horse and carts along the muddy track around the town square.

Betty had been able to describe roughly where Mary might be living and so they headed to a prosperous-looking house on the edge of the green. Large trees surrounded it, as if keeping a guilty secret. A stone wall waist height edged the front garden and ran up to a gate, worked in metal, that John would have admired, had the day been more auspicious. Instead, he barely noticed it as he gave the cart to young John before striding through the gates without a word or a backward glance.

Dressed as he was, he would normally have gone to the back door, but not today. Today, he said to himself he would go to the front, and demand what was his. Banging sharply on the high wooden door, he stood back on his heels and waited impatiently for about ten seconds before rapping sharply once more. Hearing the commotion of voices inside he turned his head in time to see the heavy brocade curtain at the nearest window drop after a head, complete with white cap, had disappeared behind it.

The door was slowly opened and a man of mature years, dressed in livery, stood there – the butler.

Trained to be polite at all times, the butler asked,

"How can I help thee sir?"

The "sir" rather took John by surprise and took the wind from his sails. After such a gracious greeting he was unable to be rude or impolite himself.

"Mary. Uz're 'ere f'Mary Hutchinson. Sir," he added as an afterthought, which made it sound almost rude.

"What age sir, and what position?"

"Ower Mary is a bonny young lass, with fair hair and green eyes, and is," and here John had to think hard, "and is twenty-six summers. She's a lady's maid."

"Mary?" He paused and thought very carefully, seeing that this answer was particularly important.

"Well sir. We do have a Mary Harrison. She's the cook. And Mary

Milner. She's my lady's maid. We did have another Mary Fothergill, of that age, but she was a scullery maid."

So, she lied about her position, and her name. He knew this was her, but the butler had said, 'did have'.

"Here no longer then, for that be she," he said, resignedly. "Dust thee know where she went, and when?"

"I believe she left just after the Christmas season. Some problem at home, she said. I remember it left the kitchen rather shorthanded. The cook was very put out."

Now he knew they would be going home without her. It was a physical pain, this not knowing where, or how she was living. All he could hope was that she'd decided this life here was not for her and had sought another position.

He gave his thanks and turned to walk solemnly back along the path. Young John could see that it was not the news they were wanting by his da's demeanour and the way he walked, hanging his head.

"She's gone, five moons ago," he told him. "That's t'end o' that. Mebbee she'll come home. But she's mad 'er choice now."

And he refused to be drawn into any conversation about her, all the long, lonely journey home.

Inwardly he was seething with anger and disappointment. Angry that Betty hadn't told them sooner, after she kept Jemmy's secret, and disappointed that Mary had chosen this life. By the time they'd reached Keld he'd pushed these feelings down inside to the place where all the bad feelings were stored. As long as he kept them there he didn't have to deal with them and could pretend they no longer existed.

Riding through the village of Thwaite he spied Betty, with a basket on her arm talking in an animated fashion to a young man who seemed to be serious about something. Finally she smiled, then shaking her head she walked away in the direction of Scarr Houses. The young man stood and watched her as far as he could until she'd turned the corner and was no longer in sight but she didn't turn her head to look once.

'There's a story to tell there too,' John mused, meaning to ask Betty about it. But again, meaning and doing are worlds apart, so it was not done.

The mood was sombre and dark that evening when they were all home. Sitting at the table with her mending Betty said little: in fact, she said nothing. She daren't speak, feeling guilty as she did about not having spoken sooner. Maybe *she* could have made Mary come home. Jane, who had been looking forward to seeing Mary, was very disappointed that her da had not brought her home.

Her first words on seeing them, "But you said...." were shut down by Peg, who was worried that poor Jane would get the brunt of his anger. But they weren't allowed to talk of Mary again.

Jane was twelve years old now, and very naïve. This experience had put her off the idea of working in a large house like her sister, just in case the same thing should happen to her. As she had no idea how it happened to any girl it was best to keep away from the lads, she thought. At present she was gainfully employed helping Peg at home, but Peggy had been asking around the village to see if anywhere needed any help, for when Little Peg could take Jane's place.

Christopher (Kit) and Edward were back from their bird scaring and wood chopping and were sitting around the large, rectangular table. Jane whispered to them that Mary had not come home, but they were more interested in their usual kicking match under the table.

"When'll thee lads give ower," Peggy bellowed at them, but that was having less and less effect on them now. She didn't shout and scream as much as she used to, having mellowed a little with the loss of Jemmy and Will, but she was still one to watch.

Edward was a shy, sensitive little boy who went wherever Kit went as his little shadow, lacking the confidence that Kit showed in everything he did.

Kit was neither timid, nor unsure, but was an outspoken seven-year-old, used to giving his opinion, whether it had been asked for or not. It didn't matter to him. And for his age he had a lot of common sense.

He and Christian spent evenings talking about things they had seen. She was trying to teach him to read and write a little. Even at five years old she was the most educated person in the family, having educated herself.

She soaked up everything she saw and remembered everything she heard. The problem, and the huge drawback, was the lack of suitable reading material for her.

Her Sunday School teacher, daughter of the present vicar, had seen her potential and offered to help, providing books, paper and pencils. With these Christian made books for Kit herself, in her large sprawling writing and gladly oversaw his learning.

They spent the rest of the summer in the usual manner, working, eating and sleeping. John still had the pastureland he was renting across the lane, adjoining Thwaite Beck, and on it Meadow grazed contentedly. Her first calf had provided meat for the last winter, but Meadow was proving expensive to feed now. He couldn't guarantee that the small piece of land he farmed would provide enough of a decent crop for her fodder.

It was time for another change. The decision was made that Meadow would have to go to slaughter that autumn, and in her place, to provide the family with milk, they would get a goat. John had even set about seeing if he could come to an arrangement with a fellow villager, to provide his services in exchange. Then they would still have milk. The taste was different, but they'd get used to it.

The next week he had some news, but not for the ears of the children.

"Lackey Joss Will says he'll gi' us a milker goat for a share in t' beef."

"How much own a share?" asked Peggy, always to the point.

"He wants half ont."

"Nah. Too much. Tell him we'll find another, and we can go three ways, but not two."

"Aye. Ah's sure he'll ken that owt's bettern nowt," replied John philosophically, with a faint smile on his face.

The third share was promised to the storekeeper. As they had no debt, it would buy them some groceries throughout the winter, at a set amount per week. There could even be some luxuries among this, such as scented soap for Betty, beef for the men, and cows' milk, as goats' milk took some getting used to. This arrangement suited the family. It meant that Peggy didn't have to spend hours each day milking, as a cow produced more than they could use or even sell but a goat produced just enough for a family. They would get used to the difference in taste and wouldn't be making butter, but Peggy was pleased about that anyway.

John thought about giving up the pastureland he was renting from Tony Metcalfe, over the lane. It was Michael, however, with his time spent working on a farm, who was a little more knowledgeable.

"Thee'll still need hay da, and a bit o'grain."

The geese lived where Bella Pig had lived so the pig pen had to be divided, with a share of the room for the goat. Thankfully it had been a large pigpen! A goat would eat most things but John listened to his son's advice that hay, and grain were needed to keep the animal healthy. And she would go to the common land in the summer.

He was happy to keep the land. That wasn't costing much, but he had no idea if it was costing more than buying the hay and grain for Jenny. He could still grow onions and potatoes though and even carrots. Kit and Edward would have to take care of that. They were good lads.

And he loved Peggy's onion pies.

That winter they had goose eggs, smoked beef, and a supply of staples weekly from the store, courtesy of Meadow. This time everyone knew where Meadow had gone.

To a neighbouring farm, of course, for a rest, and to be near Daisy!

Chapter 19

Family and Friends

"Cherish your human connections. Your relationships with friends and family"

(Barbara Bush)

1811

Peggy was forty-two years old now, and fervently, desperately hoped that her child-bearing day were over. Her body was tired after twelve pregnancies, and she was physically suffering the effect. As she walked, depending on how fast she walked, she leaked from her bladder. When necessary, she wrapped her voluminous under petticoat through the top of her legs to absorb it. But she had to go on.

Her first child Ruth was seventeen now and was living with relatives in Bowes. Or rather she was a servant in the household, or so she had heard.

She and her daughter had not spoken since Ruth left the village, three years before. And prior to that Ruth had been living with Peggy's mother, her grandmother, who had recently died.

The funeral had been a large affair. The Pedleys were great in number in the dales, and also great church goers. The address, by a visiting preacher, had been very stirring, and unlike any Peggy had heard before. It made it noticeably clear, leaving no doubt that if you had sinned at all, you were going to Hell.

Peggy had been thinking about this ever since and was worried she might end up in the wrong place. Sitting talking around the fire, as they did every evening, Peggy asked John, "Well, where duz thee reckon uz be gannin John?"

Looking at her worried face he mocked, "Were duz thee ken?

Into the ground awld lass. That's where we be gannin. And that's that."

Putting his arm around her shoulder, he hugged her. It was something he never did, so she was taken aback by this show of feeling.

"As lang as thee's there an all. That's all I wan'," sighed Peggy.

That winter the beck was frozen over, making it difficult to get fresh water from anywhere, but they had to try. Peggy came back from church and told John the news that the wide river in London had completely frozen over, so they said. It was three times as wide as the Swale but was frozen solid. And they were having a fair on the ice. Actually on the ice!

Old Dick Hamel who heard Peggy as he passed by her in the lane, had scoffed.

"There's been 'Frost Fairs' on t'river theear for yeears."

"But this yan be the biggers," Peggy threw back at him.

The drovers' report had said there had even been an elephant. She would have to ask Christian what that was. As she drifted off to sleep that night her mind took her to this fair, and she was skating along, with her John, and they were the best skaters at the whole of the Fair.

*****

There was a school in Muker and if you were lucky and deserving enough a place was paid for your child.

John had tried each year to find a place for one of his lads but had been unlucky. And it had happened again. But this time he couldn't believe that there was a lass when he had boys who were much more deserving. All lasses needed to be able to do was keep house and have babies he thought. You didn't need book learning for that.

How come Mary Clarkson, Lackey John's lass, was given a place? It wasn't fair. And when he looked into it further he found that Betty Harker had been given a place the term before that. His Kit and Edward were surely as deserving of this as anyone.

He took himself to the next select vestry meeting and asked why. John Alderson, chair of the committee took John's question. They all deliberated and then gave their answer.

"We understand that you want your boys to be educated at the township's expense."

"Aye. Poverty's nee crime, but it feels like it."

"This is for t'poor folk villagers settled in Muker. Thee has been living here for fourteen years, bit fer many years thee were settled in tha parish of Mallerstang, in Westmurlund." He finished by adding, "Cum back t'next year and we'll 'ave another gander at it."

John was utterly deflated. It seemed that he belonged neither to Mallerstang nor Muker. He had been born in Thorns, a village in the Muker parish, but that seemed to count for nothing. All he could do was accept it and watch more lasses and some boys being educated at the school, more than once,

Even though he felt that people didn't need to be book-learned to have a good life he had always wanted his children to have as much education as they could. They were learning a lot at Sunday School, but he knew they could learn a lot more. Especially Christian, who didn't seem to need to be taught anything. She just seemed to know. How he wished she could go to school.

Christian's eyesight was improving as she grew. She spent the long summer evenings teaching her siblings all about the local wildflowers that they had seen as well as any birds and insects. She couldn't just go for a walk through the meadow fields and along the lanes. She needed to have a purpose. When they all returned home from such walks she gave them each a pencil and paper, given to her from Sunday School and asked them to draw what they'd seen. Then they talked about these flowers and she gave them their names, helping them to write them. Edward tired of this, but Kit never did. Little Peg usually produced the best drawings and Jane was jealous. There was always an undercurrent of competition between these two girls.

That summer they all learned more about the place they called home from a sister who was only six years old but who knew more than any of them.

The two youngest boys wanted to be like their da and big brothers, but there wasn't much they could do except the usual bird scaring and driving the horses when they were strong enough. It brought them a duck egg now and then, and some hay for their goat that they'd called Jenny. Edward, now seven, worked at it for a full week for one shilling, and for that Peggy could buy a pound loaf. He was seven years old and there wasn't much else for him to do, unless he went to the mines. At nine years now Kit was earning money as an ore dresser at the lead mine where Miles had started. He didn't want to be a miner, but that was what young John did, and there didn't seem to be much else.

Michael was still working at the smelt mill. He went to the fairs, and had even been to Kirkby Fair a few times, but his problem was that he spent his time wagering his money at the booths where you were sure to lose your money and sure never to win.

The game he played the most was *"Find the Penny"*, and he lost every time, in common with all others who played, apart from the stooge in the audience.

He saw the booth owner put a penny under one of three cups. These were then shuffled around. The idea was you put your stake money on top of the cup that you thought was hiding the penny. The prize was a gold sovereign, and very well worth winning, with the players shown this shiny gold coin at the beginning of every game.

Talking to Lackey Will, who actually never played, he couldn't understand why he didn't win. The sovereign was always won by someone in the crowd, and they didn't seem particularly clever.

So why couldn't he win it?

He watched and watched and watched, always sure he had his eye on the right cup but when it was picked up there was nothing there. On more than one occasion, after a few mugs of ale he had accused everyone of cheating and once almost came to blows. It was up to Awld Mick to put him out of his misery and tell him eventually that the lout who 'won' the sovereign was a stooge. That he'd been planted in the crowd and was in the pay of the booth owner. And that there never was a penny underneath any cup. It was all sleight of hand. Michael would never win the sovereign. No-one could win. Feeling a fool he went back to the Inn and spent the remainder of his money on ale. At least he knew that was honest robbery.

The summer came and brought with it the much talked about goat, instead of Meadow the cow. She was a nanny goat, and they had called her Jenny. An amiable creature, she loved having her neck scratched and being hand fed and didn't need much looking after, spending the day grazing on common land.

A veritable scavenger she ate anything she saw. Anything. Peggy had to be careful if she put out clothing to dry, as if her mouth could reach it, Jenny would eat it, as sure as not. She ate any vegetable matter, any clothing and absolutely anything else that was in her way. She spent the summer tethered and then overwintered in the outbuilding behind the cottage, being brought out on fine days and she loved the fine days. Bella's pen had proved to be too small for geese and goat.

The children loved her and stroked her but had to be careful with the clothes they were wearing in case they became a snack for Jenny. One advantage of having a goat was that the rubbish heap didn't have a chance if Jenny could reach it. Kit sometimes led her round to it, just to see what she would actually eat.

Good Times

Sitting together, in companionable silence one evening, John was wakened out of his doze by Peggy, who had a suggestion.

"Whit abaht a toffee join?"

A 'toffee join' was a social evening where neigbours joined together and made toffee. She loved evenings like that where all got together and had a laugh forgetting about the trials of life, even for a brief time.

"Ah naws Betty 'n Lackey Jim'll cum. So will Bella an'her Jack," chirped Betty.

"If thear ax'n and they're be appy to cum. Thars already axed so the job's a gud yan," replied John, looking sideways at her.

"Appen un o'tothers 'll cum toa," she wondered, thinking aloud. Her mind was on Kit Guy.

He was a man who always had a ready smile for her, for all the women. Such a flirt, he was always talking to the women in the store, paying them outrageous compliments, even begging for a kiss. All in wholesome fun of course.

His wife was a lovely kind woman, and she didn't deserve her husband's reputation. Nevertheless Peggy invited them both and they said they would be happy to come. Later that week, most of

Scarr Houses gathered at the Hutchinson household, ready for an evening of merriment and jollity, bringing a chair if they had one, and a pack of cards too.

Kit Guy teased Peggy more than a little, but she, as well as the other ladies, lapped it up this evening, simpering and laughing at his saucy comments. While this was happening Betty kept out of such goings on and stirred the pan of butter and treacle in a brass pan over the fire.

"Thee hast a bonny smile," Kit almost purred to Peggy, sidling up to her and putting his arms over her shoulders to rest them on the wall behind.

"But Kit, it's awl for thee," she replied, smiling at him and laughing in his face.

She knew what her John would say if he came into the kitchen at that moment, and what he would do to their neighbour. Bearing that in mind, she ducked out of Kit's way, knowing it was all innocent fun. She knew she wasn't the only object of his affection but would have loved it if she were. All the ladies came in for the particular charms of Kit Guy that evening. It did no harm, she thought, and it made the evening.

The butter and treacle had simmered in the pan until it was the right consistency, and it was left to set. The toffee was eagerly awaited, and finally it was sufficiently cooled and ready, with the pieces that were tapped off, handed round and greatly enjoyed.

Betty had learned how to play Whist while away, and tried to teach them the rudiments, that evening, but it was a sorry affair. They knew the four suits but found it difficult to grasp the rules of the game. They just laughed and poked fun at each other, which made them laugh all the more.

"Cum om Peggy. Set thee een on thy cards," giggled her partner.

"But ahs luckin' a ma cards. What dis thee want uz t'see?" she asked, giggling back, then snorting with laughter while she tried to remember what it was she had to do next.

"This is a reet tricky game o' cards," she laughed, and snorted again. Looking at her partner, who had the same problem, she collapsed over the table, her body now almost incapacitated by this wonderful feeling of total abandon.

Betty shouted, "Ma. What's thee doin'?"

Peggy lifted her head and said, "Betty. Ah's playin cards, an ah's laffin that reyt hard that it's proper nippin me belly." This caused her to begin an infectious giggle that spread from one to the other, round the table, ending the prospect of any card game that night. Even though they couldn't play Whist at all it didn't matter. They had a night of happiness, laughter and neighbourly togetherness that made their life of hardship more bearable, and the winter for however long it lasted, seemed less long.

1812

Spring that year was very cold, and very wet. In February and March the rain was so severe, and the ground was so cold that any seeds sewn could not germinate. As well as heavy rainfall Snow had fallen in March making the ground even colder. But the weather was not the event that made the Hutchinsons sit up and take notice that winter. They were more than used to that.

It was of course news of Mary that came earlier in the year.

John's sister Jennet, who lived in the Mallerstang Valley at Hanging Lund Farm, sent them word that she'd seen Mary in Kirkby Stephen just before T'Awd Roy, and that her belly was swollen with child.

" Aw Mary, Mary," Betty sobbed. "Thee's a daft lass."

They all knew that consorting with a 'toff' would not end well. And this seemed to prove them right.

"If'n a lass's the mind t'dee it, can't nee'un stop her," commented Peggy in a commonsense kind of way.

Mary had been living with Jennet, before she left for the household John had visited, and had left that one for the same reason - being too familiar with the young men.

"Why dis she need to chase what she cannit have?"

"Ah s'ppose she's just a poor lass who wants moare," sighed Betty. "We'll have t'nip on'n'find her."

"N'fetch 'er ooame?" questioned Peggy, as she looked at John, unsure what his reactions would be.

"Why aye fetch her home awld lass. Whit else can we do? She's ma bairn. "

Once more they set off on the journey, waiting till daybreak gave them the most light. But this time John borrowed a larger cart and Galloway, in case there was a baby to transport. Betty went with them, so she could persuade, if necessary. They all knew how stubborn Mary could be. There was snow on the hillside, and in some places along the high road it was a perilous route. If it were not for the special reason John would never have attempted this journey in this weather at this time of year.

All the way he thought about the day he had held that beautiful baby, looked into her little eyes, and promised to look after her for the rest of her life. She had always been special but he'd seen precious little of her in the last fifteen years. She was a grown woman of twenty-eight years now, and ought to have known better than this.

And another thing was troubling him. They had no idea where to look once they did reach the town. Alice's sister Elizabeth lived near so they thought they may as well call there to see if there had been any news. As they drew nearer John became increasingly restless, and more aware of the leaden ball in his chest. Here was another child he had let down. Perhaps he could have made more effort to find her the last time they looked? He had let her down just like he had let poor young Jemmy down. But now he had to put it right. Now he had the *chance* to put it right.

Betty saw them first. Two women, huddled against the cold by the stone market cross, one with a tightly wrapped bundle in her arms. With a rasping, sharp intake of breath she realized that one was Mary and the other, leaning in towards her, arms outstretched and talking earnestly, was Jennet. Large, soft white flakes were swirling in the air, falling and eddying gently around them, giving the scene an almost ethereal look. As they drew nearer Betty could almost physically feel the tension between the two. John pulled up, jumped out of the cart and ran across the icy square towards his daughter and his sister.

Mary had seen the movement without moving her head and now turned away hurrying as fast as her footwear would allow. But John was faster. He caught hold of her carefully and turned her towards him gently.

"Lass. Cum home," he whispered,

He looked into the bundle but could see instantly that it was nothing but a bundle of clothing, all her possessions. But then he saw the reason for them being held so tightly. It was to try and hide, what was impossible to hide.

Very soon she would be having a bairn.

"She's cumin back home wi' me John," Jennett gently told him. "She's just agreed. An ah can tak care o'her. "

"Like thee did the last time? No. No. Mary," he almost cried. He *had* to take her home. He *had* to save her.

At least he could save *her*.

But it seemed that she was already saved.

His soul was shattered by profound sorrow and overwhelming emotions as he realized he was not needed. Mary, after all these years, did not need him.

Her aunt, who had taken her in before, was going to do the same again. And what's more, it was what Mary wanted, it seemed.

"Da", she cried. "Da. Ah cannit cum 'oame yet. A'hm so ashamed."

"Tell me that man, and a''ll mak 'im marry thee."

"Dia!" She almost screamed. "No. That's not what ah want. Leave us be."

"She'll be safe with me John. Come after the bairn's born. Ah'll send word."

Betty couldn't watch any longer. Running towards her sister, sobs wracked her frame, and her face showed the sorrow she felt.

"Mary. We love thee. Cum home," she begged and shouted after her. Running towards her, she grabbed her arm and swung her round so they were face to face, but there was something in Mary that she had never seen before. A steely resolve, and a hard look, which made her drop the arm, and simply hug her sister.

"We'll see thee soon Mary," she whispered into her ear. And then let her go.

Realizing that there was nothing he could do to change the situation, John had to admit defeat.

Watching all of this, young John was tempted to try and follow her and make her tell him the name of the man who had done this, but if Betty was to be believed, Mary had loved him once. So why had he left her? And where was he now?

Betty knew there were many girls who had got themselves into this situation, her stepmother being one. They were looked on as to be pitied, a drain on the poor rate, and their children were called bybegots or bastards. If a claim was made on poor relief, then every effort was made to find out the name and whereabouts of the father of the child so a case for bastardy could be made, and the father made to pay, through the courts. In this case, Betty doubted whether Mary would give up a name anyway.

Mary left and climbed onto the cart with Jennnet, whose son William picked up the reins and urged the pony to carry them away, towards their farm at Hanging Lund.

Both Johns said nothing on the ride home. Father John was disappointed with himself in that he hadn't picked her up and carried her, kicking and screaming to the cart. Young John couldn't believe his da hadn't done the very same thing. But both knew that when Mary's mind was made up, there was truly little anyone could do.

She'd always been independent and strong-willed. And that was the reason she was in this predicament now. Betty had tried to reason with her, two years ago, but she wouldn't listen then, and she wouldn't listen now. She would never admit she'd been wrong, even when she was much younger. Stubborn. And willful. Every bit her father's daughter. Both in looks and in temperament. And they would have to accept that for now.

It was barely a week later when news was sent to them that a boy had been born, and the christening was to be held in Outhgill church, on 15th January. Excitedly they all climbed into the cart once more, borrowed from the local farmer, in exchange for shoeing the Galloway. There was Betty, Michael, young John, Jane, little Peg, Kit, Edward, Christian, Miles, William, and Peggy with Christiana, the youngest, now almost two years old. John took the reins and led them away, along the route, towards the Mallerstang valley.

January was an unforgiving month. The snow was deep in places, and several times John thought he would have to admit defeat. The only problem with that was that he was unable to turn around once he was leading the Galloway and cart over the hillside. They were committed to their journey and with young children too. The older ones got out and walked alongside, having to scoop away the snow from the wheels every now and then. Thankfully the winds had prevented the snow from laying too deep, and they were able to finish the journey, descending into Kirkby Stephen. Then they had to negotiate the route to Hanging Lund as they were all staying the night with Jennett.

It took them another five hours to finish the journey, and by that time they were all exhausted.

They were hungry, and thirsty, and cold, and tired, and were looking forward to getting down from the cart and seeing Mary and the bairn.

Christiana was the warmest, wrapped in her mother's shawl, and held against her tightly. The older children had kept the younger ones warm, but everyone was so pleased to arrive. Thankfully, it was a large farmhouse, with enough room for them all, as well as Jennett's remaining children who were still at home, now only four of them. Her husband Will had a large fire going and Jennett had a stew bubbling on the fire, with homemade bread.

She was a marvellous baker.

Mary was sitting in front of the log fire nursing her baby boy. As yet they didn't know what his name would be. Mary had got over her predicament as she'd been made so welcome here with her aunt. But when she saw her family it all flooded back and filled her face with a red blush of shame.

"Oh da. Oh Betty," and she began to cry, silent tears.

Peggy went up to her and sat by her knee. "Thee's a grand lass Mary. Tis the men who get away with this. There's love for thee, much love for thee. Ah knaws how thee feels, and mah heart aches for thee, my darling lass."

Reaching forward, Mary hugged her stepmother, and Peggy kissed her neck.

"Now, let's be seein this bairn," said Peggy.

He was like his mother, and like his grandfather. But there was something else about him, a shape of the face that was nothing like their family. They passed him around, kissed him, smiled at him, and rocked him gently in their arms.

Jennett brought out supper with some homemade ale and everyone was happy. The young ones slept where they lay and everyone found a place to sleep for this night.

Mary tried to give her earnings that she'd been determined not to spend to her da, but he wouldn't hear of it.

"Get sum clathes fur't'bairn," he said gruffly and hugged her close.

"Oh da," she sobbed, "Ah's so sorry."

"Dinet thee be sayin that."

There was a twinkle around his eyes that she knew was tears, and to hide this, he turned away quickly and left the room.

The next morning they had to set out early to reach Outhgill in time for morning service. A name had not been discussed, but at the service, John was so pleased to hear that his first grandchild was to be called Miles. A good family name. The name of the child's great-grandfather and also his uncle.

After the service, they set off home immediately and were able to reach home late that evening. The stars helped their way, and the moon lit their path. Mary still would not come with them and was happy staying with Jenett, and now John was happy for her to stay. She hadn't felt that she could return yet. But maybe she would later.

The next morning Michael and young John set out for the mill and mine, Betty for the store, John for the forge, William for the farm, while Jane, Little Peg and Peggy got on with looking after the little ones and feeding everyone.

Life went on.

Chapter 20

Another Happy Time

"Self-belief and hard work will always earn you success."
(Virat Kohil)

It was springtime, and since coming from Jennet's Peggy had decided to sweep out the cottage every week, thinking she could make more of an effort. She'd baked more too and even tried making her own bread.

And Jane now fourteen was determined to earn some extra money.
"What about uz takin' in washin' ma?"
Peggy was not one to wash very often but understood that others did.
"If thee can find customers," she replied, "but dinnit forbye thy knittin."
At the end of that week Jane had two households who were prepared to give her a chance. They knew already that her mother was 'a stranger to wash day' and said they wouldn't pay if they weren't satisfied.
She took instructions from Betty who also loaned her money to buy

the necessary soap. Boiling the water was an issue. Jane asked her da if he had a large pan lying around the forge that she could have. And Peggy had to supervise the transferring of the hot water.

Jane took in the washing with a smile on her face, and spent an entire day with each load, boiling water, scrubbing shifts and shirts inside and out, steeping, rinsing and drying, until the whites were as white as they could be. Anything else was not such a problem. At the end of the week she had two satisfied customers and was able to add a few shillings to the weekly budget. She was proud of her small contribution and decided that if Little Peg helped her, they could add another customer. Even Christian helped. She filled the wooden water butt from the stream, sorted the dirty washing, hung the clean washing on the bushes to dry taking care not to let it drag in any dust or dirt, and generally did anything she was asked that she could physically do.

It was a huge success.

They had plenty of customers but of course they needed new customers every week, as once washed it would be a few weeks before most village folk would want their underclothes or sheets, washed again.

The venture lasted all that summer until the weather was so wet that clothes took too long to dry. Peggy wouldn't have someone else's shift steaming dry by her fire.

Mary visited them twice over the summer but couldn't be persuaded to come back to Thwaite to live. Betty thought about Jennet's well ordered, and cleaner home and thought that she would probably feel just the same!

Baby Miles was growing to be mostly a Hutchinson, in looks anyway and John was grateful for that.

And Betty. She'd spent the year growing closer to the good-looking young man who'd flirted with her at T'Awd Roy, and the Autumn Fair. Whenever these two were seen together, their heads were in close proximity, and it was either laughter or earnest words that were to be heard from either of them.

John had not spoken to her about this and was determined to do so and very soon. In fact it was his topic of conversation that very evening.

"Nah then ower Betty," he began. Betty looked up. There was something in his tone that made her listen intently.

"Thee's getting t'knaw a young man, and uz needs t'talk."

"Oh da, ah's not daft."

"Neither was ower Mary," he replied, maybe a touch too quickly "Thee's ma first lass to do sum courtin, and uz'll dee it proper."

Seeing her face he stifled a smile. She was so embarrassed, he could tell.

"I'f tha wants ta keep seein' this young lad, fetch 'im 'ome wi tha frae church, on Sunday."

Very contritely, Betty asked, "An can uz walk home t'gether?"

"Why aye, coz thee ma and sisters'll be wi'yee."

So that's how it went.

It progressed to calling for her Sunday mornings for church, their shoulders just touching as they walked along the beck side, her family tagging along behind.

After a couple of months he became more daring and held her hand to help her over the steppingstones. He'd even put his arms round her and lifted her gently over a deep puddle after a particularly heavy rainstorm.

The family were engrossed with watching the romance of this gentle sweet relationship develop. And Jane was ever hopeful she was going to be a flower girl soon.

He picked flowers for her on the way home and presented them to her at her door. She pressed some of them and gave then to him as a keepsake inside a large, red heart shape, coloured with beetroot juice and with her name below.

Betty seemed happy with the young handsome man and he seemed to be more than happy with her. He saw that she was truly kind and not the least bit selfish. He knew she worked hard and was a particularly good cook and baker. The fact that she was pretty and liked him back was all he needed for the moment.

There was no reason to believe that Betty had 'fallen'.

"Ower Betty's keepin' 'ersel right," whispered Peggy to John, one night, as they lay together.

"Aye, it seems so," he replied, and lifted himself up on one elbow so that he was looking into her eyes to let her know that he knew what this was all about. They no longer kissed. Most married couples didn't. But the rest of married love was still a frequent occurrence. Later that night as they settled down to sleep Peggy laid her head on his strong chest while he wrapped her in his arms as they drifted off to sleep. Feeling the steady pulse of his heart beating she thanked God that she'd found a good man, for as long as they may be together.

Later that year in the autumn time she felt the usual, and now remarkably familiar stirrings in her belly. She already knew what was coming but had hoped she was wrong. It would mean three years since the birth of Christiana: the longest she'd ever been without a new bairn.

But they had quite a different family occasion to celebrate before that event. Betty and her beau, William Pounder were finally getting wed. It was planned for November, and there was no reason for it, except that the two young people were in love. November was a cold month to choose, but they didn't want to wait till spring.

Betty had been sewing a shirt for her intended, almost since that first visit. She thought pragmatically, at the time, if Will didn't wear it, it would be ready for another. Later she was to berate herself about this and was pleased she hadn't told this rubbish to anyone. While she had time before she was married, she sewed a baby layette and herself some new petticoats and linen chemises. Will had paid for the making of her new dress and bonnet, all in blue. This would then become her best go to church dress.

Looking at the pile of mending made her feel guilty so she spent any time she could showing Jane, a particularly good pupil, how to mend. At fourteen years she was soon able to unpick and turn a garment to make it look like new.

The day the Hutchinsons' chose was a Thursday, the 26th of November in 1812, and the Banns had been read in church for three consecutive Sundays before.

On the day there was great excitement. Jane thundered down the stairs and scattered into the room where she began a wispy, fairy-like dance around anyone there.

"It's t'day. Ower Betty is weddin' her Will t'day," and she reeled around the room, singing this at the top of her voice.

Betty appeared at the bottom of the stairs.

"Thee looks like a fetch, ower Betty. Best get out and get theesen some water from the barrel. This was a jest, as Jane had water on to heat already for Betty, for she knew she would want a bath. The largest vessel was brought out, and the doors barricaded while Betty put fragranced oils into the water and washed herself, everywhere. Jane was the only one allowed to be there, as she was the 'bride's helper', she had decided. Clean dry rags were provided for Betty to dry herself and then it was the turn of the new petticoats, (two of them) and a linen chemise. Jane helped her into these garments and whispered, "Betty. Dis thee think ah can gan in the watter after thee?"

"Why Jane, as the bride's helper, it is expected that you will."

"Can Little Peg wash after uz?"

"Why aye she can."

Soon Little Peg and Christian had washed too, but the boys were not to be persuaded, except they would rub a wet rag over their face and wash their hands, exclaiming 'uurgh' to the lovely fragrance coming from the tub.

Standing at the bottom of the stairs, Jane bellowed, "Ma, Da, dis the want some fresh watter fetched in fur a wash?"

"Aye pet", Peggy shouted back. "Ower Jane's mor excited than the bride," Peggy whispered to John.

"Better get oot o bed then,"

Jane was wearing a dress she'd turned, from Jennet, and she looked very pretty.

There were few flowers available for a posy, so Betty had made one from holly and ivy growing in the hedgerows together with a sprig or two of fir and mistletoe. Jane too had a posy, as the bride's helper, and had decided that Little Peg and Christian were the bride's helper's helpers.

So, Jane exerted her superiority over the other girls. After all, she said to herself, she had waited the longest.

All the girls carried a posy made by Betty. She wound a sprig of ivy, with a little berry holly, around her own beautiful dark hair, and of course around Jane's!

The farmer's cart was put into use once more, also decorated with winter greenery. Ivy was wound around its sides, interspersed with berry holly, and even the Galloway had a sprig attached to her head band. Family and friends walked alongside the cart, and followed along behind, singing, the most popular song being *Amazing Grace*. It took them to the edge of the village of Muker where they left the cart and walked through the village and up to the church, Betty and her Will together, preceded by Fiddler Coaty playing the popular tunes and Betty waving and smiling all the way.

Jane, Little Peg and Christian were flower girls, but Jane said she was the 'most important flower girl,' being the oldest, and the 'bride's helper.'

Betty was an extremely popular girl and there were many people who had turned out to wish her well despite the coldness of the day. Making their way up the side of the church and inside they walked up to the altar in this small parish church where the vicar, James Bannister, read out many scriptures. Christiana fidgeted and ran up and down the church, with Peggy chasing after her, and John growling at her, "Fetch that bairn 'ere ower Peg."

Betty was totally unaware of the escapades of her three-year-old sister. She was too excited about her own escapades. For months, her days had been spent daydreaming, since she had first set eyes on him if she was honest. The idea of marriage was exciting but worrying too, and she'd spent many hours thinking of how she would spend the rest of her life with William. They repeated their vows in front of their family and friends and knelt at the altar where the vicar made sure that they knew exactly why they were getting wed. The marriage was recorded in the Marriage Register and signed in front of and by witnesses and the vicar.
Betty was as happy as she could possibly be. William was as lucky

as he could possibly be.

They just knew they would have a happy life together and it was beginning now, this very day.

After the service they made their way back to Scarr Houses where there was food waiting for them, including the usual mutton pie. The young girls were excited, thinking of their turn at this important event. They danced around the room, singing the words from the old English song, Greensleeves which everyone knew and everyone liked.

All of their neighbours had helped with food and there was certainly enough to eat.

Throughout, Mary sat in the corner of the room, with baby Miles, and although she would never begrudge Betty her day, she felt sad that she probably wouldn't have that day herself. John was so proud of his daughter Betty and made it known whenever he could, as often as he could. They were going to live in Thwaite village, near to the village store. She didn't have a bairn in her belly, but time would prove that, and that was just how it was.

That night she was nervous, but so was Will. She was also as naïve and innocent as her younger sisters. But very soon she was as knowledgeable as anyone. "Ah cannit reckon it. At wid niver have reckoned that's how uz makes bairns," she wasn't too shy to tell Will.

They settled into family life while John and Peggy announced their new arrival for the coming February. It was another girl. That made six boys and six girls for her and John. A good-sized family if all had lived.

Where had all the years gone, John wondered, looking down at this little scrap, his latest daughter, because she was so extraordinarily little. He stroked her head, and kissed her forehead, whispering, "Welcome little bairn. I wonder what's in store for thee."

Watching him, Peggy was thinking some of the same thoughts herself. They'd been wed for seventeen years and together for a year more. He'd been hers for longer than he'd belonged to Alice, yet she had always felt that she was second best. Right from the start she'd set out to trap him and she'd succeeded but had never felt proud of the fact. She wondered if it had ever occurred to him how he'd been caught. A fish on a line, he'd been pulled to shore and then finally netted.

She would have been happy if she'd known that at that moment John was thinking how lucky he'd been with both women in his life. He'd never felt trapped. He just felt loved. They had been so vastly different but he loved them both the same. There was no favourite not after all this time.

Both he and Peg had agreed on a name for their little daughter, even though she was called 'scrap' for quite a while. Her name was Alice, but she was called Elvey.

By the time that Elvey was born Betty was just becoming aware that she was to be a mother around the end of August. A honeymoon baby. Hardly surprising, as they had certainly tried. She daydreamed about what her child would be like and whether a boy or a girl. It really didn't matter to her, but her husband she knew would like a boy.

Having been at home for most of Peggy's births, Betty knew what to expect but was still wary.

She spent the months waiting in, sewing, knitting and providing clothes for the baby, while her husband William made a wooden cradle, just like the one her father had made for Miles.

Nothing much changed, she thought.

Betty kept their cottage clean and very homely, with fresh wildflowers always in a pot on the table. When anyone visited their cottage the smell of home baked bread was tantalizing, and Betty could bake a wonderful pie. She swept the floor most days, and to Peggy's amazement, washed the bedding at least once a month, sometimes more, buying strong soap from the store where she worked to try and keep the lice at bay. She couldn't abide the thought of them crawling everywhere. It was an uphill battle that she was determined to win. John was unaware of what the difference was. Men didn't seem to notice but he just knew that it was a very pleasant experience calling on Betty and William.

She had put a little by at the store and bought some matching stoneware for the table, while her pans, made by her da, were well cleaned and even scoured. She'd had good training at her previous place of work.

Jane and little Peg were very envious of her clothes, and she'd promised to make them each a new dress. Jane hoped she'd still have the time to do it now and was jealous of the bairn before it was even here. But their sister Christian never even gave clothes a thought. She was happy with whatever she had.

She'd never talked about what she heard, for the last five years, the voices. She'd promised her da, but they were getting harder to ignore. The voices in her head were becoming more insistent, telling her that she should share the messages with their intended recipients.

Alice was the most insistent, with Grandma Fothergill a close second.

'Tell him this. Tell him that,' the voice went. But she couldn't. She'd been forbidden. So how could she?

There was one person she confided in, and that was Betty, who always listened to her, but bade her be quiet,

'In case they think you be a witch, dear sister.

"Betty. What can ah dooah?"

Some days the clamours in her head was so great that she wanted it silent for good. And that was when she talked to Betty. When she couldn't stand it any longer. But mostly it just whispered into her brain and talked of people long dead and often forgotten.

She was eight years old now, and could read most things she saw, but to be fair, none of the things she saw were difficult to read. Her eyes had improved somewhat, and she had a bible that she had read, cover to cover, twice, skimming over some of the more difficult words. That was about it, really. She read the catechism when they were at church, and loved Sunday School lessons so much that she wished they were every day. Betty brought some pamphlets home from the store sometimes, and she read them out to the family. Now and again the vicar produced a news sheet with information from the drovers as they passed through, and she eagerly looked forward to that. But it wasn't enough. And it never would be.

She loved visiting Betty, just like everyone loved visiting Betty. There was always fresh bread, and sweet dumplings, pies, and even a bite of cake. Some days just the smell from her oven was enough to feed you for the day. Betty had taken the goat's milk and was attempting to make some goats' cheese, with varying levels of success, but she would persevere. She never gave up on anything. She knitted as much as she could to finish her quota and could do this as she talked and walked just like Peggy. She remembered Peggy's mother grandma Pedley, teaching her and Ruth and how they used to race to see who could knit the faster. Or they would be singing knitting to the rhythm of a popular song. Betty had taught Miles too, but Michael had never mastered it. He'd been too much of a dreamer.

She didn't see much of Michael, these days. He was over the fell at the smelt mill weekdays and so tired that he slept most of the weekend. Young John was the same now he'd gone to work there too. She worried about her brothers, but they were the same as all young men who worked in the mine or at the mill. They were pale, tired and listless and often suffered from terrible stomach cramps.

With this in mind, Peggy had bought some "cure all" medicine from a travelling man at the last market day. While she watched from the back of the crowd a man came up and told everyone that he'd been cured of feeling ill and sick after a week of drinking this noxious brew. The medicine's man's claim was that anyone who drank this brew would be in "fine fettle" within days of drinking it. Peggy was easily persuaded that there was a cure in this bottle but despite young John and Michael having downed two bottles of this black, treacly brew between them, there'd been no noticeable improvement. All it seemed to do was make them sleep for an inordinate amount of time.

She hadn't given up hope and was praying there would be another medicine seller at the Fair this back end.

But before that there was a family event that brought joy to many. Betty and William had their first bairn, and it was a boy, just as Will had wanted. He was christened on 21st August 1813, and was given the name Thomas, after William's father.

Little Elvey had a nephew, only six months younger than herself. Jane, Little Peg and Christian were in their element. They had two babies to adore. And Christiana was only three years old, very baby like still, so they had a bairn each to dote on and look after. Betty didn't want to relinquish her baby to anyone for too long, whereas Peggy was extremely glad.

The Christening was cause for a family party and get together. Jennet and family came, and so did Alice' sister Elizabeth. They were all so pleased that Mary came too. Her son Miles was a year and a half now and walking wherever he was allowed. He was also talking a little, and better than Christiana, who was twice his age.

"Well muther. We 'ave a gran' family," John said proudly, after the service.

"Aye, that we dooah," she agreed, "but Mary mun worry thee."

"That lass'll niver be happy, wantin' what she canna have. 'Neeyan cn be happy wi'that," mused John.

"Well Miles's a fine yung lad so we mun be happy wi' that f'now, if'n she'll fetch 'im moare." Peggy declared.

It was a warm summer day, or at least warm for Swaledale. There was no rain, no wind and the sky was some sort of blue even if it was also covered with large blankets of clouds.

John was proud of Betty and knew that Alice would have been too. He was proud of Mary in how she'd faced up to her problems. There was not one of his children of which he wasn't proud. He loved them all and missed those who were not still here. His heart ached, his chest was full of love but also full of sorrow. And it would always be so.

That winter they said goodbye to the village's oldest resident and a much-loved neighbour. Old Jimmy Clarkson, who they all knew as Lackey Jim, died on 29th December 1813, at the marvellous age of one hundred and thirteen.

He'd been born at the beginning of the previous century and the villagers of all ages loved to listen to the tales he had to tell of the changes over the years. Village wives cooked his meals, young men brought him peat for the fire that he sat in front of every day. It was said that he hadn't changed his clothing, or had it washed for a number of years. He's seen families come and go, had been in the militia during the wars with the French and used to sing, "Rule Britannia" to anyone who called. He could remember tales of the French Revolution and the American War of Independence that he heard about from drovers, admittedly years after they happened. There was no-one alive who could dispute his tales.

He was a character who could be crotchety and bad tempered, but his age gave him the excuse for that, it was thought.

He used to send Kit to the grocer every Saturday for a penn'th of boiled sweets, and they were dispensed to any who came to the door, for as long as they lasted.

It was certainly a means of ensuring young visitors, at the beginning of the week anyway. Christian had always visited him, even when she knew there were no sweets. In fact, especially when she knew there were no sweets. She didn't want him to think that was why she'd come.

She just loved hearing his stories and encouraged this half blind, semi deaf old man to talk to her, knowing that she would be deafened by the cacophony of voices that wanted to talk to him.

He'd lost so many loved ones in his life and there were many who wanted him to know how much they missed him. After talking to him for some months she was able to pluck up the courage and say she had a message for him, from some such friend or other. He didn't question this, just seemed delighted to hear them. And Christian was glad. He told no-one and so no-one was the wiser for their talks, but *how* he looked forward to her visits.

She had no way of knowing the names, and nicknames of these people who had lived fifty years, and more, before she was born. And like a lot of people aged in years his memory of the distant past was better than that of yesterday.

"Do you remember Thick Ligd James?" she asked him.

"Why aye ah dee. That's awld James Metcalfe."

"So thee minds when thee and he got thy feet flished, when thee walked all the way hame from Grinton. Thee took badly after. "

"Aye," he chuckled. "Me da chased uz wi the besom and gie uz a gud lam." That seemed to amuse him for quite a while as he sat with his eyes closed and a huge grin on his wrinkled, weatherworn face.

"What about Weaver?" she quizzed.

"Aye, ah ken Weaver, Hs name wuz John Hird, but that's whit he did."

His words were interrupted by a bout of coughing so severe that Christian was worried that he would stop breathing. His chest was heaving as he fought for breath but finally he was able to take a sip of his tea, at least she thought it was tea, and continue.

"Uz was reet in a pickle, cos uz pits a gadgie (*frog*) in Ma Guinners ale! It shot oot reet inta her chops." He slapped his knees and chortled away, until she could see how tired he was and said goodbye and left.

"Jagger says hello," she said to him one day.

"Ah, Jagger," he said with a sigh. "Uz both rode the jagger horses down t'hillside t't'mill. That be James Galloway."

Christian was more desolate than most when he was found dead in bed one morning, after a particularly chilly night. He was buried before the New Year and was a great loss to the village, and to Christian.

1814

That winter was a very cold one. Heavy snowfalls drifted across the dale and made life more difficult, but the dales people were more than used to such difficulties. There were stories being told again about the river being frozen in London, for another Frost Fair. But no-one living here had seen it, and by the time they heard of it, the thaw had set in anyway. In Swaledale people were trapped inside their homes for a while, and a temporary thaw allowed them egress for one day. Living in Thwaite village Betty was able to leave Thomas with her neighbour and walk to the village store to stock up on a little flour and other essentials, but Peggy couldn't manage the walk from Scar Houses. John walked along to the smithy, just over the bridge, and it was he who visited the store and took back bread, potatoes, onions and even a little pork loin for a stew. There had to be *something* to look forward to!

The fog became so dense, helped by the low hanging chimney smoke, that short journeys took many hours and only those who were very sure of their way dared to venture out into the drifts of snow. After such a memorable winter it seemed as if spring would never arrive. It certainly took its time and was much later than normal, even for this desolate part of the country. Daffodils didn't dare to break the ground until the middle of May, and no flowers opened until the end of that month when most of the snow had cleared from the roads and roadsides. The fields, however, were still covered. The Hutchinson family at Scarr Houses had been fed well enough over the hard winter. Duck eggs, goat's milk, smoked beef and their rations from the store paid for by Meadow would see them through a little longer.

Their livestock were well cared for.

The year was off to a terribly slow start. No-one had anything to spare for a neighbour. Everyone was looking out for themselves. It had been especially hard for the old and infirm, and the young.

The youngest Hutchinson Alice (Elvey) was almost a year old, and Peggy lived in dread now of the quickening feeling in her belly. Surely God would know she'd done her best.

She was forty-six years old, she thought, or thereabouts, and getting too old. Thirteen bairns she'd had. Surely to God that was enough. And John had done more than his bit too. He'd fathered eighteen. She had always done her wifely duty. Had even enjoyed it in the earlier days. He certainly had shown no sign that he was tired of her and seemed to reach for her as much now as he had always done. She supposed they were a comfort to each other. She knew she was looking much older. Her hair was coarse and grey now, and much sparser than it to be. And there were the other health problems that marked her as an old woman.

In contrast John still had a full head of hair, glossy and thick at the age of fifty years. He walked purposefully along to the forge each day, and took either a potato baked in the fire, or a cold dumpling, often flavoured with a goose egg.

On dry spring afternoons she looked at where the sun was in the sky and walked along the road to meet him coming home. They walked home together, she with little Alice (Elvey) in her arms, and

Christiana holding her da's hand, or running ahead, picking flowers, just as her sisters used to do. It was a comfortable time together, not needing to talk but enjoying being in each other's company.

They no longer attended church each Sunday. After losing Miles John didn't think that God was bothered about him anyway. They saw Mary as often as she would allow it. She wore her shame like a mantle and never took it off even though there were plenty of others in the same situation.

Jane was sixteen now: the same age that Betty had been when she had left to work in the town, but she wasn't allowed to do the same. John said it was because she was so naïve: they would buy her at one end of the road and sell her at the other, as the saying went.

She had to content herself with working at home, taking in washing with little Peg and Christian, and occasionally being allowed to go to the market. And if there were any young men interested then John would see them first. He had made up his mind on that one.

The summer was a cool one. Jane and little Peg were allowed some time to themselves and spent it walking over the hills taking Christian with them, seeing how many different flowers they could find. Jane's favourite were the purple spiked orchids, Cat's Ear and Lady's Mantle. There were so many diverse types of clover too and she and little Peg loved to see the butterflies that fed on the nectar from these.

Christian knew all their names and could describe them in detail. She more than anyone was missing the weekly visits to church and whenever possible she tagged along with neighbours as her da wouldn't let her go alone being only nine years old.

But if she didn't go then she had no new reading material for the week and she couldn't stand that. She'd read through the good book thrice now. Hymn books at Church were scanned but they gave no information or pleasure.

Therefore in desperation one day she had sneaked out, walked along to the parsonage and introduced herself.

They knew who she was. She had been such an avid scholar at Sunday school that they could not help but know who she was. It was Mrs. Bannister the vicar's wife who took Sunday school now, and she had given Christian a few books to read before they had stopped going.

"Please lady, can I beg of thee a few books to help my learning?" asked Christian.

"James, there's a young girl at the door. I'm sure we can help her." Come along inside," she offered.

"I know thee from church. Come and see if there's any titles that interest thee," said the vicar's wife kindly.

Christian was led into a high-ceilinged room, with shelves on three walls, each filled with books. She stood in the centre of this room, turning and looking at the rows and rows of books, until she felt dizzy. How could anyone read all of these, she wondered.

"I know what thee's thinking. The same thing I thought when I came here."

"There be books enuff f''twhole world," she blurted out.

"Eaxctly my thoughts. I don't believe anyone has read all of the books you see here. So, help yourself.

Now, thee can take three books, for that's all thee will be able to carry," she was told.

Christian sat on the floor of the large room, cross legged, and delved into books on many subjects, until she found three that she would take, with a little guidance from her mentor.

"And when thee's read them, come back for more," she was told, kindly. "Don't be afeared."

Christian thanked the pair, and almost cried. It was more than she could ever have hoped for. And she was very, very thankful.

Worried that she would be in trouble when she arrived home with her heavy burden, she sneaked into the cottage, but John had seen her with the books in her arms.

And all he said, when he heard what she had done was, "Well lass, that caps owt."

His heart was full to bursting with love and pride for this child who stood before him.

"Jus let'uz knaw the next time."

Chapter 21

Saint Luke's Fair

"Life is what happens when you're busy making other plans."
(John Lennon)

It was exciting. It was an adventure. For a family who never did anything except work, (in common with all other families thereabouts) it had been decided that they would take a trip together to Saint Luke's Fair at Kirkby Stephen that backend.

Jennett had said they must stay with her and Will to give them more time to see everything.

Even John was looking forward to it as he'd barely been there above four times, since he had met Alice there, thirty-two years ago. A lifetime. And he had nothing to sell this time. It was a day purely for the fun they would have.

The decision had come from a question Michael had asked one evening, wanting to know if he could take their pony and cart himself.

"Uz can awl gan Mickey," came the considered reply. Michael's reason for asking had been for the same reason his da had gone, over thirty years ago. He would look around and find himself a wife, and at twenty-seven that was perhaps long overdue.

The young Hutchinsons had never seen anything like a fair as big as this one would be, and constantly begged their father to tell them all he remembered.

The only one not going was Betty. She had her own household and baby Thomas to think about, but she would have loved to see Mary again. Also, there was a new bairn due, just after Christmas, so she didn't really want to travel in the cart.

Peggy had a particular reason for going. She wanted to see if there was a travelling medicine man who could sell her another potion for Michael and Young John. They were sickly but coping with life the best they could. And there was another reason: one she couldn't ever tell. She needed to see if he could sell her a potion that could prevent her from having another bairn. Not that she would mind, not much anyway, if it did happen, but she'd had thirteen bairns now, and it had to be enough. It just had to be.

She'd saved a little, and hoped there was someone there. There usually was, but whether he had what she needed was another matter entirely.

Jennet and William were fortunate in that they lived in a fairly good-sized farmhouse, about the same size as Southwaite. There were three rooms for sleeping upstairs, and enough room downstairs to accommodate everyone.

There were thirteen of them making this journey, and their one small cart was not really big enough. Therefore, someone had to see Dick Trot. And that someone was Young John. He was the more reliable, and at twenty-one was as sensible a young lad as you would ever find, so it wasn't difficult for him to persuade Dick to let them have a cart and Galloway for two days. As this journey was for pleasure, John felt obliged to offer a barter: he would shoe three of Dick's horses for the pleasure. Dick was more than pleased, and actually down bartered. Two was more than enough, he'd countered with!

They set off after John had closed the smithy, and the journey passed without incident. All were at Hanging Lund in time to eat a late supper. Feeding baby Elvey took no time, and soon she was asleep, together with Christiana and Mary's son Miles. It took much longer to get William, Miles and Edward to settle for the night. Although younger than some, Christian was much more at home in adult conversation and sat up along with the rest. Then there was Kit, little Peg, Jane, young John and Michel. At sixteen Jane felt that she was too old for the young people and too young for the others. It was an awkward age to be so she tried to spend some time with Mary, who was sitting at the back of the room talking to no-one.

The adults sat around the fire and talked, while those younger played "Blind Man's Buff" and "Hide and Seek" around the house. While sitting, it was not overly warm, despite being near the fire, so they huddled under coverlets, drinking warming drinks after enjoying a filling meal of bacon and potato pie with carrots, followed by a fruit dumpling.

Now they were discussing what they hoped to see the following day at the fair. Peggy couldn't tell anyone what she was really looking for, so said nothing. Jennet was hoping that there would be someone selling cloth so she could have a dress made in the latest fashion. Such quite different needs made Peggy even more aware, as she sat in Jennet's comfortable living space, of how different their lives were.

John's family, she could see, was from a background that was nothing like hers. They seemed to have more brass in their pockets, and she wondered, as she had wondered before, if John felt that he could have done better. Jennett and her children were better dressed, her house was better furnished, and clean, and their meals were always better than hers. She was not to know that Jennet was nothing like her mother, and that she had grown up in a cottage where there was little room, and truly little comfort. There was brass yes, because her da Miles had been a Blacksmith, but he had wagered away brass too. Jennet had chosen for herself a young man who was reliable and able to look after his money. He was a farmer, and as there were no more boys he would do very well. But what could Peggy say? You played the hand you were dealt in life, and she'd played hers well, right from the start.

The next morning, bright and early, with everyone excited, even the adults, they took up baskets of food and set off to Kirkby in two carts, some walking and some riding. Along by the river they went, through the valley, past the ruins of Pendragon Castle, through Outhgill and past Southwaite. There were memories there that John wasn't sure he wanted to bring to mind so he pushed them back down once more, to the dark place where all unhappy thoughts lived.

Michael looked as they passed his childhood home but said nothing. He wondered if he would be sick if they still lived there.

Peggy waited for someone to mention Alice but no one did. She was spared that at least.Past Southwaite it seemed as if everyone breathed again and   John wondered if his sister and her husband had been deliberately holding their thoughts. They chattered in a lively fashion about what they were hoping to see and do once they reached Kirkby Stephen.

The men were most interested in the street food that would be offered they said, making John remember the hot pork with crackling skin he'd eaten sitting beside Alice that first day.

It would be bitter-sweet to taste that again.

And of course, there was the ale. Dirty Maggie had long gone but it was said that she had passed her recipe on and John was eager to taste it. So were all the men including young John, who classed himself as one of the men now, being he thought about 20 summers, or so his da said.

They rumbled into the town and tied up the horses, ponies and carts in a suitable place, John remembering the sights and sounds and the assault on the senses that he'd loved.

It was over thirty years or thereabouts since that first day but things had not changed so much, if at all. There were still criers shouting out that their cloth or wool was the best. Sheep in pens bleated along the side of the square. Mummers walked around proclaiming their show would be beginning and inviting those who were interested.

"Rabbits O. A fine rabbit," shouted someone.

Another shouted, "Diddle diddle diddle dumplings O. Hot, hot all hot."

There were flower sellers, and gingerbread sellers. There were those selling mouse and rat traps, as well as others offering to mend chairs. In fact, there was barely anything you could think of that you couldn't obtain at St Luke's Fair. Comparing it to Thwaite Fair was like comparing a flea to a rabbit. There simply was no comparison.

Peggy quickly sought out her medicine man, who had a huge crowd around him. It gave her great confidence that there were at least three men who came forward and said they'd been cured of all kinds of ailments by drinking his medicine. She was a simple soul, very naïve, and was soon relieved of all her money for two, rather large bottles of "miracle" solution. At least she felt she was getting more for her money than at Thwaite Fair.

Jennet found the cloth she was looking for, and being very kind natured, after seeing her spend all her money on medicine and looking so intently as she bought her cloth, also purchased a length for Peggy who was so grateful and didn't even think of refusing the offer. She was in heaven. She would have a dress in the latest style. She couldn't wait to get home because there was a dressmaker in Muker now.

The men scuttled off to an ale house after buying their hot pork and were not seen for two hours. Betty had given the young ones a farthing each for whatever they wanted and that took no spending. John was pleased to meet up with two men who remembered his father Miles, and they spent a good while reminiscing about the man. Michael and young John remembered him too, so they were able to join in the conversation. He was a man well respected in the neighbourhood. They didn't have the money for a wager, so left their old friends in the ale house and went to meet the women folk and children who were patiently waiting for the entertainment to begin.

For Christian, the sheer number of people around her was almost too much to bear. Souls wanting to speak were constantly bombarding her with messages that she couldn't give, without being thought a witch or worse. To try and deal with this, she took herself off to a nearby field and lay down in the grass with her eyes closed, in a vain attempt to clear her head. Lying there she wondered how her life was going to end. She didn't know for how long she could withstand the pressure.

And then an answer came to her. She didn't know from where but it seemed sensible.

Just ask the spirits to back away. Tell them how much they were destroying her life.

She closed her eyes, and framed the words in her mind, asking for space and peace.

It was a miracle. For now, anyway. She could think. She could hear the sounds of the Fair, children playing, stall holders shouting. But she didn't know for how long it would last.

Maybe she would talk to Reverend Bannister the next time she collected her books. Or perhaps she wouldn't. She had a feeling that he wouldn't be very sympathetic.

The Mummers had finished their play and the jugglers were about to begin. This was more like it, thought Edward. He was ten years old and didn't want to end up in the mine or the mill. Maybe he could learn to juggle and join the travellers? He'd wanted to learn this particular skill since he'd seen it one year at Muker. Watching very, very carefully, he followed the batons they threw up in the air and caught again, never dropping one. When it was time to juggle with six he was sure they would never manage it but it proved to be no more difficult than two. With ease the brightly dressed young man threw them up in the air keeping to the rhythm, catching and throwing, catching and throwing.

How he would have loved to have a go.

Once the show was ended, he followed the lad out of the square to where he was resting, and dared to ask,

"What about a try please."

And that was where his family found him, but Edward was 'throwing and dropping', 'throwing and dropping' instead, with an earnest look on his face, that changed to one of absolute pleasure on the very very odd occasion when he managed to catch one. His face was a study in effort, concentration and endeavour. But he knew he wasn't going to make a juggler.

"Thee'll never mack thy fortune lad," laughed John.

"Ah knaw da. Uz juz wanted to try."

Smiling, Edward gave the batons back and followed them away. He'd had a go, and that's all he wanted. But he was disappointed.

They spent the rest of the afternoon walking around, looking, listening, enjoying the sights and sounds and smells. John was keen to hear any news from travellers as he remembered hearing about the great iron bridge that day. The talk today was all about the war with the French against "Boney." And that was why the Militia had been reconvened. They did say that he had been defeated and John could have cheered but wasn't sure if it was true. There was also some talk about a war with America, that big country over the ocean. And there was some talk too about a volcano erupting and killing hundreds of people. John wasn't sure what a volcano was and thought he would have to ask Christian who would surely know.

It began to grow darker and the families decided it was time for home, or Jennet's home. They reclaimed their transport and travelled the short way to Hanging Lund, a little over five miles. Evening had fallen and if it had not been for a clear starlit and moonlit night they would have had trouble on the road. All fell into bed and were soon asleep except Christian, who had some thinking to do. She was nine years old and despite knowing that she was loved felt that she did not belong anywhere.

After a bowl of hot meal the next morning they said their goodbyes, the women and children weeping and hugging. The men shook hands and off they went. The distance to Hanging Lund was roughly the same as to Muker, but the terrain was too difficult and dangerous at night. It was a Sunday, and they were home by mid-afternoon when John, Michael and young John settled themselves down for an afternoon sleep: something they never did, but today it seemed right. William, Kit, Edward and Miles went outside to play with the set of iron quoits John had made for them. Little Peg and Jane were happy to take up their knitting, along with Peggy, who could knit while she fed Elvey and Cristiana sat by her, playing with the ubiquitous stick doll.

They passed the rest of the year in the same way as usual. Peggy took a spoonful of the potion she'd bought every week, and gave one each to Michael and John, wondering how the same medicine could do such differing jobs. It had the touch of a miracle about it.

1815

There were no more bairns for her the next year but that had happened before. Michael seemed to be in slightly better health but not young John. Maybe he just needed longer she mused.

Betty, however, had her second child, a girl they called Elsey, in January. Baby Thomas had been dressed in brand new clothing, unknown before in her family, apart from the special child Christian. Elsey wore these baby clothes, but Betty swore that her dresses would be new.

She no longer had employment at the village grocer's so they were shorter of money than before but they were managing. Her husband William was a lead miner, like most of the men in Muker and Thwaite. Apart from coal mining near Keld and some farm work there wasn't much else. There was nothing else.

Having been taught by his own father, John had decided that he could start again with one of his sons as an apprentice. Edward at eleven years was interested, but so was young Miles at eight. He had to make a decision. Setting them both to work he had them fetching coal, working the bellows, scouring the hedgerows for any bits of iron, delivering pots and pans, collecting those that needed mending, bringing the horses for shoeing. At eight years old it would be a while before Miles was let loose with a hammer but he loved it. There were so many different jobs to do each day. Edward was eleven and he was ready for an attempt. The smithy at Thwaite was in John's hands now and so he had an opportunity that he did not have before when he was working for someone else. He thought back to his time at Outhgilll and how much he'd enjoyed having Miles helping him but that was another Miles in another lifetime. At times he felt that life had nothing to do with him.
All the pain and the sorrow and the heartbreak. How had that

happened to him? Why had that happened to him? And then he pulled himself up short and told himself that it had not happened to him. It had happened to his sons and his daughter and his wife. All taken too soon. Every one of them. And then he asked, why had it happened to them?

God could not tell him. What good was a god that allowed such suffering.

No-one could tell him.

But he knew that he was not the only father or husband to suffer such losses. So had nearly every other family in Swaledale.

The lead mines were the cause of some of it so they said. But where was a man to work and make enough brass to support his family if not there? John had a trade but even that brought in hardly enough some weeks. And now two of his boys were working down the mine and one at the smelt mill.

He remembered how, when he was a lad, the air in Swaledale used to be pure and clean. Now there was a pall over the village many days as the smoke from the smelt flues settled back down in the valley with the smoke from coal fire. Even walking up Thwaite side it was sometimes hard to escape it but he didn't walk up there now anyway, as that was where Jemmy had died. He knew that Betty walked that way and sometimes left a posy of wildflowers there, but he couldn't because the memory and the guilt were just too much. For now, he was loving having two sons working with him, but he could see that Edward was not enjoying been told what to do.

"All right da. Ah knaws whit t'dee," he almost shouted one day, and flung a horseshoe into a corner of the smithy.

Young Miles looked at him, his jaw dropping open.

"Gan 'get thee ma Miles."

And Miles did. Peggy arrived, took stock of the situation and dragged Edward home, not by his ear although she would have loved to. The next day he was set on as an ore dresser at the mine.

Chapter 22

Fighting Talk

"Our greatest glory is not in never falling down, but in getting up every time we do."
(Confucius)

There was never enough brass for all that a man and his wife, needed. Local men were always looking for a way to make money, and just like anyone, they would rather not work for it. One way to do this was to have a wager on a sport or on a hunt as some of the miners kept hunting dogs and chased a fox or two but John had never been fond of this sport, for the fox always came off too badly. It never seemed to have a good chance and usually died, in a bloody fashion. That was why he never placed a bet on a dog or cockerel fight either. But men fighting, that was a different matter. They could choose if they wanted to fight and weren't made to do so. That was what he was interested in.

George Kearton was a local man of legend, a bare-knuckle fighter famous in his time and well known throughout Upper Swaledale. It was said, for those who believed in such things, that he died at the grand age of one hundred and twenty-four years old in 1764. He was so good that he'd beaten the Westmorland champion and his success was one to emulate.

This bare-knuckle fighting was a popular pastime and made quite a good income for some. The downside of course was that it was illegal, so if you didn't take care you could find yourself in the lockup. But there was a place at Tan Hill, right at the top of Swaledale on the road to Westmoreland, where these bare-knuckle contests did take place and it was as remote a place as you could find. The venue was their usual place and chosen for its distance from habitation, so, if they kept calm, they were fairly safe from discovery.

The fighters trained together and fought then each other afterwards. There was never any animosity among them as they drank together as friends before and after lengthy bouts as opponents. Young John was extremely interested in the sport and had his eye on the prize purse that would make such a difference to him. He'd been training now for over six months and felt that this improved his health, despite working in the mine. He was twenty-two years old now, or something like, and supposedly in his prime.

He'd trained all summer long with Michael and anyone who wanted to help him, doing whatever he could to improve his fitness. The great tiredness he'd been suffering from still plagued him, but it seemed as if he was a little better and he hoped that this fighting would help him to shake it off.

The medicine Peggy had bought didn't seem to be helping Michael now, after she'd spent all her money on it. In fact, if she but knew, there was nothing in this brew that would help either one of them, or Peggy either, save a small amount of morphia that helped them to sleep better, and whether they felt better or not was down to pure coincidence.

John was excited and a little nervous because a fight had been arranged between him and another local lad, from Keld who was about the same age who also had never fought before and wagers had been made for weeks. Early that Saturday morning in August they rode up to Tan Hill , on a borrowed Galloway, Michael as his bottle man

It was fine and fair, with just a hint of a little sunshine when they reached the designated spot where it seemed like the whole of Swaledale were gathered to watch and bet, and hopefully win. Betty had told no-one but had wagered a whole shilling on her brother. Well, if not family, then who else, she thought.

Tom Harry Dick was there, taking wagers on the match and it seemed as if the most money was being placed on young John's opponent. This lad was much heavier and was sparring as if he were more experienced but neither lad had fought before.

Cheering on both boys were many supporters of all ages from each village, and each had their fair share of young girl followers who spent their time at such events, hoping to catch the eye of the winner and share in the prize. Their intention was to help them spend their winnings or spend it for them more like.

Young John was a clever and resourceful young man who'd spent a long time studying good fighters and there was one thing that most successful fighters did. It was all a question of balance and stability really. The object of the fight was to get their opponent to the ground and it seemed this could be made much more difficult with the following 'trick.' What John decided he had to do was lean forward, holding his arms out, making his position strong and enabling him to better keep his balance. This was what he was planning to do, and how he'd practiced, while sparring with Michael. He didn't know if it would work, but he was prepared to risk a small wager on it, and so was his family it seemed. Early that morning, as the mists lifted from the hillside, his opponent stood nearby, boxing an imaginary opponent. If it was meant to worry young John it certainly didn't. He'd plenty of faith in himself.

"Cum on lads. We mun heron afore the constable gets 'ere," shouted one spectator, keen to see if he was going to win his money.

All that did was raise a response from the Constable himself who was already in the crowd. There was no way he was going to miss the chance of a wager and the excitement of the fight. Being Constable was an unpaid position that fell to each eligible man in turn and the cash would be very welcome.

"Aye, that we dooah," he shouted back.

A loud laugh and cheer rang out from those nearby who had spied him. Spectators were now getting restless so at some unseen sign they formed a ring around the two contestants and the referee. Once he gave the signal, they began the bout.

There was much cheering and much jeering, making this an altogether riotous and noisy occasion as spectators cheered on their respective favourites and booed the other. Jostling among the crowd trying to obtain a better view of the action almost resulted in further fights taking place, of the unwagered kind, but sight of the Constable settled them down.

The Constable himself was a little uneasy as he had other things to think of. As well as watching the crowd for any signs of trouble, he was keeping an eye out for any rider on horseback approaching them. If the local Magistrate had heard of the fight he would be coming to put an end to the bout, or much worse.

"Dinnet mack si much ov a din if'n thee wants t'keep out on't lockup," he warned, reminding them that if the crowd became too rowdy, he may have to read the "Riot Act" and disperse the crowd.

And if, in one hour after that, they hadn't dispersed, then they would be locked up.

One man against so many. He didn't want to do that, but he may have to, all the same, if it looked as if spectators were going to get hurt in the melee. He didn't want to end up in the lockup himself.

He was only Constable for one year and was hoping to see it out without much trouble, as he had to live amongst the same people afterwards, but it was a responsibility that weighed heavily on him at times, as it did on every man who had to take this position.

The noise abated for a short while. The spectators knew what was at stake here. At the very least they would lose that stake. At the worst they would be imprisoned.

Young John had so far been standing his ground but after the first three rounds where no-one seemed to have the upper hand, he showed first blood with a cut to his lip. You could hardly call it 'first blood' because the cut was so slight, but it had to be noted.

The two sparred on and they rallied for the next three rounds, seemingly on an equal footing, making the crowd restless.

"Cum on John lad. Gi'e 'im yan," shouted a neighbour. "Fettle 'im nah. Thee can dooah it."

Hearing his name shouted seemed to galvanize him and his next blow landed squarely in his opponent's face. It didn't knock him over unfortunately but it did give him a black and bloody eye.

At the end of each round the betting was reassessed and John's family were gratified that he had the best of the wager after this round, but it could change very quickly.

And after a well landed blow by his opponent young John was on the ground. This was not what his family wanted to see. Nor his friends. A loud groan went up from his supporters followed by whistles and shouts of "John, lad, gerrup. Clowt 'im back. Thee can dee it."

And then, "Wha're thee deein' dawn theear? Ger up. Clowt 'im John."

And other such words of encouragement.

It wasn't over, and he did get up very quickly. He too was now sporting a black and bloody eye like his opponent, but he'd had all the fighting he wanted. Now was the time. Looking his opponent straight in the eye, he landed a punch squarely on his nose, sending him toppling to the ground, blood spurting everywhere, a red fountain. He didn't get up for quite a while after that.

The result was that young John Hutchinson was declared the victor. No-one seemed to have noticed his strategy, or worked out why he was successful, but congratulated him well at the end of the match. The prize wasn't much, but he'd wagered on himself to win, and that was where the money was. Betty wasn't there to see this as she didn't want to take her children into such a melee, but she was due quite a reward for her shilling. Peggy had managed sixpence, and John had told no-one and wagered two whole shillings on his son to win.

After this success he felt it seemed a promising idea to book himself more of the same. Michael was always there with a bucket of cold water to wash off the blood and refreshing him.He won five more fights before the end of the year and was only defeated once. By then he had a very tidy sum put by for when he found a lass he wanted to marry, and his family had their winnings. Betty had increased her wager to two shillings the next time. It certainly made for a better Christmas for all, with plenty of food, and even a few toys for the bairns. John used his winnings to buy new clothes for his whole family and once they were 'kitted out' Peggy absolutely insisted they went to Church.

1816

The following winter was severe, with heavy snowstorms that left everywhere inaccessible for a while. Windstorms blew the snow into huge, high drifts that a body could get lost in, and low temperatures, just above freezing were the icing on the cake.

Betty and her family had moved to Scarr Cottages as soon as there was a cottage empty for them. She didn't like living in the village, and she thought too that Peg might look after Thomas and Elsey when she went to the store. There was also a thought in her mind that she could get her job back. But events were to soon prove that impossible.

Spring was so cold that snow fell all day on Easter Day, in the middle of April. There was even snow into the middle of May, making it difficult to feed any livestock. Jenny Goat was lucky as she ate most things, but if they'd still had Meadow she would probably have starved, because animal feed was too frozen to use. Animals suffered, but so did people. On a lighter note, Peggy still had the length of fabric that Jennet had bought for her at the Fair. There was a dressmaker in Muker, but Peggy had done nothing about it yet as she had the new clothing that John had bought for Christmas. Help came that spring in the form of a travelling tailor, who turned up at the village, asking if anyone had any work for him: sewing up holes, darning, shirt and shift making. Anything.

She couldn't believe it. She had the cloth, and she had a little money. And now here was a tailor who said he could make her just what she needed. She showed him the cloth, telling him she wanted a dress made in two pieces: a separate skirt and bodice, with buttons down and a stomacher. She'd seen some women with dresses like this at the Fair. He measured her and soon she had a fitting. When it was made she could scarcely believe it. It was perfect.

The cloth was a heavy material, in a thin stripe, the sleeves were long, and the bodice laid on her stomach in a v shape, with a full and gathered skirt. She wore it proudly, but only for church, and was disappointed that there were no weddings at which she could show it off. Her 'other' new dress was worn for trips to market or the store, as it wasn't the newest style. John didn't know anything about style. She had never, ever been so well clothed. It felt wonderful. The dress was so beautiful, and like nothing she had ever had before. In fact, apart from a bonnet, she'd never had *anything* new before. A heavy shawl around her shoulders was necessary in the chilly weather, but she was loth to cover up the beauty of the dress. And what was even more perfect was that it was now three years since little Elvey had been born and so far, there were no more bairns. The medicine must be working, she thought.

But she didn't dare tell John what she'd done!

The 1st of April was celebrated as a special day in Swaledale. They called it April Noddy. Following the tradition, Edward and Kit had decided to play a trick on their family and were planning what to do.

"Let's mack gam that there be a boggart in the privy," suggested Kit to Edward, knowing that folks around believed in such things. He wasn't quite sure himself. "Ah'll be the boggart, and mack the noises, if thee pretend thee cannot hear it."

The privy was a small, wooden edifice at the back of the row of cottages, not too far away, and shared with a couple of other families, one of whom happened to be Betty. A hole had been dug to collect the human waste over the top of which was a bench with two holes cut out to sit on, for the 'business end'. Soil and ashes were added daily until the hole was filled. Then another hole was dug, and so on. But often, folks just used the stream. Wiping yourself down was done with dock leaves, or even grass if they weren't available. Betty at least kept the shared privy as clean as she could, and in the summer added some Meadowsweet for fragrance. Over the years John had boxed in the front of the seat so that the contents of the pit were not in view, and that minimized the stench slightly.

It seemed the boys had a good plan. They waited till they saw someone coming towards the privy and were pleased to see their first victim was to be Will. He stepped inside and lowered himself onto the seat. The boys gave him a minute or two, and then Kit began to make the noises of a supposed boggart.

"Aaaaaaaah," groaned Kit. "Oooooooooh."

Hearing the noise Will shouted, "Get thee gone. I ain't afeared o' thee."

Kit had a heavy chain for the occasion that he clanked and rattled above Will, while he continuing to make ghostly sounds, sitting and banging on the privy roof. But it seemed that Will was having none of it.

"Ah knaws it's thee ower Kit. Give ower," he laughed, and stood and banged back at the privy roof.

The next one who came was little Peg, but she was a different matter. She was about to lower herself when she heard the awful noises made by Kit. Timid in any event, the poor girl was terrified. Crying and sobbing, the girl begged for mercy and to be left alone.

"Leave uz be," she begged. "Dinna tak uz. Please, dinna tak uz."

Edmund spluttered and laughed but it was Kit who took pity on her.

"Dinna blether. Tis ainly thee brothers," shouted Kit.

Being too frightened to stay, she bolted out of the door and back into the cottage, all urgency gone.

The next person to visit was Michael but they should have known better. By now it was past mid-day, and Michael, who had known what was going on all morning, shouted out the required rhyme.,

"April Noddy's past and gone.

You're the fool an' I am none."

"Aw. Ower Mick. Spoiled ower fun," lamented Kit. "Just you wait till next year."

"If thee thinks thee can catch uz, well uz disagrees," chuckled Michael. And that was the end of that, for another year.

The rest of the year continued to be a cold one. It rained and it rained, and it rained. The old folks said they couldn't remember a colder summer. By backend there was snow, and plenty of it, with a hurricane. The stooks that were still in the fields were frozen and they could hardly feed the beasts. But they got through.

1817

Thankfully the Hutchinsons now had no crops to worry about as Jenny goat required the smallest amount of hay. It was difficult for everyone who relied on their harvest as hay stood rotting in the field after cutting because spring and summer were so wet.

The wars with the French had finally ended and so the Militia was disbanded, much to Michael and young John's regret. They had imagined themselves dressed in the 'regimentals' saying goodbye to their sweethearts and going out to fight 'Boney'. And now they'd missed their only chance for excitement.

It was a hard year for Betty. She was expecting a baby, and then she wasn't. A poor little mite was delivered by Peggy that spring, nowhere near full term, about four months, if that, but looking just like a bairn, and called a 'chrisom'.

She did what people always did with these bairns that came before their time. It was buried in the back field and a flower posy placed on the spot. She'd cried, but they'd been lonely tears because she'd told no one about the baby, except Peggy, not even her husband. Peggy was sorry for her, but she knew there would be plenty more babies for Betty before she was through. This could have been a blessing. As for herself, she was more than pleased. It had been four years since little Elvey had arrived, and there had been no more. Surely she was finished now. She was almost sure. Another year and she would be sure.

Chapter 23

Another Hutchinson Wedding

"There is no more friendly and charming relationship, communion or company, than a good marriage."
(Martin Luther)

1818

After all this time, Jane's wish was coming true: a young man who was hers, and who made her feel special. She was nineteen years old, and it was her turn at last. Her da had said, after Mary's 'problem' that he would be the one to decide if any young man was good enough for his girls. There weren't many places to meet a partner, but these two had met at a church supper, so that was a good start.

He was a young man from a very respectable village family of Metcalfes. His ma helped to run the church suppers and she was well known as an excellent cook. With dark, wavy hair and deep blue eyes, Leonard Metcalfe was quite a catch, and Jane still couldn't believe he'd chosen her, over all the young women who went to the suppers. Even above Mary Calvert who was a known beauty.

He'd already talked to her da. First, like Betty and Will, he was allowed to walk her to and from church, but now in this glorious springtime of her life they were allowed to walk together, through the meadow, past the lacy topped flowers and nodding daisies and along the beckside, looking for minnows in the sparkling water. And it felt so good. They were chaperoned of course, usually by Peggy, or sometimes by Betty if she had time for a walk.

They more often than not had Chrissey with them too, walking along hand in hand between Leonard and Jane, constantly chattering now, asking questions, making Jane feel secure. The big thing was that Jane had no idea, absolutely none, about where bairns came from, and the last thing she wanted was to be expecting a bairn when they married. She would be mortified, (if she knew what that meant) and would never be able to lift her head for the shame of it. At least that's how she felt. There were countless others who didn't have the same care.

Because Jane was so shy, so naïve, no-one had talked about anything like that with her. She was like Alice had been when she had married her da, but no one was to know that.

Peggy would never attempt it: unable to put it into words for shy, innocent Jane. Just kept telling her to 'keep theesel reet.'

Betty had tried once or twice, but Jane had just shut her down, beginning to talk about the wildflowers she was collecting, or some such other unrelated matter.

Because no-one had talked to her about these things, and she was too shy to ask, she didn't dare even hold Leonard's hand, much less let him kiss her. Heaven knew what may happen, because *she* certainly didn't! She was content for now to leave things as they were, as long as Leonard didn't become impatient. She didn't want him to start looking somewhere else.

Talking this over with Betty, sensible, down to earth Betty, she got the right advice, "Well, if that's wha he dis, he weren't worth havin.'"

It wasn't just the girls who were so woefully ignorant of the facts of life. Young John had shown an interest in a young woman from Muker, but he was playing it slow. There was no need to rush these things, he thought. Talk at the Inn, among the other young lads, was all about the experiences they were supposed to have had.

"Aye. She were reet willin," was one comment.

"How willin' were that then?" he was asked.

"Enuff fer uz," was the reply, with a laugh.

What he didn't realize was that the young girl's father was drinking at the Inn, and was just along the bar from Jimmy Alderson.

The first he knew of it was when his breeches were lifted from behind and he was hoisted along, a boot under his backside, and a kick at every step. Then he was unceremoniously thrown out of the door.

None of his friends had tried to prevent this and none of them spoke in his defence.

John had never taken part in these conversations and was surprised at those who did.

Why would you tell everyone things like that? Why would you even talk about it? It was private, and John thought it would be special, if he ever had any experiences himself.

He still took part in some bare-knuckle fights for money, and had a tidy sum now of £20, a fortune really, which his da would not accept when it was offered.

Michael had shown no interest in anyone so far, despite Betty introducing him to some of her friends. He was already thirty years old, and it wasn't that he liked it at home too much. He just didn't like change. Peggy despaired of him. She wanted this big lad, no, this man, out of the house. He took up too much room, ate too much and was too much work.

"Get thesel a lass ower Mick. Thee needs thy own hearth. Thee's ower big t'be sharin' mine," Peggy used to tease him with.

"Peggy, ah's got a warm bed, a roof ower me heeed, an food when ah wants it. Why wid ah want a lass?" and he laughed at the face she showed him.

"Thee knaws reet well," she retorted, with a cackle back at him.

The last seven children were all under fourteen, and likely to be with them for a sizable number of years yet. When Michael and young John were out of the house, and in a house of their own, at least there would be more room here.

Spring came and went. Summer was cold, and very wet. Frosts came early, in September, together with fog, day after day after day. Any harvest was delayed, causing even more hardship.

The year before had been very cold and wet, and this one was following suit. It made for a miserable, cold, wet existence, but you couldn't do anything about it except back up the fire and wear more clothes. It made Betty wonder if everywhere was like this; cold and wet all the time. She had no idea. She would love to live where the air was warm, she thought. If there was such a place. Christian would know.

John brought peat down from the hillside and Michael brought coal from Tan Hill pit. He was working there now and liked it better than the smelt mill.

Betty and Peggy spent the time in each other's houses and helped each other out when possible. Peggy looked after Betty's Thomas and Elsey for a few hours a week while Betty went back to do a few hours at the village store. And that was money for both of them.

1818

Winter came and, as well as snow, there were severe gales from January to March, causing damage to buildings, battering anything and everything in its path. It was so bad that William Pounder Betty's husband and John had to replace parts of both of their roofs. It was no good waiting for the landlord.

And again, it rained, and rained and rained.

They survived the winter, and were prepared for another wet summer, but, against all odds, to everyone's surprise, the air warmed, breezes were calm, while the sun shone. Warm weather and sunshine are a good pick-me-up for everyone. Life seemed kinder somehow. Wildflowers blossomed everywhere, and bees and butterflies abounded. Walking to work, John felt his step to be lighter, even though he was working just as hard, if not harder, than he had ever done. It was a pleasure to feel the sun on his face, instead of big fat raindrops, or misting drizzle.

The old wives spent warm evenings sitting on a chair by the door, watching everyone, eager to add a little to their fount of gossip. Men were glad of the weather to bring in the harvest. Even the beasts in the fields seemed happier.

"Settin neets" took place outdoors, making the frightening stories seem more atmospheric, particularly at dusk.

Time was passed with plenty of knitting, darning, gossiping and tale telling, of ghosts, boggarts and other things.

Christian was a different girl. She had learned how to keep the spirits away from her and allowed them to speak only when she said. She felt happy and carefree and had set herself a task.

Having spent her spare time this lovely summer, walking the fields and hedgerows, collecting one of every wildflower she could find and bringing them home, she pressed them under her straw mattress, to keep forever. She had forty at the last count and could name them all. She wondered if the vicar had a book on wildflowers she could borrow and would ask the next time she visited. Christian had set Little Peg, and Jane, if she was interested, the task of finding thirty of these wildflowers themselves. They were delighted to have been involved in this. It took them a few weeks, combing the dales and hillsides, with Jane incorporating this into her walks with Leonard, but Little Peg was finally declared a winner, as she found even more than asked. And Jane was jealous.

Christian and Little Peg were still working for Jane, taking in washing but now Jane had progressed to asking if anyone needed any work done *inside* the house. Or shopping, for a few pennies. John said that the girls could keep the money they earned as it was barely five shillings a week all told among four of them. It would be a good help when they married.

Married! The very word made Jane tremble inside. She didn't know why, and she didn't know if it was a good thing or a terrible thing. So she refused to think about it. She and Leonard had progressed to taking tea at each other's homes and Jane thought it was much more pleasurable having tea at the Metcalfe home. Leonard's ma was very amenable to Jane joining the family and promised she would show her how to bake.

The summer moved on, gently and kindly, and Peggy felt a new feeling in her breast, something she'd never felt before. It bothered her, just a little. She was unsettled, but she didn't feel worried. She sang a little, round the house and in the lane, not knowing what it was. She hadn't felt like this before and it took her a while to realize. She was just content.

****

It had to be. Anyone with half an eye could see that this day was coming. For Jane it came maybe a little sooner than she'd wanted. Was she really ready for this? She didn't know.

One afternoon in late winter, Jane received her Leonard as a visitor, and stood at the table beside him. Despite the worry of it all, and the possible consequences she decided she dared hold his hand for now.

"Ower Jane has sum news," said Peggy, standing behind Jane and her man, smiling a huge smile.

Jane stood before them, like a startled rabbit, a look of pure fear on her innocent young face. Beside her was her young man, Leonard Metcalfe. He hadn't been to see her da, even though he'd promised he would, but he stood with her now, tall and straight. He was almost as tall as her da, and had hair as dark as the night sky, and where her da's eyes were green, his were of the darkest blue. He stood there, nervous and afraid of what her da might say, but he knew what he wanted, and he wanted Jane. Dear, sweet, innocent Jane.

"Good day t'thee Mr. Hutchinson," he began, very formally. "Ah've cum to see thee on account o'the fact that ah wants t'wed thy dowter Jane."

"Oh aye?"

"Ah'll look afta 'er reet well sir."

"Aye thee will."

Then thinking he should add something to this he continued, "if thee agrees."

Not waiting for an answer Jane took his arm.

"Ahm wantin' t'be wed to Leonard da, and we want it t'be soon," she quavered, bravely looking her da in the face.

It appeared that she knew her own mind, and after waiting patiently, she now had her man, at only twenty years old.

He looked at the young girl, who seemed to somehow have become a woman, remembering her as a thin, pinched face young girl who wouldn't eat, and who constantly had a runny nose. She had never looked as if she were going to be pretty. She stood before him, no longer a girl. When had she grown into a woman, and when *had she* become so pretty?

Now it was time to let her go if this was what she wanted.

"Ower Jane. My dowter. If this be what thee wants, ah's happy f'thee." He stopped and looked at the floor for a moment. Jane didn't know what to do. Should she go? He hadn't said much.

And then John looked up, bestowing on her that smile that changed his face, lighting it up like sunlight on water. A wide smile that made his eyes crinkle at the corners. A smile they hadn't seen for a long time and never in all its glory like today.

He continued. "He's a reet good young man, ower Jane, and ah knaw thee'll keep 'im reet."

Then turning his eyes to the man he gave the warning, "Treat her proper, and din't harm a hair o'that lass's head or……" and he left the rest of the comment hanging in the air. Leonard looked at that moment as if he might run away, but sensing his fear Jane squeezed his hand and replied, "He luvs uz da." And that was all that was required.

Peggy had been watching this with interest and now wondered at the requested haste of the ceremony. "Now ower Jane. Is thee havin' a bairn? Not that it matters as he's thine."

"Oh ma. Not yet, any road," she whispered, looking down at the floor, her face red and glowing redder and redder. Peggy had spoiled the occasion with this that Jane felt was totally uncalled for. Did she not know her daughter?

Peggy crossed the floor to give her eldest daughter a hug and kiss, and whispered into her ear, "There's things thee'll need t'knaw."

Jane withdrew from the embrace as if she had been stung, a panicked look crossing her face.

She was going to have to try and talk to Betty, and soon.

It was another winter wedding, on the morning of 6th February, again at Muker. Jane was very frugal and determined that she would have no new dress for the occasion, despite Peggy offering to pay the tailor. The dress her da had bought her last year would be fine enough for a wedding. She was also determined that they should walk so there was no cost for a horse and cart.

Water was heated for baths for the girls, Jane first, then Little Peg, followed by Christian then Chrissey. Jane made Little Peg, Bride's Helper. Little Elvey managed a wash too when she and Peggy entered the warm, now fairly dirty water together: a tradition begun on Betty's wedding day. The boys, and men, were content with a wet rag and soap. It made some difference.

With a wreath of ivy in her hair, and ivy and holly with a sprig of fir as a bouquet, just as Betty had, she looked beautiful. Almost ethereal. Peggy was wearing her best, best dress and was still in love with it.

The ladies, wrapped around with warm shawls and wearing boots, walked briskly to keep warm, and even though the going was a little rough in places, they managed the route while each linking arms with a 'gentleman.'

Little Peg was so important. She felt like it was her day too, walking right behind Jane and her Leonard, carrying holly and ivy, just like Jane. Waving and smiling to any well-wishers who had braved the cold she felt as if she were a bride. A winter flower girl. Ah hope it's me soon, she thought.

The family gathering afterwards was one of the best John could remember. At one point he laughed out so loudly at something but at what he couldn't remember when someone asked him. It was a great roaring belly laugh that shook him, making his eyes water and him laugh as if he couldn't stop. In fact, he *couldn't* stop.
And it was infectious. Others who heard him couldn't help but follow, and it passed right round the room.
They were happy, and loud. But the great amount of beer and ale they had drunk may have had something to do with it.
The women gossiped, and all but destroyed the character of some poor woman in the village.
"She's gi'en up her virtue to tooa menny yung men," sniffed the oldest there, the biggest gossip.
And no-one dared dissent in case they were the next object of gossip.
The men talked, and laughed, and exchanged news. Children played outdoors in the snow. Oher adults sat in front of the fire, drinking mulled wine to keep warm, reminiscing about those who had departed and about times long gone, while smoking a clay pipe, men and women both. It was so good to have a happy family

occasion and to be able to put to the back of their minds, if only for the shortest of times, the sad events of the recent past.

Yes Peggy was reasonably happy, and she hoped that John was too.

Jane left that evening to the usual calls and whistles and alludings to what was supposed to happen that night, although Jane still had no idea. But after this she was so embarrassed that she could hardly bear the fire in her cheeks.

After the wedding, Jane moved out of her family home, and up to Keld to make a home of their own, near her husband's occupation. Fairly remote, it was quite a stretch from Thwaite as they had no transport, but it was walkable. And Peggy and Little Peg missed her very much.

Jane and Leonard visited as often as they could make the walk,

Betty confided in Peggy that she hadn't been asked for any 'information', and neither had Peggy. But the babies came along anyway.

Chapter 24

Family Misfortune

"It is not death that a man should fear. He should fear never beginning to live."
(Marcus Aurelius)

All seemed to be well with everyone, except young John. All was definitely not well with him. He was hiding something.

His winter had been a hard one at the lead mine, and he was tired and drained every day. Every night his shirt was wet with sweat, and he coughed so much. There was no way he could have had his fighting bouts like this. He knew he worked hard, but the others didn't seem to be as tired as he was – not at his age anyway. He'd tried to carry on, but now he found it impossible. This illness had crept up on him but now it was galloping its way towards some sort of a conclusion.

One morning in early May he was so weak that he couldn't work. He wanted to, but his flesh and bones wouldn't allow it.

"Aaahm sick muther," he said softly, and lay down in front of the fire. "Ah need t'rest."

Peggy looked properly at him and saw the same look she had seen on the face of Miles, twelve long years ago.

"Keep thissen warm, lad. Aah'll fetch t'medicine," she said as she reached for the bottle on the shelf by the fire.

"Nay. Not that foul brew ma."

It was the bottle she'd bought from the medicine man at the last fair, and now he was refusing to swallow any more of it.

Clutching his stomach, he lay there. He hadn't been able to eat anything for a while but had hidden the fact very well. And when he tried to eat, he just vomited.

By now he was a shadow of his former self and going downhill fast. As he lay shading his eyes against the light that he said made his head ache so much, he asked his ma to hold him.

"Gi'uz sum comfort ma," he whispered.

She saw now that his skin had lost its normal colour and had a strange pallor. For two weeks he only moved to visit the privy. They waited, stupidly, hoping he would improve, but of course, he didn't. Finally, John was so worried that he sent Peggy to fetch the doctor before he had to set off for work.

Dr Makepeace was in no hurry to arrive. He had two difficult birthings to attend to, and a mine accident that needed stitching and repairs. After an examination Dr Makepeace put away his stethoscope and looked at Peggy.

"Is the lad's father not here?"

"He's at t' forge."

He looked down, and then up into Peggy's worried face.

"All right Peggy. You must know he has the lead lung."

Peggy's eyes blurred, and she gasped, "No, not another. We canna loss another un."

"Aye, Peggy. But you know he's incredibly young to have such a condition," said the doctor in puzzlement. He carried on with, "I believe he has underlying consumption too."

Peggy knew what consumption was. She'd heard about it before.

"You know Peggy that he needs fresh air and good food."

"Ower Miles were even yunger," Peggy added.

"Before my time Peggy I'm afraid. Was he the same as this young man here?"

That was when John returned, and after being brought up to speed with the doctor's diagnosis, told him about Miles, and Alice, and her father too.

"More than likely had the same," Dr Makepeace replied.

"He probably has consumption and has had it for quite a while" the doctor went on. "So his lungs have been affected more easily. It could even have been caught from his mother at birth." He continued, "This disease can lay asleep in a person before making itself known, wreaking its havoc on the body, and coming out years after."

He stopped for a few seconds, looking from one to the other, considering his words carefully.

"This boy could also have caught it from your son who died. Over all my years as a doctor, I have seen this tragedy so many times." He stood and beckoned for them to follow him.

"Just make him comfortable, talk to him, say anything you need to say, now, while you have the chance."

Peggy thanked him, paid him, sat down next to young John and took the boy's hand.

"Ah'l look after thee. Dooant worry thee sen."

"Aye ma," was all he could reply.

They managed to take young John outside and lay him on the grass. They did this every day of that early summer. Despite their best intentions the air was heavy with smoke from housefires and the smelt mines, and some days it hung so heavy in the air.

He did his best to eat a little, but the achievement of eating was undone by evening as he vomited back all that he had eaten. They tried to get him to eat the fresh fruit and vegetables they bought but he couldn't make his jaws chew the food.

His pleasure was lying outside having Christian tell him stories, with little Peg listening too. Michael sat with him when he could. After seeing Miles suffer, and now John, he wondered if the same thing would happen to him.

Then came the day when young John couldn't open his eyes. He couldn't speak or talk to anyone. Coughing caused him to choke. That day John went to the smithy, fearing unwelcome news before the day was out, and it came.

Lying outside, with Peggy beside him holding his hand, little John had to finally give up.

When she was sure he'd passed, she laid her head on his chest and said a short prayer. It was no good crying and lamenting. There had been enough of that over the years. Now it was best if they tried to just say their goodbyes and move on. At least that was what she told herself.

The funeral was on the 3rd June, and the year was 1818. John was only twenty-five years old.

Once more they walked the road to Muker, with family and friends walking beside the coffin, pulled on a cart by Sorrel, borrowed from Dick Trot. He refused to let John pay for the cart, saying that John had suffered enough without paying for it.

Finding the guinea for the funeral was easy because the lad had given his fighting winnings to his da.

Because Young John was a popular lad, he had a good send off in the local Inn, with drinking, singing, tears, and even some laughs as they remembered the daft things they'd done as lads. There were so many mourners at this wake that it spilled out onto the road.

There was money left over and they didn't know what to do with it. John had thought about a headstone for Alice, but after all this time would he know where she was? Probably the church would. And what would Peg say to that?

"Uz'll keep it for a happy time," John decided. "Whatever that mun be."

As for Peg, John wasn't her bairn, but she'd been his ma since he was two years old, and he'd known no other. It was no use being sad for what they'd lost, for young John had lost more than they: his life, his future, his wife and his bairns.

Chapter 25

A difficult decision.

"I must have a prestigious amount of mind; it takes me as much as a week, sometimes, to make it up."

(Mark Twain)

After saying goodbye to John, they watched Michael very closely for any indication of the disease. He was the last of Alice's boys, and had lasted the longest, and that was because he'd worked in the open air for a lot of his life.

There was only Betty and Mary after that. The doctor had said that it was highly likely Miles was suffering from consumption together with lead lung disease when he'd died. Apparently it could lay asleep within you for years, they were told, and then finally take its strangle hold.

Talking among themselves, they knew Michael was pale, but that was because he worked at the Smelt Mill all day and didn't see much fresh air, wasn't it?
He'd never had a big appetite. Well he loved his food.
He needed to rest weekends because he worked so hard; that was why he was so tired wasn't it?

And he coughed was because he worked in dusty conditions, didn't he?

This was what they told themselves, and all of it was true, up to a point.

The warm summer continued, up to August, when it was a little cooler than normal. And finally, the weather broke in autumn, with the ubiquitous rain upon rain upon rain. There was nothing now to look forward to except cold and wet, and eventually snow. Once again, when the festival came around the family didn't want to take part in T'Awd Roy, but it did make the long dark days of winter less hard to endure. Betty was a girl who loved dancing and had managed this year to persuade her reluctant husband, (who told anyone who would listen, that he couldn't dance) onto the dance floor on the Saturday night. It was perhaps unfortunate that she chose such a vigorous dance for his first attempt.

The willing dancers were flung around the room, until William lost his footing, and skidded right along the length of the wooden floor on his rear end, with Betty just able to keep her feet and prevent herself from joining him. The dancers carried on dancing, seemingly oblivious to the spectacle, but Betty could do nothing for laughing. Will gingerly picked himself up, looked around and saw that all had averted their eyes from his misfortune by now.

It was too much for Betty. She snorted with laughter, held her belly and wiped away the tears. Watching her, so did John and Peg, and many others. Laughing made you feel good. It was good for the soul, so they said. And it was definitely what they needed.

1819

The Hutchinson family was smaller again, now that half of Alice's children had passed on, and a quarter of Peggy's.

There were still nine children, and that included Michael. Some of them were now grown, plus two adults, and that was fine. They could all be well fed. They were clothed, and cleaner than before, by choice and Betty's example. Jane and Leonard visited on Sundays for tea when they could make the walk with Jane carrying a basket on her arm containing a homemade cake. The basket contained a few duck eggs and potatoes when they left. And Peggy was proud of her eldest daughter.

Betty had helped with the clothing before, but she had her own family now, so she was making sure Little Peg learned how to darn. She was eighteen and actually quite a good sewer already. Peggy was still proud of her 'new' dress, only worn for church and she wanted to get the same for Little Peg, by putting aside a penny here and a penny there from the sale of her goose eggs. By the next fair she hoped to have enough, but there were cloth traders at weekly markets too.

As soon as she had enough money she was determined to take little Peg to choose something.

During a wet but unremarkable spring, something of note happened that made everyone sit up and take notice. A carriage drawn by two fine horses came thundering through Muker and stopped at Scarr Cottages. As everyone in the row watched, the carriage door was opened and out stepped Mary, fairly-well dressed, followed by a tall young man looking to be about seven years of age.

Stepping down carefully, he stretched, and excitedly asked those around if he could see his grandfather. He knew who he was to be meeting. As for John, he immediately recognized his first-born daughter Mary. Putting aside his surprise, he came rushing forward to put his arms around her, lifting her off her feet and twirling her around.

"Steady. You'll make me dizzy," she said, in a voice not like any of his other children.

Peggy watched and waited her turn. She knew who this was but wondered if she would be acknowledged. It seemed not.

"And who's this young man?" asked John, looking down and raising a quizzical eyebrow, although of course he already knew.

"My name is Miles Hutchinson, Sir," the boy replied, putting out his hand in greeting, a stern look on his face.

Quite surprised at this formal tone, John took his young hand in his and shook it, seriously and carefully, after which they all followed Peggy into the cottage.

Once sat down, Mary was questioned about her health, the health of Miles, on Jennet and William's health: anything except what they really wanted to know, which was, had she had any contact with Miles' father, and more importantly, who was he?

"Young Miles be too fine speakin' for uz," Peggy said, as she and John stood in the kitchen of their small cottage.

"Appen that's because of his da," replied John. "Appen he's a gent an' is teachin' Miles his ways. We did wonda."

Miles was mixing in much different company to theirs. If Mary wouldn't tell him, he hoped that Jennet could. But when he delved into this later it seemed that she knew nothing either, despite Mary living under her roof. Mary had kept her counsel and told no-one.

In spite of the sense of confrontation in the air, they spent a good family day together: Miles with his young uncles, Will, Miles and Edward, who took him along the lane to where a fell pony was tethered.

Mary was sad that she hadn't been able to come and say goodbye to her youngest brother, but she couldn't make any better of it now. Now that they had her to themselves, the important question was asked, and answered, in some part.

Yes, he had seen something of his father.

No, she would not tell who that was.

Yes, he was someone 'above her station'.

The problem here was that his parents had wanted more regular contact with Miles, who happened to be their only grandson, and they wanted to provide for him. But the thing that was really the issue here was that they wanted to send him away to a prestigious boarding school. That was what she was here for: to ask their advice.

"Will they still want him if he doan't go," John asked, and the question remained unanswered.

"Why send the poor scrap away? Doan't thee love im?" Peggy asked, unable to comprehend the idea.

Betty burst in through the back door, and stood in front of Mary, drinking in the sight of her sister who she missed so much. Then they clung to each other, with whisperings that no-one could hear. She was told of the impossible decision Mary had to make. The decision was just too hard. Of course she wanted what was best for Miles. What were his life chances now? Was she hindering them if she said no?

Betty sat, weighing it up. "If he do go, he'll be neither one nor t'other. E'll be ower poor for them, an' ower rich for his own kind. Ah think it'll be better to keep 'im with thee."

"That's what ah think," Mary said, almost crying. "But he wants to go. He may niver forgive me if ah deny him this."

They sat together all of that afternoon, mulling over the problem. The advantages. The disadvantages. The problems. Those that seemed insurmountable and those that were mere practicalities. At the end they still hadn't agreed. Finally, when it seemed that they would never decide, John asked the only question that made any sense: the only question that would settle the matter.

"Well Mary. What wid thy ma say?"

It was such an easy question. It was such an easy answer. Considering for the shortest time, she replied, "That's just so easy. She'd say, give him all the chances he can have."

"Well there you have it," sighed John.

They talked on through the evening, but the decision was made now. The next morning the footmen, having stayed at the Inn, arrived for them, and they were both packed off in the carriage with plenty of hugs and kisses, and promises to see one another soon. As they left, Peggy wiped away a tear. "Oh my. That poor soul. We may never see him again," and she turned and led the way into the cottage.

Chapter 26

Twice the Joy

"Twins have a special bond. They feel safer together than with their peers.

(Jeanne Phillips)

Babies keep on coming. It *is* the miracle of life, but did folks wonder how it happened, or even, why it sometimes didn't happen for couples? There was no way of knowing how, and the common folk had no 'concept' of conception and birth. Yes, it *was* a miracle, but the well-being of a family was in direct opposite correlation to the number of babies born to the family. And there was only one sure way known to women of preventing babies at that time. But, men had to have their needs met, and women had to meet them!

Betty had the usual news for them. There was to be another Pounder baby at summer's end. It was only May time, and already she was looking as if she were about to burst, finding it hard to push herself to do the jobs that needed to be done now, without thinking of what it was going to be like when the new baby arrived.

"Ah cannot think ah was as tired as this afore ma. What's wrong wi' me?"

"There's nowt wrong wi'thee but the bairn making thee tired. And there's Thomas and Elsey an awl."
She was not to know that Betty was worrying she had the same illness as the boys.

Privately Peg thought that perhaps Betty was going to have a child sooner than she thought and was prepared for that. But the weeks moved on, and no baby came. At midsummer there was still no baby, and Betty was too big and too tired to even make the walk next door. Every step she took was a major effort, and, as she walked, she used both hands to cradle her huge belly. Some days she needed little Thomas to walk in front of her, so she could place one hand on his shoulders for support. Peggy had birthed both Betty's children, but she was loth to do this one alone. There was something not right: she worried that the baby would be too big and that Betty would not be able to manage the birth without help. And Peggy knew enough to know that she was not experienced enough if there was such a problem. As soon as Betty started to groan and rub her belly, Peg ran next door, shouted to Little Peg with urgency in her voice. "Run. Fetch the midwife," just hoping that someone had the three shillings to pay her. But it was either that, or risk losing Betty, and she couldn't do that. She sat with her, rubbed her back, felt the strength of the contractions and knew it wouldn't be long.

Eventually, just as Peggy was convinced she was going to have to do it herself, the midwife, a large woman, the mother of seven children herself and who had birthed, she said, "most of the bairns around here," arrived just in time to deliver an average, if not even on the smaller side, baby girl.

Both Peg and Mary the midwife, looked at each other with puzzlement at the outcome, but Betty took hold of the baby, wiped and wrapped in a cloth, with a smile of gratitude that "Eve's curse" was over.

Except it wasn't.

"Peggy," Betty screamed, "what's 'appenin? Ah'm still pained."

The midwife took one look at her face, felt her swollen belly, and came to the conclusion,

"There's another one!"

This was another girl, exactly like the first.

"Well. In God's name Betty. Thee's had twins. And lived to see them."

Both were swaddled now, and Betty held one in each arm. Thomas and Elsey were next door with Little Peg, so they couldn't hear their mother's cries of pain. Now Peg brought them to see their two new sisters.

"By God. Thee's got two now. One in place of the bairn you lost last year," Peg smiled in wonder. "Praise be," she said, her Methodism coming out before she could prevent it.

The midwife gave Peg a sideways look and continued her ministrations to mother and babies. "Was that reported to the coroner," she asked, while looking at no-one.

Betty looked at Peg in exasperation and volunteered, "It weren't a bairn. It were no more'n a couple of months. There were no need."

Muttering a "Hmmmmmmph," the midwife carried on, and Betty wasn't entirely sure if the midwife believed them, even though indeed it wasn't true.

Now the question of names was raised.

"It mun be Mary, for Will's ma," replied Betty. "And then Elizabeth, for her sister. But ower Will comes hoam soon, and we'll decide, afore kirk on Sunday."

The bloodstained shift and cover were crumpled up in the corner of the room, ready for someone to wash. 'Probably me,' thought Betty. "Pit 'em in some cowld watter ma, please, and ah'll wash them the momorra."

The two babies had by now both begun to cry. Feeding two at a time could have been a problem, but the midwife had some sound advice.

"Pit ain unda apiece arm Betty and dee it this way," she advised, and demonstrated for her.

"That'll save thee time lass. Thee'll need time in't'next year or moar," watching as Betty put one under each arm, and nursed them together, exactly as the midwife advised.

Peggy had no experience with twins. Was it harder, she wondered to have two at once or one every year, as she had nearly managed? 'But of course, it's harder. Dinit be a barmpot. She cud have twooah moar next year,' she said to herself.

No-one knew why twins appeared. It wasn't a regular occurence and for some old women in the village, and even those not so old, it was something to be wary of. Peg was a little that way, but trying not to show it, hence her comment about the baby lost. The midwife was a little more informed, but unable to explain what had happened. Various stories about twins were passed around. That when one gets sick, then the other does too. That they must be dressed alike or one will get annoyed and die. That they brought bad luck. That they would be opposites, one good, one bad, one a leader, one a follower. Betty knew all of this, but she was more sensible than most, having spent some time away from the confines of the village, and village mentality.

"You're beautiful," she whispered to them. "Ma twooa pritty

lasses."

Tom and Elsey sat next to her, each stroking a soft downy head. "There. You have one each," Betty laughed." No need to share."

Will rushed into the room, still dirty from coal. He'd left the pit as soon as he could and didn't know if he yet had a son or a daughter, but he knew that it would be soon.

His eyes took in the sight of the two babies, but he didn't understand.

"Which ain's ower bairn, an where's the ma on't'other? He whispered, as Thomas and Elsey had their eyes closed, almost asleep.

"Which ain dis thee mind is ower bairn?" she asked him, mischievously.

He looked carefully, and slowly raised his finger to point at one of the girls, watching her face for any clues. She nodded.

"An this ain," she nodded towards her other bairn. "They're both thy bairns."

He was shocked. "Nay Betty love. Nay. Ah's been true t'thee. Ah has. They's spinnin yarns Betty,"

"Oh Will," she wanted to laugh, but daren't. "It's uz whee's spinnin yarns. They's both thy bairns, an they's both ma bairns."

He still looked puzzled.

"They's twins. They're reet alike. They's verra verra alike." And she finished with, "an they's lasses, if thee want to kna." As he hadn't even asked.

A look of comprehension flashed across his face, followed by a look of annoyance at having been made a fool of, and then his face settled into one of pride and joy.

"Saints above. Two dowters. Double to love."

"Double to love," repeated Betty. "Meet Mary, the older one, and her younger sister Elizabeth. If thee agrees."

There were traditions about the naming of children, and there was little choice but this, so the names were agreed, and duly given to the girls five days later, on the 1st of August 1819.

John was now a grandfather to two boys and four girls. The year before, Jane had produced a daughter, surprisingly nine months after the wedding and called Nancy after the baby's grandmother. That christening had been at the Methodist chapel at Keld, almost a year ago, and now there was another bairn on the way. John wasn't keen on the Methodists, but he had no real religious feeling either way, having seen God take so many of his children already. Grown children too, taken before him, was an abomination. And that he would never forgive.

Chapter 27

Michael and Nanny

'Family is not an important thing. It's everything.'
(Michael J Fox)

Praise the Lord. Peggy said to herself. Finally the big lad had found himself a lass: Nanny Calvert from Muker. He was thirty-three years old now, and she was beginning to think he was never leaving. John hadn't set any conditions on this courtship. The lad was a man after all and would soon have a man's responsibilities. And there would be no more of this 'big lump' crashing through the door shouting, 'What's ter eat. Ah's fair clemmed.'

Peggy went very carefully. She didn't want anything to get in the way of this courtship! She welcomed the lass: even cleaned up a bit if she knew Nanny was coming.

Michael hadn't worked in the mill and mine as much as Miles and John, but still, she and John watched him to see if he was showing signs of the same disease that had taken his brothers.

Once Michael had found somewhere to live that he thought he could afford, John spent time helping him to make it more presentable. The cottage had been empty for a good while because of its condition so John negotiated a rent-free period (with free horse shoeing too) for John Alderson who owned a few cottages in that locality.

The ceiling was open to the sky in places, so the roof was the first job. "Thee'll ha t'dee wi'out a room upstairs our Mick. There's ainly the two o'yee."

The roof was fixed. The door was fixed. The windows were mended where possible. The fireplace was fixed up and John provided them with a cooking pot to hang over the fire.

There was no privy, but they were allowed to share the one provided for the row.

"That's thy first job. Thee needs a privy if thee wants t'keep thy wife."

Michael tried to help but found he was standing on the sidelines watching for most of the time.

As Peggy said, he could be a bit gormless.

Nanny brought a besom and a scrubbing brush and set to work cleaning where she could. Little Peg was delighted to be allowed to help, pretending she was preparing her own accommodation for her and her husband.

Michael put on an act of wanting to marry but he wasn't as keen as Nanny was for this match, as he'd told Peggy and John they weren't in a hurry and would wait till the next year.

In fact, he wasn't overly keen at all, but felt he ought to do it, just so people would stop asking him why he wasn't wed.

Not that it was anyone's business but his.

The reason was that he knew he didn't earn enough money to raise a family. Babies seemed to come along every two years, he had noticed. With everyone! So how was that? He was very naïve and didn't want to ask.

So, there would be babies to feed, he and his wife to feed, rent to pay, and he would want a mug of ale now and then.

He'd seen how Betty and Will were struggling, and Betty had been working too for some of the time. When he last saw Jane, he'd been struck by how different she looked. What was it? She seemed to be tired, not as clean as she used to be, and if it was possible, she was even thinner. Either she was unhappy, or she had no brass, or maybe she was unhappy because she had no brass.

It wasn't the kind of thing men talked about together. It seemed their minds were rigidly fixed on two things: the Inn and the marriage bed, and not about whether their wives were happy.

Of course, if there was a lack of brass then they might talk about that.

Little Peg was desperate to marry a man of her own. He felt like warning her not to: to stay at home where at least she would be fed and clothed and have no worries about finding the brass. But he knew he couldn't.

His da, as a Blacksmith had plenty of work, and they were better off than most in Scarr Houses.

She would eventually find out for herself, the same as all the lasses round here.

****

At Christmas Tide, the Hutchinson and Pounder families had a festive day together with John treating them to a loin of pork, received as part payment from Salty Will, the local butcher for shoeing his horses, and a goose reared from the eggs, especially for this purpose. The vegetables, potatoes, leeks and carrots were from their garden plot, and Betty made some sweet dumplings for after.

After the clearing away, with the plates scraped to keep for Jenny Goat, Betty asked if they could do *"The Twelve Days of Christmas,"* taking a number each. Little Peg thought that was a particularly clever idea, while Thomas and Elsie jumped up and down with delight when they began.

"On the Firtht Day of Christhmath my true love gave to me" said Elsie with her delightful lisp, as she pointed at Thomas.

"A partridge in a pear tree," said Thomas" in his confident voice. He

pointed to Betty, and she began, "On the Second Day of Christmas……" and so it went on.
Green grow the rushes Oh," was the next favourite of everyone, half sung, and half chanted.
Gifts were not given. They seldom ever were, except sometimes for the children. This year John had made a set of quoits for the boys and a hoop and stick, to share. Although Christian knew that any gift was precious, she'd been a little disappointed with her rag doll, and had been hoping that any gift may have been a book. The other girls were more than pleased with the dressed rag dolls, made by Betty. There were even tiny peg dolls for the babies. And Little Peg just loved her new dress in a dark rose pink. Much ale was drunk, and the kirk was not even mentioned. How times had changed.

At the end of a carefree day a toast was raised to all those who were not with them any longer, with a short bowing of the head. Finally, Will Pounder produced his fiddle. They were determined to enjoy the rest of the evening, and they did. There wasn't much room for dancing, but someone had the promising idea of opening the door to dance outside. It was certainly cold, and snowflakes were coming down, slowly, whirling and dancing in the air like white delicate fairies, making it seem even more special.
If you caught one on cold clothing, you could see the shape of it

and its crystals.

Edward was the curious one who wanted to know more about this sparkling wonder that came every year so he and Christian stood together, taking turns to catch one and examine it.

"Whit dis thee ken ower Christian. Whit is't."

"It's wet, and comes from't sky, like rain. That's arl it is."

"Mebbee," he replied, trying to get a good look before the one on his arm completely disappeared.

She had told the voices to recede, and they had, to a point. But it was she who wanted to hear them, in case it was Jemmy, or Will, or any others of her kin. But it never had been, so far.

The dancing continued, round and around, while Will played. Betty organized them into pairs and arranged them opposite each other, along the lane, then gave them instructions for the dance. The end couple hitched along the middle to the music and when they reached the top they danced and swung around, taking their places opposite each other, which signal led for the next couple to begin. Someone began clapping in time to the music, and it was taken up by everyone.

Betty had seen something like this when she was away, working at Kirkby Stephen, and was incredibly pleased at her organizing ability and her memory, (although it didn't really matter if it wasn't right), while John was transported back to Southwaite, to when Jack, the fiddler from Scotland, gave them a night to remember. Neighbours, coming outside to see what the music was about, joined the top of the line. Till finally, when everyone present who wanted to dance was satisfied, they went inside and warmed through, trying to dry their clothes, but it didn't matter.

They were all tired enough for sleep to seem like a clever idea. Betty picked up baby Mary and baby Elizabeth, who had slept through the whole affair but had been carefully watched over by Little Peg, while Will collected a very sleepy Elsey and in the case of Thomas, a very bad-tempered boy.

Jane, and her family of two now, was loving being back 'home' once more, among those that she loved. She felt it was very lonely up at Keld and decided she would visit more often. It was such fun all being together.

The next morning the goat was to be milked, the geese eggs collected, but no-one felt up to the occasion, except Christian, who milked Jenny and then took her outside and tethered her on the grass opposite. Then she took the besom and brushed the covering of snow away so that Jenny could get to a small area of grass. It seemed that despite those flakes the evening before it had not lain or drifted.

Christian was determined again to talk to Reverend Clemitson who she hoped would give her some advice. She needed more reading material so needed to go to the vicarage to choose more volumes to keep her busy. And then maybe she could talk.

John knew Christian was 'different', but he didn't know who else knew. So far it was only Betty who knew. He worried about her and he had reason to because he knew how people viewed anyone who seemed to be dabbling in the "dark arts", as they may call this. He didn't want her to be labelled a witch.

She'd told him of her intention to speak to Reverend Clemitson and although he wasn't in agreement, he knew that short of locking her in, he couldn't stop her when she was determined.

"Ah cannit abide it da," she sobbed. "How can a live the rest o'ma life wi'these voices?"

"Thee mun be canny dowter. There's many as won't unerstan."

"It's the bein' canny that's killin me da. Ah cannit gan on."

"Mebbe if thee gives the family some messages thee'll feel better."

"Ah have un f'thee then," she smiled. "Alice says, 'Get thee head up. Life's not abaht knowin misery. It's abaht bein' thankful.'

And putting her arms around him, as high as she could reach, she hugged him.

"And" she went on, "she says, mind what thee drops in the mud in future."

The Fair thought John. He'd made her drop her parcel of cloth at the Fair. But Christian couldn't know that. So, he tested her.

"Thee means the loaf o' breed ah spoiled in the lane."

"Nah barmpot. The parcel o'cloth fr 'er weddin' dress."

"Aye it's true dowter. Thee has a gift. But ah still warn thee abaht keepn' it safe."

With a smile from ear to ear, she took hold of his hand and they walked along the lane together.

1820

Michael was lying in bed, thinking about the coming day. An important day. He wanted to smile, and yet he didn't want to. His stomach was turning over, and his mouth felt strange. All the old worries, mostly about brass or the lack of it, were coming back.

At the end of the day, he would have a wife! He, Michael Hutchinson, would have a wife.

Having always been a dreamer he was amazed that anyone would want to marry him. Her name was Ann Calvert, but she was called Nanny by everyone, and she was pretty *and* clever.

He didn't know if he felt happy or not. There were so many 'what ifs'. He knew he was 'gettin' on' to not be married yet, but that was because he was content. Peggy called him her 'big lump ov a lad', and worried he would never leave. That did happen. Jimmy Miller lived near where Betty had lived, in Thwaite village. He was knockin on forty, and still his ma was cooking for him'. Michael was thirty-three.

'All saints above, help him to find a decent girl and marry her,' was Peggy's prayer most nights. And now it had been answered.

But it was no saint, it was Betty who'd pressed him to be brave and ask her to go courting. And now they were going to be wed.

Nanny seemed to have faith in him, and he liked her very much, so that was all that mattered. The future couldn't be told, and he would just have to do his best. And the best thing was that she'd had a choice, and she chose him.

Michael and Nanny were wed on the 8th ^{of} January 1820, a Saturday. It was another morning wedding because all weddings at that time had to be held before noon, by law. Everyone was away from their occupations and could take part in the ceremony and celebrations. Again, there were no flowers available for a posy, but Nanny's mother had taken holly, fir and ivy, much like Betty, with one or two Christmas Roses, tied it with thin twine and made trailing ivy fall down from the posy as Nanny carried it.

She wore a thin circlet of dark green ivy in her beautiful blond hair. Her pale green dress, waisted and collared, set off her amber eyes, and the thick woollen shawl she wore had been knitted by her grandmother before she passed away, and lovingly kept for this day since then.

When she looked at Nanny Little Peg couldn't help the tears that fell and she uttered Jane's words from any wedding she'd been to before her own: "She's reet pretty, Chrissey."

"Orl brides 're pretty."

Jane watched, thoughts of Betty's wedding day making her smile. But then dark clouds covered her face as she thought about Miles, and Mally, the girl he was set to marry, but never got the chance. She was happy enough with her choice but knew now how different the dream from the reality was. Her Leonard worked hard, but life was hard, especially with two bairns. She really didn't want any more, and she thought about her ma. Twelve she'd had. Maybe she should talk to Peggy about that.

The family were all together once more. Even Mary had made the journey from Mallerstang for her younger brother. Her son, Young Miles was now away at school, and she missed him. It was as if there was a hole in her heart, a dead place inside her. He'd been gone since September. She'd seen him, but not for long, at Christmas, and she wondered when, and even if, she would see him again.

The weather was poor, so Michael borrowed a horse and cart from

Dick Trot, 'for old times sake' and he and Nanny travelled, with Little Peg, Christian and Chrissey as flower girls. This was Little Peg's dream, and in it she was transported to a future occasion, with lots of sighs and smiles. Mary had her own horse and cart transport, courtesy of her new family who were treating her very well. She took Betty and Peggy, complete with little Elvey, with her but the rest, family, friends and neighbours, either walked or begged transport from someone.

That route had been travelled many times by this family, although not as many happy as sad. John was so proud to be walking with them, and couldn't stop himself from saying a silent prayer, despite his current lack of belief, that all would be right with this son of his and Alice's, the only one left.

As they travelled back, rays of watery sunlight broke through the clouds to reflect on patches of ice, with an almost blinding intensity. As they walked along the riverbank, a river shaded by trees, John noted that the snow still covering the ground was hiding signs of spring with its sparkling white mantle. Soon the willow branches by the water's edge would dangle their catkins. Those who knew used the bark and leaves of Willow trees to ease aches and fever, and it worked. John had seen it used to significant effect when Alice had cured fevers and helped ease pain. Wild daffodils with their pale-yellow petals, would grow beneath. Pilewort, with its waxy yellow petals, as well as delicate primroses, would be next. The wedding party made their way to the Calvert's home in Muker for the wedding breakfast. Looking at his now eldest son, John felt a mixture of pride and pain equally, even though it was supposed to be a joyful day. A toast was made to the happy couple, and then Michael raised his mug, looked all around at the crowd who were waiting on his word, and proposed another toast to all who could not be there, naming each one by name. It was touching and it was sad, but it was a testament to the feelings of all those there that a huge cheer went up. Then they resumed eating, drinking, dancing and music.

Michael and Nanny lived in Thorns till their cottage in Thwaite was habitable and Michael greeted the arrival of his first child, a boy, in October that year, ten months later, called John. This was the start, he knew. An extra one wasn't too bad, but when it got to four or five, then that was trouble. Peggy had now been child free for eight years. She'd known for a while now that her childbearing days were finally at an end. She was fifty-three years old, or so she believed, and a grandmother, with her youngest child only seven. Her eldest, a daughter Ruth was twenty-seven, and she didn't even know where she was. She'd never told who Ruth's father was and had vowed to take that to her grave.

Chapter 28

Christian

"Be kind, for everyone you meet is fighting a hard battle."
(Attributed to Plato)

All mothers know how much work a baby is: feeding, changing, comforting, loving. The Pounder twins were everything a baby is, only twice over. They were fairly content, not crying much, but Betty, trying ridiculously hard to keep her home looking like her home, was run ragged trying to look after them both and perform the usual tasks she'd always done to achieve this.

Her husband Will could see what this was doing to her, but there was no way Betty could be persuaded to slacken off on her daily tasks.

Every morning Little Peg walked along to Betty's to help her with anything she needed. She didn't need to be asked. She just loved doing it for her sister, and because she loved babies. But it seemed to her that two babies were more than twice the work of one.

The girls were absolutely identical to outsiders, both in how they looked and how they expressed themselves. But Betty could tell them apart with no trouble at all. And in time so could Little Peg.

But Betty had to cheat for Will, and tie a red ribbon in Mary's hair, and hope it didn't fall out.

Their moods were aligned, seeming to smile at the same time, and if they did cry it also was at the same time. But all Will said about that was that 'one set the other off'.

They were dressed the same, not intentionally. It was just what all babies wore. Her older two, Thomas and Betsy, kept Betty busy sewing, and she was glad of their hand me downs for the twins. No 'new clothes' snobbery now.

Little Peg could sew, producing a very neat line of stitching. She'd sewn baby clothes for Jane's little boy, and also for Betty's girls, and she was so looking forward to sewing for her own. As yet there was no young man who had shown an interest in her.

She, Elvey, Christian and Christiana loved taking the twins to see the geese and the goat, Jenny. They had five geese as well as one gander, and had given them all names too, after wildflowers, but still often got them mixed up.

"Look, There's Meadowsweet," cried little Peg, only to be told it was in fact, Daisy. It was difficult because they moved around so fast, and all looked very much the same. So that summer they decided to spend a day learning the differences, so they could tell them apart. And they did.

This is what they found out.

Meadowsweet was the goose with longer feathers in her tail than any of the others. Where the other geese were so fast as they raced around looking for bugs, Daisy was slow and always at the back of the line, while Buttercup was always at the front. It was Sorrel, named after their pony, who was always faster to the feed bowl than any other and recognizable by her injured left wing, gained in a fight with the gander, while Sage meandered lazily around the edges, in no hurry for anything.

But what was the same about all of them was the honking and wing flapping noise and scurrying together, en masse, letting everyone know if a stranger was coming.

This summer was warm. John was no longer paying rent for the pastureland across the way, but the children still played there, and no-one seemed to mind. Little Peg led Jenny Goat to the common land to graze each day, talking to everyone she passed, being very sociable and enjoying the walk. If the weather was wet though she tethered Jenny on the pasture, and John said that he was helping by providing 'fertilizer' for the grass to grow.

Kit, Edward and Will were lead miners all, and Miles was an apprentice Blacksmith with John while Christiana was eleven years old now and helping at home looking after little Elvey.

And now to Christian. Sixteen years old and looking for an answer to the issues that still plagued her every single day. Although granted not as much as before, as they did leave her when it got too much for her. Despite advice to the contrary, she had eventually talked it over with Reverend Clemitson, but he'd been of no help at all. His only suggestion had been to perform an exorcism! There was no devil inside *her*. Of that she was very sure. What she wasn't happy about, in fact she was very unhappy about, was that he said he would consult with his Bishop and then let her know. And if he did that then people would know about her. Not just her parents and her sister. But people!

After all the years she'd kept this a secret, for it to be let out that way, was what her ma would call, a 'cryin' shame'.

What would they do to her? What would they do to her family? She was terrified. It was time to leave. Now.

That was all she could think of doing to protect her family from this 'curse'. She didn't dare wait until she was better prepared. That might be too late. Sneaking down to the kitchen that night she packed a little food in a cloth: some bread, a hard piece of cheese and one small piece of bacon. Looking longingly at the two slices of onion pie set aside for her da's snap, (she could not resist her ma's onion pie) she took one and left the other. Finally, a carrot and a small apple completed her food haul. When she was sure that all were sound asleep she crept along past the sleeping quarters of her ma and da, gave them one last look almost hoping they would wake and stop her from leaving and then sadly left the home she loved. She hadn't taken much. She didn't have much to take anyway, not wanting to leave her family with less than they needed.

She had only the clothes she was wearing when she left, not knowing where she was going, just following the river to the east away from anyone who might know her.

She'd tied up her hair and had 'borrowed' a pair of breeches from her younger brother Will while he was sleeping, trying to look less like a girl as she set off along the path that dark, moonless night.

Life was not certain, was never certain and never could be, but she knew she had to get away from so many closed minds. She had been lost on a sea of fear and worry and she needed to escape.

Later in her life she'd been asked and had tried to remember how she'd felt that night, but she couldn't. She was simply numb.

After leaving Scarr Houses and walking all day, (it was surprising how much land could be covered in twelve hours with a rest or two) she spent the first night sleeping under a hedgerow. She'd been anxious and hadn't slept much that first night, had just lain there, looking up at the night sky, covered in those twinkling lights that were called stars, according to a book she had read from the vicarage. It had been too difficult to understand but she loved the pictures. Listening to owls hooting, she was deeply sorry when she heard mice screaming when they became the owl's dinner.

When she woke the first morning it was with a sickly feeling and she was certainly not refreshed. Trying to make herself feel a little better she'd eaten a little bread and drunk some water from the nearby stream. But she rationed herself as she didn't know how long it would have to last.

On the second day she was able to gain a ride further east in the back of a hay cart and that was quite pleasant. Now she was a little more at ease, and after travelling for seven days, and sleeping out in the open under those beautiful stars every night she was beginning to feel the peace and solitude of just being alone. Maybe this was the answer? She loved the open air and thought that if there were no people there would not be the clamour of voices in her head.

That was partially true, but if she passed a farmhouse along the road, then it began again. They would not, or could not, leave her alone. She was very hungry, but she was more at peace with herself, away from villages, away from people. It wasn't so bad, really. She knew she would have to find somewhere for the winter, but for now, she fed herself by foraging. She knew which mushrooms to eat, which berries tasted the sweetest, and even which wildflowers were edible. And there was always a supply of fresh water.

Her days were filled with wandering. Nights were sometimes starry, and sometimes overcast and warm. She came across flowers she hadn't seen before, trees even, that were new to her. Birds entranced her with their unknown song. Some Romany travellers took pity on her, gave her food and let her travel with them. A cooked hedgehog was something she hadn't eaten before, but she was extremely glad of it. Rabbits, birds, mice, anything went in the cooking pot with a few potatoes, and produced a satisfying meal which they didn't mind sharing with her, but eventually they had to part ways.

Even on her own she felt safe and was never threatened. There was protection from somewhere: she was protected by something, but by what she didn't know. It would have been enough, wandering like this for ever, but she knew it wasn't possible, and that she would have to find shelter for the very wintry weather coming.

Abandoning her solitary route one day, she dared to venture into the nearest town. By now she was dirty, in torn clothing, looking every inch a vagrant, but with such an angelic smile and such beautiful eyes, that, despite themselves, people stopped and listened to her. She thought she'd find some help at a local church. Seeking out the holy man she asked his advice but he looked at her, only seeing a vagrant in rags. Unfortunately, he was certainly not the sort to be kind to anyone like her, despite his occupation.

"Thankee sir," she whispered, as he ushered her away. "Thee has a true callin'."

It was one of a group of old women at the wash house who knew what she wanted. They were working hard, but chatting as they worked, when one lifted her head and looked straight at Christian, so intently, that if felt as if she'd touched her very soul.

'She knows,' thought Christian. 'She knows how ah feel.' The thought didn't alarm her but rather comforted her, because she could only know that if she was the same herself, she reasoned.

After watching her for a while as she chatted to the rest of the company, and pounded her washing in the chilly water, the old washer woman pulled Christian aside and whispered in her ear.

"Tell no-one, my little love. It be a blessing but can be a curse. A curse to me these many years, all my long life, but ah've learned to live wi'it."

Gasping, Christian took hold of the old woman's shoulders.

"Tell me how to live with it. Please, please tell me," she begged and sobbed.

Looking around to ensure no-one was listening, the old woman finished with, "There be a place, at the next town, at York. They calls it, *The Congregation o' Jesus*. They'll understand ye. So a'hve been telt mind. Get theesel there and may God's love go wi'yee."

"Thanks to thee old mother," she replied gratefully, and accepted the hunk of bread and cheese proffered to her.

"Ah winnot starve, but thee might," she whispered croakily to Christian, and waved her on her way.

After asking directions and making sure the road she was travelling was leading her to the place she was seeking, it took another seven walm balmy nights to reach York. Another full day was spent wandering around roads, past houses, past inns. A place so big, she wondered how people knew how to reach home at night.

They musn't go far, she reasoned.

It was nightfall before she found someone who was able and willing to direct her. All the while the voices spoke to her, clamouring to be heard. She'd tried, mostly without success, to shut them out once she entered the city gates.

The town had its own sounds, some comfortingly familiar and some not. It was like a huge fair she thought, so loud and busy, with many street sellers and many beggars. This helped to mask, just a little the din in her head. By now she'd been on the road for two moons, and it was getting colder at night. If these people couldn't, or wouldn't take her, then what would she do? What could she do?

Following confusing directions, she had eventually found herself standing by two high, grey, stone steps, in a narrow, dusty thoroughfare, edged on both sides with tall, stone buildings.

This was where she'd been told to come.

The steps were before an old door, very tall and very wide, the wood of which was warped and cracked. She had never seen a door as tall as this and was sure that even the front door at the vicarage was not as tall as this. Looking up at the windows, she'd never seen a house as big as this. It seemed even taller than their church, the largest building she'd seen, before now. The house was built of stone, a golden colour that seemed to reflect the light. The windows, edged with wooden shutters, were much taller than her and topped with huge stone lintels. The houses on either side were similar, she noticed, only they were a little better cared for.

As she stood there, tired to her soul and debating with herself what to do, a street seller passed by, offering nosegays of sweet-smelling flowers, but Christian was ignored. She was a dirty vagrant and not worthy of recognition. People bustled past as she stood there: a woman with a basket on her arm, a man with his dog, children playing. Everyone ignored her. She wasn't worthy of anyone's attention. After so long away from her family, and not knowing what was to become of her, she gave into the terrible exhaustion that she'd been fighting for days. Slumping down at the side of the stone steps, she leaned back against the wall, feeling the warmth from the stone, and gave in to a body numbing weariness that sent her into a deep sleep.

Woken by strong hands roughly shaking her awake, she felt herself being dragged her to her feet before she could even open her eyes.

"What're yee deein' 'ere. A vagrant? Yee cannit sleep 'ere. "Get thee gone" shrieked a voice in an indignant manner.

"Where yee from?" shouted another, bending down, his toothless mouth inches from hers and staring through her eyes.

"Show us thy papers, vagrant, thy deed o'settlement."

Half asleep, exhausted, hungry and confused, she hardly knew what had been asked of her. What was her deed of settlement? She was just a child and didn't know.

"Sir," she began, rubbing her eyes. "Ah's ainly a girl. Ah dinnet knaw whit thee wants."

She looked up, her pale blue eyes blinded by the sun, but could see they were not friendly.

"Where's thee from vagrant?"

"Muker sir," was all she could answer. Somewhere of which they had no knowledge.

"And where's that then? "one asked her.

How could she answer that? She didn't know, except that it had been her home for all of her short life.

"Thee needs to be getting back to Muker," said the first.

Looking at them in bewilderment and confusion, she didn't know what to say, how to respond. Was this the end of her quest? To be sent back home again? Was this defeat? Had she lost? Even her parents wouldn't want her now after she'd brought shame on them. They would never want to see her again. She was too engrossed in her own misery to be aware of the imposing door behind her creaking open, just a few inches. She saw no-one but she heard someone speak. It seemed to be a disembodied voice behind her, speaking softly but with confidence.

And it said, "Thank you constable. You can go now. This girl lives here now, with us."

An arm reached out, took hold of hers, gently and carefully led her up the steps. She felt herself almost lifted up those stone stairs, or at least she had no memory of climbing them, and entering the wide doorway. She didn't have time to feel afraid, or worried, or wonder whether she should shout or run. She just knew that she was safe.

"We've been waiting for you," the voice said.

Later she wondered at how easily she had accepted her fate.

Putting up no resistance and letting the arm lead her inside, she stepped into a wide, dark, cool hallway, with a flagstone floor.

Without knowing how, she just knew that this was to be her new life, and instantly felt at peace.

Chapter 29

A Scandal

"A lie has no legs, but a scandal has wings."

(Tom Fuller)

It was coming to the end of that warm summer, and no one liked to lie in bed when it was relatively warm outside – often warmer than inside, so they'd missed her early the next day. She was always the first up to milk Jenny goat.

She wasn't outside when John left for the smithy, and that was a wonder in itself as this was the time she was usually milking Jenny to provide warm, creamy milk for breakfast.

As he left, John shouted to Peggy, "Ower Christian's neewhere 'ere. The lass niver lies abed. Is she badly?"

A great bellow went up the stairs. "Christian. Get theesel down. There's fettle t'be dun."

All that did was produce a sleepy-eyed Chrissey and Elvey at the bottom of the stair, yawning and complaining at being woken. their hair having escaped from its nighttime plaits and hanging loosely around their faces.

"Her's not 'ere ma."

"Dinna be a barmpot. Where else c'n her be? Gan 'n look proper."

Thundering back up the stair, Chrissey shouted back, "Her's not 'ere ma. Ah's already telt thee."

"Her mun be wi' ower Betty."

At that very moment Betty came inside and was adamant that she had not seen Christian that morning.

A shout came from up the stairs from Will. " Ma. Where's me britches?"

"Gan an' tell thee da his dowter's gone. Run lass," she shouted with urgency at Chrissey, pushing her out of the door, still just wearing her shift.

"But ma," complained Chrissey, to no avail.

It took until midday before they were sure she was a runaway.

She hadn't gone early to the vicarage for books.

She hadn't walked to the mine with Kit and Miles as she had done on other days, after leaving word with Chrissey.

She wasn't washing in the waterfall where she could go to drown out unwelcome voices.

She wasn't visiting any of their neighbours.

They were now sure that she was gone. But where?

John, Edward and Kit had borrowed mounts and ridden all over Swaledale, looking for her, asking for her, searching for her, talking to anyone they saw. For four weeks they searched every day and hoped that nothing had happened to her. It was an impossible feeling. Not knowing if she was alive seemed as bad somehow as knowing that she wasn't.

Peggy had sobbed for weeks. Her golden child gone. Little Peg tried to comfort her but was sobbing too much herself. How could they live without knowing what had happened to her? Had she been taken by gypsies? There were always tales circulating of these things having happened. But none had been seen for a year or more. She'd been in her bed. Chrissey and Elvey had seen her. Kit, Edward, Miles and Will were abed much later, and on the other side of the curtain.

So when had she gone? Why had she gone? And then there was the mystery of the missing britches.

A young girl did not wander away alone. It wasn't safe.

John knew how unhappy she'd been, but Peggy didn't. He knew she'd not come to terms with the voices, but had she run away? Why would she? So, they searched, and tried to comfort each other, and waited. Finally, they had news. A letter was delivered to this house where no letters ever came. Fortunately, John had the brass to pay for it, but unfortunately neither he nor anyone else there could read it.

Holding it very carefully and feeling optimistic, although he didn't know why, John took it to the vicar in Muker and asked for his help. "Reverend. Can thee tell uz if this is from me darlin dowter, missin' these six months?"

Reverend Clemitson was more than glad to help, feeling guilty as he did about what he now saw as his part in the matter He'd told his Bishop, who had wanted her to go to the Palace and be interviewed, and that hadn't helped. She'd begged him not to, and he now saw that by telling he'd only made things worse.

The Reverend carefully opened the letter and skimmed it himself before looking up at John, whose face showed the signs of a man worn down with worry.

"Yes, this is from Christian."

"It's bad news. Ah naw it's bad news," John whispered, seeing the Reverend's face. His heart thumped in his chest, and he could hardly breathe.

It was true that the Reverend thought some of it was unwelcome news. Unbelievably shocking news indeed in his mind. But nevertheless, he was happy to tell John that Christian was very much alive and living with a religious order of nuns in York. Then he read the letter aloud in its entirety.

On the way home John went over in his head the contents of the long letter. He had to remember for Peggy and for Christian's brothers and sisters.

She was living in York, with some nuns, and she was happy!

That was all *he* really needed to know. She was alive and she was happy. She'd described her journey and some of the good people she'd met on the way. Her love for her family was the main thing that had spurred her on as she didn't want to bring shame on them. But now she knew there was no shame. She was just closer to God. As he walked home he wondered what her life was like now. Living among nuns he was sure she would be safe, but the space created by her leaving was infinite. She had been the 'golden child', beautiful, kind and caring. Just talking to her, or even sitting beside her gave you a feeling of peace and calm and she'd certainly had a favourable effect on Peggy, he thought. She would be so missed.

But there was one aspect of her life that was hard for him to understand and come to terms with.

She was turning to Popery, to the Catholics. That's what the nuns were: Catholic. She said clearly in her letter that it was what she wanted and that she would be a nun herself one day. The voices were still there, but they were a part of her life now. This was her life forever, with the *Congregation of Jesus*. She prayed that her family would understand, but there was no turning back now.

It was a closed order so she would be confined to the Abbey, but she would have all the books she could read in a lifetime.

Reverend Clemitson had been visibly shocked as he read that she would become a Catholic. Popery? How could she? What a scandal.

John didn't care what religion she chose. It was all the same to him. Religion hadn't helped him or his family, despite what Peggy said.
Religion didn't stop your sons from dying too young.
Religion didn't put food on the table, not ordinary folks.
Religion didn't pay the rent.
Religion didn't stop people from starving.
What good was religion?
There was both a lightness and a heaviness around his heart as he walked home. That she was alive was the lightness. That she would never return, the heaviness. How could he give Peggy that news, that she would never see her golden child again? It could break her. Once a year they could visit, on her Saint's Day, the letter said.
But they didn't have the brass to do that.
It was too far.
He'd asked the vicar to reply, saying how happy they were for her because he didn't want Christian to think otherwise. To tell her how much they loved her and missed her. How they were glad that she was safe, and not carried away by robbers. That they would visit But he knew they wouldn't.
Giving Peggy the news was hard. He saw the first emotion of relief

on her face, pushed aside by the stronger emotion of grief, as she realized she would never see Christian again. This family news was something that John and Peggy would have rather kept to themselves, but as in all small villages, news travelled like wildfire. Despite none of them talking outside the cottage, Christian's fate was the talk of the place. She'd been gone quite a while now, and curiosity had reached almost fever pitch.

The talk veered from Christian being clandestinely married or being with child. It was even said, quite knowledgeably, that she had eloped and sailed to America, or that she had joined a band of travelling players.

No-one could even touch on the real reason for her disappearance as it was more bizarre than anything they could make up.

They knew it was something to wonder about because Reverend Clemitson himself had said, what he should not have said. He called it *a scandal,* so what were people supposed to think.

He wouldn't be drawn any further, but it was indeed a scandal to him that a child who had been baptized into the Church of England, followed a Protestant religion, and attended church regularly should turn her back on all of this and join the' incense swingers and followers of 'idolatry.' Catholicism was seen as a threat because it was associated with countries such as France and Spain, which were enemies of England.

But, despite the uproar, once the wind had settled, life went on as before.

Once more Betty was expecting a child. After having twin girls, the last time, she was understandably concerned about the possibility of this happening again. Being heavy with child in the summer months, even in Swaledale, was difficult, so she was grateful for a speedy, timely birth, in August once more, two years after the twins.

This produced another boy, Miles, after her grandfather, as tradition dictated,

She had her hands full, and no mistake, and with no Christian to help she had begun to rely even more on Little Peg, who at nineteen was more than capable. Chrissey and Elvey, at ten and seven years old, relished the responsibility and were able to carry out their childcaring roles competently, helping Peggy too with housekeeping chores such as bringing a pail of water, brushing the flagstones with a besom. They added Meadowsweet without even being asked.

Summer segued into a winter that was unseasonably warm. There was snow, but not of the thick drifting kind. There would always be snow, but this winter it didn't severely inconvenience anyone, just left a sparkling carpet over the fields and along the lanes. Jenny Goat left her cloven hoof marks around her winter housing, together with what they thought were the footprints of a fox. She was milked, the goose eggs collected and the geese watched carefully for predators, with Edward sitting for a couple of hours each night, with his gun. He didn't manage to shoot anything, except the old Oak tree, and frightened a family of Squirrels.

Despite the lack of snow, the winter was long and dark. Nights in front of the smoking peat fire made the family think once more of the boggart, but they had lost all heart for this since John had died. "Knitting," pronounced Betty. "Uz mun knit to mak brass fr summer."
"Aye, uz can knit. An uz can sing too," Peggy added.
In this way the long dark winter nights were made bearable, and it wasn't long before the first signs of Spring were reported.

1823

Little Peg was twenty-two years old. The last year she had found to be desperately sad. She missed Christian so much and was finding the realization that she would never see her again difficult. And she was wondering what her life was going to be like.

She still went to Church with Peggy and Betty and had recently been seen in the company of a young man. John had made sure she was aware of how to conduct herself, and she knew she was to bring him to meet her da before anything further could transpire. However she didn't know if she wanted to. She needed to talk to Jane about this: not Betty because Betty would be annoyingly positive about married life, or at least she thought she would be.

She begged Peggy to let her visit Jane that weekend, and was allowed, as long as Chrissey helped out, which she always did. Peggy was never on her own looking after her family.

Jane was still living at Keld, and it was a long walk for her to get there and back in one day so she would stay overnight. Allowed to take two goose eggs, she chose them herself and put them carefully in the bottom of her basket, almost skipping along the dirt road. She was excited as it was a good many months since she'd seen the sister she had been so close to when growing up. It was also a little bit worrying, making the journey all by herself.

She set off early, making sure she milked Jenny first, and made Chrissey promise to take her to the common.

It was well into spring and the days were warming up, but only slightly. She needed her warm shawl wrapped around her tightly but even then she felt the wind right through to her ribs. Not wanting to break the precious eggs, she was careful not to run too fast, and it was late afternoon when she walked into the village of Keld.

There had been no way of letting Jane know she was coming, and she was met with hugs and kisses at the doorway. Leonard was home already, sitting in front of the smoky fire, in his dirty work clothes, puffing on a clay pipe, his face black with the grime from his collier's work. Looking around the room Little Peg was surprised to see how unkempt it was – not like Jane at all. She watched her ladle a plateful of a tasty looking stew onto a plate and put it on front of her husband, who began eating as if he hadn't eaten for a week. Looking up she saw Jane watching her, and she knew that if Jane had known she was coming, the floor would have been brushed at least. A plate of stew was placed in front of Little Peg and she ate it gratefully.

Baby Maggie and toddler John were both asleep on a mattress in the corner so she stood looking down at them, thinking they looked well fed at least.

But Jane didn't. She never did.

"Uz can kip here, in front o t' fire, thee and me."

Leonard took himself off to the steep stairs after using the chamber pot, right there, in the corner of the room.

Little Peg had gladly accepted her supper and had been looking forward to the goose egg for breakfast but Leonard had clapped his eyes on the egg and said the same himself.

'Ah well' she thought. 'Ah'd rather ower Jane had t'other.'

As they joined the children on the mattress, she wondered if she dared ask Jane what she wanted to ask her. But Jane surprised her by saying first, "Dis thee 'ave a lad yet? Iz thee luvsum yet ower Peg?"

"Ah want t'hear abaht thee first Jane."

"Well sista. Thee can see there's niver enuf brass. The cottage is reight cowld and draughty. Leonard is as black as coal after fettle. Them bairns is two scamps."

She stopped, smiled and continued, "But, ah love 'im, an 'e luvs me. An those two bairns is ma life."

She stopped and looked down at her belly. "An there's another cumin. Ye dinna get bairns by holdin' hands ower Peg," and she proceeded to tell her exactly how you did 'get bairns.'

The next morning Peg insisted that Jane ate the egg, if not for her then for the bairn she was expecting.

'If thee's getting'wed, give uz till spring t'get this one awt," she laughed.

It was with a lighter step that Little Peg set off down the hill towards

Thwaite. Jane was happy.

******

When she turned into Scarr Houses there was Peggy watching for her, a look of relief on her face. There had been angry words the night before when John discovered his daughter was walking to Keld, alone.

Little Peg was now set on finding herself a husband. Peggy was happy to see her sweet, shy daughter, who had blossomed into a prettiness to rival any other, do just that. Peggy had seen the young men at church looking to see who was walking her home, with Peggy always in attendance. Remembering how plain she'd been when young made Peggy wonder when she'd turned into such a pretty lass. It seemed to have been a gradual metamorphosis, so slow that no-one realized, until they looked at her one day and saw a young woman with a beautiful smile, beautiful eyes. a pretty face and hair that shone like the sun.

She was so shy it was a wonder that any proposal of marriage had been made at all, but so pretty that it was a wonder there hadn't been many more.

In the end it was a collier from Tan Hill, Thomas Metcalfe, from a good family, who won the prize. He was the one she'd chosen. She had patiently waited her turn and here it was. It was all she'd ever wanted, from the time that she and Jane had played together with their stick dolls.

He had asked leave to marry her after she'd walked home with him (Peggy following behind) a total of only three times.

She was totally in agreement with the situation, although her shyness had prevented her from any meetings on her own. Even at T'Awd Roy she was too shy to dance with him and they had only stood together, talking.

They all decided on a May wedding, but they weren't to know it was going to be one of the coldest summers ever, so the old folks said. Spring flowers had just managed to poke their heads out of the soil and snowdrops were still flowering, their drooping white heads held on green stems that stood out from the snow around. It could have been so colourful, with daffodils, pilewort, and any amount of flowers. Yellow cowslips would be appearing soon, but Little Peg contented herself with a small posy of snowdrops and a few primroses in her hair and felt herself oh so fortunate to be marrying her Thomas, with Chrissey and Elvey as her flower girls. She had a new dress, a beautiful cobalt blue, and Peggy brought out her 'new dress' once more.

Her sister Betty managed to make it to the church, as her belly was swollen once more. She held on until June to give birth to William. And as young as they were, he was to be their last child.

Little Peg and her Thomas began their married life at Pit House, Tan Hill, where Thomas worked as a collier, turning coal into charcoal, like his brother-in-law, Jane's husband. They had a snug little cottage, and enough coal to keep them warm even though it was a windy, cold part of the dale.

She hadn't needed to talk with Betty, and Betty just couldn't bring herself to tell her anything, but Little Peg knew everything she needed to know anyway, from Jane.

Thomas was a very patient young man because he knew the prize was worth the wait. And he loved her very much.

Chapter 30

Ups and Downs

"There is something about poverty that smells like death."
(Zola Neale Hurston)

Michael was struggling. He knew he would. Even before he wed he knew he would struggle for brass. Since he'd married in 1820, he'd worked as a coal miner and it had been a good start. He had a pretty young wife who seemed to love him, a cottage that was better than those on either side of him, thanks to his da, and he had steady employment. That is, until he didn't.

Now, there was no work for him. And while he had been working there was none left over to put by for the tough times. There may have been if either of them knew how to manage the little money they had. Like Peggy said, he could be a bit gormless, and his 'pretty young wife' liked to spend his money.

Nanny gave him a farthing, or sometimes two at the weekend, and that was all he had after a week of work. That was soon spent. There was no more gambling for Michael.

After three years of marriage, he and Nanny had increased their number by the usual of one every eighteen months and had two tow haired boys: a toddler and a baby.

But by now his nightmare had come true. He couldn't afford his house rent.

Sitting with his head in his hands, he moaned, "What's we ganna dee Nanny? We canna buy food, nevva mind pay rent."

His wife wasn't one to be beaten and also couldn't abide any shows of self-pity, such as this. She took a much more pragmatic approach to the situation.

"Mickey. Shake theesel up thee big lump. Dee whit anyone else wud dee and gan t't' Parish."

He was loth to do this, and being the dreamer he was, decided to wait and see if the money fell from the skies for him. He could wait a little longer.

After all, he was unafraid of hard work and had spent long shifts down the mine. Even with that they hardly managed. How was it that as a working man he couldn't afford to pay rent and feed his family too? Could it be done he wondered?

"Mickey, 'as thee bin yit? Get thesel t't'Parish. If thee disn't ah'll shame thee by gannin' mesel."

"But Nanny", he pleaded. "Neen in our 'ouse 'as iver been t't'parish, Me da says that's his pride. He'll be shamed."

"Aw, Mickey, Mickey. Thee big lummox. Will thy da pay for uz food an' rent? Gan t't'parish or starve us out o' this cottage."

With his cap in hand, and really more afraid of what Nanny his outspoken wife would do, he did what all others in his situation did. He paid his first visit to the Muker Select Vestry: a committee appointed from churchwardens and land holders, by law, to take care of the unemployed, the sick and the destitute. Michael came into the last category and because he had been born in Muker Parish they had to hear him. Standing before them, he felt the shame flood through his body because he couldn't provide for his family. But, as Nanny said, as she pushed him out of the door, pride didn't fill empty bellies and it didn't pay rent to keep a roof over your head.

The Select Vestry only paid out to what they considered were 'the deserving poor.' Thankfully, that was him, because they paid his whole rent owing, one pound and six shillings, directly to his landlord, John Alderson, covering arrears up to September 1823. The relief he was given lasted for one month. The rent was paid, for now, but they still had scant brass for food.

Since he'd married he'd thought back often to when he'd been a single man. Even then there had been challenging times. What on earth had made him think he could support a family? In fact, he'd known even then that he couldn't. And now there were two small children he was responsible for, for many years to come. That thought itself was terrifying.

Very soon the situation necessitated a second visit to the Select Vestry which was even more demeaning than the first. They were convened at their weekly meeting when he entered, head lowered, eyes on the floor.

"Michael Hutchinson, his father from Thorns. Born at Southwaite but resident here for over 20 years," said the curate. And to Michael, "And what do you want this time." He went on, "Did we not already pay your rent arears?"

They were very parsimonious when handing out relief. The feeling was that if they made it too easy, they would be inundated with requests. You didn't have to mind their comments.

"Yes Sir," he replied, "but work be so scant and payin' so poor we have nutin to feed the bairns."

"Well, the young must be fed. They ought not to suffer because of your lax ways," snorted the most prosperous landowner there.

'What would he know about hunger, or hardship?' thought Michael, but he wisely held his tongue. It was the best way.

"We'll gi' ye a peck o' meal, until thy work pays more," added another, and they all agreed.

He thanked them and left. What could he say? That it wasn't fair? That he worked hard? That there wasn't enough work to support them all? That it was even harder trying to work when you were practically starving?

It was talked about that some families had agreed to be relocated by the Select Vestry to the factory towns and coalfields of Lancashire, with any removal costs paid.
For some it had been a success. For others it hadn't.
Although their home parish still had to provide relief if they needed it, now they may be away from family and friends that had made the situation more bearable. Many had found themselves in the same situation as the one they had left behind.
Michael had so far resisted. The last thing his family needed was to be uprooted from everything they knew: father, mother, brothers, sisters, left so far away.
So he continued to look for a way to earn the brass he needed to put food on the table and pay the rent. Living in hope, and with his best efforts, once the work as a collier had finished, all he found was a few days here and there as an agricultural labourer. That was all there was to be had: unless he went back to the mine, or the smelt mill, both of which were killing him.
Walking to the nearest farm he had managed to secure a day or two labouring, as he already had experience. That fed them for a while longer with Michael having meals at the farm and smuggling

food home. He wished he could do this for ever. It was perfect for him. But now it was the quarter end, and they had no money for rent. He wouldn't go to his da, and he had no-one else to ask.

Betty

Betty had been married for just over ten years to the gentle soul who had taken her dancing that year at T'Awd Roy.

She was happy, living with her good husband and their six children. Her twin girls were a major help to her, and she'd made sure that they and Betsy had learned her ways of keeping a clean house and feeding a family, as young as they were.

When their sixth child William came into this world, in September 1823 her husband Will had been feeling 'badly' for a few months, but because he seemingly wasn't as ill as Miles or Young John had been, Betty saw no reason to worry. She did stop him from sitting over the smoky peat fire and made him walk outside in the open air.

When the day came that he couldn't go to work because he was so short of breath, she began to wonder, and to worry, and to see what had been in front of her eyes the whole time.

But not Will. Not her Will.

"Lass," he whispered that morning. "Ahs got such gripe in me chest."

Watching him suffer like this was as bad as seeing him struggle out of the door each morning, to be returned home, unfit for work.
He had a cough. Then he had a fever.
He was half the man she'd married, so ill that he'd spent the last ten days in his bed. Betsy and the twins did all they could to make him comfortable while Thomas brought in peat for the fire.
Bu she could see the way it was going now.
All she could think of was how to make this man that she loved, comfortable: how to ease his pain and help him. He was such a good husband. She'd been lucky, as that wasn't always the case.
But apart from using the bark of the Willow tree, and a warm drink of Meadowsweet infusion, she just couldn't.
That did seem to help but she knew that no-one got away from this. The Angel of Death was not finished with this family. At the end of 1823, spreading its wings, it came a little nearer and swooped down onto another Hutchinson residence. This time it didn't take a Hutchinson, though it was a Hutchinson who suffered.
As he lay, his breathing short and laboured, she cradled his head on her chest, and talked to him, softly, as they used to whisper to each other in bed when the children were near. She said all the loving things to him that she was used to saying and kissed his cheek.
At the end, clutching his chest in agony, he couldn't breathe.
The medical man, brought by young Thomas, was too late, but

there was nothing that could have been done anyway. There never was.

She felt she should cry but was in too much shock. Thinking it was better done sooner she brought the children in to see him, and to say their goodbyes. Then he was laid out in the kitchen until the burial.

John paid for the service, because Betty would spend the brass on food for their bairns, and on the appointed day he was lowered into the ground, while his family watched. There were prayers from the vicar, meant to be consoling. There were songs. The children asked for one they liked from Sunday School, Amazing Grace, singing it with their clear sweet voices and as it was so near Christmas, Hark the Herald Angels Sing. The vicar said some words about Will: how he was a good family man and husband, a kind neighbour and a stalwart of the community. It made John remember the Sunday School lesson when the children were small, where they had to write about someone being *a good man.* He couldn't remember who, but he did remember thinking it would be good to be remembered that way. And it was a fitting tribute to Will.

There were plenty of tears, but the walk home was completed in silence. John didn't know how to comfort her, his capable, reliable daughter. She was always the one who gave comfort. He knew himself what it was like to lose a life partner, but he didn't know what to say, or what to do. He had no words of comfort for her, none that would help. After all, they hadn't helped him. Muker churchyard had so many of his family there now.

Peggy bustled around, providing practical help, looking after the children, sending Chrissey to the store, or to take one or two of the children down the lane.
Seeing that Betty was numb, that she was unable to think beyond day to day, all they could do was help with the children. She'd been so happy, but now she was desperately unhappy. If she didn't have the children she felt she would just lie in bed all day.
'Why can't I go to sleep and wake up on a day when this hadn't happened?' was her thought.
The children asked for their da, but accepted he was in heaven, as Peggy told them, 'wrapped in the arms of Jesus.'
How could they not miss him like she did? But if they did, their little lives would be broken. Then, like all young children, as long as there was someone there to love them, and their needs were met, they could eventually live with the memory of their father.
It was enough for them to know that he loved them and that he sent a bright star to remind them.
After a month or two she let her mind go to the place where it

didn't want to go. She'd travelled there, a bit further every day, until she was in that place.

There was still a lifetime to live. Would she have to live the rest of her life alone, with no comfort? At the moment she couldn't bear the thought of another man.

But for now, she had to think of her six children, and not of herself. The parish helped out a little, a shilling here, a shilling there. But for the most part she took in washing, with help from Elvey, and did charring at the Inn in Muker.

Peggy and Chrissey looked after the children, and she told anyone who asked, that she didn't know what she would have done without her. But that's what families did.

They saw in the New Year together for 1824. Michael and Jane were happy to be back home with their families for a short while, and the little cottage was full to the rafters once more. It was Edward who was the master storyteller this year as Michael was too short of breath, but he said he was "letting the wee uns 'ave a go."

And he marvelled at how Betty managed to keep her household going with the little money she had.

'How dis she dee that' he wondered, but he couldn't ask her.

January was a bad month for Michael, who was once more asking for relief. It was either that or starve. And who would let their family starve to save their pride? That's what he kept saying to himself.

Once more they granted the peck of meal, the difference between food and starvation, as well as a weekly sum this time, to help with his family for the rest of the year.

Nanny looked for work, but they lived in such a small place that there were no opportunities,

The Overseers of the Poor were very generous, giving him an extra five shillings in August to go to apply for work wherever he could find it, with another peck of meal at summer's end.

Michael had always been a dreamer. He still was, but his dreams these days were of a much different calibre. He dreamed of a wonderful life,

where there was bread every day,

where there may be a little meat at the end of the week,

where he could afford to pay the rent,

where his children were clothed and not in rags,

where he could afford to burn coal for a fire instead of selling it.

It wasn't a lot to ask.

He would feel like a king, but this dream was impossibly out of his reach.

He found a few weeks' work repairing the highways, but that didn't earn him enough money to keep everyone and pay the rent too. It was a vicious circle.

As he worked digging, he often daydreamed about his time at Southwaite, in the valley, when he was young. Animals were his passion then, and they would be now. He'd been such a carefree boy, loving to wander, spying any kind of wildlife, watching the birds rather than scaring them.

Now his years down the lead mine and in the smelt mill had ruined his health, just like most of the men he knew.

His visits to the Select Vestry, cap in hand and looking contrite, had earned him a regular pension of two shillings a week, 'until a change in his circumstances should happen.'

It wasn't enough. It could never be enough to keep them all and pay his rent. His boys were still very young and didn't eat much. He worried too much to even want to eat, and Nanny wouldn't eat until the bairns had eaten as much as they wanted. How did families manage who had more children? How did they afford to pay their rent and their taxes? He thought back to when he was still 'at home' with his ma and da. They had twelve bairns. He should have been a Blacksmith then maybe he could manage. Their Miles was going to have a better life when he finished his apprenticeship with da.

"How dust they ken uz can live on this," he moaned to his wife Nanny.

"Juz be grateful we have this," she replied. "There'll be graft somewhere. Thee juz muz find it." She had past the point of being sympathetic and was tired of his moaning. "Grup th grund t'put sum veg in't'garden, naw thee has nee fettle."

So he did.

Hay timing was another way, and thinking back to when he and his da were cutting the hay together, windrowing, turning the grass to dry it in the sun that summer, just made him unhappy for what he had lost. He'd been so proud when his da had seen him working with the men, working almost alongside each other.

A lifetime ago. Another world ago. That was someone else, not him. He hadn't felt carefree at the time, but now he realized that he just hadn't known then what carefree felt like.

At the beginning of September 1825 he found some regular work, but his meagre pension of two shillings a week was stopped. The work he'd found was back at the Smelt Mill, and with his scarred lungs, he just couldn't do the work. He was thirty-seven years old and already an old man. His body was broken.

Jimmy Alderson gave him a little work as a farm labourer that very dry summer. He managed to stumble through it, earning just enough. One of the best things about farm labouring was that meals were part of his pay, incredibly good meals. Not only was he well fed, but again he was smuggling food home for the family.

They were lucky, all of them, to avoid the smallpox that raised its head in Muker, in 1826. She took both old and young in her indiscriminate grasp. A vaccination had been developed and Dr Rudd had vaccinated those who could pay, or sometimes the Parish paid.

"Ma! Ma! "shouted Chrisey running in one afternoon. "Chris Harker has the pox!"
"Stay away our lass. Diven't thee be gannin near."
"But ma, whi abaht them yung bairns? Them poor yung bairns?"
"Whit abaht them poor young bairns?"
No-one would go near for fear of this terrible disease. No-one knew how it was caught, or spread, or where it came from.
But Peggy surprised herself. Every morning she took a loaf, just a small one, to the house, knocking on the door and leaving it on the doorstep. That was the least she could do she thought because no one else seemed to be doing anything. They had themselves to

think on. She did this every day for two weeks. John would have been so proud of his wife, but she didn't tell.

Children died. Adults died. Old people died.
It swept through the dale: another angel of death.
The Hutchinsons avoided this curse, but many of their friends and neighbours died. Some survived but carried the pitted scars as evidence and constant reminders of their fight. And then the scourge swept out again, along the dale, to another village.

As a testament to the circle of life, in early 1827 Michael's third child, Alice, was born. All he could think was more mouths to eventually feed, and less money, without thinking of his part in this! To earn a shilling, he sent his two boys bird scaring, as he'd done. They worked a full seven days for a bag of meal. Nanny made their own bread, and the meal made porridge for the boys. She also cooked oatcakes on the backstone of the hearth, made from oatmeal and water.
She tried to keep their bellies full with flour and water dumplings, to which she could add stewed windfall apples, or a goose egg, for flavour: anything really.
She had managed, when Michael was too weak to do it, to till a small amount of soil to grow a few vegetables and grew potatoes

in a bucket. A walk to see Peggy and John took all her energy but at least she came home with a few eggs, onions and anything else they had growing. But at the end of the summer Michael was once more destitute, or more destitute than normal. He couldn't pay his rent again at quarter end, and this time he was afraid his family might be sent to the Workhouse. He'd tried putting a penny by each week for rent, but always seemed to need it for something else.

And Nanny was terrified. She'd been told more stories about how they would be treated. Her children might be taken from her and made to work. They would have to wear a workhouse uniform.

But, she reasoned, they would be housed, fed and clothed, even though the work may kill them.

Walking into the meeting, Michael was greeted with, "Naw then Mick. 'Ere agin? Hast thee no pride?"

"Aye ah has that Sir, but it's brass ah needs, not pride."

"Impudence, mind, will cost thee lad."

He was forced to apologize to everyone there, and abase himself once more, to have his rent paid.

"We'll pay thy rent for the year. To thy landlord, Richard Fawcett, twenty shillings."

"Ay," said another, "and get out there and find thee self some graft. Thee's still a yung un."

As bad as it was, he felt he could put up with the indignity, as long as they continued to help his family. His children and his wife needed this. He could have slept in the fields, but not them. Now he was constantly, gnawingly hungry, but made sure the bairns got most of the little food they had.

He wanted to work. What kind of a man was he if he didn't, when his wife and children were always so very hungry.

Bringing berries home he'd picked for the children and a few mushrooms meant a little to eat. A truly little.

Because they lived up at Tan Hill his da didn't know how bad things were, but Peggy had worked it out. She'd seen how thin and how pale the young woman had become when she visited.

"'Ere lass. 'Ave a bowl o' broth", and she fed whichever child Nanny brought with her. Michael did have pride, and so far it hadn't let him ask his da for help, but he must have known where the goose eggs, potatoes and vegetables came from. It was a veritable feast when Nanny returned from Thwaite! Doing the best he could, he even managed a shift or two a week down the mine, but his lungs were addled. He thought a lot and often about Miles and young John, and how they'd suffered and died so young with miners' lung disease. And by now he knew he had it too. He thought he probably had the consumption too, just like them.

1828

The year ended at Tan Hill, and another began. They had no Yule Log this year. There had been no holly and ivy to cheer their cold cottage. They had no heart for the season.

In early January the Select Vestry had seen him again.

"Nah then Michael. What's it t'be."

"Sir," he began. "Ah's starving. Ower lass is starvin. Me three bairns're starvin'."

He spoke so softly that they could hardly hear him.

"What abaht the mines? What abaht the colliery? What abaht the fields?" retorted one.

"All those places to find work, and yet you say you're all starving?" asked another.

"Look at me," Michael pointed to his chest. "Ah can hardly breathe." Whee's ganna gi'me any graft?"

"And what are ye deeing wit'brass we gi' yee?" asked a corpulent landowner, who looked as if he'd never missed a meal in his life. This question seemed to shock even the other Vestry members. Ignoring it and not expecting any answer, they awarded Michael two shillings a week.

"Get thy lass owt t'graft. She can dee sumat," the corpulent farmer suggested.

The money bought them a bag of meal, and they existed on watery porridge.

He was too weak to even look for work and unable to do any work if he could find it. Nanny went to the local Inn and managed to persuade the Innkeeper that he needed yet another char lady. He didn't really, but she could be very persuasive.

While life seemed to hold no more for Michael, his younger brother Miles, born just after the death of his namesake, was beginning a new chapter in his.

*****

Although it was common knowledge that they were always together, Miles had been extremely excited to tell John and Peggy that a young woman, Hannah Cottingham, had agreed to be wed. John had kept out of this apart from giving his son a 'gypsy's warning' about treating the girl right. The rest of it was on her father's shoulders and he'd spoken to her father who was happy with the arrangement.

Hannah was a sweet, shy young girl, not unlike little Peg, and only twenty-one years.

Although he was also young, at twenty-two, after what had happened to his brothers, Miles and John, he didn't want to wait too long.

They were married by Banns in September 1829, at Muker church, by Reverend Lowther.

Summer hadn't quite ended. The days were still long, sometimes quite warm, and a wedding was a good enough reason to sing, dance, eat and drink.

Peggy was excited, because it was the first of her own boys to wed, but for John it was even more of a happy occasion. Miles was his apprentice and was by now a good Blacksmith. He could give the position and the smithy to him, and that would be a great start to their married life. Miles had a trade and would never be out of work: the most recent in the long line of Hutchinson Blacksmiths.

"Lad. Ah's right proud o' thee. Thy grandfather would be too," he said, ruffling the young man's hair with affection as if he were a child.

Miles was inwardly glowing with pride himself, just as his father had when the same was said to him, all those years ago. As always, a young man could bask in the knowledge that his father was proud of him. Some never heard those words, whether deserved or not.

"Aye. A Blacksmith is all I want t'be. So da, thee's done a good job wi'uz."

Looking at his son, he replied, "Thee'll be a grand Blacksmsith. It's in thy blud."

John was now sixty-nine years old. He hadn't expected to live as long as this, and that had made seeing some of his boys meet the Lord before him, as Peg called it, even harder to bear.

He tried now to find joy in the simple things, like the early morning birdsong, or holding his grandchildren, or poaching a rabbit with Edward, or an evening with his family around him singing the songs they loved while Edward played the fiddle.
Never, ever in religion, or the Lord, or the Church.
They'd done nothing for him.
As a younger man he'd been too busy, earning the brass they needed, or the barter needed, to feed them all and pay the rent. He knew he'd missed these things then and wanted to make sure he didn't miss them now. He thought about his parents, how much they'd supported him and how it had been more of a partnership with his own father as it was with Miles now.

It was early 1830. Signs of spring were all around them, but snow was still to be seen on the hills and in the hedgerows.
And by now Michael was very ill. It was the same story.
He coughed, sweated, shivered and vomited all day, laying on a pallet in front of the fire. He didn't want his children to see him like this but there was no choice. As with young John, they made him lie outside as much as he could, away from the smoky fireside,

trying to breathe cleaner air to heal his lungs.

Nothing helped. Nothing could. His family had seen the signs beforewith Miles and young John, but Nanny had not.

She refused to believe her young husband was going to die and still hoped for his recovery, spending money she didn't have, to call Doctor Rudd.

He told her plainly that her husband was extremely ill, and that she should prepare for the worst. And, seeing the circumstances in which they lived he sent his bill straight to the new Poor Law Guardians.

Following that the overseers had increased his pension slightly, in an attempt to help the family, but Michael was unable to struggle any longer and in March 1830 he died.

Nanny had no money to bury him, but she was determined he would have a proper burial. She went once more to the Select vestry, now called the Poor Law Guardians.

"Now Nanny. Thee's got a man t'bury," pronounced Dick Alderson. "Ah suppose thee needs the brass t'dee it."

Swallowing her pride, which was exceedingly difficult when faced with this attitude, she cried the customary few tears, wiped her face and asked for help.

They must have been feeling generous that morning as they paid for the whole event. There was even a service. This plus the coffin and hire of the Muker funeral hearse, amounted to one pound eleven shillings and eleven pence.

The service was short, with a prayer for his immortal soul, and a song chosen by John, at Nanny's request.

'It's a great pity they couldn't give him this money when he needed it. When we all needed it,' was her thought.

The final one of Alice's four sons was now gone. Only Betty and Mary remained, and they'd both had their share of heartache.

Michael's wife and three children were left destitute, alone and with no means of support, except the Poor Law, and family, just like Betty. Nanny was a Calvert, and the Calverts were a well-known family, but her mother didn't visit, and she hadn't the energy to walk into Thwaite to visit her. It was just too far. She didn't know if her ma was aware of their visits to the Guardians of the Poor, but she hadn't offered any help. She was perhaps embarrassed that her daughter was in such dire straits.

Swallowing her pride again, Nanny walked into the meeting with her three children and made her elder son Simon ask for the help they needed. To support herself and their three children she was given a pension of four shillings a week, double what they had allowed Michael, and that was how they survived in the short term.

How blind did the overseers have to be to see just how ill he had been, and how there was no way he could work. The Hutchinson family were known as good workers, yet that hadn't helped at all. Every time it was decided that it was the pauper's fault that they needed money: that they were lazy and unwilling to work.

She'd been married for only ten years, and again, like Betty, and many other women in the dale, was already a widow. She and Betty were living the same life, suffering the same hardships, and dependent the same way on the Guardians of the poor.

However, Nanny was a very resourceful young woman and was determined she would still make something of her life.

She didn't need to wait. While looking around her for opportunities, she heard that the school master at Angram, Anthony Wharton, had recently lost his wife and was looking for a housekeeper. He wasn't young. In fact, he was much older than her, and that was perfect.

A housekeeper's position was an excellent solution to her predicament. She had no experience, apart from running her own household, but she was determined to have that life.

Having often been told that her amber eyes were one of her best features, she made sure to obtain, by any means, a ribbon for her bonnet that matched the colour of her eyes. Her clothing needed mending, so she mended it, cleaning up her one dress as best she could: the green dress she'd been married in ten years ago. She was pale after years of malnutrition, so she used a trick she had seen ladies use at the Fair, of pinching her cheeks, so they had a deceptively healthy glow. The trick could be reapplied as often as necessary.

Leaving her three children with Peggy, she walked up to his house and presented herself at Mr Wharton's door for the position.
She knew she was still pretty, even though a hard life had faded her looks a little.
"Gud day t'thee sir. Ah wud like to come work for thee in thy hoose, t'mind thee, and cook for thee. Ah hears thee is wantin' a lass for this."

Speaking respectfully to him, she remembered to lower her eyes. On her arm she had a covered basket, containing a selection of pies she'd baked, and these she offered to him to taste. Giving away food that would have fed her children was hard, but the taste of them and the sight of Nanny was enough to persuade him. She was lucky that his reputation as a strict, authoritarian had meant there was not much interest in the position.
"I will need a written character for thee, young lady. Can thee

provide one? "

She produced a letter from her skirt pocket

"Sir, from the vicar, sir, t'thee."

By now he was enraptured, and captured, and could see what he was meant to see: a shy young girl, looking for a respectable way of earning money to keep her.

She worked for him for two months, with the children living with Peggy, but eventually she took them to his door, not knowing for certain what his reaction would be.

She need not have worried. He was pleased to have a family, and by now would have done anything to make sure Nanny stayed with him.

The children and Nanny had been living at Angram in the schoolmaster's house, for three years, before Anthony and Nanny were married, and it was a much quieter affair than the last one.

She missed Michael, but her children came first, always. Living where she did, the children didn't see their cousins much, and links with the family were not strong. John had three grandchildren he now did not see, and that was a cause of sorrow for him, as he thought of what Alice would make of it. No doubt she would have insisted they visit Angram, despite feeling unwanted. Family is family.

More News

"Ma. Da. Thee'll niver ken," shouted Betty, as she burst into their cottage like a whirlwind, cheeks rosy, hair windswept and bonnet trailing.

"Nay dowter. Neither will uz. Settle theesel down and tell," laughed Peggy, pleased to see Betty in such good spirits. It wasn't long after the death of Michael, and good news was welcome.

"Ower John, thee ken him, my Will's brother, is gannin t'America, to Philadelphia and takin his lass and bairns," she shouted, hardly able to contain herself, the news had been so unexpected and extremely exciting.

"America? America?" Peggy screamed with disbelief. "Arl that way? So whee's payin' for that then? They cannit."

"The parish is. The Poor Law Guardians is payin," she answered."

"Well, that caps owt."

Sitting on the settle, in front of the fire, John opened one eye and took in the sight of his hardworking daughter, who'd had her own share of heartache, and proved he'd been listening all along. "Why's he gannin' ti America?"

"Why d'ya think da? There's jobs there. Thee knaws there's neen here."

Sitting down at the table with her head in her hands, she continued wistfully, "Liverpool first, then onto a ship, the Delaware. And then the Guardians is givin' him £20."

"What? That's a fortune" Peggy shrieked.

"Aye, but he's ganna need more brass than that," added John.

"Eeh, ower Betty. Thee'll miss that family," sighed Peggy, taking her hand.

"That ah will ma, and thee knaws, ah's a bit jealous. A lot jealous. It's an adventure that mah Will 'nd ah could ah had."

Betty found this news very unsettling, and she spent many a night thinking about the possibility of following them: daydreaming about the life they would have, in a far-off country. Her brother-in-law was a farmer, and he and his wife were already forty years of age when they travelled.

But what opportunity was there for a widow and her six children? She talked and talked about this with John and Elizabeth, his wife, who also had a family of six children, from eleven years to a child of only one year. It was a perilous journey for young children, and some may not survive. But Betty too had six children and would never leave any of them behind. That was too much to risk. But it was still good to dream. To journey from Liverpool to Philadelphia in North America was a journey of two weeks and would be in the worst accommodation: below decks, cramped and with no comfort. They didn't know where they would be living, but they hoped for a better life.

And Betty just hoped for a letter.

Chapter 31

Miles and Hannah

"Each morning we are born again. What we do today is what matters most."

(Buddha)

Miles and Hannah were now wed and had set up their home at Scarr Houses, just along the lane from John and Peggy.

They were poor. They had nothing but a life together ahead of them but they were happy. Miles was a Blacksmith now, out of his apprenticeship and ought to be thinking of his experience as a journeyman but he didn't want to leave the dale, not yet anyway.

The lead mining industry was stumbling on and opportunities for work were few. Some, like John Pounder went to America. But many more left for the coal fields of Lancashire. Miles was fortunate. He had a trade. Others were not so fortunate.

It was a tragedy that, in order to prevent them from being a drain on the poor rate, some children as young as nine years old were being sent to the coalfields, without their parents.

"Them power bairns," Peggy lamented when she heard. Some were already in the Workhouse, but others weren't. Parents just couldn't afford to keep them.

His brother Kit now a grown man of twenty-six and a lead miner, was thinking of moving to the coal mines, and was trying to persuade his brother Edward, just a year younger, to go with him.

"Ah cannit abide on't that both ower lads might leave," Peg lamented to John all day every day.

He was thinking too, how quiet the place would be if they did go, and such a distance. They wouldn't see either of them again.

It was because Kit's friend had gone to Colne with his family the year before and was working down a coal mine. Sending a message through the Poor Law Guardians, who visited regularly to take care of those they had relocated, Kit had been invited join them as a lodger until he found a place.

Looking on it as a bit of an adventure was the only thing to do. He knew all about lead mining. How different could coal mining be? What else was there to know? You were underground for most of the day, hacking out the lead, or the coal with a pick, while your bones ached so much that it felt they were in a vice. You came up dirty, covered in the dust that had already got into your lungs, day after day.

"Cum on, Eddy lad," he chivvied his brother. "There's nowt hereabouts, nee fettle, nee brass. We'll mak sum money in't' coal mines, and mebbe meet some reet pretty lasses," he added, hoping that would persuade him.

Kit hadn't seen a lass that had turned his head yet, but there may be someone in Colne.

At that Edward smiled. "Ah've already got ma pretty lass."
Kit thought he'd kept that one a secret, and wondered if he was joking. But Edward followed it up with a name.
"Annas Milner is ma pretty lass."
Kit had seen her. Her family were from Thwaite and he was, as Peggy loved to tell anyone who'd listen, "reet smitten wi the lass". He couldn't be persuaded to leave for Colne. And who could blame him. He seemed to have regular work in the lead mines and wasn't affected like Alice's boys had been.

And while brother Kit was coal mining in Colne, having decided to make the move, Edward married Annas the next year at Muker. She was just nineteen and her parents' only child. Again, John left it all to her own da to put restrictions on their courtship, but he didn't. He trusted the Hutchinson lads.

At seventeen years old Elvey appointed herself a 'flower girl' for her brother's wife, just because she wanted to be, like she'd been for Miles and Hannah.

Miles and Hannah were the very picture of a happy young couple. And the hopes of many young men were dashed the day she met Miles at the altar and agreed to be his wife. She was so pretty that some actually called her beautiful. She had hair as dark as the night sky with no moon, almost to her waist. Despite being quite slim, there was no doubt that she was a woman, and not a girl, and as she walked, her hips swayed slightly, but not too much. She was totally unaware of the effect this had on the men who watched her, and that was part of her charm.

Making sure that she brushed her hair and with a flower behind her ear, every day she walked along to the smithy to meet her man. John recounted to Peggy the bashful looks of both when they met, how Miles' face lit up when he saw her, and how she blushed when she saw him too.

"Aye Peg, they's right sweet on each other. "

"They's more'n that, ye barmpot," laughed Peggy.

And that was the end of the Hutchinson weddings for rather a long time.

John and Peggy were getting on in years and, with Miles as the Blacksmith, John did little work.

Now there were only Will, Chrissey and Elvey at home, and all were working, so John thought that maybe he could take life a little easier. All the children were grown up, and they didn't need him.

With free time on his hands, something he had never had, having worked all his life from a child, he spent some time in the village Inn, some just walking, sometime just sitting on his "hunkers" on the front step, chewing the sweet ends of the long grass.
He'd never smoked before, but recently he'd taken to a clay pipe now and then, as he sat mulling over his long life.
There was a profound change of pace in his life, and it wasn't unpleasant. In Peggy's too. There were no children to rear, and there was no work to do. John helped Miles out now and again, for a little bit of money. They didn't need much.
They helped Betty with her children, but she could manage really. They hardly saw Nanny and the children. And they never saw Mary. Edward had settled down with Annas in Thwaite and was working in the lead mines. His brother Will was working there too.
Yes, life was hugely different now for John and Peggy, but for others it was very much the same.

Miles and Hannah were a couple whose happiness made everyone smile, and after a year they had their first child: a blond-haired boy, who took after his grandfather John. Peggy loved to look after him, sitting him on her knee, stroking his hair, kissing the top of his head. As soon as he could walk he tottered around chasing the geese, with no fear of them at all. He ate his dish of meal porridge which he seemed to love, with his grandparents. John took immense pride in walking along with him aloft on his shoulders, to Thwaite and then back along to Muker.

It could be said he was the favourite grandson if there was such a thing. He had been named John after all.

Miles was a good Blacksmith and had plenty of work, spending his days as his father had, making horseshoes, shoeing horses, making picks and hammers, ironing cartwheels, as well as the smaller, but no less important jobs of ironing clogs, and making nails. Life continued with its usual rhythm of the days, weeks and seasons. Little John was a sturdy boy who loved his food and loved to play. He was often to be seen running along the lane, chasing birds, and even rats, clutching a hunk of hard dry bread in his little hand.

On warmer days Peggy and his mother Hannah stood at their doorway, chatting to each other, and to anyone who came by.

On chilly days they stayed inside, by the coal fire, and were often joined by Betty who needed some company, now her husband was gone. But she didn't have as much time on her hands as they did, with six children and no man in the house.

Those times were pleasant, convivial, family times, to be enjoyed and remembered. And if they had a laugh or two, then so much the better.

"Awld lass. Peggy awld lass, "shouted John. "Hannah needs thee."
It was September 1833, and she was birthing a second bairn.
Bustling into the cottage, a miniature whirlwind, Peggy immediately took charge, helping Hannah with the birth while little John was at Betty's being fed.
It was fairly quick, an unremarkable but painful birthing. The midwife had to be called, as was the rule now, to check the baby and mother over, and ensure both were healthy.
She arrived just as this baby, a second boy, came loudly into the world, with a high-pitched keening cry. Giving the baby to Hannah, who put him straight to the breast, the midwife finished off the necessaries, making sure of the afterbirth, and left.

"Where's ower Miles?" Peggy asked Hannah, who could hardly keep her eyes open.
"Alang the road," meaning at the smithy.
"Has neebody been t'tell im thee'd started?"
"He kenned, but he was badly this mornin, so ah telt 'im t'go

t'work."

Outside she went and screamed up the lane. Her voice was not to be ignored when it was at this pitch.

"John. John. Jooohn."

"Aye, ma pet?" This was his greeting when he was a little cross with her and trying not to be.

"Ower John man, gan and see t'thee son. Hannah reckons he was badly this mornin' and he needs t'knaw he has a son, at least," and as she spoke she waved her arm in the direction of the smithy,

Off he trudged to the smithy. Walking inside he looked all over for Miles, but it was too dark to see anything.

"Why hasn't thee lit the fire?"

At that, he heard a cough, seeming to come from behind the forge. Walking around, he was shocked to see Miles lying there on his side, his knees tucked up and his arms around them, and he seemed to be shivering.

"Aw lad," he whispered, as he knelt down beside him. "What ails thee?"

Miles was unable to answer, and John was sufficiently worried to call in the neighbours, two grown lads who hadn't yet set off for work, to help him transport Miles back home. It wasn't far, but he was tall, and dead weight.

"Fetch 'im in 'ere." Peggy had been scouring the lane waiting for him to appear and was standing at the doorway of Miles' cottage. The fire was on, and when she saw him shaking, as if with cold, she fetched a blanket and stirred the fire to make it burn brighter.

It was September, and not yet so cold, but Miles shook, as if unclothed in the middle of a snowstorm. Pulling his shirt around his neck, with one hand, and holding his other to his forehead, he groaned with the pain of the fever.

Peggy knew there had been others like this in the villages around, and that it happened regularly. Her son-in-law, Jane's husband Leonard, had been ill with the fever that March, and he'd recovered, as had many others.

Everyone just called it "the fever", and like all ailments, they didn't know what caused it. All they knew was it came and went, and often took a poor soul or two with it.

Some recovered but were totally exhausted for a good while. There was nothing you could do to prevent it, they thought. You either got the fever, or you didn', but there was a theory that it was because of something in the air.

"How long's he bin this bad," she asked Hannah.

"Just this day ma. Not long. And it's got much worse the day lang."

"Has thee called for the medical man?"

"Nay ma. He'll be well."

Peggy looked into his face and knew he had a long road to recovery before him. Smoothing his hot brow with a cold wet rag, she tried to soothe him with comforting words while Hannah attended to the bairn.

Peggy was so worried that she stayed by his side, day after day, that whole week, nights too. She was sometimes with John and sometimes alone, while Hannah looked to the two little boys. Her husband couldn't eat and had to be forced to drink even a sip of water.

His fever made him delirious, shouting out about things she couldn't see, pointing his weary arm into the shadows.

He called for his sister Christian, but she had left long ago.

Betty came for a little while, but she had enough work at home.

"Aw John man," Peggy sobbed. "He's nobut a bairn himself. My own bairn."

"Dinna fasch theesel, awld Lass. He winnet dee. He canit dee," and maybe he believed it himself.

And then, while Miles was in the throes of this fever, Hannah began to take ill herself. Very soon she was as delirious as he was.

For one week they lay side by side, suffering together, but each unaware of the other, getting weaker and weaker.

As Miles, the first one to take ill, was not improving, and a rash had appeared, all over his trunk and limbs, John thought it was time to see if the medical man, Dr Rudd, could help.

But it was Typhus, he told them, and only a few recovered. Jane had been lucky that her husband had, but Miles, and Hanah did not recover.

John and Peggy were beaten again.

That was five of their grown boys who had died: and not just died but had suffered terrible deaths, long, lingering and painful. Another light had gone from their lives. A young life, with a young family. This time John almost cursed a god who could let this happen to poor young folks who had done nothing but good in their short lives.

But he stopped short at that.

Later that week another young Hutchinson boy joined his brothers in Muker churchyard. His little baby boy was only two weeks old. His pretty young wife, pretty no more, joined him one week later. She'd called the new baby Christopher.

The curse that took them was Typhus fever. It had a name and was noted in the Parish Records.

Now things had changed once more. John and Peggy had a new

role. Or rather they were back to their old one, as 'parents' to John and Christopher, the two young orphans, their grandsons. They'd had a short hiatus, a period where they'd left the parenting of young children behind them. But fate had a different idea.

Putting aside their grief was something they were used to doing now, so they picked themselves up, and carried on, having the two boys to live with them.

They weren't young and had already passed the age where they'd expected to die. John was now seventy-three, and Peggy sixty-six. They had some help from Chrissey, now twenty-three and Elvey, twenty, but both girls were working too, in domestic service, along in Muker, to help keep the family in food and rent.

And John was back at work in the smithy.

That wasn't the only problem for the family. Work was scarce everywhere around them. Young, fit men, who desperately wanted, and needed to work, to support their children, and their wife, were unable to find employment, or enough employment, to keep them from starvation. Few folks were more than a meal or two away from the beginnings of this fate, just as Michael had been.

Jane's husband Leonard was one such young man. He was a collier at Keld when she'd married him. Now there was no work there, so they'd been forced to rely on Parish support for quite a while. They'd moved down from Keld to Thwaite, with Leonard chasing employment, but were now receiving regular payments of five shillings a fortnight.

This was becoming quite a drain on the poor rate for the Township of Muker.

Just like Michael, Leonard wanted to work, was desperate to work, but there *was* no work. However, those responsible for the 'doling' out of the Poor Rate, the Poor Law Guardians, believed they had an answer: in the short term anyway.

They were aware of their responsibility to the local poor and carried out these responsibilities dutifully. However, in this one instance it could be said that they acted over zealously.

They visited all 'pensioners', removing all furniture and goods that in their opinion, were not necessary.

All these items were auctioned off at Muker Fair, in January, and the money raised put into the pension fund.

It was legal.

It was heartless.

It was never repeated.

Of course it caused much upset in the parish of Muker, and also a little black mirth, as John repeated when he came home from the Inn one night, with a smile on his lips.

"Awld lass. Thee'll niver believe this."

"Gan canny barmpot. Dinnet wake the bairns."

"Tham as knaws 'ave penned a rhyme abaht the Guardians."

"Nah then. Let's 'ave a listen."

John did his best to remember the long song, and managed the first two verses, launching into it with,

"Come all honest men who have cesses to pay

Let your care be attention to what I shall say.

Your wise Vestry laws, restrictions and rules,

Are left to a parcel of asses and fools.

These hard-hearted monsters pursuing their plan

Seized clocks sir, and cupboards and the frying pan

Fire irons, hand irons, kitchen table and all,

With various articles they made up the whole.

It raised a smile on Peggy's face, and she mumbled, "Thee knaws ower lads wid 'ave sang that wi'thee."

It was only a few short weeks later that Betty once more whirled into her ma and da's cottage.

"Whit is it now dowter?"

"Ower Jane has t'gan away."

"What's tha on aboot lass, away?"

"The Vestry, theh're sendin' the family, all on 'em, ower Jane says, ova a hund'ed mile away t't'pits an mills, t'look for work, t'scour for graft."

"Bradford happen." John sighed. "There's others gone there. Leonard could find work down a pit."

Looking at her angry face John felt the loss to come, but knew there was no work here in Muker parish.

She said the Guardians, or the Vestry as folks still called them unaware of the change in the law, would also pay for a few clothes for the children.

It seemed to be a done deal. And if they became destitute when in Bradford, Muker Parish was legally bound to help them: a bit of a safety net, meaning that they should be no worse off in Bradford than in Thwaite, apart from they were so far from family.

All they had to look forward to here was a lifetime of Parish payments, and a life of hunger, because it was never enough.

At least Leonard might get a job in the mines, and Jane could work in the mills, when the children had grown.

Later that day Jane came to see them.

"We have t' gan ma. We cant 'bide here. The bairns are sufferin."

She went on, "And the're going to pay for sum clothes for'em too."

"When do ye be gannin ?" Peggy asked," and what if thee needs brass down there, if there don't be work f'thee?"

John knew the answer to this and told her.

"Muker parish'll dee the same as they be deein' now so they'll be nee worse off."

"Except they'll be so far away" Peggy said, beginning to cry, just a little, and putting her arms around her eldest daughter's shoulders, wondered once more, how that little scrap of a thing, who always looked as if she wasn't going to survive, was now a mature woman. This was just too much.

"We muz bide till a carrier can be sorted, and they say they'll tak the one that is least brass."

It ended up costing the parish well over one guinea. They knew this outlay was worth it, as it was costing them that amount each month while the family lived in Thwaite and out of work.

A life in Bradford would be a lot different to a life in Muker, but they had no choice, and they were moved by cart later that year, saying goodbye to family and friends they knew they would not see again.

Chapter 32

Chrissey (Christiana)

"The pain you feel today will be the strength you feel tomorrow."

(Marvin J Ashton)

Jane left for Bradford, and the family settled back into their routine. The trees got out their best gowns for autumn, before the village prepared for winter.

Chrissey was a hard-working, bonny and independent woman, who, at twenty-five years, had not yet married, although there were young men who would have asked her, if they'd dared.

She worked as a barmaid now, in Thwaite Inn, enjoying sparring and bantering with the customers, but knowing how far to go.

As far as husband material went, she found none of them suitable, until a newcomer caught her eye. He was lodging with Dr Rudd as an apprentice medical man. She loved the way he spoke, so different to the S'wardle she spoke, and his manners seemed so different too.

Looking back, she couldn't believe what had happened. She was a girl who knew how things went and had never got herself into something she couldn't get out of. Until he came, that is.

All the young, unmarried girls crowded around him if they saw him walking alone. They didn't dare if Dr Rudd was there, as he could terrify them with a look. She'd spent hours talking to him at the Inn. He seemed to want to spend his time with only her, and it was a good feeling. His background was so different to hers, but that didn't seem to matter to him, or at least, that's what he told her. According to him, they had a future together. He told her she would make a great assistant for a country practitioner. It would be like a partnership.

She was so excited, and she let this excitement take her further than she should. But it didn't matter because he was going to marry her. Peggy could see that her girl was in love and didn't worry, because she knew Chrissey had a good head on her shoulders.

But she'd forgotten how love made you feel, like it had made her feel with her first child Ruth.

When Chrissey realized that she was 'havin a bairn', she told the young man. He was a little shocked, although, under the circumstances, a doctor ought not to be. Nevertheless he said he would have to tell his parents at his next weekend visit, which was soon.

She waited for two months for any news of him, hearing in the Inn eventually, that he was not returning. He'd taken a position closer to home, he'd told Dr Rudd.

It was a double desertion, and she really did want to end her life. She'd lost the man she loved, was going to wed, and the father of her child. But she'd also lost the life he had painted for her, and how happy she would have been. There was nothing left for her now.

But it wasn't just her life. It was the life of her unborn child.

There was no hiding away from this, 'unless ah joins Jane in Bradford,' she'd considered as a very real possibility.

Betty was the one she went to first. It was always Betty. But Betty couldn't help and told her that she couldn't keep her secret: not after what had happened to Mary, so it was no good going to Bradford.

It was a secret that no unwed girl wanted to have and was a secret that her sister Mary had shared.

Soon she wouldn't be able to hide it any longer.

Peggy was already suspicious. Living in the same cottage, it was the absence of the usual signs that made it obvious to her. John of course was oblivious.

Peggy waited patiently for her daughter to tell her, remembering how it had been for her, all those years ago. She would do it in her own time, she knew. And that happened one evening as they sat at the old pine table, having a bite to eat. Looking down at her hands, as they twisted round and round each other, she struggled to find the words.

When she finally did blurt out her news, all she said was,

"Ma. Da. Ah's in trubble. Ah's brung shame on thee."

Hanging her head, she waited for what seemed like forever, but it really wasn't more than a few seconds.

John continued chewing the lump of bread he already had in his mouth, looking down at the table. Then, turning a quizical look to Peggy, who returned the look and nodded, he looked Chrissey full in the face he said,

"Well, dear dowter. Ah can see thee's in good fettle, so the bairn'll be fine an all. And thee winn't be aleean."

Leaning over to her, he took her hand in his old, leathery fist, bent with the effects ofarthritis, and breathed, "Did thee think we'd be fashed? Doesn't it 'app'n to t'best," looking over at Peggy and smiling, about something she knew nothing of.

"But Da, whit will ah dee?"

"Dowter, lass, thee has a ma and a da. " he murmured, looking into the lovely, but worried face, of his daughter.

"But the'll needs muz tell on the man. The Vestry will want that."

She knew that, and didn't want to, but knew there may be no financial support for her child if she didn't. That was just the way it was. Peggy listened, thinking back to her time. She'd refused to name Ruth's da; hadn't dared name him. He'd given her money now and again, in thanks, but not enough. Now of course, she knew she'd been wrong to shield him.

Chrissey knew her da wasn't happy. Who would be? Now she would give up the name of the father of this bairn. There was no reason not to, and every reason why she should. The Select Vestry Guardians would make her anyway, if she expected to receive any money for the child's upkeep. But she needn't tell them just yet.

A "Bastardy bond" would be taken out against him, and if he didn't pay then he would be taken to the Quarter Sessions at Northallerton.

Her baby boy was born in January 1835, and the only name she wanted, and the only name she would have, was Miles.

John and Peggy's family was growing again.

They had their grandsons, little John and Christopher, living with them already, and now another baby, another Miles, for Chrissey and Elvey to look after. Peggy was having problems moving around now so the girls had to give her a lot of help.

John hoped that this Miles would have a happier life than his two namesakes, his uncles.

T'awd Roy was celebrated, with Peggy and John wanting to have the family, what was left of them, together for this.

Edward and Annas brought their little ones, William, not married and not wanting to be, paid them a short visit. He lived in the cottage next door. There was Chrissey and Elvey, and the three young boys, one a very small baby, just days old.

In January Chrissey went to the Poor Law Guardians' meeting for a Bastardy Examination, giving the name of her baby's father.

There was quite a bit of 'tutting' and some eyerolling when she gave his name. It was demeaning. It was demoralizing. She wondered what they thought about the bairn's da: if *he* was less than he should be?

The law had changed, she was told, and if she had wanted to she could apply for this bond herself. That was something she didn't really want to do, applying to the Petty Sessions.

The arrangements for transporting Chrissey and John were made, engaging Henry Harker, at a cost of one guinea, to the Petty Sessions in Northallerton. There, a Bastardy Bond was produced for Chrissey and Jonah Jeffries to sign. He did not attend, but his father did, and gave his guarantee that his son would take full share of the responsibility, as Chrissey had been forced to do.

He would have to make monthly payments to the Select Vestry, or Guardians of the Poor now, for the upkeep of his son. And Chrissey would be entitled to regular payment for his upkeep, until he was old enough to be apprenticed out.

She received two shillings a week for his upkeep, and none for hers. They couldn't be seen to support a girl who'd fallen so far from grace, now could they!

The Guardians continued too with their other responsibilities to the Hutchinson families. There were payments to support Michael's children, even though their mother had remarried. Betty and little Peg's families were also receiving assistance, a few shillings here and a few shillings there, supplemented with a load of coal or a peck of meal.

Edward seemed to be doing better, supporting his family as a lead miner, and Will, at twenty-seven, was employed as a lead miner too, unmarried and living next door to John and Peggy.

They had heard nothing from Jane, in Bradford, for the last year, but Peggy thought of her often, as she lay in bed, listening to the rhythmic breathing and slight snores of John, lying peacefully next to her. But she didn't know that John lay, in much the same frame of mind, when she was asleep, thinking about the first daughter who'd taken his heart, and who he also never saw, his Mary.

This was 1835, and the family had a peaceful, and uneventful three years. John still continued with his smithing now that Miles had gone. He had mouths to feed. He did work for the Guardians too, ironing the clogs of paupers in the village. It was getting paid that was the problem.

He and Peggy tried to be parents to the two orphan boys, but in reality, they were too old, so this was left to Chrissey, Elvey and Will.

But John did make little John a hoop and stick, just as he had done for hos son, the boy's father, and a set of quoits. Christopher was much younger, and preferred to play in the dirt, although he followed his brother around, as younger brothers do.

John loved hearing stories from his grandpa of the Militia, and the French Wars, and playing at soldiers with sticks as swords.

In the late spring of 1838 Peggy began complaining about her feet and legs swelling, a common complaint among the elderly of the day, but one which had made walking difficult, and walking to the village impossible.

Not only that, when Peggy and he went up to bed at night, it was a battle for her to climb those steep, narrow stairs. Undressing to their shifts, they lay together in companionable silence, each unaware of the other's thoughts. They'd been together for forty-five years and he felt they were more than lucky that they were still together. They'd never talked to each other about how they were feeling. Emotions were always well hidden and after all their sadness they'd learned how to push these thoughts down into a place from which they could not escape. They'd coped with a lot, but then so had many of their neighbours. It was just life.

Every night as he lay in bed John listened to Peggy breathing, and the little whistles her breath sounds made. It was familiar and always lulled him to sleep. When he woke the next morning, after having a long stretch and yawn, he usually nudged her with his elbow, and said something like,
"Nah then, awld lass. What's to do? Ower bairns needs their porridge. Lazy awld woman," knowing well that Elvey would have seen to that.
She would nudge him back, or complain, but If she didn't he would give her another playful push, and then usually decide to let her stay, getting up to see if Elvey had done it. He knew Peg was finding it hard to get around now.

Each morn the same thing. She was not well, and had been very tired lately, finding it difficult to rise in the mornings. She was getting breathless too, just walking to the door, and had complained of pains in her chest.

She had liked to walk next door to see Betty in the evening, but even that was now too difficult for her. She was confined to her chair almost. It was worse at the end of a long day, when her feet and lower legs began to swell, making the skin look shiny, and stretched, and the muscles in her legs ache so painfully. As well as that she was always dropping things. She said, they 'juz flew out a ma hands."

Dr Rudd had visited but had no remedy for what ailed her so they just ploughed on: two old people doing the best they could.

This particular morning, John carried out his usual actions, nudging her to wake up. As he did, he felt her rock back over to him, without opening her eyes. Shaking her shoulder as he usually did, he made the remark about the bairns' porridge.

Then he realized, with instant clarity, that she had gone.

It was a shock, but perhaps it shouldn't have been.

He sat up and looked down on her, at her wrinkled, weather-beaten face, her hair, wiry and grey now. She looked peaceful, as if she were just asleep, and would open her eyes any moment. But there was no rise and fall in her chest, and her body was cool to the touch.

And now, as he processed what had happened, he felt almost jealous that she had gone first.

As he and Peggy had aged, he had begun to think about what would happen when he died. He knew Peg had no doubt about it, but he hadn't been able to believe it. That is, until he was nearing the age of death himself, and wanted to believe that there was something else for him. It was a comfort too, as he could then think he may see his lads and lasses again.

As for now, realizing that Peg would see their lost ones before he did, he felt sad. There were no tears for the missing of her, and the thought of his kin, but leaning in towards her he whispered in her ear, "Say hello t'the bairns fr'uz."

He rose and called for Chrissey.

A new system had been put into place only the year before, for the official notification of any deaths, as well as births and marriages. Prior to this, all significant events had been recorded when a visit to the kirk, for a burial, a baptism or a marriage, was required.

There had been petitions against this General Registry Bill, in 1835, with one sent from Muker Parish, but nevertheless, the law had been passed. These important life events were still registered in

Parish Records, in individual churches, just as they always had been, but the Bill imposed on everyone, or their families, the legal requirement to ensure they were recorded officially, and registered, for the Government.

The local Registrar appointed was Dr Rudd, who was also the local medical man for the chapelry of Muker, and perhaps the only man thereabouts with sufficient education to ensure the job was done properly. Because of this new Bill, the cause of death had to be recorded. Sometimes it had been, as in the case of Miles and Hannah and their Typhus, but usually it wasn't. It was he who officially registered Peggy's death, and as a doctor, decided the cause of death too.

He decided, and recorded Peggy's official cause of death as *Dropsy*, which was more like a description of the effects of the disease. Yes, she was now prone to dropping things, but the main effect of *Dropsy* was an accumulation of fluid, causing more than a little pain, and affecting her heart. It seemed that poor Peggy's heart had just given out, after all those years of childbearing.

Chrissey, or to give her full name, Christiana, was recorded as being present at the death.

Once more they made the journey along to the churchyard, with a borrowed horse and cart, as they could not afford the hire of the

Muker parish hearse, and there was no way John was going to ask the Guardians to pay. He hadn't asked for a penny all his life.

He missed her. Of course he did. But she'd been old and had lasted longer than she'd expected to. Old people died. That was how it was meant to happen. It was the proper circle of life.

The fact that so many of his children had died, and some as young men, had hardened him to any emotion. She was gone.

He'd found after this that he'd lost the fight, the will.

He couldn't work.

There was no-one in the smithy now. No Hutchinson anyway. The Hutchinsons had been Blacksmiths for well over a hundred years. But no more.

At the end of May that same year, at the age of seventy nine, he made his first request to the Poor Law Guardians for help and became a pauper, for a pension of one shilling and sixpence a week. Not a lot to live on after a lifetime of work.

Chrissey looked after them now. As a mother to her own son Miles and as an aunt and surrogate mother to her nephews, John and Christopher, she was doing the best she could. Three young boys who needed a lot of love and attention, got as much as she could give them. Elvey was making money charring, with Chrissey working some nights at the Inn. Will, living next door, was lead mining.

Chrissey had all the work at home. She was a mother with no husband and poor prospects if any, of finding one but she had her son Miles, and she would make him her priority until he was grown and settled. And she did.

A few months later, as John sat on the old wooden settle they'd brought from Southwaite one cool summer evening, he looked back over his long life.

He'd begun as an apprentice Blacksmith under his own father, Miles. He remembered that. He felt old, and knew he was a good age, but wasn't sure how many summers he'd seen. They'd said Peggy was seventy-one when she'd gone, and he knew he was a few years more than that.

Maybe Betty would know.

Alice's name came to mind, but her face was lost. She'd been the first to go, he remembered. A long, long time ago. Tears pricked his eyes when he realized he couldn't bring her face to mind, but he did remember that she was pretty. That at least. And that he'd been lucky that she'd wanted to wed him.

He and Betty had sat here just the night before and counted up all his bairns.

It was an incredible eighteen all told, but they weren't all here now. Betty had reminded him of little Edmund, who'd lasted only two weeks, and then Peggy who had stayed for six months.

But it was the mention of Jemmy's name that had made the now frail old man cry real tears. Jemmy had been a free spirit, but it was being such that caused his death. John had never been able to forgive himself for that, and nor did he want to. The thought of the young boy's suffering, all alone on the hillside, for two whole days, continually turned like a knife in his chest. To remember it was his punishment. Then there was Will, a few years older, who'd gone with the Red Rash too, and had been buried with him.

He knew Miles and young John had gone too, but he wasn't sure who went first. They had both been strong young men, until they weren't. Cut down in their prime, by Lead Lung, Betty reminded him, before they'd had a chance to have their own life.

And then Michael, the dreamer, with Lead Lung too. He could tell a good tale o' the Boggart, John remembered. He knew there were bairns, and that Nanny, his widow, had remarried, for the sake of those bairns. There was a Christopher. He hadn't died, so where was he now?

He'd had another boy called Miles, he knew that, but what had happened to him? Just as he was thinking this through, Betty came for her nightly visit. Turning towards her he spoke his usual greeting,

"Nah then our Beth" and asked her to help him remember.

"Miles was took by the fever, with Hannah," she reminded him. "And little John and little Kit are their bairns. "

She went on, "and Christopher, he went to the Lancashire pits, and is lodging with the Harkers, who moved from here too.

Dinnet forgit ower Jane. She's in Bradford wi'her Leonard and bairns. He's down t'pit an all."

Her thoughts were, we will never see Jane again, that's for sure.

"Aye, so whee's left wi'uz?"

"Our Will and Edward, workin' in the lead mines. Little Elvey, Little Peg, an' me. Ower Mary, I reckon she'll be an awld woman now. She's abaht five year older than uz. Ah knaw she would have left a message wi' someone to tell uz when she was gone. Her posh son, another Miles, wad uv done that."

She didn't want to remind him of her personal tragedy, of losing a husband of only twelve years, who had left her with six children.

But there was another, whose name was scarcely spoken, who'd run away, who'd converted to popery, and who now lived with *The Little Sisters of the Congregation of Jesus,* in York. Family were allowed a visit once a year on her name day, but it was too far to go, and they didn't have the money for such things. Beth remembered what a special girl she was, and how she absolutely could not have lived here any longer. They had received a short letter from her, but nothing recently, but at least she was alive, or the Convent would have let them know.

While Peggy was alive Betty had considered asking the Guardians for the money to visit her, but she never had, and now it was too late.

And Mary, John's first daughter? There had been no news of her for many years. All they knew was that her bastard son was being brought up as a gentleman, by his grandparents.

He was tired now. He would sleep and think it over again tomorrow.

He wondered who he would dream of tonight.

He was a man poor in money, but rich in the love of family, and had no regrets. He thought how funny it was, yes funny, that he was so sure now that he would see his kin again.

He chuckled slightly, wondering what Alice and Peg would make of each other.

Giving Betty, or Beth as she now preferred to be called a kiss on the cheek he pulled himself up the steep set of stairs to the room he used to share with Peggy, and now he shared with little John and Kit.

Barely six weeks after Peggy had gone, Chrissey found him propped up on the settle, in his usual place, a clay pipe on his knee.

Dr Rudd was summoned and he certified the death as "Old age."

He was seventy nine.

Final Words

This book is as true as it can be. Spending many hours at Northallerton, Carlisle and Kendal, I traced living history, and this family came alive once more for me, as I hope they did for you. Dates and places of all births, Christenings, deaths and marriages are from Parish and Government Records and places the family lived are faithfully recorded. The only actual causes of death available officially are Miles and Hannah (Typhus), Peggy (Dropsy) and John (Old Age).

While re-reading before publication of the Second Edition, I felt, keenly, the pain of a family who had lost so many children: eight all told. Four of them as men in their early years of a grown-up life. What a cutting pain. There was no way I could know what had killed these boys, but working where they did, Lead Lung was a good contender. Even a daughter, Betty, was not allowed to have a life, when her young husband died, probably of miner's asthma, leaving her with six children to rear.

The pattern and events of daily life are from research which provided a knowledge of how people lived at that time.

Yes, a Blacksmith had a trade, and in those years he could be the most prosperous man in the village, but that was not necessarily the case. It was also dependent on the people who wanted his services and whether they could find the 'brass'.

Many families, including some of John's, needed help from the Select Vestry, who later became the Poor Law Guardians.

And many families, including John's, were torn apart, when they were almost forced, by the same people, to move away, hundreds of miles, to mining and mill areas to try and find work.

Others were given the 'opportunity' of a life in America, for better or not. (Select Vestry and Poor Law records, Northallerton)

The weather is referenced much in this account and comes from records produced by *"weatherweb"* who give a record of general weather conditions.

I am proud of the accomplishments of these family pioneers, leading the way through the Hutchinson dynasty. It was Miles Hutchinson, the young Blacksmith who produced my family heir. His first son John was born into a family that contracted Typhus when he was two years old. It shows that life was a lottery, as neither he, nor his baby brother suffered this terrible disease, although both parents died of it. It was just called *'The Fever'* and as they had no idea how this disease was spread there was no way they could have protected the boys. Again, another winning ticket in life's lottery. If little John died, or if both he and his brother Christopher died, the line would have been extinguished.

Not a lot was known about Typhus at this time, and it was still often confused with Typhoid before eventually being recognized as a disease in its own right. It could be that they did indeed have Typhoid and it was wrongly diagnosed by a country apothecary Doctor.

I know these people very well now and I admire their tenacity and resilience in times that were difficult.

As my friend Richard Gibson remarked, *"exciting time in the dale. The souls long since buried in the churchyards have a second chance to live.... Living through the pages of your book....*

Appendix

Bibliography

- A glossary of words used in Swaledale, Yorkshire 1873 By Captain John Harland, of Reeth, near Richmond
- Minutes of the Select Vestry, Muker District (Northallerton Records Office
- Christenings, Burials, Marriages, Parish Records as above
- Births, Deaths, Marriages, General Registry Office, (after 1837)
- Census Records 1841 – 1891
- Upper Dales family history group (a new URL in 2018
- Christine Amsden's original Swaledale and Wensleydale census transcripts and her main website
- The Gunnerside website a very useful resource for family historians
- Free BMD which is the fastest (and free) way to search for English BMD records after 1837
- Swaledale lead mines
- *Life behind the cottage door* by Valerie Porter 1992
- *Traditional Food in Yorkshire* by Peter Brears
- *Swaledale* by John Hardy 1992
- www.johnhearfield.com essays about Swaledale's people and communities.

Printed in Great Britain
by Amazon